Silence

I0598249

Book III of the Orbit Series

J.S. Collyer

Published by Dagda Publishing, Nottingham United Kingdom.

For my grandparents

CONTENTS

Prologue

The air was cold and smelt like iron. The chill seeped through Hugo's skin, saturated his flesh and bored into his bones. He ached. He couldn't remember the last time he'd woken and not ached.

His breath misted in the frigid air. His fingers were white but he didn't reach for his gloves. Disassembling and cleaning the rifle was delicate work and he managed better without a constrictive layer of fabric. He also wanted his nerves to know each flat surface and sharp angle in the weapon so that every level of him understood what he was about to do.

The metal made soft clicks as each part disconnected from the rest. All the segments slotted into the carry case as neatly as the bullets in the magazine. His foggy breath shuddered in and out, but his hands were steady.

He fastened the case and let it rest on the bench. His stomach was knotted. He took a deep breath then looked up and met the eyes of the fair-haired man watching him intently from the doorway.

"I'm ready," Hugo said.

The man eyed him a moment longer then nodded, apparently satisfied. Hugo hoisted the carry case onto his back and followed the man out of the room, icy water flowing through his veins where once he remembered there being warm blood.

I

Webb shifted higher up on his elbows and adjusted the zoom on his binoculars. The compound gate, just visible through the trees, was shut. What windows of the complex he could see had the blinds drawn.

"Anything?" the commander at his side asked.

"No," Webb sighed, adjusting his angle to try and get a view of the roof. He could make out three flyers but no people. "All their flyers are grounded. They must all be holed up. I don't think we're going to see any action today."

"Surely that's a good thing, sir?" the young commander said as he wiped sweat out of his eyes.

Webb frowned, lowering the binoculars. "Not knowing what they're doing is far worse than having them out in the field where we at least know what they're up to."

The commander shuffled and muttered, clearly hoping for Webb to issue the order to return to camp. Webb brought the binoculars up again to check the windows for a third time, ignoring his subordinate cursing the clinging heat and buzzing insects.

Minutes slid by. Webb thought he saw a blind twitch but then all was still again. Sweat dripped down his neck.

"They still haven't found Kaleb Hugo have they, sir?"

Webb's grip tightened on the binoculars. "We're on point here, Commander Matsuo."

"Do you believe the rumours?" the commander asked after a pause.

"I don't normally hold much truck with rumours."

"Seems his family does," Matsuo mused. "Otherwise why would Erica Hugo send her husband out to Mars?"

"If you are talking about Special Commander and General Hugo," Webb said, lowering his binoculars and levelling a heavy look at Matsuo, "how about you refer to them correctly, Commander? And me too, whilst you're at it."

"Yes, Captain," the young man said, shrugging himself back round to face the compound again. "Sorry, sir."

"Take a note of the flyer reg numbers," Webb ordered. "If we're facing a few days of inaction we could at least look into who's supplying these bastards."

"Yes, sir," Matsuo said, pulling out a panel and keying in the reg numbers Webb read out. "You know him well don't you, sir?"

"Who?"

"Kaleb…I mean Vice-Admiral Hugo."

"It's probably ok to leave titles off of AWOL Servicemen," Webb muttered after a pause.

"What do you think then, sir?"

"About what?"

"About how people are saying he's run off to join Red Star?"

Webb sighed and glared. "What I think doesn't matter, nor is it any of your damn business, ok? Focus, dammit. We're - "

"Sir! Captain Webb, sir!"

Webb hissed as two Eclipse agents scrambled up the rise behind them, breathing heavily and calling over each other. "Keep it down, goddammit. Wanna let the whole jungle know we're here?"

"Sorry sir," the breathless woman said, but the man that had followed cut her off.

"Sir," he said. "I've just found Midshipman Jin investigating inside the designated perimeter."

"What?" Webb snapped. "Jin, is Vergennes right?"

Jin swallowed, took a breath. "Yes, sir. I'm sorry - "

"Are you out of your mind?"

"Sir, I was careful," the young woman said, cheeks flushed and not just from the heat. "Please, there's something you've got to see."

"I recommend Midshipman Jin be ordered back to base for official reprimand, Captain," Lieutenant Vergennes said, looking down at Jin from his considerable height.

Jin bristled and she, Matsuo and Vergennes all began hissing whispers at each other.

"Quiet, already," Webb said, checking the compound once more but it was still locked up and silent. "Fall back. Now. Not you, Matsuo," Webb said, gesturing toward the gates as he got up and brushed leaf mould off his combats. "You keep watch on that gate. Anything moves, you signal me. Jin, Vergennes, follow me."

Webb led the two young soldiers several paces back into the jungle then turned on them. "Ok, you two. Tell me what exactly was worth risking the mission for?"

"Sir," Jin began but again Vergennes stepped forward, back straight and chin tilted up to look down at Webb. His intense blue eyes, the colour of cobalt, were cold.

"Captain Webb," he said, "I recommend again that Midshipman Jin be ordered back to base for breach of orders."

"Ok, ok, Lieutenant," Webb said, pushing sweaty hair out of his face. "I heard you the first time. Jin, spit it out. What's going on?"

"Sir - " Vergennes began again.

"Stow it, Lieutenant," Webb snapped. "I said your objection is noted. Jin?"

Jin didn't quite manage to stop herself throwing a victorious look at the young lieutenant before continuing. "Sir, I've seen something. It's important. You need to come and see for yourself."

"Is this 'something' outside our perimeter?" Webb said, warning in his voice.

"Yes, sir," she said, ducking her head. "I exceeded your orders -"

"Breached them you mean, Midshipman."

"Vergennes," Webb said. "Don't make me order you back to base."

Vergennes clenched his hands behind his back, cool look still lingering on the other officer.

"As I say, I am sorry, sir," Jin continued, "but I found a blind spot in their surveillance, south of the rear gate, and got pretty close. You won't believe what's happening. Please hurry, sir, before he goes."

"'He'?"

Jin nodded, pulling out her panel and showing him some blurred pictures. Webb frowned at them, tapping on the screen to zoom in on the image of a man through the window of a Jeep that had pulled up at the rear gate of the compound.

"Wait. No way. Is that Ambassador Matinez?"

"I think so, sir. But I can't be sure myself."

"Show me," Webb ordered, pulling his visor down over his eyes.

Jin set off into the trees. Vergennes visibly restrained himself from speaking but Webb could read his disapproval on his face. Ignoring his lieutenant, he scrambled after Midshipman Jin as she took them on a round-about route looping towards the back of the compound. The map on the inside of his visor signalled when they reached their surveillance perimeter and Jin dropped flat to the forest floor and started up a scrubby incline on her belly. Webb ordered Vergennes to hang back followed her.

Webb could just make out the narrowest of gaps in the compound's surveillance nets displayed on the inside of his visor caused by a clump of bamboo that no one had thought to clear. Jin crawled up to its roots and peered between the thick stems.

She gestured for Webb to join her, urgency on her face and Webb shuffled up and put his face to the gap. The back gates were just grinding closed. He caught a glimpse of a man in civilian clothes and a designer sun-visor shake hands with one of the compound's uniformed soldiers before the gates clanged shut. His chest tightened.

"Fall back," he whispered to Jin and they crawled back down to join Vergennes. "Lieutenant, we are heading back to base. Radio through to Major Tremaine that I'm coming to see him right away."

"Why him, sir?"

"Just do as I say. Jin," Webb said turning to the midshipman. "Good work."

"Yes, sir," she said, saluting and smiling. "Thank you, sir."

"But if you risk your ass like that again on my watch, I promise I'll kick it to Silence City and back, ok?"

Her smile slipped. "Yes sir."

"Back to your post. Finish the surveillance sweep then head back to camp. Commander Matsuo is in charge until then. Vergennes," Webb said as he turned and marched back into the trees. "Why aren't you on that radio?"

"Sir, whatever Midshipman Jin found she discovered whilst breaching regulations. We can't report what she saw without opening ourselves to official reprimand - "

"You've got an irritating habit of offering your two cents when I've not asked for it, Lieutenant," Webb muttered as they reached the guarded clearing with a dozen quadbikes parked up in rows. "Can you just do as you're told? And do it now. You're accompanying me back to base. I want eye witnesses."

"Yes, sir," Vergennes mumbled then began tapping commands into his wristpanel communicator as he mounted his quad. Webb started his own engine then accelerated off through the trees.

Vergennes's quad roared after his through the undergrowth. They bumped onto a dirt track between the close-growing trees. They reached a clearing clustered with pre-fab buildings surrounded by a wire fence studded with cameras and sensors. The sweating sentry at the gate waved them through. Webb braked the quad in the dusty yard. Some Ground Corps cadets came forward to attend to the quads whilst Webb hurried to the command unit, pulling off his visor and gloves as he went.

"Sir," Vergennes called as he caught up. "The major's aide has replied to say he's in a meeting."

"Meeting over," Webb replied, hurrying through the mercifully cool corridors of the command unit. Ground Corps soldiers moved to let them past, some with disdainful looks that Webb was well-used to. He turned a corner and stumbled, black spots dancing in front of his eyes. Lightening forked thorough his head and he gasped.

"No," he murmured, "Not now."

He clenched his eyes shut, pinched the bridge of his nose, putting a steadying hand against the wall, but the pain rose and blinded him. He staggered.

"Sir? Captain Webb? What's wrong?" Vergennes's voice sounded far away. Webb blinked. He was on the floor, back against the wall. The pain receded and his vision gradually returned.

"Dammit," he cursed, getting to his feet and trying not to shake.

Vergennes's well-trained face revealed nothing but a questioning look lingered as they moved on.

"I'm fine," Webb growled. He burst into the major's ante-office to the splutters of his indignant aide.

"Captain Webb," the round man scrambled up from his desk to block the door to the main office. "He's in a meeting. He can't be disturbed."

"The major's used to be disturbed by me, Knowles. Move."

"I'm sorry but I must insist you come back later."

"Move your butt. That's a direct order, Corporal."

Knowles stiffened, narrowing watery eyes.

"With respect sir," he said, with absolutely none in his tone. "You are not my CO."

"Vergennes," Webb said, stepping aside. "Would you be so kind?"

Webb didn't miss the disapproving look that large youth flicked him before moving to do as he was asked. The tall, wide-shouldered young man had no trouble removing the protesting Knowles from the door and Webb stormed into the office.

Major Tremaine's hulking frame, barely contained by his grey-and-black Service uniform, tensed at the intrusion. The three officers with him looked up, surprise melting to anger as they recognised Webb.

"Major, we need to talk."

Tremaine's large face and balding pate flushed red. "I'm busy, Captain. Knowles," he bellowed.

"I'm sorry, sir," a flustered Knowles said as he scrambled into the room. "I couldn't stop them."

"This is urgent, sir," Webb said, stepping forward.

"Is the unit under attack?"

"No, sir."

"Is anyone in immediate physical danger?"

"No, sir, but - "

"Then I'm not the hell interested. Come back in an hour."

"Listen, you giant ass," Webb snarled. "You may be in charge here, but I represent the Eclipse Division. You will damn well listen to me or I'll be on the comm to my Divisional Commander before you can swallow another ration cake."

Webb didn't think it was possible but the major turned an even deeper shade of puce. The three other officers and Knowles stood by, struck dumb.

"Gentlemen," Tremaine said after taking a very deliberate breath. "I apologise for this. Would you excuse us?"

The others left the room, all shooting Webb disgusted looks as they passed. Webb nodded to Vergennes and he left with them and Knowles shut the door.

"You've done it this time, Webb," Tremaine started in immediately. "Command may have ignored all my reports on your insubordination this far, but they can't ignore this. I will have you removed from this operation before the day is done, mark me - "

"Fine, you do that chubs. But since the paperwork for that is going to take the rest of the afternoon, listen to me first." He ignored Tremaine's indignant mutterings and pulled out Midshipman Jin's panel. "We've just had visual confirmation of Ambassador Martinez arriving at the guerrilla stronghold to the north."

The major's face flattened. The rushing sound of an aircraft landing could be heard through the thin walls, but the big man raised his voice over the noise, a dangerous look on his face. "Say that again, soldier."

"Just as I said," Webb said, thrusting the panel into his hands. "He shook hands with them. He's meeting with them willingly. Take a look."

"Not possible," the major said, staring at the grainy image on the panel. "Martinez is in Beijing with the rest of the delegates."

"I'm telling you, I saw him. I'd know him a mile off. And he shook the bastards' hands."

Tremaine continued staring at the picture. The colour had drained from his round face.

"You must have been mistaken."

"Sir - "

"This picture," Tremaine said, cutting him off and handing the panel back. "How was it taken? Your patrol area doesn't go anywhere near the back gate."

Webb took a breath. "One of my unit took it upon themselves - "

"Stop right there. Are you telling me one of your men breached the perimeter?"

Webb swallowed his first response and forced himself to remain calm. "That's not the issue here, sir."

"It's say it ruddy well is the issue," he growled. A bleeping started up on his desk comm but he disconnected it without looking. "This isn't the first time your damn Eclipse unit has breached orders."

"Major - "

"Silence," he thundered. The bleeping started again. "I've had enough. The Service has trusted me and my men with containing this guerrilla force whilst our ambassadors negotiate with the New Republic's leaders and you wretched good-for-nothings breach protocol time and time again, threatening the lives of your own unit, mine and the outcome of the negotiations. You can't laugh this one off, Captain Webb. I don't care what your connections are. Your unit is done here, understand? Done."

"Tremaine," Webb tried again.

"Enough. I don't give a damn how vital Command thinks your intelligence is, I want you and your unit packed up and heading back to Sydney HQ within the hour or I'll throw you out myself."

"You can't do that. We answer to Divisional Commander Hudson, not to you."

"You answer to me in the field, soldier," he said, prodding Webb in the chest. "This is a Ground Corps op and it's my unit you're endangering. Now get the hell out of my office before…what?" he roared in response to an urgent knock at the door.

"Sir," Knowles quavered, opening the door a crack. "I'm sorry sir but…but…"

"What the hell is it?"

Knowles swallowed, glance darting between Webb and the major. "It's SC Erica Hugo, sir."

"What about her?"

"She's here, sir."

The major's fleshy face fell. Webb blinked.

"What do you mean, 'she's here'?"

Knowles took a tentative step further into the room, kneading his hands. "She's in the mess hall, sir. She just landed in her copter."

They stood for a moment in shocked silence. Tremaine visibly shook himself and threw a glare at Webb.

"This isn't over," he said, before starting toward his aide.

"No sir," Knowles said, looking even more nervous. "She wants to see Captain Webb."

Webb felt his eyebrows climb up his face.

"That can't be right," Tremaine said, glowering.

"Sorry, sir," Knowles fumbled, clearly as confused as Tremaine. "No mistake sir. She's waiting, sir."

Webb stood frozen a moment longer, pulse beating in his ears, bewilderment struggling against unease.

"Sir," Knowles prompted.

Webb shook himself and followed the corporal out. Tremaine called something after him but he was too dazed to listen. There was a cadet almost bouncing with excitement in the ante-office, waiting to take him to the mess. Vergennes gave Webb and the cadet a questioning glance as he followed them from the room.

"Get back to the unit, Vergennes," Webb ordered. "Grab as much intelligence as you can with what time we have left."

"Sir?"

"I want anything and everything you can record on that compound whilst we have the chance. Get me the make of their underwear if you can. I want everything."

"What's happening, sir?"

"I have a feeling we won't be here much longer."

"I don't understand, sir."

Webb blinked as they stepped back out into the solid heat and light of the dusty yard. The soldiers stood around were all gawping at the sleek RoterCopter that was powering down on the helipad beside the barracks.

"I don't either, Vergennes. Just get going. We need to use every second we have left."

"I should come with you, Captain. I could radio your orders to the team - "

"Just do as I say," Webb said, pushing as much sweaty hair as he could up under his cap and trying to dust off his combats. "I don't have time to argue."

Vergennes's sculpted jaw tightened but he nodded and hurried back toward the quadbikes. Webb watched him go then followed the cadet toward the mess.

He wiped sweat off his face with his sleeve as they entered mess hall. The building wasn't as nicely conditioned as the command unit. It smelt of unwashed bodies and overcooked protein gruel. Webb straightened his stained shirt before shaking his head and giving up. If she was going to drop in on them in the middle of a jungle op, she could take him as she found him.

There was a small crowd gathered at the doors to the canteen, all trying to sneak looks in the windows. The cadet wrestled her way through.

"Don't you guys have better things to be doing?" Webb growled to the gathered soldiers. The crowd disbanded but didn't move far. The cadet held the canteen door open for him. He took a breath and stepped in.

The room had been hastily abandoned. Plastic trays still half-filled with gruel, vegsticks and Nutripaks were scattered across the benches and the serving counter still steamed with trays half-full with the lunch rations. Webb hadn't eaten since before sun-up but his appetite was quite gone as he stood there faced with four of the Hugo brothers and SC Hugo herself.

The Special Commander stood at one of the windows, stat-ue-still and staring out to the wire fence and the jungle beyond. The brothers were lined up like they were on parade, grey-and-black uniforms pristine and studded with rank and reward pips with matching appraising looks on their dark features.

Webb suppressed the uneasiness that settled in his gut. Their heavy dark brows, serious eyes and straight backs all put him in mind of their youngest brother Kaleb, who he preferred to keep out of his mind altogether.

"I'm flattered," Webb managed to say, plastering a wry grin on his face. "I'm worth almost the complete set, huh?"

"Silence, Captain," the oldest brother retorted.

"Verne, right?" Webb said. "I can always spot Giles," he nodded at the tallest and youngest in the line. "But I forget which of the rest of you is which."

"We said, *silence*," the middle one with the square jaw barked. "We are here to make you answer some questions, since you saw fit to ignore the all official summons."

"*Riley*, right?" Webb said, rubbing his chin. "And then…Francis?"

"Our Christian names are of no concern here," Verne, the eldest, continued whilst all four continued to glare. "And if you wish to address us at all, you should do so appropriately."

"You'll have to refresh my memory on your ranks too, pal."

"Enough," Giles raised his hands. Webb has always liked Giles. He considered the serious set of the other man's face and wondered if that was destined to continue. "Webb. Why have you ignored the summons?"

"I've been kinda busy. You know, getting the intelligence the Service needs to secure all these new allegiances and shit."

"Your belligerence won't serve you here," Riley said.

"You still mad for losing at chess on Becca's enrolment weekend, Riley?" Webb shook his head. "Should have known that would come back to bite me on the ass."

"Take this seriously," Riley retorted, drawing himself up. "You're on wafer-thin, ice Captain. The complaints we have had on you have their own section in the Analysts' files. The only reason you've never been suspended from duty is through SC Hugo's intervention. And now this is how you repay her?"

Webb pushed the brim of his cap up with his thumb and crossed his arms. "Can your mom not speak for herself?"

All four men stiffened. Webb wondered if he'd finally gone too far.

"Enough." Erica Hugo's voice wasn't loud. It was never loud. It never needed to be. Her sons all clamped their mouths shut. "Leave us alone for a minute."

"Ma'am - " one brother protested.

"Wait outside, please."

They all exchanged glances. The eldest frowned heavily at Webb before gesturing at the door and they all filed out. Giles hung back a second to spare Webb a glance that was either loaded with sympathy or warning, he wasn't sure which, and then the canteen door shut behind them.

Webb felt his nerves start to thrum. SC Hugo continued staring out the window. He fought the urge to shift on his feet. A serious of sarcastic remarks that he would have reeled off to any other commanding officer rose in his mind, but the thought of saying them out loud to her gave him chills.

"I didn't respond to your summons, ma'am," he found himself saying as the silence stretched on, "because I think I know what you want. And I can't see how you expect me to help."

She turned to face him at last. She wasn't as tall as him, but she had always managed to make herself appear a head taller than anyone else in the room. All her older sons had the square jaw, heavy brow and broad shoulders of their father. The two youngest, Giles and Kaleb, as well as their sister Dana had the look of Erica. She had the same dark colouring, though her hair held more silver than mahogany these days, but their builds were more wiry, their looks sharper, the women most of all. The thought of Dana Hugo caught him off guard and he suppressed the inevitable kick of pain.

"Did it not occur to you that you could find that out if you'd come to the meeting like I asked?"

Webb took a breath. "So you flew the whole clan out to the middle of the jungle instead? What for, to intimidate me?"

"To tell you that even though your work so far has proved valuable enough for you to keep your position, ignoring a direct summons from the Special Commander which has necessitated her and four of her commanding officers to make a trip out to you to prove she is serious is unacceptable."

"With respect, ma'am, no one made you."

She regarded him for a long moment. Nothing about her look or stance changed but Webb suspected that he had pushed too far. Apparently, she was able to read as such in his face because she took a step closer to him, cool glance sliding away to survey the cluttered room.

"It's no secret that the increasingly fractious attitude of Mars colonists under Governor Rose is cause for concern. I need to be able to depend on my officers, all my officers, at this time. Not have to chase them down to make them listen to what I have to say."

Webb ducked his head but didn't speak.

"I'll tell you what I want to know, Captain. And you will answer me truthfully. Look at me when I talk to you, please."

Webb raised his head, straightened his back. His throat was dry but he held the woman's steady gaze.

"I want to know…" she said, regarding him levelly. "Have you heard from my son? And no jokes about which one. You know very well which one."

Webb's throat tightened. "No, ma'am. I have not."

She surveyed him for another achingly long minute. "You're sure?"

"I'm not lying, Special Commander. I wouldn't lie about this."

"No, I don't suppose you would." Her eyes went far away for a moment then he saw her drag her focus back to him. "Not that you've not done much to inspire my confidence of late."

"My commanding officer is happy with my performance."

"Of course she is. DC Hudson's operated on the underground her entire career. She's used to dealing with soldiers trained to defy protocol."

"To provide vital intel," Webb said deliberately slowly, feeling his face go hot.

She held his hard look with a stony one of her own. "Eclipse might well have facilitated much of the Service's expansion, but that doesn't stop some of my generals disliking the way it operates."

"I think it's been proved that blasting independent governments and separatist movements into oblivion isn't the best way to win their allegiance."

"I don't know why you're arguing with me, Captain. I agree with you. And with DC Hudson. I always have, which, again, is why you continue to have support from Command. However, my favour does not give you freedom to ignore my direct demands."

"I - " Webb started, but she cut him off.

"I've had enough of your arguments. I believe you when you say you haven't heard from Kaleb. But in light of your unique relationship with him, I have an assignment for you."

Webb didn't bother to argue that he was already in the middle of an assignment. Her manner told him it would be useless.

"As you know, General Hugo has journeyed to Schiaparelli City on Mars to meet with the Governor Arcadius Rose to discuss the rumours of an armed insurgent group gathering force in the colony there and to investigate the claims that my son…" she stopped a second and schooled her face to blankness again before continuing, "claims that my son has defected and joined them."

"You don't believe those rumours, I'm guessing?"

"I am keeping an open mind. But either way, my only concern is getting him back. If he has defected, he is to be returned for court-martial. If he has been kidnapped, it is a rescue operation,"

"I take it you've not heard from him either then, ma'am?" Webb asked quietly.

"No," she said. "No one has for over a year. Not even his wife."

Webb felt chilled, despite the heat. He blinked to hide it. "No one at all?"

"We were hoping perhaps by now you might have."

Webb winced. "We didn't exactly part on the best terms. If there was anyone he was going to reach out to, there wasn't much chance it'd be me."

"Disagreement or not, you were his closest friend. The fact that he has not contacted you in some way makes me believe it more likely that he is being held against his will."

"Red Star actually exists then?" Webb said, daring to look her in the eye again.

"As I say, I'm assuming nothing," she said. Her face was closed up and unreadable.

"So, where do I come in?" Webb said, already knowing and

dreading the answer.

Webb followed her glance through the window in the canteen doors but the corridor has been cleared of curious faces.

"Your new assignment is to find my son, Captain Webb. Find him and bring him home."

Webb stood still for a long moment. "What makes you think I can and General Hugo can't?"

"My husband has faith in Governor Rose's cooperation and the Service's influence over the Martian colony."

"And you don't?"

"If Mars were that loyal to us, my son would have been delivered back to us months ago."

Webb chewed on the inside of his cheek. Emotion rose up his throat despite his attempts to choke it off.

"You know him better than anyone, Captain," she continued. It was clear from her tone that it might be the truth, but not one she liked. "If Rose fails to deliver Kaleb, or can't, I think you are the one with the skills to locate him and bring him home. Before it's too late."

Webb rubbed the back of his neck and stared at the floor. He closed his eyes and couldn't help but see Kaleb Hugo's face rise in front of him, expression twisted with fury and hateful words spilling from his mouth. Guilt rode through him like sickness.

"I…can't."

"This isn't a negotiation, Captain."

"No," Webb snapped. "It's not that I won't. It's that I can't. I haven't spoken to Kaleb since well before he disappeared, Special Commander. And we were almost strangers to each other at that point as it was. I thought I knew your son, but I was wrong. I'm not the person who can figure where he's gone or what he's doing. And, even if I found him, there's nothing to say he'd come back with me."

"I think you misunderstand that situation, Captain," SC Hugo replied, taking another step closer to him. Her iron-streaked brows had drawn together a fraction. "I'm not asking you to do anything. I'm ordering you."

"Ma'am," Webb started, desperately.

"The situation is simple. Either board my copter ready to return to Sydney HQ to prepare for your mission within the hour, or you will be discharged from the Service. Dishonourably, with no pension or reference."

Webb stared at her, opening and closing his hands like he was drowning and trying to grab onto something to keep him afloat.

"Gather what you need," she continued with a glance at her wristpanel. "I have arranged a debrief for you with DC Hudson and Captain Harvey to fill you in on what little we have so far."

"Right now?" Webb started, "But - "

"Your unit can handle what's left of this mission on their own. We will supply a story to explain your transfer. From here on out, everything is under strictest confidence. In fact, once you launch from HQ there is to be absolute radio silence about the true nature of your mission until it is complete. General Hugo's negotiations may still deliver and if they do, I don't want Rose or any Martian sympathisers finding out I subverted them. These are the parameters of the mission, Captain. If you do not comply I will be forced to review your situation."

"Ok," he started, hurrying after her as she paced toward the door. "Ok, I get it. I'll do it. But I - "

"You now have fifty-eight minutes," she said as she pulled the doors open. Her sons were stood to attention in the corridor and saluted as she came out. "Don't make me wait any longer than I already have. Cadet?" The girl that had brought him from the command unit hurried forward from where she'd been waiting. "Take us to Major Tremaine, if you'd be so kind."

The flustered girl nodded, saluted and turned on her heel to lead them away. The brothers all filed after her mother. Giles hung back and smiled, held out his hand. Webb hesitated then took it.

"Thanks, Ezekiel," he said. "I told the others we could count on you."

Webb gave him a searching look. "I wouldn't say I have a huge amount of choice."

Hugo's brother held on to his hand a second longer and Webb wondered how much he knew of what his mother had said to him, then clapped him on the shoulder.

"I know you'll deliver."

"Hey," he said softly, stopping the other man from following his brothers out into the yard. "What if he doesn't want to be found?"

The man's mouth tightened. "It's not about what he wants. Not anymore."

Webb nodded, looking at the floor. "Giles…"

"What?" Giles frowned at the look on his face.

"I gotta tell you something. One of my unit photographed Ambassador Martinez in enemy territory."

"What?"

Webb waved out toward the forest. "The guerrilla compound we're monitoring. We think it's the base of a group that's been making raids around here. Martinez just arrived to meet with them. I saw him myself."

Giles frowned harder. "Are you sure?"

Webb rolled his eyes. "Yes I'm damned sure. I have a photo…" Webb trailed off, patting his pockets. "Shit, Tremaine has it."

"I'll get it off him."

"If he hasn't wiped it. Look, Giles, it was him. I remember him from the Memorial Ball last year. The guy spent thirty minutes trying to tell me real soldiers fight in the open, not underground."

Giles smiled slightly. "Yeah, that sounds like Martinez." He shook his head. "He was here? Really?"

"Really."

"Ok…" Giles said. "I'll look into it. Maybe the talks are just going better than planned and he's gone to discuss terms."

"Through the back door?"

"Leave it with me, Webb. You have other things to worry about.

Now go. We'll see you on board."

Δ

Webb stared at his open pack. All it contained was two spare shirts and his cargo boots. He was already wearing his knives, dog-tags and gun. The rest of the stuff in his footlocker: visors, gloves, data panels, grips and other assorted tech, belonged to the unit. He looked at the clothes in the bag and felt his jaw tighten. He couldn't think of anything back at his apartment in Sydney he'd want either.

It had never bothered him before. The Service always provided him with what he'd needed for the mission at hand. He'd never needed to own anything. But seeing this jumble of meagre possessions suddenly struck him as pathetic. He zipped up the pack, pushing away the thought and slammed the locker shut.

"Damn you, Hugo," he cursed under his breath.

"Sir?"

Webb started. Lieutenant Vergennes's large frame was taking up most of the doorway, a tiny line between his fair brows.

"Did you get another headache?" the young man asked carefully.

"No, I'm fine," Webb said, shouldering his pack and grabbing his cap off a hook in the wall. Then he noticed the pack at his lieutenant's feet. "Vergennes? What are you doing?"

"Colonel Hugo said you'd been reassigned and needed a number two, sir."

"Which one's Colonel Hugo?"

Vergennes raised his blonde eyebrows. "Colonel Giles Hugo, sir."

"There's a mistake," Webb said, rubbing his eyes. "This isn't a two-man mission."

"The colonel was quite specific, sir."

"Look, Vergennes. This isn't exactly...well. Let's just say it's a sensitive assignment."

"I've served undercover ops in Eclipse since I graduated from the Academy, sir," Vergennes continued, straightening to his considerable height, his face hardening.

"Yes, and you've been great, even if you have a rod up your ass like no one I've ever met, and believe me I've met some rod-bearers in my time - " Vergennes coloured but otherwise didn't react, " - but seriously, Eclipse needs you here. And no matter what the Hugos say, I'm better off doing this alone."

Webb moved to leave but Vergennes didn't move.

"Lieutenant…"

"I'm coming with you, Captain. And, with respect, I don't think there's a lot you can do about it. The number two on this assignment is in the mission parameters."

Webb sighed. "You're a royal pain in the ass, you know that, Vergennes?"

"Yes sir. Shall we get to the copter, sir?"

Webb shook his head. "Lead the way."

SC Hugo's copter was environmentally controlled and had a motion smoother than any flyer Webb had ever piloted. He watched the jungle base and then the trees drop away out of the porthole until it was nothing but a sea of green beneath them.

"Well I bet Tremaine is cracking open something expensive and bubbly right now," Webb muttered.

"Sir?" Vergennes replied.

"The major's been waiting to get Eclipse out of that base for weeks. Now I'm not there to head him off at every turn I bet he'll get his way."

"Matsuo will take care of it, sir."

Webb snorted. The green turned to blue below. The copter hummed around them. It was blessedly cool. He leant his forehead against the bulkhead and felt the smooth movement and the endless blue calm the edges of the roiling in his head.

"Captain Webb, wake up."

Webb blinked and the copter compartment came into focus around him.

"Jesus, are we at Sydney already?" he said, peering out the porthole at the multitude of glowing bands of skyways weaving between towering megablocks.

"I believe Special Commander Hugo gets priority skylane use."

"I bet she does," he muttered, rubbing away the last of the fading dream that was still flashing on the inside of his eyelids.

"Captain Webb?" Vergennes asked after a pause.

"What?"

"What exactly *is* our mission?"

Webb looked at his lieutenant. The younger man sat calmly, blue eyes clear but guarded, his broad shoulders square and back poker-straight, even when sat down.

"Are you sure you want me to tell you? Cos if I do, there's no getting out of tagging along for the ride."

"Again, Captain. I believe I've proved I'm capable of completing all manner of assignments."

Webb sighed. "I know you have. It's not your capability I'm worried about. It's your readiness to jump head-first into a potential snake-pit of a political shitstorm. And a dangerous one at that."

Vergennes just said, "I'm ready sir."

"Are you sure? Really sure? Cos this shit won't wash out of your uniform, believe me."

"I wouldn't have joined your unit if I wasn't prepared to bear a certain amount of disdain from the establishment, Captain Webb."

Webb eyed him, trying to figure out if there was an insult in there.

"Ok, fella. You asked for it. Here's the deal. We're off to find

Kaleb Hugo, wherever he might be and in whatever company he might be keeping. And no one is to find out what we're doing. How's that for fun?"

Vergennes blinked slowly. "Isn't his father General Hugo - "

"The general's good wife doesn't have the utmost faith in his success, it would seem." Webb looked out the window as the top of one of the megablocks in Service HQ rose to meet them, feeling his belly begin to tie itself into knots. "And, Jesus help me, she's probably on the money. Hugo's gone to ground. His angry dad is hardly likely to flush him out."

The copter landed with a smooth rock on its landing gear and the thrum of its powerblades faded.

"He's an associate of yours, yes? Vice-Admiral Hugo?"

"Was," Webb replied, feeling the knots tighten further.

"I studied Pharos's Lunar Uprising at the Academy," Vergennes said into the silence that followed. "You both achieved some great things during those times."

"Don't believe everything you read, kid."

They left their compartment and disembarked from the copter. Erica Hugo and her sons were already halfway across the open space of their landing platform, surrounded by grey-uniformed servicemen who were thrusting panels at them and yammering questions. Not even Giles had hung back.

"I guess that's the limit of our executive-access time," Webb muttered.

"Sir," a waiting Servicemen called over the noise of the wind. "If you and the lieutenant would follow me."

"Where are we going?" Webb called, holding his cap on his head so it wouldn't gust away.

"Guest quarters," the guard replied, striding toward the express lift shaft ahead of them. "I've been ordered to escort you there so you can refresh yourselves and then to your meeting."

"There's no time being wasted on this," Vergennes observed as they stepped into the lift after their guide.

"That's because it's probably too late already," Webb said.

The sleep on the copter had restored some of his energy but he was still more relieved than he could express by the sight of the guest quarters suite with its private washroom. All thoughts of Hugo and Mars were firmly shelved whilst he stepped into the shower to wash the last of the jungle off him. When he stepped out from under the steaming water, he felt almost human again.

He caught sight of himself in the mirror. Harvey was going to tear a piece off him for losing weight again. It didn't matter how many times he explained to her there wasn't time to eat properly in the field, she never believed him.

The thought caught him off guard. He hadn't seen Marilyn Harvey in almost a year. He wondered if they were still friends.

He stopped himself touching the scars Ariel had given him on the Tide. It had been an age since he'd even noticed them, but with Hugo planted firmly in his mind for the first time in months, they suddenly felt as fresh as when they were newly healed.

His crew-cut has grown out enough to flop in his eyes and he pushed the wet hair back from his face, still disliking that short hair felt unfamiliar to him. He'd cut his pirate tail off when he'd signed up with Eclipse seven years ago. Technically, he'd had shorter hair longer than he'd worn it long…but the false memories of his predecessor nagged at him to feel otherwise. An old bitterness rose but he was well-practised at pushing it away and did so.

He rummaged in his pack for clean clothes, only to notice that some had been laid out on the bed. He frowned at the captain's uniform, grey slacks and jacket, stiff black shirt, grey tie and the peaked hat. He hated the hats most of all.

He dumped his pack on top of the uniform and pulled out his own black combat trousers and a white t-shirt. He pulled on his cargo boots, so old now they were scuffed to grey in places but were still the comfiest things he'd ever owned, then shrugged on his old jacket he'd had since the Zero and pulled his baseball cap on over his still-damp hair.

He looped his dog-tags over his neck then looked up at a knock on the door. He opened it to the same guard that had led them down from the landing platform with Vergennes standing to attention in full uniform behind him. They were both too disciplined to give his own attire more than a glance but he didn't miss it.

"Any chance of some food? I'm goddamn starving."

"I believe food has been laid out at the meeting, sir," the guard said.

Webb heaved a sigh. "Lead on."

II

One thing Webb had always liked about being in Service HQ was the chance to be faceless. The complex of megablocks consisting of docks, meeting halls and command rooms was always teeming with high-ranking Service officers like the Hugos and their generals. Webb was just another captain in the melee and rarely got more than a vague glance of recognition.

He followed the young Serviceman through the broad, well-lit corridors and in and out of express lifts, revelling in the feeling of not having disapproval roll off everyone who looked at him and trying not to let his mind wander either back toward his unit or forward to what he might have actually said yes to.

The Serviceman preceded them into one of the smaller meeting rooms on the conference level, announced them and left. Webb stood near the door for a moment, gathering himself.

Marilyn Harvey was sitting in one of the high-backed chairs around the table. Divisional Commander Hudson was standing at her shoulder. They had apparently been talking but stopped when they entered. Hudson looked collected as ever: uniform spotless and creased just right, brown hair pulled back from her face and tied in a knot at her neck. Webb's commanding officer basically looked as she always did, but Webb wondered if there was a slightly more pinched look about her mouth than usual.

He almost didn't recognise Harvey. He swallowed the choke of guilt. The former smuggler, usually vibrant with energy looked small and stooped and there were grey smudges under her green eyes. Her cheek bones were more prominent than he remembered and her yellow curls were pulled back and tied in a tight tail, making the new angles of her face even harsher. Her green eyes, once so vital, were dull and pained.

She'd looked more alive when she'd been recovering from her torture at the hands of Ariel. Webb wanted to rush to her and take her hand, hug her, anything, but he stood rooted to the spot and let her examine him the way he was examining her.

"Zeek," she said. "You've not been eating, huh?"

Webb tried for a smile. "Speak for yourself."

Harvey's mouth turned up in half a wan smile. "It's been a while, right?"

"Yeah. It has."

She looked away and Webb felt a stab, wondering what she didn't want him to see.

"Well this is something we can fix, at least for now," she said, nodding toward the plates of food and jugs of water and fresh juice on the table.

"Not a Nutripak in sight," he said. "I could cry, guys. Thanks."

"You've been assigned a number two for this?" Hudson said, weighing up Vergennes.

"Lieutenant Blaise Vergennes reporting for duty, ma'am," Vergennes said, saluting. "Colonel Giles Hugo said I was to accompany and assist Captain Webb."

"Do you understand the nature of this mission we're about to discuss, Lieutenant?" Hudson asked.

"I do, ma'am. My understanding is it carries the highest level security rating and has both personal and professional implications for some prominent Service Commanders. I'm honoured to have been chosen for this mission."

"He volunteered," Webb said, trying not to make it sound too apologetic.

"I am familiar with your service record, Lieutenant Vergennes," Hudson said. "Captain Webb is lucky to have you along."

"Thank you, ma'am."

Webb muttered under his breath.

"Take a seat, Captain," Hudson said to Webb. "Help yourself to food. We have much to discuss."

"Don't we just," he said, taking a seat.

"You too, Vergennes," Hudson said, indicating the last free

seat. "I know how field work can take it out of you and we're all grateful you've joined us so speedily."

"Not all that speedily," Harvey said, giving Webb a look as she pulled a plate toward her. "Erica came to me weeks ago about organising this."

Webb winced whilst loading his plate with cold meat and fruit.

"I want to get one thing straight," he said, taking a breath and not looking at anyone. "Ok, so SC Hugo has asked me to find Kaleb. I'm touched in some ways. Really, makes me fuzzy that everyone still thinks of me as part of the gang. But, seriously, what do you think I can do that you haven't already tried?"

Harvey stared at her plate and Webb regretted the words, but watched Hudson.

"It's the truth, Cheryl," he said around a mouthful of orange. "If the Analysts haven't found any trace of him, no one's made any ransom demands and he hasn't even got a message to his own wife, what makes you all think I can do anything?"

Hudson pulled back a chair carefully and sat. She leant forward on her elbows and looked him right in the eye. "No one's tried an Eclipse approach yet."

"You're trying to tell me Eclipse hasn't been trying to dig up his trail from the second he left?" he asked, filling a glass with juice. He made himself take a sip and a bite of bread. He knew he needed it, but he couldn't taste any of it.

"We've had an Eclipse Analyst trying to track him down for over a year," Hudson replied wearily. "But they haven't found anything. Not even a hint. It's time for a manned mission, Webb. And you're the one most qualified to take it on. Try not to think of it personally."

"Yeah, but it damn well is personal," Webb said before he could stop himself, slamming his glass back on the table. "Sorry Marilyn," he said, seeing her flinch, "but the bastard vanishes without a word? To any of us?"

"He was taken, Zeek," Harvey said. "He didn't leave. Someone took him."

"How do you know?"

Harvey's tired glance went round them all, finally landing on Hudson who gave her a tiny nod of encouragement. She looked back to him, eyes heavy.

"You didn't see him for months before he disappeared," she began. Webb tried to decide if there was judgment in her tone. "He wasn't himself."

"How so?"

"He was moody. Cold."

"And your point is?"

Harvey managed to glare. "I know you fell out, Zeek, but you know he's a good man. You like him, really. Love him, even. So cut the schoolboy crap and get your head in the game, ok? He needs you."

Webb glowered at his plate.

"As I said, he was acting weird for weeks before he vanished," Harvey continued. "I tried to get it outta him but he just shut me out. He spent hours in the shooting range and on the simulators. Once, not long before he went, he was gone for days and I didn't know where. He wouldn't tell me. The girls were due home for the summer break…" Harvey choked for the first time. She put her knuckles to her lips. Hudson hesitated then put a hand on her shoulder and it seemed to steady her. She drew in a noisy breath and continued. "Becca and Ayme knew something was wrong and I didn't know what to tell them. And then one morning he was gone. No signs of a struggle and he took nothing with him."

There was a silence. Webb risked a glance at Vergennes. He was watching Harvey but he still wore his professional Service mask. Webb felt a stab of envy, wondering if the guilt crawling under his skin was showing on his own face.

"I think he was contacted by whoever took him months before he vanished," Harvey continued. Her eyes were dry, but the knuckles of her hands where she clasped them together were white. "I think they tempted him, then blackmailed him then threatened him and when none of that worked, they just took him."

"Any idea who?" Webb asked, afraid he already knew the answer.

Harvey raised her head and looked at him. "Red Star."

Webb drank a mouthful of juice. His throat was dry.

"I've had Anita Rami look over their domestic comm systems," Hudson put in. "There have been transmissions from Mars to their apartment. But whoever it was is too good at covering their tracks to leave any workable traces."

"I thought Red Star were just a rumour," Webb said, not very hopefully.

"Everything we have found, which has amounted to not much more than rumours it's true," Hudson conceded, "indicates the existence of some sort of separatist movement gathering sympathy in Schiaparelli City. Whether Governor Arcadius Rose is actively involved isn't clear, but he's vocal about his stance on using the Martian colony as an example of a new way of life, away from Service control. Its population and power are growing every day. And with it also grows the support for Rose's Orbit Alliance ideology."

"Orbit Alliance?" Webb asked.

Hudson visually schooled her face. "Rose has resurrected the campaign for a democratically elected circle of representatives governing the Orbit. An 'Orbit Alliance'. He has openly stated that he believes the Service is outdated and oppressive."

"Well, if that ain't a political hot potato," Webb said, tearing up some cold meat with his fingers.

"The Service is the only organisation in history that has managed to establish and maintain stability for all of humanity," Vergennes put in. Webb blinked at him. There was a slight flush on his cheeks. It was almost an emotional response, but not quite.

"The idea of a democratic Orbit Alliance is not a new one,"

Hudson hedged. "It's just Rose is currently the most prominent advocator for it. But either way, his political views are not Eclipse's concern."

"The only thing we care about is if he's hiding a private army ready to fight for his little philosophy." Webb sighed and pushed his plate away. "You'd think the damn politicians would be bored of this dance by now, wouldn't you? Ok, ok…" He laid his hands flat on the table and attempted to order his thoughts. "There's clearly a rich mix of crap being stirred up out in Silence City. Any info we have about Kaleb's involvement is just guesses. But with the Service securing new allegiances every other day with the promise to relieve overcrowding by shipping folk out to Mars, I guess what everyone wants is to track Hugo down, if he really is out there, and bring him home under the radar, so it doesn't rock any boats?"

"There are already mutterings amongst the generals," Hudson added with an assessing glance at Vergennes, "about SC Hugo's own family getting mixed up in the likes Red Star. They're not happy, even if it is only a rumour. And their suspiciousness certainly isn't helping our relationship with Mars."

"Erica's got a hell of lot to lose," Harvey said. She looked a little calmer, sat a little straighter. "We all do. But she trusts you to fix it. And so do I."

"No pressure then."

Harvey almost smiled. "You're never happy unless you're neck-deep in something nasty, Zeek. Admit it."

"Well, this is nasty alright." Webb slumped back in his seat and closed his eyes a second. "Ok. I'll do it."

Everyone shifted in the room and looks were exchanged.

"Let's not kid ourselves," he said with an edge in his voice. "The Special Commander has ordered me to do it. It's not like I can really say 'no thanks, sweetheart', is it? But I just wanted it on record, officially, that I warned you that even if I do find him, rescue mission or not, he ain't exactly gonna be thrilled to see me."

"You think too much of yourself," Harvey said. "You think your fallout was such a big deal he wouldn't want your help?"

Webb shrugged a shoulder. "He's a stubborn asshole, is all I'm saying."

He was gratified to see an actual smile brighten Harvey's face for a second. "That makes two of you."

"Good," Hudson said, standing. Vergennes followed suit, then Harvey. Webb got to his feet too, stuffing one last meat strip in his mouth. "I will have Anita Rami issue you with everything you'll need for an infiltration and extraction mission. Report to Central Docks at 0800 and everything will be ready."

"Hold your horses. That's it?" Webb said. "You don't have any more information?"

"Everything we have on Red Star, Mars, Schiaparelli City and Governor Rose will be sent to the systems on your ship. But I'm warning you, it's not much. And remember, your orders are to maintain radio silence after launch."

"Christ wept, do you not even know where I can start?"

"You know where to start," Harvey said, something flickering in her eye. "The one person who's most likely to have heard something is one none of us have been able to get to talk to us."

"No…" Webb started, stomach clenching.

"Grow a pair, Zeek," Harvey said, looking tired again, edge of desperation creeping into her manner despite her attempt at a casual tone. "She might be glad to see you."

"All the Hugos hate me right now, Marilyn," Webb argued. "But they're practically strewing flowers at my feet compared to her."

"Dana Hugo is not only Kaleb's only surviving sister but is also an extremely well-connected freelancer," Hudson said, heading for the door like the matter was settled. "She's quashed all our attempts to communicate with her, but she'll talk to you."

"None of our regular points have been able to give us anything solid on Kaleb or Red Star, Webb," Harvey said, pushing her chair back in at the table. "But I'm willing to bet Dana's made it her business to gather everything there is to know since this all happened. And her reach is greater than ours."

"Then why can't you talk to her?" Webb tried, trying not to whine.

"Like Cheryl said, she won't talk to us. She's not spoken to any of the rest of us in years, she's hardly likely to start now. She still operates out of Sunside 3 though, I know that much."

"Aw man," Webb dropped back into his chair. "This mission just keeps on giving."

"You'll be fine," Harvey said, moving toward the door. Vergennes fell in against the wall and saluted her. "At ease, Lieutenant. Why don't you go and get some rest?"

"Yes ma'am," the lieutenant responded. "Sir?"

Webb waved in the direction of the door. "Go on, get out of here."

Vergennes left. Harvey lingered with her back to him. He saw the stiffness which had eased whilst they talked was back in her shoulders.

"Marilyn," he heard himself say, his voice quiet. "I'm sorry I never came by. I…have no excuse. I just didn't…" He groped for words.

She wandered back and took the seat next to him. She paused before taking his hand. She held it in her lap and looked at it and not his face.

"I think I understand, Zeek. Though I didn't at the time." She raised her head. "The girls have missed you."

Webb winced. "I just…after everything with Kaleb. After what we said to each other…he told you, didn't he? What happened?"

"Whatever went on between you two was always just between you, Ezekiel. You should know that. We've known each other long enough."

Webb clutched her hand and covered it with his other. He couldn't think what else to say so he just sat still, holding their hands clutched together.

"You'll look after Eclipse while I'm gone? Major Tremaine and some of the generals would love a chance to clip our wings."

"I can handle the generals," she said. "Thanks, Zeek," she added softly. "For doing this."

Webb swallowed. "Why not save the thanks for if I actually manage it?"

She smiled a lop-sided smile. Her eyes were dry but hollow. "Thanks for trying."

Webb nodded stiffly and patted her hand but couldn't think of anything to say.

"If…if he's dead," she said, her voice catching. "Bring his body home. If there is one."

Webb's throat tightened. "He's not dead, Marilyn. I know he's not."

She nodded firmly, like she was making herself believe him, then rose and went to the door.

"Good luck with Dana," she said.

"I'll damn well need it," he replied after she'd left.

Δ

Webb slept better than he expected, though the night in the soft bed with proper pillows left him with a crick in his neck and an ache in his back. He didn't like to think about the fact that his body preferred travel cots and shipboard bunks than anything civilised. He also neatly side-stepped thinking about the fact that they hadn't let him back to his own apartment, probably so SC Hugo could make sure he didn't run off.

Like he was likely to do that now, he thought bitterly.

He took his time showering, despite the chrono nearing his launch time. He allowed the hot water to wash away some of the tension that built whenever he thought of what lay ahead. He told himself he just had to be objective. It was just another job. He's done infiltration and extraction missions more times than he cared to remember.

It's just this time the thing to extract happened to be an old friend. An old friend who he'd hurt. And who was currently a political grenade with the pin pulled out.

Vergennes was waiting for him outside his room. Webb took a second to take him in, consider him, for the first time, as his partner on the mission. He was very tall, with a steel-blue gaze and fair hair. A strong jaw. Almost too good-looking, Webb thought. He wondered, not for the first time, how a man with such striking features and straight-laced thinking had made such a successful career in a rag-tag, undercover unit like Eclipse.

Webb told himself that the other officer's ability to adapt could only be in his favour right now, though something in his gut nagged at him. Pushing aside the uncomfortable suspicion that the feeling might be bourn from jealousy, Webb made himself examine his partner objectively. He was in civilian clothes: a nondescript jacket, shirt and black combats, but stood straight as any soldier on parade, as usual.

"Blaise, I've told you this before," he said. "Real people, you know, with real spines, don't stand like that. Try and relax a bit, will you?"

"Yes, sir," he replied and Webb didn't miss the overtones of disapproval in his voice.

Webb shook his head and they stepped onto an express lift which whisked them down to the shuttle platform levels.

"No personal flyer or priority skyways now, huh?" Webb muttered as they joined the queue of Service officers and civilians waiting for the inter-city shuttle.

"We're operating off the radar now, sir," Vergennes said. "I checked our Service profiles this morning. Officially, we've been assigned to Patrol Duty at Tranquility Hall."

Webb blanched. "I've never been assigned to Patrol Duty in my life."

There was the suggestion of amusement in Vergennes's blue

eyes. "I suspect it's meant to look like a reprimand, sir, as a result of your confrontation with Major Tremaine."

"Oh. That."

Webb stepped aboard the shuttle and found a seat near the back away from the other passengers. The vehicle's doors hissed shut and it slid out from the platform and into the city's skyways.

Webb checked the personal comm on his wristpanel, but there were no messages. He wasn't sure who he was hoping to have heard from, but he pulled his sleeve down over it with a jerk and watched the skyline of Sydney slide by the window.

They disembarked at Central Docks with the majority of the shuttle's passengers.

"Have you been told which is ours?" Webb asked as they moved through the grid of walkways between the berths holding everything from civilian cruisers to short-hop skiffs.

"This way, sir. Ours is the Duty."

"The what?"

"The Duty, sir. A Class Two sloop with duplex engines and berthing for three. I believe that's it there."

Webb felt a real smile start to form on his face when he spotted the sleek runner Vergennes indicated. It was a neat craft with clean lines, gleaming silver-blue hull and some impressive hardware.

"Well, she looks fast at least. I think our chances of success just received some much-needed boosting."

"Captain Webb? Captain Webb, sir?"

Webb swung round. A woman a little older than him was making her way toward them from the nearest walkway. She bobbed through the foot and moped traffic easily in her tall heels, disarming all the disgruntled moped drivers with a wide, flashing smile. When she reached them, she turned her smile on them. She looked vaguely familiar, though Webb couldn't put his finger on why. Her teeth were perfect and white, with an ornamental silver one near the front. Her eyes were wide and a deep blue, like the Earth sky just after sunset, and she wore a simple but elegant suit in a shade of blue that complimented her eyes, though it looked ridiculously out of place amongst the sweating and grimy spacers in their coveralls and flightsuits.

"Captain Webb?" she said again and glanced at Vergennes. "And…I'm sorry I don't know you?"

"Who exactly is asking?"

Webb's bluntness did not appear to put her off. Her smile widened and she pulled out a stylish datapanel with a silver-plated stylus.

"My name is Vee Osgard. I'm an Analyst for the Now network site."

Webb scowled and turned away. She hurried after them both as they paced down the side of their ship.

"Please, Captain, I just want to ask you a couple of simple questions."

"You're not an Analyst, you're a reporter," Webb countered, speeding up.

She matched his pace, easily, tapping commands with her stylus without even having to look.

"Now is a highly accredited site, Captain. We have a lot of reach and a lot of influence. I'm interested in getting your take on the disappearance of Vice-Admiral Kaleb Hugo."

"You need to back away, ma'am," Vergennes began but Webb stopped in his tracks.

"No, hold on a minute. What do you know about Hugo? And why are you asking me?"

She brightened, consulting her panel. "I have background on you and the Vice-Admiral which suggests you have had a long-standing relationship. Bumpy, it would seem, but pretty solid. Would you say that's right?"

"Cut the crap, lady," Webb retorted. "Tell me what you know and how you know it."

Osgard's eyes flickered toward the Duty and then back to them.

"I think you mistake my intention here, Captain. I'm dedicated to getting the truth. There are rumours going around about what's happened to SC Hugo's youngest son, and what the implications of that might be. I'm keen to help the Service deliver its message and to keep the situation under control."

"The Service has its own Analysts and PR units for that."

Osgard put her head on one side, like she pitied him. "They need more than their official spokesmen to speak to be believed. I'm offering you an opportunity here. I don't suppose many networkers will be so keen to help the Service as I am."

"See ya," Webb said, turning back to his ship. "Contact Erica Hugo's press office if you want statements."

"Is it true you've been assigned to find him, sir? Is it true that SC Hugo doesn't think her husband's investigation will succeed? Where are you going to start looking?"

Webb hunched his shoulders and mounted the boarding ladder, skin crawling. He heard Vergennes intercept Osgard and tell her firmly to back away before launch. She called up to him as he opened the hatch but Vergennes kept her from following him up. For the first time since leaving the base, he was grateful the imposing lieutenant was with him.

He paused just inside the hatch until Vergennes had joined him, sealed it and retracted the mounting ladder.

"Reporters sniffing around already. That can't be good," he murmured.

"Have they approached you before, sir?"

"Yeah," Webb said, stepping to the nearest porthole and watching Osgard stand just out of range, taking pictures of the ship with her panel. "People have asked me about Hugo in the past. But how does she know about our orders?"

"She might just be taking an educated guess, sir."

"Maybe. I don't like it though. Let's get out of here. And I need to make some calls so I can get a new reg for the ship."

"Sir?"

"She's got all our details down now," Webb said, nodding out the porthole as the blue figure of Osgard slipped away into the foot traffic. "She could track the ship. Besides, 'Duty'? No way I'm piloting a ship call Duty."

"If you think that's best, sir."

Webb gave him a look and moved past him toward the cockpit. He took the time to look the sloop over and had to admit he was grudgingly impressed. She was small, but with trim lines and every weld and bolt in her was brand new and lovingly finished. The stores of tech were all top-grade and the weapons more advanced than any he'd had access to in months. When he opened the small hold to find two motorbikes, black chassis gleaming, secured to the deck for flight, he felt his first surge of excitement.

"Captain?"

Webb looked up from the bike to see Vergennes stood in the doorway.

"Analyst Rami is on the comm for you sir."

Webb followed Vergennes back to the cockpit and sat at the comm station, smiling at the image of Anita Rami's face on the display. She had some more lines around her eyes and a streak of white in her black braid, but looked otherwise unchanged. He wasn't sure how that made him feel so shied away from trying to decide.

"Hey, Anita," he said instead. "It's been a while."

"It's good to see you," she said and he almost felt she meant it. "I trust the *Duty* meets your requirements? Hudson only gave me the brief yesterday. I had to pull her together pretty quickly."

"Looks like we have everything we'll be needing. For what good it will do."

She pursed her lips. "Officially I don't know what your assignment is, Webb. I'm an Analyst now and there's a…wall…between us and Eclipse. But, unofficially, I will say watch your step out there. All my information says tensions between Mars and the rest of the Orbit are growing since General Hugo's arrival in

Schiaparelli City, not lessening as we'd hoped."

"I love how everyone's going out of their way to make me feel hopeful about this job."

"I believe in being prepared. I know you do too."

There was a moment of silence in which he wondered which version of him she was talking about.

"Yes, I do. Thanks, Rami. And the bikes are…well. Let's just say the mission just got more interesting," he added with half a smile.

"Thought you'd like them," she said and he was rewarded with a soft smile of her own. "But the bikes aren't for play. Schiaparelli City's skyways won't be for months. Most of the traffic is still on suspended groundways."

Webb rubbed his bottom lip and glanced around the cockpit. "Anything else you can give us, Rami? There seems so little info right now."

Rami shrugged one shoulder. "We're still digging. All mentions of Red Star are just that: mentions, gossip. The poor connection to Mars communications doesn't help matters either. Everything we have so far is in your databanks, along with SC Hugo's electronic seal. You've been given permission to use it if absolutely necessary. I've also been told to inform you that you are free to use any means necessary, but that if you're caught, the Service will deny all involvement."

"Always good to know where I stand."

"This is serious, Webb."

"I know it is."

Impatience mixed with what might have been sympathy tightened her face.

"There are some IDs for you both in the locker in the hold: some fake Service ones, some civilian. The cards should pass even a Service inspection. I'm telling you all this because once you launch you won't be able to ask me, or anyone else, anything until you complete your mission. Radio silence must be absolute: we have no idea who might be watching out for someone attempting…what you're attempting."

"I reckon they'd be surprised the Service waited so long," Webb muttered.

Anita pursed her lips. "I think this was a last resort. Not that I would presume to comment on SC Hugo's motivations."

"Sure. But…Anita," he said after a pause, glancing at Vergennes who was busy running start-up checks on the command console. "Do you believe the talk? Forget your facts and probabilities, or the fact you're not supposed to know what we're doing. Do you think Hugo's turned coat? Is the man we knew even capable of that?"

"I don't know," she said after a long pause in which she stared off-screen. "I…no. I don't know."

"Ok," he said, and watched her face close back up. "Anything else?"

"No," she said, a little stiffly. Then her face softened slightly. "Good luck."

She cut the connection. Webb stared at the blank display, annoyed at the wash of guilt that was still left in the wake of talking to Rami, even after all these years.

"Sir?" Vergennes prompted.

"Where are we at?" Webb said, shaking himself and moving to stand behind his lieutenant's chair.

"Start-up checks almost complete, sir," Vergennes reported. "We will be ready to launch shortly."

Webb watched Vergennes's hands skate over the panel. The young man's face was blank, focused.

"Why are you doing this, Vergennes?"

"Sir?" he looked up with the faintest of frowns on his fair brow.

"You've heard it from the horse's mouth: we're flying right into a hurricane of epic proportions. If we screw up, we're on our own. And we can't afford to screw up. I can't turn back…but you can."

"I have my orders, sir," he replied, turning his attention back to the control panel.

"It's not too late for you to step away. I wouldn't blame you and I know you wouldn't blab about what you heard."

"I'm not stepping away," the man stated.

"Explain to me, then. You signed up for this almost before I knew what we were signing up for. Why? Career advancement? Kudos with the Hugos? What? Because I warn you the chances of us achieving either are pretty damn emaciated."

Vergennes levelled an unreadable look at him. "I volunteered to do my duty for the Service, sir."

"I can think of easier ways to do that."

"Do you have a concern about my abilities?"

"Again, no. Jesus. You've frightened me in the past, even. This is just…different. I need to understand why you're here if I'm to trust you. And out there, with just each other to rely on…I need to be able trust you."

Vergennes's face changed slightly. "I can understand that, Captain Webb. I wanted to be your number two on this as soon as I knew SC Hugo was involved personally."

"Oh yeah?" Webb said, letting a smile show on his face. "You got a crush?"

Vergennes's look hardened again. "I believe in her, sir. The Service is stronger than ever, but I've heard what some people are saying about SC Hugo and her family. If I can be of any assistance in stabilising their position, I am honour-bound to do so."

Webb blinked a couple of times. "Ok, then."

"And you, sir?"

"Me?"

"Are you sure you don't want to take the chance to 'step away'?"

"I feel you're dancing on the boarders of appropriateness here, Vergennes."

"Hardly, sir. I understand the nature of this mission. If it's not something you're committed to, it is best we abandon it now."

"I'm committed, Blaise," Webb said, indignity flaring.

Vergennes eyed him for a long moment, then nodded, apparently satisfied.

"Checks complete, sir," he said, voice once again cool.

"Move over, I'll pilot."

Vergennes moved to the co-pilot chair and Webb took the pilot's chair. He took a second to marvel at the sleekness of the controls. They responded to the lightest touch. The engines powered up with a noise no louder than a purr.

"Are we clear?"

"Clearance in thirty seconds, Captain."

Webb pulled in a breath, held it. He looked up at the sky. "I guess this is it, then. God help us both."

Δ

Webb stared out at the white-specked blanket of black nothing ahead, fighting hard to keep his mind blank and not feel like he was being sucked into the suffocating vacuum of his thoughts. So much had been resurrected in his head that he had had firmly stowed for so long, it was almost disorientating. Even the launch and space flight, normally a balm to any tension he might be carrying, weren't quite enough to still the stirrings of anxiety rippling under his skin.

He found he was actually glad when they finally began the approach to the string of shining space stations that were the Sunside colonies, which gave him something else think about. Even so, the sight of the uniform space stations, strung out in a giant daisy chain of gleaming metal with links of thruster flashes from the inter-colony traffic, brought a clench to his chest.

"Starting final approach to Sunside 3," Webb said, flicking controls. "Don't suppose you noticed any body armour in the hold, huh?"

"No sir."

"Figures. Are we ready to close in?"

"Setting in approach vector now, sir. Hailing Harbour Control."

Webb watched the wheel-shaped colony grow larger and larger in the viewscreen. They dropped into the orderly line of craft heading to the nearest docks. The other vessels in the line were mostly passenger shuttles, cruisers and luxury long-haul liners.

"The recreation scene out here must still be alive and kicking, even with Mars promising to be the next Eden."

"Yes sir."

Webb steered the *Duty* closer and closer and then allowed the tracking signals to guide them to their designated yard, throat tightening the whole way. They touched down and the ship gently sighed as the engines cooled. Webb spent a long moment gazing at the wide dockyard, full of neatly-berthed runners and shuttles. Teams of technicians moved amongst the ships, busy with scanners and tools. A series of bright displays high on the internal bulkhead reeled ads for repair companies, service rates and tool hire, as well as features for shows and barhouses that all promised him the time of his life.

When the red-and-white logo of the *Lagrange Lounge* flashed up, he could almost taste stargazer cocktails, citrus-flavoured ice and a mouth that grinned at him as often as it scowled.

"Sir? Are you ok?"

"Let's get this over with," he said, standing. He moved to leave, checking his weapons out of habit then turned to Vergennes. "On second thought, you stay here. I'm better off doing this alone - "

"What is it we're doing here, sir?"

Webb blanched. "Making a deal with the devil."

"Sir?"

"Hugo's freelance sister has a nightclub here. I'm gonna see if she's heard anything. If she'll let me in the door. And if she'll see me without ripping my balls off. Neither of which is certain."

"It is procedure in such circumstances to bring back up - "

Webb raised a hand to cut him off. "As unlikely as she is to talk to me alone, she definitely won't if I bring along such and obvious Serviceman. No offence."

The slight pinching about the mouth told Webb that offence was taken either way.

"What should I do then, sir?"

"Go through the data in the ship's computers and get surfing on the solarnet. See what normal people are saying about Red Star."

"I'm not an Analyst, sir," he said, bristling further.

"I'm not asking you to hack in Haven's credit banks, man. Here…" He paced over to the workstation set into the control panel and booted up. "Come here. Sit. Look." Webb loaded a generic search engine as Vergennes lowered himself into the chair, either not quite disciplined enough to hide his scowl or, on this occasion, not caring to. "Just try and get in the mindset of someone pissed off with the Service. If Red Star really exists, they're recruiting somehow. Search social network sites, rumour boards, discussion forums, anything."

"This is not my area of expertise, sir. And I'm not likely to find anything Analyst Rami hasn't already found," he insisted.

"Just do your best, ok? You will look in ways the Analysts won't. You have no idea what could be in places a normal person might stumble upon that an Analyst wouldn't think to check. Just have a go. The ship's system's encrypted to Pluto and back so it's not like you're going to leave a trail. See what you can come up with."

Webb left the younger man glaring at the workstation display like it had turned up to parade in a rumpled uniform.

An ID swipe and weapons' license check later and Webb was stepping into the colony, finding himself on a wide platform high above ground level, boarded by illuminated decorative fencing. Sunside 3 lay below, from this height looking more like a work of art than a colonial city, lit up in thousands of different coloured lights in dazzling patterns with artificial stars arranged in decorative constellations blinking in the hull above. On his right were a number of shuttle lines bound for different sectors of the colony as well as luxury low-flyer hire booth and a line of waiting taxiflyers. From a chrono he passed he discovered the night-cycle was just getting started and the place was packed with healthy-looking, well-dressed people, all looking like they hadn't a care in the world.

He wondered how many of these people were rich enough to be enjoying Sunside 3 as their regular recreational escape and how many had saved up for months for a chance to spend a couple of days rubbing elbows with the rich and powerful. In his boots, combats and battered cap he drew glances from the Servicemen that guarded the shuttle boarding points and customs entrances, but no one deemed him important enough to stop and question.

He boarded a shuttle with a crowd of people in suits and gowns heading for the nearest rec level and kept his gaze on his toes.

The *Lagrange Lounge*'s entrance had been refurbished since his last visit. The sign over the entrance was new. The red-and-white logo lit up the elegant people filtering in and out of the wide doors, as well reflecting off the visors of the private Enforcers who stood to on either side, bulging out of their tailored suits. Webb stood across the street, looking at it for longer than he knew was professional, with his stomach doing rolls.

"Christ, man, grow a pair," he muttered to himself, took a deep breath and strolled toward the door.

"Hang on there, chum," one of the guards said, stepping into his path and giving him a deliberate up-and-down. "This is a classy joint, ok?"

"I'm here to meet Ms. Lagrange," he said, fighting a sneer.

"Is she expecting you?"

"I guess on some level she might be," Webb said with a half-smile.

"And what is that supposed to mean?"

"Hey, Cliffe," the other Enforcer interrupted, frowning faintly at Webb. Webb recognised his face but couldn't place the name. "I'll handle this." The first man gave them both a doubtful look before returning to his original position. "You're that Serviceman, huh? Webb? I remember you."

"That's me. Can you let me in? I have some important business."

"You're barred from these premises, sir."

Webb blinked. "Say again?"

The man's meaty shoulder rose in a half-shrug. "Sorry. I can't let you in. Leave quietly now, let's not have a fuss."

"Look, can you just tell her I'm here?"

"I'm sorry - "

"Don't 'sorry' me, man. Get me Ms. Lagrange. Radio through to her now. Tell her I have a business proposition of personal interest to her. She will want to see me." He put as much confidence into his voice as he could muster to mask the fact he had none.

The man eyed him a moment longer.

"Wait here," he said, then stepped away and pulled up his sleeve to tap a couple of commands into a wrist comm. A mumbled exchange followed. Webb tried not to shift on his feet or hope that he might still be refused.

The Enforcer took just long enough on the call that Webb was already rehearsing ways to tell DC Hudson they'd fallen at the first fence, before coming back to him.

"Ok, Mr. Webb…"

"Captain," Webb corrected, before inwardly flinching.

The man narrowed his already-narrow eyes.

"Sorry, sir. *Captain* Webb. Please take a seat, with our compliments. Ms. Lagrange will be down momentarily to meet with you. We're sorry for the delay."

"Thank you," Webb said, with as little sincerity as the man had put into his apology and swept through the doors.

He was so wrapped up in getting in, he hadn't thought to prepare himself for succeeding. He had been hoping that she'd refurbished the interior too, neatly wiping all the memories, but it was exactly as he remembered it. The sight of the fine room with the subtle under-floor lighting, marble bar, deeply-cushioned booths and the light-up murals of an eternal sunset on the walls hit him like a blow. He stood on the pristine tiles just inside the door long enough to have the people at the nearest table sending him quizzical looks.

He shook himself and headed straight to the only empty booth. The panel in the top of the table welcomed him and asked for his order. He was suddenly aware of how dry his throat was and punched in an order for a beer then huddled himself deep into the booth and rubbed his temples.

A waitress appeared at the table wearing a silk oriental dress and a dazzling smile, carrying a tray with two drinks. She placed the tall glasses containing a light orange liquid on the table and moved to leave.

"Uh, miss, I didn't order stargazers."

"You don't come to the *Lagrange Lounge* and drink beer, Ezekiel."

Webb started when a woman lowered herself the seat opposite him. Another Enforcer took up position next to the table, staring out over the milling pleasure seekers. The woman wore a fine dress of black and silver, cut low and sleeveless so the Chinese dragon tattooed onto her right arm was fully on display. She wore diamonds in her ears and her dark hair was shaved round the sides and long on the top, styled into spikes with just the right amount falling into her eyes to look effortless and deliberate at the same time.

"Hey Dana," Webb said, voice tight. "You look…good."

Dana pulled her drink to her and raised her glass and took a drink, not taking her eyes off him. She looked older. In a good way. The last of her girlish leanness had filled out into curves. It looked good on her. Damn good, in fact. He picked up his own drink, feeling himself flush. He raised it to his face and the citrus smell smote him, raising more memories, not all of them unpleasant. He took a mouthful and it burned down his throat. As it settled in his belly he felt a measure of calm spread through him.

"What do you want, Ezekiel?" Dana said.

"What, social visits aren't allowed?"

"It's been two years. You haven't just dropped by for a drink."

He clenched his teeth and took another mouthful of the stargazer. "Even if I had, it wouldn't have done me much good. I'm barred, huh?"

"I was angry."

"You were always angry."

Her only reaction was something stirring deep in her eyes, but he knew that would cost him.

"You have five minutes to tell me what you want. I have a meeting scheduled."

"Who with this time? Lunar 1 deadbeats or corrupt governors? Or both?"

She leant back in her seat and regarded him with a faintly incredulous expression.

"You were always one for self-sabotage, Zeek, but I didn't think even you would fly all the way to Sunside 3 just to ask me to kick you into the street. But have it your way." She tapped a command on her stylish wristpanel. "Cliffe? There's a scruffy gentleman in booth 4B who is ready to leave."

"Wait," Webb said holding out a hand. "Wait, look…sorry."

"Could you say that again? I didn't quite hear you over the noise."

"I'm *sorry*, Dana," he said, more forcefully.

She narrowed her black eyes ever so slightly, then cancelled the order and clasped her hands on the table. A diamond ring winked on her right hand in the light from the projections.

"See, that wasn't so hard, was it? Now, do you want to try again? You now have four minutes."

"You're still wearing the ring," he said, without inflection.

She lifted her hand and looked at it.

"Well, it is mine. You gave it to me. It was you I didn't like, not the ring."

His teeth clenched. She had the decency not to smile but he could see the satisfaction in the line of her mouth.

"The clock is ticking, Captain Webb."

He huffed out a big sigh, glanced around and leaned in, lowering his voice. "You must know why I'm here."

She watched him closely for a moment and took another deliberate drink. He watched the muscles in her throat swallow and felt something run over his skin that he quickly suppressed.

"I suppose it was only a matter of time before Harvey sent someone to ask me about Kale."

"You didn't respond to her calls."

Her mouth took on a harder line. "She made them all through Service channels or on Service machines. She should know better than that. I was expecting her to come herself."

"She's been a little busy, Dana. The father of her children has gone missing."

Her eyes dropped to her drink. "You know better than most I have nothing to do with my family or the Service anymore, Webb. You might not have the spine to extricate yourself from that rats' nest, but I got out years ago and I never intend to go back. Kale going missing is nothing to do with me."

"I don't believe you don't care."

"I don't believe you do."

Webb bristled. "I'm under orders, here."

"At least you're honest about that. But then I guess there's no use in you pretending you give a damn around me."

"Have you heard from him, Dana?" Webb said after taking a pause to martial his reaction.

She looked at her glass and didn't speak.

"You have?"

Dana drank, watching him.

He let out an impatient noise. "Will you please just tell me? For Harvey's sake?"

She laid down her glass, slowly. "Yes I heard from him. Just before he vanished."

Webb's stomach clenched. "And?"

"He wanted what I'm betting you want. Info on Red Star."

"Why?"   Webb said, hand tightening on his glass.

"I don't know. I never returned the call."

Webb wondered if there was a flicker of regret in her eyes.

"So you think he went to them? Or was taken by them?"

She shrugged one shoulder, not looking at him. "Hard to say. But it would be a pretty big coincidence if they weren't involved in his little vanishing act."

"We fell out because of you, you know," Webb heard himself saying, unable to stop himself, bitterness rising in his throat. "That's why I haven't spoken to him in forever. That's why I wasn't around when - "

"Don't blame me for your problems, Zeek. That got old many years ago. And you have three minutes left."

"What did you tell him?"

"Who?"

"Kaleb," Webb said, feeling gall rise. "When we broke up. What did you tell him? He almost pulled his gun on me."

"I just told him the truth."

"And what's your version of the truth?"

She didn't even blink. "That you're the worst kind of coward. The hypocritical, self-righteous kind that refuses to admit when he's scared."

"I'm not a coward, Dana," Webb replied, not recognising his own voice. "I just wasn't gonna lie back and say nothing whilst you got into bed with the likes of Councillor Pope."

She gave him a hard look. "I also told him about that baranium trader from New Tokyo."

Webb started. "That wasn't even any of your business. It sure as hell wasn't your brother's."

"Yet something else we can't agree on."

"I'm not going through this again," Webb said, kneading his

temples.

"Are you still getting those blackouts?" she suddenly asked.

Webb blinked then dropped his gaze and glared at the table top.

"Thought as much. And you've still not told anyone about them?"

"My physical wellbeing is not on the table here."

"No it isn't. And I couldn't care either way. But how do you expect me to take you seriously when you refuse to accept responsibility for yourself?"

"You want to talk about responsibility?" Webb countered. "You cut all ties with the Service and your family and set up as an underground freelancer. You turned your back on everything you grew up with and everyone who you mattered to."

"It didn't put you off at the time," she said with a slight narrowing of her night-black eyes.

"Not to begin with," he countered.

"I only came to meet you tonight because I thought you might have grown up some in the last two years. But I see we still can't discuss things. It's not like you can't see what's around you, more like you refuse to see."

"See what, exactly?"

Dana huffed out a sigh and swilled the orange liquid round in her glass.

"See everything. War is coming. Again. And after that there will be another, and another. The Service will win, probably. It always does. But only for a time. And I refuse to nail my colours to the mast of a ship that is just fated to sail in destructive circles forever."

"You and your brother both told me that the Service isn't perfect, but it's the only chance the Orbit has for any kind of stability. If you're not working for it, you're just feeding off the poor suckers that it leaves twitching in its wake."

"You don't believe that. I know you don't. You're not a born-again Serviceman, Zeek. You're just so messed up about what you are that you're desperate to belong somewhere."

"Don't pretend you know what it's like to be what I am," Webb said, feeling a dangerous stillness steal through him.

"You can't play the 'clone card' whenever someone confronts you with an uncomfortable emotional truth," she said, face calm and collected. "Whatever you are, you're still human. You once told me the happiest you've ever been was that two days spent in the cottage in the Highlands with your father. You were happy because you were *out* of everything. Away. Free. You nearly didn't come back."

Webb felt heat rise in his face. "What's that got to do with anything?"

"You want out of the Service just as much as I did. You want your own life, deep down. But you're too scared."

"Enough of this, Dana. Since you've not heard from Kaleb, there's no point in me being here." He rose to leave.

"Unless I could tell you about Red Star?" she replied quietly.

Webb blinked and sat again. "What do you know?"

She leant in, slight smile on her mouth. "I know Red Star are real and more dangerous than anyone knows and are at the beck and call of the governor of Mars."

"Rose? You have proof of this?" Webb's skin tingled.

"Proof enough for me. Not enough for the likes of Mother. But then, she's too wrapped up in keeping track of us kids to do anything sensible about it."

"SC Hugo is doing just fine."

Dana cocked an eyebrow. "You think so do you? Well maybe she doesn't know about what people are saying. But if she doesn't then she's even more blinkered than I thought."

"What are you talking about?"

"My, my. You really are lacking in info. Ok. Let's talk business here then, Captain Webb. What are you offering me in return for my information?"

Webb took a breath to keep himself from reacting immediately. He saw satisfaction dawn in her face but refused to be baited. "What do you want?"

She rubbed her lip in thought. "I'm struggling to think of anything you can offer me that is worth my time."

Webb shifted on his seat muttering. "I can get you a pardon. Wipe your slate clean."

"I could ask Mother for one of those any time I want."

"Don't count on it," Webb replied in a low voice.

"Next offer. And hurry. You're running out of time."

Webb made an impatient noise. "What do you need, Dana?"

She pursed her lips a moment then smiled. "What everyone needs right now. Prior knowledge."

"Of what?"

"Of what's coming."

Webb bristled. "Who am I supposed to get that from?"

"Kale," she said simply. She leant in further, lowering her voice. "I'll help you find him, on the condition that you bring him to me before you take him back to my mother."

"What if he doesn't want to tell you anything?" Webb said, watching to see if the blow would land but she didn't react.

"That's my concern." She held out her hand, the diamond winking on her ring. "Do we have a deal?"

Webb paused, then shook her hand. The skin was smooth and warm.

"I'll get him to come to you," he said. "If I find him. And he's still alive."

"He's still alive," she said, checking her wrist panel. "I know that much."

Webb's wrist panel bleeped. He swiped the *Cancel Call* command in frustration.

"You know that for sure? How?"

"Ok, Webb, since we have a deal, here's what I know. Listen carefully because I do not intend to repeat myself. First: you'll want to be careful where you tread chasing these leads, Service mission or not. Rose and Red Star are not Mother's only enemies. Several of her generals are getting restless. My defection was embarrassment enough, but Kale's is dangerous. They think if she can't control her own family what chance does she have to do what's needed in the face of the likes of Rose and his supporters?"

"I already know this, Dana. I'd have to be deaf and blind to miss the fact that Servicemen are antsy about the state of the Hugo clan. Big deal."

"But do you know there are active plans to supplant her?"

"How do you know *that*?" Webb snapped. His panel was bleeping again but he ignored it.

She smiled softly. "It's amazing what you can overhear when Service officers have had a drink or two."

Webb shook his head at that.

"And your brother? You said he was alive. Do you know if he's gone to Red Star? Or where he is?"

Something flickered in her eyes. "I know he's alive because I've had assurances through channels I trust. But I have no direct links to Red Star or anyone that knows them. The general talk suggests they're everywhere, but I don't know who their leader is, if they have one."

"It's not Rose?"

She wrinkled at her nose. "Think, Webb. He's the political face. Good family, academic education and strong connections with Earth and Tranquility. No, he's not the sort to be in charge of anything as sordid as an underground guerrilla war force."

"So what can you give me?" Webb asked, curbing his own impatience. "You've not giving me anything I don't already know. I might as well have just set a course straight for Mars."

"Did you listen to what I said, smartass? They're everywhere. Not just on Mars."

"Rose is out there."

Dana rolled her eyes. "Exactly. If they have a Hugo in their midst, would they be dumb enough to hide him right where anyone could look for him?"

"Schiaparelli City is as good as independent. I'd say it was a great place to hide a political playing card."

She sighed. "Fine, believe what you want. I'm not here to try and talk you out of anything. But I thought you wanted my help?"

"You've as good as told me you don't even know anything."

She paused. "No. But I can name someone who has information about them. Maybe one of the only people who has info who would talk to you."

"Who?"

Dana straightened her back and tapped her fingernail on her glass. "Nam Webb."

Webb blanched. "That bag of crazy?"

"She worked as a mercenary for years before they put her away. My information tells me she was contracted by Red Star for some dirty work not so long ago. If anyone knows who's in charge of them or where they'd hide Kale, it will be her."

"That woman's tried to kill me more often than I can count. She won't tell me anything."

"Use your imagination Webb. Make her an offer she can't refuse."

The Enforcer stepped up, finger to his ear piece. "Ma'am, Councillor Pope has arrived."

Webb scowled. "Still cozying up to that lowlife?"

Dana stood in one fluid movement. "My investors are people with vision and understanding. They know the Orbit's on the verge of overhaul and always will be. We're here simply to grab what we need to survive while we can. And your time is up, Captain. You know the way out."

"Dana, wait." He'd stood and taken a hold of her arm before he'd realised he was moving. The Enforcer stepped up but Dana raised a hand to stop him. Webb kept his hold on her arm. He tried to think of something to say. Frustration surged through him but it was damped by something cold he had a sneaking suspicion was regret. Her eyes were dark and unreadable but he thought he detected some stifled emotion in the stillness of her face, though it could have been a trick of the low light. Or his wishful thinking.

He swallowed, opened his mouth but no words came out.

She gently pulled her arm out of his grip. She took a step closer, reached up and pulled his cap off. His hair fell in his face. She reached up and gently brushed it out of his eyes. He could smell her spicy perfume.

"Get in touch when you have Kale," she said, voice soft but she was close enough that he could hear it. "I know you know how to get hold of me. And tell a medic about those blackouts. That's just some general advice, one business person to another. Your life is on you, Webb. And that is the last time I will ever even take a polite interest."

She tossed his cap on the table, turned and strolled away. The crowd of people parted to allow her and her Enforcer bodyguard to pass. A few gave her bows and greetings which she returned. Then she was gone through the doors to her private rooms.

He shook it all away, grabbed his cap and stumbled for the door, blinded momentarily by things he hadn't let himself think about in years. He careened head-first into a solid body that took him by the arms before he could fall.

"Captain Webb? Are you ok?"

Webb blinked up into the passive face of Vergennes, that slight crease between his brows again.

"Lieutenant? What are you doing here?"

"You didn't respond to my calls. I tracked you using your wrist-panel."

Webb blinked, stepped away from him and pinched the bridge of his nose, breathing in and out slowly.

"Sir, have you been attacked?

Webb let out a bitter laugh. "She'd like to think so," he said before hurrying away from the club.

"Sir, where are you going?"

"Back to the ship."

"Were you able to get any information?" Vergennes asked as he caught up with him.

"Somewhere to start, maybe. Did you find anything?"

Vergennes frowned. "I don't know, sir. Nothing solid."

"Anything liquid?"

Vergennes looked at him questioningly.

"Anything at all?"

"As I say, sir. Maybe. I'll show you."

Δ

After making a quick stop at a ridiculously overpriced off-license, they were back on the *Duty*. Webb leant his hip against his lieutenant's chair as the man tapped commands into the cockpit workstation. He swallowed another mouthful of his clear, strong drink, grimacing as it burned a path down his throat and willed it to scour away his thoughts of inked skin and the feel of a diamond ring pressing into his flesh.

"See, sir?" Vergennes was saying, pointing at the screen. "I've found a few threads on some social forums debating the existence and intentions of Red Star. But from what I can see not a single user has any facts. But this site seems to have an awful lot of information on General Hugo's visit to Mars."

Webb leant in and looked at the screen, frowning. "Is that the Now network site? God dammit. That's that woman…Osgard. It's her site."

"I've read through everything. On the face of it, it's just news reporting. But it's very well informed."

"I see what you mean," Webb said, skimming the text. "Damn, where does she get her information? I don't believe for a second the press office gave her General Hugo's travel dates."

"I don't know, sir."

"You don't have to answer every question I say out loud, Vergennes," Webb muttered, refilling his glass. "Most of the time I'm talking to myself, anyway."

"Yes sir."

"Oh for God's sake. Have a drink and unwind for a second will you? You're as bad as Hugo was."

"I'd rather not, sir. Analyst Rami has stocked the databanks with all the information they have on Rose and Schiaparelli City. I'd like to get through it all tonight."

Webb let out a noisy sigh and rubbed his eyes. "Fine - " he started, then his wristpanel bleeped. He frowned at it, reading the code that popped up and then smiled, went to the ship's control panel and started tapping commands.

"Sir?" Vergennes asked.

"We have our new name."

"New name?"

Webb paused to drain his drink and pour another, then started in on the controls in earnest. Window after window flashed up on the ship's display and data scrolled and buckled, highlighted and vanished as he worked.

Vergennes came up behind his chair and stared at the display.

"What are you doing, sir? Those are the ship's base commands."

"I'm renaming the ship."

"Is that possible?"

"It is if you know who to ask for registration codes."

"You're using forged reg codes?"

Webb narrowed his eyes at the screen as more code obstruction flashed up. "It's called 'undercover work' for a reason, Vergennes."

Finally, Webb got around the authorisation protocols and a display blinked: ENTER NEW VESSEL ID

Webb sipped his drink for a moment then typed in: Job. He entered one final command and the code turned green and the windows began to close down.

"That should stop any more reporters catching up to us every time we stop for gas."

"'*Job*', sir?"

"Aye," Webb said, stretching. He was aching already. His eyes were heavy. "As in he who was dealt disaster and told to suck on it."

Vergennes' eyebrows rose again. "Is it wise having a name with religious connotations, sir? What with the strife with Councillor Pope and the Nova Catholica church?"

"I'd rather people thought we were from Lunar 1 than the Service right now. Didn't you say you had work to do?"

Vergennes's jaw clenched but he turned and went back to the workstation. Webb finished his drink. He stared at the empty glass for a moment, chewing the inside of his cheek. Then he sighed and grabbed the bottle, standing.

"We launch at the start of the next day-cycle," he said and headed toward the cabin, feeling the lieutenant's disapproving look on him the whole way. He sat down on his bunk, pulled off his boots, made sure the bottle was in reach and fished out a new datapanel from the tech locker and started to work. He sunk himself into it and the taste of the liquor to head his mind off from wandering back to Dana.

He caught himself staring at his panel until the text on the screen had started to blur. He blinked and reached out and refilled his glass with the last of the bottle. His stomach was rolling and his throat was burning but he leant back and emptied the glass in one go. He coughed and clenched his eyes shut, shook himself and tried to focus on the panel again.

The tiny cabin was quiet around him. Job's atmosphere controls didn't even buzz as they kept it at a pleasant temperature and pressure. The bunk he was narrow but comfy. The bulkheads were plain, the single locker functional. On some level it all felt familiar: his searches processing on the high-tech panel, the neat and ordered lines of the chamber and even the neatness with which he's stowed his possessions. It was all habit. It all made sense. It was all pre-ordained and all dictated by someone else.

That used to comfort him.

He shook his head, the alcohol swilling through his mind and dulling his movements but not the thoughts. He peered at the screen again, pressed the 'Save Info' command, then dropped it on the deck, rolled over so he was facing the bulkhead and shut his eyes, willing it all to go away.

Vergennes forbore to comment when he dragged himself into the cockpit the next morning. He'd showered and changed his shirt but he knew his eyes were red and dull and the hangover had quashed his need to shave. He swallowed some painkillers as he came up behind the co-pilot chair.

"Move," he muttered. "You can pilot today."

Vergennes again said nothing, vacated the co-pilot chair and settled in the other. Webb tried figure out whether he found the man more annoying when he was openly questioning his methods or when he didn't bother voicing it. He dropped into his own chair and buckled in.

"Set in a course for Lunar Alpha. But schedule in a stop at Tranquility on the way."

"Lunar Alpha?" the lieutenant repeated, seemingly forgetting to hide his surprise.

"Aye. One of the prisoners might have information that could help us."

"Was this the information Dana Hugo gave you?" Vergennes asked as he started inputting commands.

Webb narrowed his bleary stare. "It's incredible how you can call me an idiot just by the way you say things, lieutenant."

"I don't think you're an idiot, sir. I just don't know whether Dana Hugo is someone we can trust. It's well-documented that she's…legally questionable."

"Legally questionable?" Webb laughed. "Good one. But she's also a businesswoman, whatever else she might be. She's telling the truth."

"Who is this prisoner then, sir?"

Webb suppressed a shudder. "An old acquaintance. And apparently one once employed by Red Star."

"And the meeting in Tranquility?"

"To obtain some leverage." He gestured limply out the viewscreen. "Get us clearance to launch right away. Wake me if anyone tries to kill us before we get there."

With that he slumped in the co-pilot seat, pulled his cap down over his face and let himself drift away again to where it was blank and dark.

III

Vergennes attempted to concentrate on piloting the *Duty*…
no, *Job*, he mentally corrected himself…along the long-distance
space lane and not on his growing discomfort. He glanced at his
captain, slumped in the co-pilot chair with his hat over his face,
snoring gently. He clenched his jaw and looked away. As the ship
glided along its course, approaching top speed, he kept one eye
on the display in the control panel which he had streaming data
on Lunar Alpha. The prison manifest was not public and not even
with the privileges installed in the *Job*'s processors had he been
able to find a list of inmates.

It was only after adjusting their heading slightly to open out
into a direct lane to the moon that he noticed the message light
was blinking on his wrist panel.

Can you talk? The message read.

Vergennes glanced at Webb. He hadn't moved. He'd stopped
snoring but had sunk even lower in the chair. Vergennes tapped
in a couple of commands to slow the ship and straighten it up so
he could switch to autopilot then typed his reply.

He's asleep.

Anything to report?

Vergennes hesitated then typed: *He was drinking last night.*

Noted. Where are you now?

We're on way to meet a contact DH gave him.

There was a pause. Then: *Regarding Red Star?*

Vergennes swallowed, tried to think how to explain. *He's taken
the mission, sir. I've tried, but he wouldn't turn it down.*

Stick close. Watch his back. Keep me informed.

The message window closed down.

Vergennes let a breath out through his nose, a familiar prickle of irritation riding across his skin. The chrono showed him they were still several hours from Tranquility. The moon and its string of Lunar colony space stations were just slightly bigger dots in the spread of stars ahead.

He took control of the ship back from autopilot and then booted his language course up on his wrist panel, placing an earbud in his ear. A soft voice began going through Russian verbs and nouns, syntax and conversation frameworks. He repeated softly after the voice, letting himself sink into the rhythm of learning.

"Are you talking to yourself?" Webb hadn't moved. His cap was still over his eyes and his voice was creaky.

"Good afternoon, sir. We'll be entering the moon's orbit in three more hours."

Webb groaned and sat up, rubbing his neck. "Shit. So it wasn't all a dream, huh?"

"Sir?"

"Nothing. Keep us on course. I'll get us some docking space sorted." With that he hauled himself upright and began entering commands into the communicator, yawning widely as he did so.

Vergennes shut off the language program and pocketed his earbud, watching the captain's hands as he did so. The man was half asleep but went through all the communications and remote dock protocols barely without looking at the screen.

"What are we doing in Tranquility, sir?"

Webb yawned again, rubbed his eyes. "Leave it to me. I've got this much in hand at least. Why were you talking in Russian anyway?"

"Sir?"

"Before. I heard you."

"I'm learning."

"Oh yeah? They don't teach you languages at the Academy?"

"Only Japanese, Chinese and English, sir. The old Slavic and

European languages were not held in priority but I've tried to learn one a year since joining Eclipse."

"That's why you always take monitor duty. You can always understand the bastards," Webb replied. Vergennes thought he registered grudging admiration in his captain's tone. "They taught you English, huh? It's not your first language?"

"No, sir."

"What is?"

"French, sir."

"Should have guessed." Webb stretched then scrubbed a hand over his face. His eyes went far away for a moment. "Did you like the Academy?"

"'Like it', sir?"

"Yeah. Did you enjoy it?"

Vergennes blinked. "It's not a place for amusement, sir. But the training was high quality."

"That I believe. Shame, really…" he added, almost to himself.

"Shame?"

Webb shook himself. "Nothing. I just don't understand why graduates never mention the mountains round there. I've passed through them. They're quite something."

Vergennes frowned slightly. "I suppose so, yes sir."

Webb chuckled softly. "Hugo had the exact same reaction. Guess it's hard to enjoy the scenery if the only time you're out in it is live field exercises."

"I suppose so, sir."

"Like I said. Shame. Anyway, I've got us docking in the Northside harbour in Tranquility. They'll hail us when we get close. Get us docked. I'll need a few hours, a half-cycle at most, then we'll head on to Lunar Alpha."

"Yes sir," Vergennes said. "And after that?"

"That rather depends on what Nam chooses to tell us."

Vergennes made a note of the name then increased their speed. He docked Job in the Northside harbour without trouble. All official Service visits he'd made in the past were through the more commercial Southside harbour and he looked round at the scrum of varied ships, towering customs sheds and the unfamiliar skyline of spacescrapers with mild interest. He followed Webb to the hold where he began arming himself from the weapons locker.

"What are you doing?" the older man asked as Vergennes began to select his own weapons.

"Getting ready, sir. I understand this sector of Tranquility is quite dangerous."

"You're staying here."

Vergennes felt himself flush. "But, sir - "

Webb shook his head, shutting the locker as he did so. "No arguments. Once again, this point would not appreciate me dragging a Serviceman along to the meeting."

"You're a Serviceman," Vergennes argued.

Half of Webb's mouth curled up in a wry grin. "Not in this guy's eyes. I'm going alone. Go through the data and network sites again if you want something to do."

"It's not about being bored, sir. I'm here to help."

"I don't need help."

"My mission statement is quite clear, sir. I'm to protect you as well as aid the investigation."

Webb raised his eyes brows. "*Protect* me?"

Vergennes kept his face blank. "Yes, sir. It was bad enough you went to your meeting in Sunside alone, but I allowed it as that's a safe colony. This city is not."

"Well, it's appreciated Vergennes, but unnecessary."

"Sir - "

"No more backchat," Webb said, turning on his heel. He punched the release on the exit hatch and patted all his weapons as he spoke. "I've been doing this since…" he stumbled a moment, frowned and then carried on, voice a little strained. "Well, as long as I can remember. Eclipse might always insist on the buddy system, but this isn't an Eclipse mission. And I do better with points like this on my own."

"How long since you met them alone, though, sir? The world's moved on since the *Zero*."

Webb's face flushed. "I have no idea how you know so much about me, but it's gone beyond flattering to annoying. Now follow my orders and stay here."

"I insist you call me for backup if you need it, sir."

"I won't need - "

"Nevertheless. I want your word on that. Or I will see no option but to abort the mission and report in that you were being reckless with your mission parameters." Vergennes kept his voice calm, but it didn't stop his captain visibly bristling from head to toe.

"Goddamn all Servicemen," Webb cursed. "Yes, I'll call you if I get into trouble ok? Now get on with something useful that doesn't involve being around me."

Webb left. Vergennes peered out at the lines of foot traffic, zooming flyers and mopeds all zig-zagging across the vast harbour before the hatch hissed shut and blocked out the sight and riotous noise.

Vergennes took a moment clenching and unclenching his fists, a small nagging feeling in his belly, then went back to his cabin, resolutely ignoring Webb's suggestion to get back on the workstation. He changed into his workout wear and strapped on some combat gloves. He set up his collapsable fighting pole in the space available in the hold then went through his hand-combat routines one after the other, letting the heat in his body build and the sweat wash away some of the frustration.

He resisted the urge to send a message that he'd been charged with an impossible task. How was he supposed to guard someone that wouldn't be protected? He stopped himself by remembering that he'd made this argument a number of times since starting his commission in Captain Webb's unit, and had always been met with short shrift.

He paused, breath heaving and hair plastered to his forehead and watched the fighting pole slowly thrum back to stillness in its brackets. It would all be so much easier if he didn't care.

He made himself do all his routines again, keeping himself focussed on the swings of his fists and the impact of his kicks, counting his paces and trying to beat his timings. When he'd been through it all again and there were no messages on his wrist panel and Captain Webb hadn't returned, he re-stowed his gear, took a shower, dressed and went back to the workstation in the cockpit.

He frowned and closed down all his previous search data on Red Star, Lunar Alpha and Mars and instead loaded up all the official Service profiles, articles and reports he could find on Vice-Admiral Kaleb Hugo. A lot of the newest information was speculation about his possible defection and disappearance, but there was also plenty there from his service history: his role during the Lunar Uprising, his now-public work on the *Zero*, the undercover vessel that had been set up by Admiral Pharos and was the pre-cursor to the whole Eclipse movement. There was also older information on his roles in the Space Corps since graduating from the Academy. On the face of it, an exemplary soldier who had earned some high honours and recognition. But at every stage there was something nagging at him, like there was more to the story.

He remembered a briefing he'd sat in on when the vice-admiral had drafted in men from Webb's unit for a reconnaissance mission in the Lunar Strip. Hugo had commanded the attention of the whole room. He stood tall, though he wasn't as tall as some, his dark features eternally stoic with just a hint of tightness that made his expression permanently grim. His approach to their mission parameters, strategy and responsibilities was solemn. During the execution of the mission he had brooked no wavering from the guidelines.

The total opposite of what it was like serving in Captain Webb's unit, Vergennes mused. The younger man insisted on professionalism, smart thinking and hard work, but he also encouraged free-thinking and the use of initiative. This was not a practice Vergennes believed was always appropriate, but it meant that their unit had a high success record and low injury and loss stats. Vergennes attributed this way of working to Webb's unorthodox past. He had read up on the man's orphan upbringing on Lunar 1 and then recruitment to the *Zero* at an early age before defecting after the Lunar Uprising. Then he joined an early incarnation of Eclipse and enjoyed a significant role shaping it into what it was today.

He also knew more about his captain's heritage than he was prepared to be the other man realised, but even with that Vergennes wondered how these two very different men, with such different backgrounds and life experience, could have ever been friends. He drew the same conclusion he always drew when considering this: that there was something more about their history that wasn't public knowledge. He felt a familiar frustration surge through him, one which came from being charged with a mission whilst having potential vital intelligence kept back from him.

But he knew it was no use. He'd researched both men in many ways over the years, officially and unofficially, but had never found anything that wasn't already public or that he hadn't been fed confidentially. This time was no different. He closed down his searches on Kaleb Hugo, then put the name *Nam* through his search engine.

There were too many hits to filter. Even with a cross-search he couldn't narrow down which Nam might be the one they were seeing at Lunar Alpha. He shifted in his seat again, chafing at feeling unprepared and resenting that they couldn't call upon a systems expert to process their data for them. But he calmed himself, putting the undisciplined frustration aside. He'd know soon enough. Then he might have a better understanding of just what exactly he was caught in the middle of this time.

Webb waited to try and catch an express lift on his own, but the foot traffic was never-ending. Imbrium Block was notably busy the last time he'd visited but now, just a couple of years later, the megablock was swarming. The parking pools were rammed and every level was crowded with more stalls, vendors, dealers, boarding pods and storage units than the block probably had capacity for. The air smelt like a thousand different foods and bodies as always, but now it was, if anything, even closer.

He decided he'd be less noticeable in the crowd than out of it and crushed into the next car that arrived with eleven other passengers. He stepped off at level 102 and moved with the crowd into the wide passageway. He peeled away from the main flow of bodies when he could and ducked down a narrower, dark passage between two banks of utility outlets. He passed a couple of people, one dressed in torn coveralls and another in a stained cook's tunic, both bent with the weariness of someone coming off a too-long shift, then turned a corners until he was faced with an empty passage, brightly lit with smudged walls and shut-up steel doors. The doors had unit numbers and buzzers on them. He stopped at number 57, took a breath then pushed the buzzer.

"*What is it*?" a tinny voice barked through the comm speaker.

"I'm here for a meeting with Jaeger."

"*Name?*"

"He knows who it is. He told me to come this way. I sent a message."

Silence for a long moment and then the door opened. A large woman in a much-washed apron and gave him a long look.

"He's in the office," she eventually said, stepping aside.

Webb squeezed past her. She followed him down the corridor, almost too close, but then pushed open a door open that spilled noise, steam and the smell of cooking and disappeared through it. Webb continued to the next door down. It was propped open with a breeze block.

The man that rose from behind a cluttered desk when he entered the room had broad shoulders, now slightly stooped, dark hair and brows shot with grey and frown lines and old scars etched deep into his face.

"Jaeger. What the hell, man? I gotta come in the back way now?"

"I don't want my customers seeing you," the older man grumbled, his voice deep and gravelly and tinged with a German accent.

Webb frowned. "What's the problem?"

The bartender raised his bushy eyebrows but didn't say anything.

"Ok, maybe I've come at a bad time. I just need something real quick."

"You've come to ask a favour?" the older man said, voice low.

Webb folded his arms and put his head on one side. "Ok, spill. What's with the attitude?"

"I don't have to explain myself. I'm a businessman, Webb. You are not good for business anymore."

"But I was two years ago when I helped you out with your license?"

Jaeger strolled across the room. Webb flinched out but all the man did was heave the breeze block over so the door banged shut. He turned and stood in front of it, face heavier than ever. "The only reason I've let you in at all is to tell you to your face that you are never to set foot in my block again. Is that clear?"

Webb blinked. "I don't understand."

"You don't have to understand."

Webb opened and closed his mouth a few times. "Jaeger, I just need to sort a place for someone. Someone with a…sticky past. She won't get work anywhere else."

"And why should I take her?"

"Because you've taken on lost causes before. Found them work, given them direction. And because you owe me."

"For the license? I paid you back for that already with the Councillor Pope info for your Analyst friend."

Webb pushed his cap up with his thumb and stared at the man. "Well, if not from that then from forever and everything else we've done for each other over the years. Come on, man. How long have we been watching out for each other?"

The man glowered a minute longer then huffed and sat back heavily at his desk. He stared at the grimed wall and not at Webb.

"I'll take your stray on, Webb. She can have a place here and I won't ask any questions. If in return you forget we ever met."

Webb blinked. "Why? Why now?"

Jaeger's dark gaze lifted to him. He felt it go right through him. "I don't want any more dealings with Duran McCullough's bastard."

Webb stared. "You…what did you say?"

The man's hands formed to fists. "You heard me. The *original* you knew just how I feel about revolutionist bullshit that's torn Tranquility to pieces too many times to count. Bad enough I dealt with McCullough's son at all, even if he didn't know who he was at the time. But you. *You.*"

"What about me?" Webb breathed.

"You're not even a real person. You were created to be a pawn in another rebel's game. A game that nearly destroyed my city. And you were the one that steered the *Resolution* right at us. You nearly killed us all, Webb. Need any more reasons?"

Webb's head swirled. His palms were damp. "How do you know all this?"

A nasty half-smile turned up a corner of his mouth. "Someone saw you do it."

"But the only other person on the *Resolution* was…" Webb felt his chest clench. "Hugo?"

The older man sneered.

"Jaeger, you've heard from Kaleb Hugo? When?"

Jaeger narrowed his eyes. "I agreed to one more favour in exchange for you turning *Sturm Hafen* to your rudder and never showing your face in Imbrium Block again. I owe you nothing more."

Webb collapsed onto a stool. He put his hands on the desk, palms down and looked the man right in the eye. "Please, Jaeger. Hate me, I don't care. I don't blame you. I hate me too, most of the time. But tell me about Hugo. Then I promise I'll fuck off forever."

Jaeger didn't move. If anything, his look got blacker.

"Please," Webb breathed. "Not for me. But Kaleb. He was Webb's friend. The real Webb. The one you liked. He didn't know he was McCullough's kid, you know that. He died not knowing. He was your dictionary definition of a victim of circumstance. And he loved you, man. I know…I remember what he remembered."

Seeing the old bartender's face soften a moment only made the bitterness in Webb's mouth that much sharper. But the expression was gone in a flash and the man was pulling a panel out from a pocket. He frowned at it, skimming through data Webb couldn't see.

"Your Service friend came by the bar one day about nine months ago. He was looking pretty bad - thin, beat up - but I recognised him."

"He was here?"

The big man nodded.

"Alone?"

Jaeger laid the panel down on the desk. A blurry security image was on the display. It showed a hunched figure at the *Sturm Hafen* bar, hair shorn close to the head and dark smudges for eyes, tack-tape holding a cut on his forehead closed. It was dated earlier that year.

"He was alone. He stayed all evening. When I told him we were closing he looked at me, right at me, with his eyes looking…dead."

"And?" Webb asked quietly.

Jaeger glared at him. "Then he told me everything. Told me

who you really are. *What* you are. I chucked him out and told him neither of you were welcome here anymore."

"Vice-Admiral Hugo has been MIA for a year. Why didn't you tell anyone you'd seen him?"

"Nobody asked me. And I'm not about to throw myself into any political mires." The big man rose and nodded at the door. "Leave. Now. It's your last chance to get out of here with all your teeth."

Webb rose. His knees felt weak. He paused at the door, leaning on the doorjamb.

"Have you told anyone? About me?" he asked in a low voice, staring at the floor.

"Like I said, I deliberately avoid stepping in piles of political shit. I'm not keen on anyone knowing I know this stuff. I can't make the same promise for anyone else he might have spoken to, though. Now leave. I won't ask again."

The steel rear entrance to Jaeger's bar slammed shut behind Webb. He stood in the service corridor feeling boneless. He blinked at wall and the cracks in the sealant faded in and out of focus. He made himself pull in a couple of breaths then started to move.

It seemed to take an eternity to make it back to *Job*. He wandered on and off shuttles and shuffled along walkways in a daze, trying to make sense of it all.

He found Vergennes at the workstation in the cockpit, skimming public information on Lunar Alpha.

"Get us ready to launch," Webb said. "We've got no time to lose."

Vergennes jumped. "Sir, you're back. I didn't hear you." He frowned at the look on his face. "What happened?"

"Get us launch clearance. Now."

The young man's frown deepened before he did as he was told. Webb moved to the workstation he'd vacated and dropped himself at the controls, feeling like his limbs were weighted with lead.

He paused, hands hovering over the touch-keyboard, but then he swallowed and started typing.

The searches returned nothing he hadn't seen before, but he kept looking, broadening the filters whilst the hair on his neck continued prickling.

"Sir, what are you looking for?" Vergennes was stood behind his chair.

"Me."

"What is it you're - "

He cut off when Webb clicked on a link that opened up a page of text and a blurry picture of Webb in full Service uniform standing to the side of an event platform, saluting. He'd seen the picture before, it was taken at a public event years ago and was used whenever he was mentioned in the press. But it wasn't the picture he was worried about. He squinted at the text, the fear in his belly building.

"What language is this?" he said in a low voice as he typed in the translate command and nothing happened.

"Bantu, sir. It's an African language."

"How long ago did we secure the treaty with Johannesburg?"

"Almost a year, sir."

"The translate command has been blocked. It must be a restricted article. Can you see the date it was posted?"

Vergennes pointed to some numbers under the headline. "It's dated about nine months ago, sir."

Webb went cold. "Can you read it?"

"Yes, sir."

Webb hit a key, wiping the screen. He sat there a moment, staring at the blank screen and chewing the inside of his cheek. He turned to face his lieutenant, searching the younger man's vaguely bewildered face.

"You need to understand before we go any further…if you read this and it contains what I think it does…"

"You can trust me sir," the young man said.

"I know I can trust your loyalty. But right now that needs to be to me, not the Service."

Something flickered in the lieutenant's eyes. "You're my captain, sir."

Webb weighed him up for a long moment, trying to decide if that was enough. But the prickling was too much to endure. He braced himself, let his breath out in a rush and booted the page back up. Vergennes leant in and started to read, lips moving as he translated in his head.

"What does it say? Is it about me?"

"Yes, sir."

"Well, tell me what is says, dammit."

Vergennes straightened, looking grave. He hesitated a moment then said: "It questions your prowess as an officer. It…urm…discusses the quality of your upbringing and implies…"

"Spit it out, man."

Vergennes cleared his throat. "It calls into doubt the quality of your background and questions the motivations of the Service for giving you a rank with responsibility."

"That's it?"

Vergennes nodded.

"So it just calls me a bastard street-rat? Nothing more…specific?"

"The conclusions they draw are inaccurate and disrespectful."

"But they're not claiming anything out of the ordinary?"

Vergennes frowned slightly. "Like what, sir?"

"I don't know," Webb said, feeling his face go hot. "Anything about…my physiology? Biology, even? Family?"

Vergennes frowned. "No, sir."

"Well that's something," Webb murmured, though he didn't feel much reassured.

"What's this about, sir?" Vergennes asked. "How does this African journalist even know who you are? You're not that prominent a figure."

"It seems I've been badmouthed on the sly. I'm just trying to figure out what's been leaked…and how far it's gone."

"Badmouthed? By who?"

"I don't want to talk about it anymore," Webb said as he stood and shut down the workstation, wiping the history. "Do we have clearance to launch?"

"Yes, sir."

"Then let's get going."

Webb piloted the ship from Tranquility to Lunar Alpha. It helped to distract him from the feeling that he was itching all over whilst thinking about Jaeger's revelations. It was almost a physical pain refraining from breaking radio silence. He felt Vergennes watching him as they travelled and fought to keep his face blank.

It was short trip, the inter-city lane hugging the moon's surface closely. Job could have done it in even less time, but the all the lanes within the moon's orbit had new speed restrictions. Webb wondered whether he was pleased by the delay or whether he'd prefer to have the visit over with. The whole damn mission over with, even.

They passed through the moon's terminator and he couldn't suppress a shudder. The hulking, windowless structure that was Lunar Alpha appeared on the horizon. The blank walls were lit up with floodlights, slicing the buildings into harsh angles of black and white. There was only a supply vessel in the space lane ahead of them. He twitched when the base's security team hailed them for a systems check. Vergennes stiffened.

"Don't worry," Webb said, more to reassure himself than anything. "Rami's the best programmer I've ever known. She's got our systems sown up tight. They won't find out why we're really here."

"And what about our new reg codes, sir?"

"They're good. Just watch."

Webb pressed the *Accept* command and the Lunar Alpha autoscan appeared on every display in the cockpit and began filtering through their ID codes, manifest and specs.

Vergennes didn't move until the final check had finished and the authorisation pass bleeped on the main display. Webb smiled inwardly at the relief on the younger man's face.

They followed the supply ship into the docking hanger. The airlock was big enough to allow both them and the other vessel to enter before the mammoth metal gate closed behind them and the chamber pressurised. The sound of the rushing gradually gained volume as the space filled with air. Lights in the walls blinked from red to green and the gate ahead lumbered up, allowing them into a large hanger.

The supply vessel used its thrusters to steer slowly to where a group of people in coveralls with lifters waited for it. Webb steered *Job* toward the berth they'd been allocated, carefully scanning the milling workers moving between the supply and transport vessels for anyone that might be their welcoming committee, but none of the workers looked up.

Webb was powering down and acknowledging a growing trepidation in his belly when the comm finally bleeped.

"*Job* here, Captain Webb responding," he said with as much authority as I can muster. "I have a meeting scheduled."

"This is Lunar Alpha Administration. Your permission to enter the facility has been revoked."

"Why the hell?" he barked, trying to sound merely indignant.

"You have not supplied enough information. Access to the prisoners is only granted when - "

"I was told it was all in order," he cut them off. "I'm on the clock here, guys. I'm not just here for kicks."

"Nevertheless, sir. We are not a Service institution and your status does not allow you access without a warrant. And the information you supplied has been designated insufficient."

He could feel Vergennes's eyes on him which just made his frustration mount higher. "Look, whoever you are. I have an agreement. Check with Supervisor Loade."

"Sir, I appreciate - "

"'Appreciate' nothing," Webb snapped. "You're messing with stuff way above your paygrade here. And I I've had a pretty shitty day. You do not want to make it worse."

"Sir - "

"Why did you even let us land if we didn't have clearance?"

"The problem with the application was only highlighted when you hailed us on your approach sir. I've only just had the decision from my superiors."

"Supervisor Loade is your goddamn superior. And I have an agreement with him. You sure you want to screw up his agreements without consulting him?"

"Sir, Supervisor Loade is in a meeting."

"You get him on the comm with me right now. I ain't leaving until you do. I know some stuff about your boss he trusts me to not let get back to my own bosses. It would be terrible for us both if I felt the need to come clean. Relax, Lieutenant," Webb said after he'd cut the transmission, taking in the rigid set of Vergennes's face. "I told you, I got it under control."

"Webb? It's me." A gruff voice came from the communicator.

"What the hell, Loade? You said I could get in."

"Don't get shirty. I'll get you in. It ain't my fault if your last-minute applications with no information or warrant look dodgy to our Analysts. Seriously, Eclipse usually give us much tidier work than this."

"I'm on this one solo," Webb replied. "It's all strictly under wraps. Eclipse isn't involved."

"Well I'd say you're bloody lucky I owe you a personal favour, huh? But you start blabbing to my comm officers again about what you know I'll skin you alive. Clear?"

"Clear, man. Now can we get this over with?"

"Head out the hanger through the south exit. Your passes will be waiting at reception. There's just the two of you, right?"

"Yeah, me and my lieutenant."

"Good. Any more than two Servicemen walking about Lunar Alpha gets the governor twitchy. You're gonna keep it brief?"

"This woman has tried to ice me at least five times. I'm not staying in a room with her a nanosecond longer than I have to."

Vergennes didn't react but Webb could see him mentally taking notes.

"So long as we have an understanding," Loade replied. "I'll get the cameras diverted too. She'll be waiting in interview room 7B. But then we're done, you hear? Square. I don't want to hear from you again unless you have an official request and an air-tight warrant."

"You got it, Loade. Ain't like I'm planning on making a habit of visiting."

"Just be careful where you step if you don't want to become a permanent resident. I gotta go. You're on your own now."

The channel cut off. Webb stood and took a breath. "Ok. Let's get this done. And, yes, you're coming with me. A coward I ain't but I'm not facing this woman alone whilst the cameras are diverted."

They disembarked and crossed the hanger to a set of guarded double doors marked as the south entrance. One of the guards consulted a pocket-panel, gave Webb and Vergennes a suspicious look but then waved them through. The lobby beyond was busy with prison officers coming and going from their shifts and supply workers lugging lifters stacked with boxes and bottles. Webb stepped up to the large reception desk where a man in a black uniform was talking into a head set and frowning at the expanse of computer displays in front of him. He gave them one glance, not stopping his conversation, checked a different screen, then handed them a couple of passes and waved down the corridor.

They followed the signs to the interview rooms. Vergennes was looking round, tense with alertness like he was on point. People hurried past them in both directions. Two prison officers passed escorting a prisoner in blue coveralls. The man shuffled along, head bent, muttering under his breath. Webb stood to one side to let them pass. The prisoner looked up at him, sneered, then spat at his feet. The guards yelled and slammed the man against the wall. Webb and Vergennes hurried on.

"Have you been here before, sir?"

"Unfortunately," Webb replied, turning them around a corner to the passage of interview rooms.

"There are no windows," Vergennes observed.

"You don't want to see into the cells, believe me," Webb said, then stopped as they passed an admin booth at which two clerks were watching a live newsreel on a large wall display.

"What the…" Webb stared. "Is that Major Tremaine?"

"The Service is committed to keeping the peace along the New Republic of China's boarders whilst the talks continue," the major was saying to a reporter off-screen. His face was red, his collar too tight and words clipped. "I authorised the deployment of three more Ground Corps units myself. The show of force is regrettable but necessary, given the increasing amount of evidence of underground forces seeking to undermine the New Republic's position with the Service."

The shot cut to an aerial view of a series of clearings like pock marks in a large stretch of jungle, crawling with figures in grey Service uniforms that swarmed around prefab buildings, flyers, tanks and artillery.

"The bastard," Webb muttered. "He's rolled out more force? China will take it as threat. What the hell is he playing at?"

Vergennes stood silent, watching as the reporter speculated on whether these were still peaceful negations between the Service and the New Republic of China.

Heat swirled in Webb's belly.

"Tremaine was just waiting for a chance to turn this into a pissing match. Idiot. I hope SC Hugo has his balls for breakfast. Come on. We need to get this over and get back to our ship."

Webb muttered under his breath all the way to the interview room marked 7B, then he fell silent, thoughts of Tremaine abandoned. He took a deep breath and it shook a little as he released it, then pushed the door open.

There was a plastic table bolted to the floor in the small room. There were two chairs fixed to the floor on either side. A lean figure stood against the far wall, her eyes sharp as shrapnel. Webb kept his face neutral with an effort. He always forgot how tall she was. Her blood-red hair was cut in a ragged bob, falling in her face but not masking her glare. The blue prison coveralls were shapeless and dirty but she stood with her back straight as a poker, arms straight at her sides and chin tilted up so she was looking down at both of them.

"Nam," Webb said as casually as he good. "It's been a while."

She stared at him without blinking, the faintest trace of a sneer curling up a corner of her mouth. "What in the name of all the hells are you doing here?"

"Isn't it obvious?" Webb said, dropping himself into one of the seats. Vergennes stood at his shoulder, watching Nam warily. "I missed you."

"If you came all the way here just to mock me then you're even more of a disgrace than I thought."

"Says the woman sentenced to a term in Lunar Alpha for terrorism."

"Why are you here?" she repeated.

Webb let out a sigh and shifted forward in the hard seat, resting his elbows on the table. "Why don't you sit down?"

Nam raised her head again, eyeing him like was either prey or a predator, he couldn't decide which.

"Relax. I'm not going to hurt you, am I?"

"You should be more scared of what I might do to you."

"You've never managed to land more than a scratch."

"You've been lucky so far," she said. "But locking yourself in a room with me was either foolishness or foolhardiness."

"Cut it out. You can't do anything and you know it. Vergennes is more than capable of stepping in."

Nam gave the lieutenant a very long and cold up-and-down look. "A guard dog. Wise. But I wonder how much damage I could do before he stopped me?"

"Sit down, will you? I haven't got long."

"Not until you tell me what you want."

"I have a proposition for you."

"You have a proposition for *me*?" she asked, lowering herself into the chair. Her movements were all slow and deliberate, the way a shark circles or a snake stalks. She crossed her arms on the table and the sleeves of her coveralls rode up to reveal the wide silver bands of force manacles on her wrists. Webb looked at them then glanced about the room and felt under the table.

"There's no control for the manacles in here," Nam sneered. "They monitor everything from the admin station. But they're not monitoring us. I can tell. The lights on the cameras are off. So right now they're just jewellery. Or…" she looked at him, smile revealing all her teeth, then started forward.

It was so quick Webb didn't realise anything was happening. He blinked, heart thumping against his ribs. Her wrist with its band of thick metal was an inch from his face. Vergennes had reacted and caught her by the coveralls, but he wouldn't have been quick enough. She only hadn't hit him because she'd stopped herself.

"Let her go," Webb ordered, voice a little shaky. "She's just trying to scare me."

"'Trying'?" she said, settling herself and straightening her coveralls with exaggerated dignity. Vergennes's jaw bulged as he stepped back behind Webb's chair.

"You don't scare me," Webb said.

Her bottomless eyes narrowed. "Are you still getting headaches?"

"What?"

She looked at him through her dark-copper lashes. "You wake up at night. You sweat. You keep painkillers and Vod in the bed-side table."

"Stow this crap," Webb growled. "Do you want to hear my proposition or not?"

"I don't know if I care either way."

"You want out of here, don't you?"

"You don't have the power to get me paroled."

"Under my mission parameters right now, I can do almost anything."

"Is that so?"

"Just *listen*. I've found a position for you. In Tranquility. It's not much. Bar work. But it's good work, real work, where no one will ask questions."

Nam regarding him for a very long moment. "You think I want bar work?"

"I think you want just about anything that gets you out of here and gives you somewhere to lay low and earn some credit."

"And just what am I supposed to do in return?"

"Give me information on Red Star." Webb watched her closely for a reaction. Nothing showed on her face but she'd gone still. "I have intel that they hired you," he pressed.

"I don't ask for details of my employers. It keeps me alive."

"I don't believe you. You don't do anything you're not in control of. I need the name of a base, a leader, anything."

She watched him for another long moment. "You are extraordinary, you know that?"

"Huh?"

Nam leant forward. Vergennes tensed but all she did was look right into his face. "You know if I get out, I will find you again."

Webb winced inwardly but kept his face blank. "As I've said, you don't frighten me."

"Yes I do," she said softly, running a finger across the table to stop an inch from his hands. He pulled his hands back without thinking and she smiled wider. "I've been so close to you whilst you've slept I've felt your breath. Your guards and alarms have stopped me in the past, but I'm patient, Ezekiel. Infinitely patient. You know all this, and yet you're willing to help get me out for the sake of one of your Service operations?"

"What makes you think this is anything to do with the Service?" Webb said, hoping he wasn't looking as pale as he felt. "Everyone wants information on Red Star. Maybe I'm just getting ahead of the curve."

"You're the first one to come to me."

"It's not like you've advertised your association."

"No. I may be mad, but I'm not stupid." She put her head on one side. "How do you know about it?"

"I had information from a…reliable…source."

Her lips pressed together. Her eyes were like flint. "When was the last time you went to Lunar 1, Ezekiel?"

"Nam - "

"Indulge me. Answer my question and I'll think about answering yours."

Webb let out an impatient noise, rubbing his forehead. "I don't know. Four, five years?"

"So you haven't seen what Councillor Pope has done with the place, huh?"

"No."

"It's special, I can tell you. The church keeps him in check, where it can. And the backstreet warfare has died back to next to nothing now, I've heard. But it took a lot of…controlling. Blood ran in the streets. And everyone stood by and let it happen. All because Lunar 1 is independent and sorting out its own affairs was easier than trying to take it back."

"Nam - "

"What *happened* to you?" she suddenly snapped. "You're a *Webb*, like me. Lunar 1 is our mother and our father because the Service took our real ones. And yet you turned your back on your colony and sit there with Service dog tags around your neck and a pet Service hound at your back because you're too scared to face me alone." She leant forward again and whispered. "You make me want to throw up blood."

"I'm not here to talk about me," he said, voice tight. "Do you want this deal or not? Because if not I'll take it somewhere else."

She didn't move. She blinked, once, eyes deep and dark and swimming with emotion too intense to name. Being close enough to see it had always made Webb's stomach flip over. He made himself sit in silence and wait for her answer. But none came.

"Ok, Nam, cards on table. There must be something you want. Tell me what you want in exchange for telling me what you know about Red Star."

When she spoke, her voice was only just above a whisper. "I want my sister back."

Webb sighed. "I can't do that."

"Someone can," she said.

"Huh?"

Another slow, red smile spread over her face, like blood spilling across metal. "There's someone who can bring her back."

"What are you talking about?"

"Do you know where I was when I was arrested?"

"Laying explosives under a research lab, I heard."

"Yes, but what *sort* of research lab?" she asked, smile as sharp as a knife wound.

Webb blinked. "A gene research lab...?"

"The researcher was just lucky some of his files caught my attention before I pressed the detonator."

"What researcher?"

"The cursed man that did the operation that destroyed my sister."

"Dr. Yoshida?" Webb started.

Nam grinned. "Took me years to find him. Your Hugo Service friend may have rescinded the ban on cloning, but it's not popular. Yoshida kept himself and his work well hidden, but I found him. I always find my man."

"Just hold up here - "

"He took my sister away," Nam hissed. "It's only right he give me back what he took."

"I don't understand, sir. Does this mean…?"

"Lieutenant," Webb snapped. The tall man was staring hard at Nam but looked up with a start at Webb's sharpness. "Leave us."

"Sir - "

"Leave. Now."

Vergennes's jaw worked as he looked between them both but he left, clicking the door shut behind him. Nam was regarding him with an odd expression.

"Nam," he said slowly. "No one can bring your sister back."

"Yoshida can. I've read his research - "

"No, he can't. He could make a clone, sure. But it wouldn't be her."

She glared. "How do you know anything about it?"

Webb took a deep breath, staring at her hard. "You really don't know? About me?"

She frowned, leaning forward, trying to read his face. "Know what?"

"I was on Haven to track the Ghosts down, remember?" Webb said, relief washing through him when he only read bewilderment in her face. "He was working with them. I found out all about his cloning when we found his lab."

Her brow clouded and her shoulders tensed. "You lied about the lab."

"Only about where they'd stashed it. Listen to me. He…Yoshida," Webb made an impatient noise and scrubbed a hand over his face. "Whatever he could make, assuming you could pay him enough and assuming he didn't report you, it wouldn't be Magdalena, ok? She's gone. She should stay gone."

Nam was silent again. When she did finally speak her lips barely moved. "You realise you're talking me out of my incentive for taking your deal."

"I've already given you incentive. You've got a chance, here. A chance for an actual life, somewhere away from Lunar 1 that doesn't revolve around revenge. Wouldn't that be what your sister would want?"

Nam's face flushed almost red as her hair. "Don't you dare talk about her like you knew her."

Webb looked her in the eye. "We both know you can only count on number one in this wretched fuck-up of an existence, right? Do right by you. Take this chance to have a life. I have it as fact you won't be offered another."

She was looking at the surface of the table now. She'd gone very still. "I can go to Tranquility. I can work in your bar. But you have no control over what I do then or how I spend my credit."

Webb rubbed the back of his neck, scowling at the floor. "I can't stop you. But I want it on record that I've told you that cloning your sister would be a big mistake."

"I want this agreement in writing."

"You can't have it in writing."

"Then I want your word, Ezekiel Webb. Your honest word." She held out a hand. "And I will know if you lie."

Webb eyed her long-fingered hand like it might bite him. His felt like he'd swallowed rocks but he held out his hand and shook hers. She gripped it tightly for a second too long then let it drop.

"Now, what do you have?" Webb asked, praying he'd made the right decision.

"I have a name," she said. "The name of the man that gave me my contracts. He operated out of Silence City."

"Was he a member of Red Star?"

"He never said so. But he didn't have to."

"That's not enough."

She laughed. "You never met him. If you had, you'd know he was a man ready to make war. The work I carried out for him was…" she smiled again. Webb wished she wouldn't. "Bloody. And telling."

"What was the name?"

"Coale," she said softly. "His name was Coale. Christof Coale."

"And he was their leader?" Webb pressed.

Nam raised an eyebrow. "He spoke like a leader. Made decisions like a leader."

"And he's on Mars? They're based on Mars?"

"That's all I have. He met with me, he gave me my contracts, he gave me my credit. I never asked anymore."

"Where, exactly, did he meet with you?"

"My life's not worth anything if I give you that much. Out there or in here."

"Come on," Webb said, standing and leaning over the table. "It's my neck that'll be on the line on Mars, not yours. And I know you don't give two snaps about my neck."

She considered for a moment. "*House of Remus*. A constructors' bar in the north-east quarter of the city."

Webb rubbed his mouth, mind racing. "Ok. Ok, that will have to do."

"You'll sort my release?"

Webb ducked his head. "I will. Along with passage to Tranquility. When you're there, head to Imbrium Block, a spacer block, and find a barhouse called *Sturm Hafen*. Ask for Jaeger. It's all arranged."

Nam chewed on her thumbnail, eyes burning into his. The sound of the nail snapping shot through the quiet in the room.

"This changes nothing, you know," she said, spitting the nail onto the table. "You still scuppered my retribution on Yoshida and the Ghosts. Thanks to the little civil war kicked off, most of the Ghosts were lynched or expelled from Haven by the Elders. I'll never find the ones that are left. You cheated me out of my revenge. I will take it out of your flesh. Someday."

"Good luck trying, sister," Webb said, turning for the door. "I said I'd arrange your release and wouldn't interfere with your insane choices after that. I didn't say I could stop you getting flung back in here the minute you take a step out of line. That shit's on you."

"Be careful, Ezekiel Webb," she called after him. "No one hears you scream in Silence City. Literally."

Vergennes stood to attention when he came out of the interview room. Webb shut the door and leant on it, rubbing his forehead.

"Sir?"

Webb blinked at the floor, gathering himself, then raised his head. "Guess we're going to Mars after all."

IV

"We're heading to Mars, Captain?" Vergennes asked as he followed Webb back through the busy corridors of Lunar Alpha.

"I'll tell you about it once we're out of here," the captain said. His stride appeared more determined and he stood straighter, though he still had a slightly haunted look that only left his face once they were back aboard *Job*.

"That woman threatened you, sir."

"She always threatens me."

"But what she said…about watching you waking up at night? She's been stalking you. She sounds serious."

"She's deadly serious," Webb said. "But don't worry, I can handle Nam. Get on the comm and get us a launch window for getting out of here," he continued, seating himself at the workstation. "Then once we're in drift set a long-haul course for Mars."

"It's a two-day cruise there, sir, with the engines on full. We'll need to stop for supplies and fuel."

"We'll stop at Pole-Aitken."

"There are restrictions to landing at Schiaparelli City too, sir."

"General Hugo can get us in," Webb said, pulling off his cap, brushing his hair back under it, hands shaking slightly, then pulling it back on. "Get a secure comm channel to his people."

"But there's a radio silence order, sir."

"Sweet Jesus, Vergennes, must you argue everything? The RS just covers communication back to base or about the mission. His staff know who I am. They'll get us landing permission with no questions asked."

"Well in that case, sir, protocol would dictate meeting with the general when we land."

"I don't need to meet the old man," Webb muttered, not looking up from his screen. "He's trying to track down Kaleb the official way. I guess he won't be too jazzed to find his wife has sent us out after him too."

"He's the commanding officer on the scene, sir," Vergennes insisted. "And the one best placed to brief us on the current situation in the colony and on any revolutionary activity he may have already found."

Webb made an impatient noise. "I guess. Fine. Arrange that too, once you get. But stress we're undercover here. Everything needs to be hush-hush."

"Yes, sir," Vergennes said and began to do as he had ordered. On the short journey to Pole-Aitken, Captain Webb never rose from the workstation or looked up. He became increasingly tense and Vergennes wondered which situation in particular it was that was unnerving him.

"No response from my attempts to hail General Hugo's staff yet sir," Vergennes reported as they landed in Pole-Aitken.

"What's that?"

Vergennes frowned slightly as he cut off his latest attempt to hail General Hugo's aide. "No response so far."

"Leave a message. Coded. Attach SC Hugo's seal. It's in the databanks. That should get a response."

"Yes sir," Vergennes said, and fired off the message, keeping one eye out the viewscreen on the busy supply harbour as he berthed *Job*.

Webb reeled off a list of supplies whilst still typing and Vergennes inputted them into a computer panel then pocketed it.

"Be as quick as you can," Webb said. "I want to get on our way."

"Yes sir," Vergennes said, taking note that Webb was scouring an information web Vergennes didn't recognise for the name Coale. "Do you think Vice-Admiral Hugo's on Mars, sir?" he asked quietly.

Webb was silent for a moment before he answered. "I don't know. But it would seem that the leader of Red Star is after all, so it's as good a place as any to start looking."

Vergennes hurried into the city. Once all the supplies were secured and delivery arranged, he slipped into a quieter side-street off one of the busy trading squares, took a breath, pulled his ear-bud from his pocket and typed a comm code into his wrist panel from memory.

It connected almost immediately.

"What is it?" a familiar voice said in his ear.

"We're heading to Mars, sir. I thought you should know."

A pause. Vergennes felt his heart rate speed up.

"When?"

"We're launching from Pole-Aitken within the next few hours. We're currently don't have authorisation to land in Schiaparelli City, but I think Captain Webb knows how to get it."

"My specific instructions to you were to keep him away."

Vergennes winced. "We couldn't predict SC Hugo would put him personally on Vice-Admiral Hugo's tail, sir."

"Yes, I know, Blaise," the voice said, a little softer. "I'm sorry. I just…" an impatient noise. "I guess it couldn't be helped. Just stick to your role and make sure he doesn't find out about our arrangement."

"Of course, sir," Vergennes breathed. "As I have always done."

"You're a good soldier. I should thank you more often for doing everything I've asked of you."

"It is my privilege, sir."

A laugh. "You are too good to an old man. Especially for a Serviceman. You don't have to tell me how hard it can be leading a double life."

"You are…" Vergennes paused, throat tight, then rephrased. "I owe you so much, sir. I promised I would always do as you asked. And you have never asked me to compromise my position."

"And I don't intend to. I suppose there was no way of avoiding Mars once he got assigned to this mission. The lad's not daft, he knows his job."

"Yes, sir," Vergennes replied after a moment.

Another laugh. "Rubbing you up the wrong way, is he?"

Vergennes paused. "He's very dedicated, sir. Just…unconventional."

"Yes, that's one word. Major pain in the backside is another. Why couldn't the lad just stick to running Eclipse?"

"I suspect he would have if he'd had a choice."

A sigh. "You're probably right."

"I'll protect him, sir," Vergennes insisted.

"I know you will," the soft voice answered. "You're also a good lad. I'm proud of you."

Vergennes felt a swelling in his chest.

"Keep me informed. We obviously can't stop him now. I strongly suspect the mission will fail and he'll be returned to Eclipse where he can carry on ferreting about in the undergrowth of the Orbit out of the way. In the meantime, the priority is just to keep him safe."

"I'll ensure he's safe, sir," Vergennes said. He hesitated, then asked. "Do you know anything that could help us?"

"What are you asking me, exactly?"

Vergennes swallowed, feeling himself flush. "I know you have an extensive information net is all, sir. Do you know anything about where Vice-Admiral Hugo might be? It could help us complete his mission quicker."

"And how would you explain coming across this information?" The soft voice had taken on a dangerous edge.

"He's beginning to trust me, sir," Vergennes said. "I could easily tell him I - "

"No," the voice replied harshly. Then, slightly kinder. "I'm sorry, but no. Under no circumstances can I help you with any investigation, Blaise. You know this. Anything I give you could lead him back to me and he cannot find out about my involvement."

"Would it be so bad, sir?" Vergennes risked. "Don't you think after everything he's been through he'd be glad to know he has someone watching out for him?"

"You don't know him like I do. He's more pride than me, and

that's saying something. Stay on mission, Blaise."

"Yes, sir. Sorry for asking, sir."

"Is there anything else? I can't stay on much longer."

"Just one thing you perhaps should know, sir. Webb has a name. 'Coale'?"

There was a longer than usual pause.

"Sir?" Vergennes prompted carefully, turning slightly into the wall as a group of spacers passed the mouth of the alley, laughing and jostling each other around a lifter full of broken ship parts.

"Noted, Vergennes. Thank you."

"Does it mean anything to you?"

"No," the voice in his ear replied, Vergennes felt, a little too quickly. "Not familiar. Now get back to him. And stick close to him on Mars. Your main concern is his safety."

Vergennes clenched his jaw. "He doesn't make it easy, sir."

A soft laugh. "No, I imagine not. Just do your best. Especially in Silence City. I understand it's not the paradise colony the PR companies are portraying it as. Or at least, not yet."

"Yes, sir," Vergennes said and the connection cut. He leant against the wall, breathing in the air that smelt of old oxygen and oil. Pole-Aitken's atmosphere shield glowed orange between the tall buildings and shining bands of skyways. Just for that second, whilst he stared up at the dull orange shield with the suggestion of black space and stars beyond it, Vergennes wondered exactly who he was.

Then he straightened, shook himself then hailed a taxi-flyer to take him back to the harbour.

Δ

Webb stared at the workstation display, fire rekindled in his belly. He had abandoned his search for Christof Coale, not finding anything useful or even concrete, and was re-playing Major Tremaine's statement after reading up on all the official press releases about the increase of Service troops at the New Republic of China's boarder. He rubbed his mouth, the man's voice echoing in his ears. He couldn't help but see the image of Ambassador Martinez rise before his eyes again. Service Ambassadors sneaking around meeting private armies on one hand whilst the Service Ground Corps increases their armed presence on the other. *Something* was going on.

Frustration mounted and he reached out to key in a comm call to Harvey at HQ then cursed and kicked the console.

"Damn this radio silence order," he muttered, rubbing his temples. He felt powerless. And alone. It was a grey, cold feeling that seeped into his pores and threatened to suck him into itself. It was all too familiar and he hated it.

"Screw this," he said and started typing commands he hadn't used in years. He wanted to be surprised when he still remembered the codes to hack into the underweb, but he couldn't even pretend. Of course he hadn't forgotten. Of all the things he'd lost, he didn't know whether he'd ever forget that most of what he'd done in the past had been done using the underweb, shadows, doubt and deceit.

It bothered him that it now bothered him, but he put that aside too, and typed in a long number that he also knew he was never likely forget.

The screen greyed and buzzed for a few moments, before a connecting window opened up. Dana's face appeared on the screen. Her breathing was heavy and there was a faint sheen of sweat on her face. She was wearing grey track-gear, darkened at the chest and neck with moisture. She smiled, not entirely pleasantly.

"Zeek. Didn't expect to hear from you so soon, though pleased you remembered the right way to get in touch. Have you found my brother?"

"No," Webb replied. "Did I interrupt something?" he added, bitterly, eyeing her sweaty clothing.

She snorted. "Only a workout. Don't blow a gasket. If you don't have Kale, what do you want?"

Webb bit his lip, sighed then launched into it. "How much do you charge to get information?"

She raised her eyebrows. "We've already got our deal for the info I've given you."

"Not that. I need something more."

"I told you, I don't have anything more."

"Not on Red Star. On something else. How much?"

"Well that depends on what sort of information it is and where it needs to be extracted from. Oh, and who's asking for it, of course."

"Stop playing me, Dana. I'm serious here."

A small frown appeared across her dark brow. "I'm serious too. My business is serious. And you of all people aren't in a position to be calling out of the blue for a personal favour."

"It's not a favour. It's a business enquiry. I need information on a Service unit's status."

Her eyebrows raised even higher. "You need what?"

Webb shifted in his seat, looking over his shoulder at the readings on the command console to check Vergennes still wasn't back. "I need to know what's happening to my Eclipse unit. Something's happened to the mission I was on before your mom redeployed me."

"So contact Harvey. Or my mother, even."

"I've been ordered to radio silence for anything more than landing requests, with a flat out ban on phoning home."

Realisation dawned on her face. "I see. You're afraid your unit's being screwed like a pooch whilst you're out of reach, huh?"

"Yes," he replied through his teeth.

She had the decency not to smile but he wasn't sure he liked the business-like mask she adopted any more than her mockery. "Very well. I can find out what's happening to your unit. It'll take me a couple of cycles."

"And what will that cost me?"

She narrowed her eyes. "I'll think about it and let you know. Is that all?"

Something on the console bleeped and Webb started. "Yes, that's all. I gotta go."

Webb rose from the workstation, feeling all wrong, then went to the console and pushed a button to stop the hold alarm bleeping. Bringing up a camera feed he saw Vergennes ushering in delivery carts and instructing the lifter pilots where to unload.

He dropped into the chair and rubbed his eyes again, feeling dog-tired. He contemplated heading to the captain's cabin and sealing himself away with another bottle of spirits until they got to Mars. He could drink and sleep and then drink again. It was more tempting than he wanted to admit. But the lack of results of his search on his display glared at him. He glared right back.

He chewed his lip, then brought up a new search. He hesitated, then typed in: *Lunar 1, latest news.*

Thousands of articles on Councillor Pope popped up as well as news pieces on internal conflict, crime, oppression and the Nova Catholica church's attempts at damage control. His stomach tied itself in knots but he made himself read.

"You grew up there, is that right, sir?"

Webb jumped and turned. Vergennes was stood behind his chair, eyes on the screen.

"In a manner of speaking," he murmured, opening a report on the demolition of the rimside slums. He groped through his mind for what Webb remembered of them. He had a feeling his predecessor had stayed there with some other boys the first time he'd ran away from a youth unit. But when his search for concrete memories came back blank he felt cold.

"What was it like?" Vergennes's voice sounded different.

"Like it is now," Webb said, closing everything down including his reactions. "Same shit, different bastard at the top doing the stirring. Are we ready?"

"Yes sir."

"Good. Get us launched."

"Any word on our access to the Martian colony, sir?"

"Not yet," Webb said, moving over to the co-pilot chair. "You pilot. I'll chase them."

Webb tried the hail again as Vergennes started the engines, but no answer came from the general's aide. He muttered curses, did a quick search through the contacts in his own wristpanel, then typed in a new comm code and sent out an urgent hail. He got no answer. Webb ground his teeth and typed a message, attached SC Hugo's Code seal and sent it.

He sat with his arms crossed and watched the comm station, aware of the ship humming into life around him. The moon city of Pole-Aitken fell away out of the viewscreen and the orange backdrop of the atmosphere shield faded to infinite black pin-pricked with stars. As Vergennes laid in their course, the comm finally bleeped and a light started to flash.

Webb plastered a grin on his face and opened the video connection. A harried-looking oriental man with a thin face and even thinner hair appeared on the display.

"Captain Webb, this better be good. What do you mean pinging me with the Special Commander's seal at this time of the night-cycle?"

"Ah, sorry Hazuki. Is it night-cycle there?"

"You ruddy well know it is, the comm will have told you. What do you want?"

"It's not our fault, man. You think I wanted to hassle the admin support? We've been trying to get an answer out of General Hugo's aide for hours and getting no response."

"Then you should understand from that that Lomax is busy. The general too."

"Too busy to answer a mission hail sanctioned by his wife?"

"You don't want to use that angle with the general, Webb. That is the fastest way to get your ass fired."

"I'm under her orders. I need to speak to General Hugo, or at least to Corporal Lomax. I'm on my way to Mars."

"You're what?"

"Strictly top secret shit here, Hazuki. I wouldn't have called you except I know you won't blab. I need to check in with the unit out there. You've got to help me get in touch with them."

"General Hugo's doings is way beyond my paygrade, Webb. I may owe you, but I can't go poking Corporal Lomax just because you ask me to."

"Come on, man. I got you out of that sticky spot, didn't I? You could have been court-martialled for being on duty under the influence."

The man winced. "I wouldn't have *been* under the influence if it wasn't for you."

"Come on, Hazuki. This is important."

"Everything you do is important," the thin man humphed.

Webb could sense Vergennes's eyes on him.

"Ok, so you can't get us in with Lomax or Hugo. Just get us into the city, ok? Just any old berth will do. We ain't fussy."

"Webb - "

"You're head clerk. You can get us on the Service's manifest. I know you can. You did in New Tokyo."

"I always regret letting you in places," he grumbled.

Webb pulled out his most playful grin. "Only in the morning, man."

The man muttered and looked over his shoulder. "Fine, I'll get you access to land. You'll officially be part of the Service detail here in attendance on General Hugo. Tech crew is all I can wing, though. Don't expect access to the general. And I'm only doing this because the seal tells me you're not bullshitting."

Webb crossed himself, still grinning. "On my honour."

The man raised an eyebrow. "I know all about your honour, Ezekiel Webb, so I'd be careful how you use it to buy faith. I'll transmit the details and a pass via return frequency. But I'm warning you, I'm sending a memo to Lomax so he knows you're coming. I'm not hiding anything from the officers."

"Hey, it was Lomax we wanted in the first place. Not our fault he didn't get back to us."

Hazuki shook his head. "I gotta go. And watch yourself when you land, Webb. The Martians aren't keen on a uniform, if you know what I mean."

The connection cut.

"Well that's that taken care of at least. What?" he said as he saw Vergennes's lips pursed. "You know what? Never mind. I know what you're going to say."

"We should have waited for official permission, sir - "

"*Trust* me, will you? Erica Hugo assigned me to this because she knew I can get round the stumbling blocks. She's counting on it, in fact."

"Yes, sir."

"Good," Webb said, feeling something go out of him and his shoulders slumped. "Did you get my Vod?"

The lieutenant straightened his back, gazed fixed out the viewscreen. "I did not, sir."

Webb blinked at him, slowly. "Run that by me again?"

"I didn't get the alcohol, sir. My official assignment is to provide assistance and protection to you. I didn't think buying you Vod was the best way of doing that"

"You are not my mom," Webb growled. "We're on a two-day cruise to Mars. I want a damn drink."

The man turned his blue gaze to him and met his dark look with a frank one of his own. "I've got a better way of blowing off steam, if you're interested sir."

"I'm sorry?"

"It's physically stimulating, as well as improving stamina, balance and wellbeing."

Webb raised his eyebrows. "What exactly are you suggesting here?"

"Change into your track gear, sir," the younger man said, a little haughtily, before turning back to the controls. "Meet me in the hold as soon as we're cruising the long-distance space lane and I'll show you."

Webb clenched and unclenched his hands a couple of times. But then he told himself he couldn't hit his lieutenant for not buying him alcohol, however much he wanted to, so went to do as he suggested, not knowing what else to do.

While he waited in the hold for Vergennes he took a moment to look over their supplies and the weapons locker. He half-hoped to find a supply missed or inappropriately stowed but the man had even organised the ammunition in calibre order. Webb muttered and slammed the weapons locker shut.

"Sir?"

Webb span, blinking. Vergennes was stood in a clear space near the doors, dressed in black Service-issue track gear, immaculately clean, with bare feet and something folded in his hand.

"Ok," Webb said. "What are we doing here that's better than drinking?"

Vergennes eyed him a second longer before unfolding the object. It opened out into a tall pole, taller even than the lieutenant, with a frame at the bottom that Vergennes activated and magnetically sealed to the deck.

"A fighting pole?" Webb frowned.

"Yes," Vergennes said, giving it a test shove. The pole gave a little then snapped back to its start position, lights and readings flashing along its length and base. "Keeping in good physical condition as well as well-practiced in hand-to-hand combat is a standard expectation of all Service soldiers."

"Hey, there' ain't anything wrong with my physical condition, pal," Webb said, folding his arms.

Vergennes gave him an openly assessing look. "Your active duty keeps you fit enough, sir. But you do not nourish yourself correctly and your strength could be improved." Webb began to sputter but Vergennes continued, unabashed. "Take your shoes off, sir. We'll start by working through basic jujutsu systems. When I've got an idea for your form, we can work out a training routine to keep your reflexes sharp."

"Well that's too bad. I don't know any jujutsu," Webb said.

Vergennes raised his eyebrows slightly. "What about judo?"

"No judo."

That slight crease between Vergennes's fair brows. "Wing chun? Taekwondo?"

Webb let out a sigh. "Jesus, man. No, I don't know any of that shit."

Vergennes raised his eyebrows. "Marital arts and hand-to-hand combat was standard training at the Academy."

"Well, news flash, bub. I didn't go to the Academy."

"Very well," Vergennes said, ducking his head. "But I know you can fight. Show me."

Webb rubbed his temples. "Can't I just go to bed?"

"After this, sir. I will feel better heading into Schiaparelli City if we both take some time to sharpen our skills."

"Fine," Webb said, pulling off his shoes and throwing them aside and padding up to the fighting pole. Vergennes handed him a pair of fighting gloves and he strapped them on, glaring at the pole. He'd used one before, there were half a dozen in every HQ gym, but he'd never had someone watch him before.

"Don't think about it," Vergennes said, stepping back. "Just fight."

Suddenly all the frustration, fear and rage that had built in the last few days overloaded him like a dam bursting. He struck at the pole, punching, kicking, swearing. Soon there was sweat pouring down his back. The pole was high-quality, with a good action and response. It snapped back in place after every strike and he kicked it again, not thinking, not framing a single thought, letting it all pour out.

"Send your kicks round the side," Vergennes's voice came from somewhere nearby but Webb barely registered. "They have more power if you feed through from the side."

Webb obeyed and watched more lights flash up the pole with the increased power of his strikes. The score on the base climbed. He kept going until his breathing was heaving, his clothes were plastered to his skin and his heart hammered fit to break out his chest. He leaned over, hands on his knees, watching moisture drop onto the deck and realised not all of it was sweat.

He rose slowly, wiping his forehead and then his eyes on the back of the fighting glove. He felt surprisingly…empty. And tired.

Vergennes was stood to the side, that assessing look still on his face.

"Go on then," Webb said between pants. "Tell me I fight like a rat."

"You don't fight like a rat," Vergennes said calmly, stepping up and putting the pole aside. "You fight like a man. But a desperate man. You have speed and force but you need more discipline. If you have more control you could easily subdue a bigger and stronger opponent."

"You mean like you?"

"Yes, like me."

"You're ten feet fucking tall. If I saw someone like you coming at me, I'd run, not fight."

"Wise," Vergennes said. "But you don't always have that choice. Come, sir. Step up here." Vergennes placed his feet apart, balanced on the balls of his feet and raised his fists. "Let's try."

"I'm not fighting you," Webb said, rubbing his face. "I'm tired. I need a shower."

"Not something an enemy will consider, sir."

"Why are you so hell bent on this?"

"I want to know you can protect my back as well as I can protect yours."

"We've got guns, Vergennes," Webb muttered. "And knives. And more guns. I can watch your back just fine."

"You're not naive enough to think that having a weapon makes you prepared. One bout. For practice. It pays to understand a partner's strength and style."

Webb shook his head. "You're a strange man, Vergennes."

"I'm a Service soldier," the younger man replied, matter-of-fact-ly, dancing a little on his feet. "And so are you. And SC Hugo is depending on both of us."

"If we do find Hugo," Webb said, putting his feet apart wearily. "I think you two would get on just great. Ok, Blaise. Hit me."

And he did. The speed shocked Webb. As did the young man's strength and reach. All Webb could do was duck and try and turn aside hits. Vergennes didn't punch hard, but instead used open-handed slaps that sent Webb's ears ringing and his flesh stinging. Webb cursed the air blue and was unable to think about anything but trying to read the man's movements and slap aside his blows. The younger man's face was a mask of focus and cal-culation. When Webb's heels knocked against the weapons lock-er and there was nowhere to turn, Webb wondered whether Vergennes actually intended hurt him. The answering surge of adrenaline made him duck and deliver a blow to the man's so-lar-plexus. Vergennes turned and avoided the full impact of the strike, but Webb felt the connection ride up his arm and stag-gered forward. A strong hand grabbed the back of his vest and then he was slammed again against the weapons locker.

When the world stopped spinning, Webb was blinking into Vergennes face. It was centimetres from his own and, for the briefest moment, crumpled with hate. The spell broke and Ver-gennes released him. Webb slumped against the locker and they both stood there, panting.

"Very good sir. I suggest a meal and a protein bar then we'll practice again tomorrow."

"What the hell was that?" Webb panted. "You nearly planted me into the deck."

"I'm sorry sir," Vergennes said. "It's easy to get lost in practice. But it helps to relieve stress and frustration."

Webb had to admit that now the adrenaline was fading he felt a curious calmness stealing through him, but he still watched his lieutenant fold up the fighting pole with mixed feelings. There had definitely been something in his face that wasn't about training.

Too tired to think too hard, he retrieved his shoes and cap and padded from the hold. He went to his cabin with only a cursory check of the autopilot controls. He was too tired to eat anything more than a Nutripak before collapsing on his bunk. An urge to hunt for any unfinished bottles of Vod in his cabin crumbled away half-formed and he fell into a deep sleep.

*

He woke hours later. The cabin was still with only the low hum of the ship's systems to be heard. He became aware of stiffness in his limbs and bruises forming along his ribs and arms from the bout with Vergennes. However, inside he still felt calm. Empty.

No messages or warnings waited for him on his wristpanel. When he booted up the ship's system reports on the cabin display he found they were still cruising their space lane with no hails or summonses waiting. A message from Huzuki containing their landing codes and a clearance pass was the only thing that had changed since he went to sleep.

He splashed some cold water on his face, dressed and padded up to the command deck. Vergennes was sat at the console.

"All well?"

"Yes, sir."

Webb stood behind his chair a moment, watching him work. "Thanks for yesterday," he heard himself saying. Vergennes paused and looked up. "I feel…well…good." Webb rubbed the back of his neck, looking away. "Well, apart from beat to shit."

"Apologies, sir, but the practice only has real benefit if it feels real."

"It felt real alright," Webb muttered, rubbing the meaty part of his left thigh where a bruise was forming.

"Good. We shall do another, later. And, if you'll follow my advice, you'll continue to practice with the fighting pole as regularly as possible."

Webb would normally have been irritated, but this time he just laughed. "Sir, yes, sir," he said with a mock salute. Vergennes frowned but Webb waved the reaction away and sat himself at the workstation. He sighed before putting his hands to the keys and roping together his focus.

"Do we have a plan, sir?"

"Wouldn't that be nice," Webb murmured as he skimmed an article in their databanks put out several years previously by Apollos Outreach, the company that had established the Martian colony. There were pictures of grand buildings, well-equipped iron fields and refineries with smiling employees and rec areas, all captioned with promises of plentiful work, credit, good fortune and safety. As he looked through the pictures he wondered where Red Star had managed to find a place to hide amongst all the classy conference centres, accommodation blocks and civic halls. "All we have is a name Nam gave me. Chistof Coale."

"Who is he?"

"Red Star's leader. I hope. And if we find Red Star, we'll find Hugo," Webb replied, skimming to the next info slide. It was Hugo's Service profile, complete with picture of him stood straight and tall in full uniform, dark eyes and solemn expression staring straight out at him.

"You think the Vice-Admiral really has defected then, sir?" Vergennes asked quietly.

The calm that had settled Webb's insides took a punch. "I don't know. If he had gone willingly, I would have thought we'd have heard something by now. You don't keep a political playing card like SC Hugo's son joining your ranks a secret."

"Unless they're waiting for an opportune time to play the card,"

Vergennes suggested.

"I'm keeping an open mind," Webb said, crushing the sneaking fear that tried to return.

"Yes, sir," Vergennes said, finishing off his system check. "We will be arriving at Mars in just under forty hours."

"Fine. I'm going to grab some food. You need anything?"

"I've eaten, thank you sir," Vergennes said without looking up from the console. Webb made his way to the tiny galley, opened the food locker and stared at the ration bars, Nutripaks and vitamin shake bottles without taking them in, the picture of Hugo still all he could see.

Δ

True to his word, Vergennes insisted on another fight stick and then hand-to-hand combat practice a few hours later. Desperate for anything to get him out of his head, Webb complied. This time Vergennes remained distant and closed, even when Webb managed to land a couple of hits. The young soldier rattled off some dispassionate advice about his defensive blocks but then packed away in silence, perhaps sensing that Webb wasn't really listening.

He was standing in his cabin, staring at his bunk and thinking about climbing into it when the cabin display started bleeping. Blinking, he loaded up the specifications of the communication signal, but they were all coded.

He paused a moment before pressing *Accept*.

A video window opened up to reveal Dana's face wearing a cold, business-like expression. The screen flickered and pixelated then Dana's image was back. "This connection's dreadful. Where the hell are you?"

"A long way away," Webb hedged, reaching and fiddling with some of the settings with the on-screen display. "What have you got?"

"I have what you asked for. Major Tremaine is now in charge of all the operations along the Chinese boarder. Eclipse has been withdrawn."

"What?" Webb snapped. "By who?"

Dana paused a moment then looked up. "Admiral Myles Osgard issued the order."

"That stuffed shirt? He doesn't have the authority - "

"He's my mother's second-in-command, Webb. He absolutely has the authority."

"Son of a bitch," Webb muttered. "Does the old ass not care about us being caught with our pants down? Cos that's what's gonna happen if these talks go west and we're without Eclipse intelligence - "

Dana frowned. "I'm just the messenger, Webb. Save your rants for someone who cares."

Webb just swore again. "I can't believe your mom allowed that."

Dana heaved a sigh and he heard her tapping at keys, looking off-screen. "Well she did. Or, more likely, she's had her hands too full to stop it."

"What else do you know?" Webb asked, seeing the look on her face.

"That it's not just your unit. Looks like Osgard has withdrawn a total of seven Eclipse units on active missions from their posts."

Webb went cold. "What?"

Dana's face was still carefully blank, the light from the screen she was looking at washing her skin white and sparkling off the diamonds in her ears, but Webb thought he saw the start of tightness in her mouth. "They were all units that were aiding peaceful negotiation with local authorities in Eurasia."

"But why?"

Dana shrugged again. "Again. Messenger. Took more than I'd hoped to get this much, too. You asked for whats, not whys."

Webb cursed and slumped onto his bunk, elbows on knees and

head hanging, thoughts racing. "What the hell?" he murmured to the deck.

"I gotta go," Dana said after a pause.

Webb raised his head in time to catch a look in her eyes that might have been concern, but was gone to quickly to be sure. "Ok. Thanks."

She looked at him a moment longer than was comfortable, then her cool gaze slid away. "I'll be in touch when I want the favour returned. Don't forget this."

The connection cut.

He collapsed onto the bunk and lay staring at the bulkhead above him. "Myles Osgard, what in seven hells are you up to?" he muttered then paused, the name catching at something in the back of his mind. The thought didn't lead anywhere so he shook it away continued to stare up the bulkhead, listening to the almost-silent purr of the ship around him until, despite everything, he once again slept.

Δ

"It's confirmed. He's coming."

"Yes, I know."

"What do we do?"

The two voices were somewhere nearby, but Hugo was only aware of them as ripples on the edges of his consciousness. Some level of him, buried so deep he wasn't even sure if it was real, suggested he should care about what they were saying. But he didn't.

All he was sure of was the cold in his bones that made it feel like they'd been grafted with iron. He clung to its familiarity. It was all he knew. It was all he wanted to know.

"We do nothing," the coarser of the two voices snapped in reply. "Let the bastard come. He's just one man, and a street-rat besides, whatever his connections. And anyway..." There was the scrape of a boot step close by. Somewhere there was the sensation of a gloved finger under his chin, tilting his head up, but all he saw was white light and all that mattered was the cold that stiffened his flesh to armour. "…this will be the ultimate test for our friend here."

A moment of silence then the first, lighter, female voice said: "Do you think he'll deliver?"

The grip on his chin tightened. Hugo just stared into the light.

"I know he will."

His chin was released and the sounds of booted feet and the two voices faded away. Hugo was left with the white light, the chill, the pain and emptiness.

Δ

"Sir? Captain Webb, sir? Wake up."

Webb heaved himself up, breath ragged and sweat plastering his hair to his forehead. He blinked until the cabin came into focus and his breathing slowed.

"You were having a nightmare."

Webb looked up, shame and the fall of adrenaline both crashing like cold breakers into his stomach. Vergennes was looking down at him with a slight crease in his brow. The chrono on the cabin display said he'd been asleep for almost nine hours.

"Jesus, I must have needed that," Webb said, swinging his feet off the bunk and shivering as the connected with the cold deck. "Where are we?"

"We'll be entering Mars's orbit in a few hours, sir. I thought it best we get ready," Vergennes said, then left.

Webb got shakily to his feet and staggered to his locker for a bottle of water, lamenting the lack of anything stronger. After a few swallows, he felt himself calm and his muscles ease. He stood with his eyes closed, gripping the door of the locker, waiting for the images of the dream to fade and yet fighting the despair that followed when they did. His head throbbed dully. He might have escaped a full-on blackout but not its aftereffects.

Shaking it all away, he went through the motions of pulling on a clean shirt, boots and scraping his hair back under his cap. After he'd strapped on his gun belt and arm-sheath with knife and checked the extra dagger in his boot, he felt a different sort of calmness descend. He pulled his beat-up jacket over all his weapons and paced up to the cockpit.

Once he got there, he stood and stared.

"Sir?"

Webb shook himself, not realising he'd muttered out loud. He took a step closer, eyes fixed out the viewscreen. "Christ. That's it?"

Vergennes nodded, following his gaze to the view of the planet ahead. Webb leaned forward to gape at the expanse of rust-covered landscape that filled the screen. He'd seen a hundred vidfeeds, newsreels and still-shots of Mars over the years. The footage from the early scouting expeditions had been doing the rounds when his predecessor had been resident in a youth unit on Lunar 1. Him and the other children had all sat in a semi-circle around the rec room display screen, eyes wide and hushed as the Apollonauts' footage was played whilst they spoke through muffled mics about the brightness, the sand and the springy lack of gravity. They also repeated the promises that had been made about the opportunities the red planet offered, how humanity would get a chance to start again.

It was one of the few times he had felt wonder and hope growing up. At least, one of the few times he could remember. But nothing of what he or the original Webb had seen compared to what the expanse of copper-coloured sand and rock looked like close up. It was like a vast, crumbling dune or empty river bed, like the ones he'd seen on a ground mission into one of the fallout areas in North America. But…darker. A shade of red like nothing he'd encountered elsewhere, somewhere between a hot Australian sunset and fresh blood.

He fumbled his way to the pilot chair, swatting Vergennes out of it with a distracted gesture. "It's…weird," he said.

Vergennes settled in the co-pilot chair with a disgruntled expression, giving the planetscape barely a glance. "Yes, sir."

"Don't you think, though?" Webb prodded. "It looks…dead." He could feel his lieutenant giving him another odd look. "Never mind. How far out are we?"

"380 kilometres, sir. Standard orbit."

Webb pushed a few commands, skimming more close-up images from his scopes and frowned out at the red desert again. "Where the hell's Schiaparelli City? It's not coming up on my readings."

"It's in the Northern Plains, sir. We're not far. But I don't believe there are any public beacons and the spaceways are all restricted. You can't find it unless you're registered to be out here. Your contact gave us landing codes and coordinates for the dock within the colony, but no coordinates for the city itself or an approach vector."

Webb swore, casting his scans wider.

"What are we going to do, sir?"

"Just wait. Ha. There."

"Sir?"

Webb took the ship off autopilot with a flush of pleasure, revelling in her smooth response, then steered her to starboard. "Heat signatures."

"From where?" Vergennes asked, scanning more surface reports.

"Not down there," Webb said, nodding out the viewscreen as they swung round and slightly bigger flecks of light could be seen moving amongst the stars. "Over there. Other ships. There's only one place they'd be going."

"They could be coming from the iron farms, sir. We should hail your contact for directions."

"Where's the fun in that?" Webb said, increasing their speed as they chased the other ship to the horizon. "Besides, I don't think Huzuki will cut me any more slack."

Webb steered toward the other ship. The brightness of its engine exhaust increased as they got closer and his instruments told him they were descending. He felt his heart start to speed up.

The surface below them, closer than ever, had become more pitted, carved out with seas of shadow between peaks of coppery rock. In one of these shadows, lights were strewn about like stars in the sky. It was an indistinct web of flashes and strings to begin with, but as they got closer, they formed into floodlights, guidance lights, beams and beacons, a thousand flecks of brightness in the dark, lighting up a confusing tangle of metal and concrete that Webb could not make sense of.

"That's it?"

"Yes, sir."

"Where's the atmosphere shield?"

"It's invisible, sir," Vergennes said, leaning over to look himself. "They've used the newest Haven-built generators that produce a clear screen for the city until the planet-wide atmosphere generators are built. I understand it's so the residents can experience the Mars day and night, which is about the same as Earth. To make it feel like home."

"It don't look much like Earth," Webb murmured.

As they approached, what had looked like a giant dropped box of machine parts slowly formed into miles upon miles of scaffolding, building platforms and access frames. Metal spires, girders and cables stretched up like skeletal fingers from the dense layers of construction, giving shape to what would one day be truly monstrous spacescrapers and megablocks, bigger than those even on the moon. And they were only the structures he recognised. Some of the other shapes could be the beginnings of anything. Walls, levels and floors were taking shape lower down, but mostly it was a web of skeletons, blistered with lights from construction machinery, small, one-man worker-flyers and countless elevated groundways, busy with traffic, and narrow rails over which shuttles were racing. They stopped at platforms, disgorging or picking up dozens of faceless figures in visors, helmets and long coats with loads of unidentifiable cargo.

"It sure doesn't look like the brochures."

They descended further. Webb noticed that the lowest levels of the city, still far below them, were wreathed in some sort of mist or fog. It moved almost imperceptibly, like clouds across an Earth sky in summertime. It looked utterly surreal, drifting between the feet of the giant, distorted half-constructs, lit up in patches by the artificial lights.

"What the hell is that?"

For once, Vergennes didn't have an answer. Webb blinked when something started flashing on his comm panel.

"Someone's noticed us at last," Webb muttered. "Send our ID and codes."

Webb breathed a sigh of relief when the hail turned out to be an automatic beacon which confirmed the pass codes and beamed them coordinates of a harbour and berth for *Job*.

"All appears to be in order, sir," Vergennes said with what might have been grudging admiration.

Webb humphed. "I get more nervous when things go to plan than when they don't."

He activated the ship's close-quarters navigation system and loaded in the coordinates and steered them along the generated course. It took them lower and lower until the city of scaffolds and suspension cables rose up and swallowed them. Webb couldn't shake the sense of claustrophobia that wrapped round him as *Job* was guided down narrower and narrower landing lanes to a harbour on the outskirts of the North East quadrant. They passed the half-built constructions so closely he could make out the individual workers in the cockpits of the cranes and industrial welders.

"There're no flyers," Webb observed, looking round and still seeing the only airborne vehicles were little one- or two-man worker flyers, small, manoeuvrable craft labourers used for the close work on the constructions.

"No room for skyways until the buildings are finished, sir," Vergennes said. "Look," he said, then pointed ahead. *Job* was flying between two of the elevated groundways, thick bands of polymer suspended by huge cables, over which drove scooters, mopeds, two-wheelers and bigger caterpillar vehicles transporting workers and equipment. There were low-flyers scattered amongst the wheeled vehicles but they were having trouble manoeuvring amongst the grounded traffic. Vergennes was now staring with his mouth slightly open, craning his neck to watch a Jeep and open-bed truck loaded with girders jostling at a junction.

"It's like the groundways on the moon," Webb said. "Only…. not on the ground."

A few more twists and turns which required them to slow to a crawl and they were finally joining the queue of smaller spaceships waiting to dock. The harbour ahead consisted of a platform suspended amongst a cluster of structures that one day might be supply warehouses, but at the present moment were the same skeletons and ghosts of buildings as the rest of the city. The glow of electrical fences hemmed the platform. All the foot and motor traffic was funnelling through a single set of gates where some temporary checking units had been erected. Webb berthed *Job* and looked around, noting that all the neighbouring ships had Service reg plates and logos.

"This must be where General Hugo's unit are berthed," Webb said. He got up from his seat, did one final check of his weapons and tech then headed for the hold, Vergennes following.

"Guess Rami was right about needing land vehicles," he said as he unclasped the holders securing one of the motorbikes in place. He straightened and caught the lieutenant eyeing his own vehicle suspiciously. "You know how to ride, right?"

Vergennes looked up, lip still curled. "In theory."

"You've used quadbikes on land missions. This is just like

them."

"Indeed. Bumpy."

Webb wasn't able to stop a smile as he pulled on a visor and gloves. "Sure, bumpy. And fast. Real fast, if you know what you're doing. And it's best we have the capacity to stay ahead of the game."

Vergennes didn't comment but put on his own visor and gloves with a distasteful air. Webb shook his head and wheeled his bike over to the hold hatch and hit the control. The hatch clanked and rolled open.

The air that swept in was very still, cold and smelt of iron. Webb shivered and activated his visor. Data flashed in front of his eyes, environment readings down once side, scans of the surrounding area on the other, then mounted his bike. He pushed the engine starter and the vehicle sprung to life. He engaged the accelerator and steered down the ramp. Their tyres hit the harbour platform with a dull noise and he steered them toward the nearest thoroughfare, busy with scooters and trucks.

On the surface of it, it was exactly like any other dock or harbour he'd visited. There were ships and spacers, pilots, dock-workers and machinery on every side. The people were all absorbed in the myriad of activities a busy harbour generated: loading, unloading, haggling, cursing, greeting and gesticulating. But there was something…off about it. The distant sun was small and cold, the sky a sickly shade of ochre-yellow that made him feel slightly ill and the sense of the bike under him didn't register right. At first he thought it was the machine, but when they had to come to a full stop and he put down a boot to steady himself, his foot connected with the ground too hard and he realised the gravity was all wrong.

But what made his insides swirl the most was the strange quality of the sound. Twice he dug a knuckle in one ear then the other, shaking his head to try and clear his hearing, but still everything sounded like he was the other side of a sheet of plexiglass. When he held his nose and tried swallowing to pop his ears Vergennes pulled up beside him and leant in to speak directly into his ear.

"They're still getting the atmosphere controls right, sir," he said, sounding even at this close range like they were speaking to each other underwater. "The air's breathable but the high levels of carbon dioxide and iron oxide in the planet's atmosphere have had unexpected effects. The pressure and the gravity haven't been stabilised entirely yet."

Webb coughed, drew in a breath, shaking his head trying to make himself adjust. "This is why people call it Silence City instead of Schiaparelli City?"

"One of the reasons I believe sir, yes."

"Even Haven's got better environment controls than this," Webb muttered, digging in his ear again at the uncomfortable sensations, then pushed the accelerator as the traffic moved forward.

They came up to the gate. On either side was the dull blue shimmer of the cheap electric fencing and beyond that, the disjointed and heaving half-built metropolis spreading to the hazy orange horizon. Their IDs were checked. Webb handed his over with a smile. Vergennes was somewhat stiffer.

"Service, huh?" the customs officer, invisible and shapeless behind a black mask, armoured suit and gloves, said through his mask's speakers. "You're a bit late to the party."

"Additional tech crew," Webb said with another smile. "We had another job to finish up first."

The blank mask paused. "That's a lot of weaponry for tech crew to be carrying," the man said, mask tilted toward the guns at Webb's belt.

Webb went for an easy, one-shouldered shrug. "You know how careful the Service is with its tech crew. We're at a premium, you know. Most guys want to drive the ships or shoot the cannons."

"Flares?" he said, poking the charges at his hip.

"Homemade," Webb grinned. "Great at parties. Look, guy. It's all for work, ok? And it's not like there's an official safety rating for this place yet. Your governor seems pretty keen on keeping the official position on personal firearms under wraps until the city's finished. Now, do you want us to just accept that and do what we can to watch our own assess, or do you want us to start asking questions and pointing fingers?"

The man was silent for a while, then shifted on his feet. "The rest of your lot are boarding in the Conference Centre accommodation on Appollos Square," the man said, and Webb heard the sneer in his tone. "Try not to get too fat off our rations whilst you're here."

He waved them through.

"I don't know if it's wise to antagonise people, sir," Vergennes commented as they emerged into the colony.

"If there's one thing I've learnt about customs, it's that they like to think they have more power than they do," Webb commented, looking around. "Threaten them with actual action, they crumple like paper. Now, where the hell are we?"

They came out onto a junction that joined one of the elevated groundways with several others snaking off in other directions. The traffic was heavy, all shapes and sizes of vehicles thundering and zooming past. The noise should have been deafening but it was oddly muted in the thick air, making Webb uneasy again.

A thin pre-fab rail was the only barrier between the traffic and the dizzying drop down into the shadows and fog of the foundation levels. There was a honk behind them as another vehicle became impatient. Webb gestured to Vergennes, then pulled an earbud out of his utility belt and put it in his ear.

Vergennes nodded, tapping his ear indicating he already had one in. Webb frowned a moment but then shrugged, activating his own by double tapping it and pulled the bike out into the traffic.

"You hear me ok?"

"Yes, Captain," Vergennes's voice, a little strained, buzzed in

Webb's earbud. His visor displayed traffic stats, the angle of the road and the details of the vehicles around him. Now it had had a chance to analyse the atmosphere it was bleeping various warnings down one side about the pressure and gravity. It took him more time than he liked to get the hang of steering and braking the bike in the unbalanced environment.

They rounded a bend and a gap between two empty spacescraper frames revealed a wide square ahead. Surrounding the pedestrian area were the first complete buildings Webb has seen. They were tall and elegant, finished in a white polymer layer that shone blindingly against the dull sky. The square, from what he could see, was dotted with fountains and benches and statuary. He couldn't tell what the statues were of from that distance, but the whole spectacle was utterly surreal set against the jagged, confused backdrop of scaffolds, cranes and frames that formed the skyline.

"Where are we going, sir?" Vergennes's clipped voice came in his ear as he turned left at another junction where the groundway sloped steeply down, taking them away from the square. "The Conference Centre is the other way."

"We're not going there," Webb said. "I want to do some digging of our own."

"Then where are we going?"

Webb swallowed, not wanting to say out loud that he didn't really know. It darkened around them as the groundway took them further down. The half-built structures rose up and blocked out more of the weak natural light. The trucks and bikes around them turned on headlights and Webb did the same. Floodlights on tall arms swept blinding spots in the gloom, illuminating areas of work and the engines on the jetting worker flyers flashed making Webb's visor darken and lighten over and over again to try and compensate.

"Sir?" Vergennes said again and Webb noticed with a start the man had sped up enough to be driving alongside him

"House of Remus," Webb said, taking another turn that took them still further down. He glanced around, noting that the traffic heading this way was mostly scooters and other bikes. The way was narrower and the traffic moved faster. "We need to find the *House of Remus.*"

"What's that?"

"A constructor's bar," Webb replied. "And Rami's data said the constructors are all housed on the lower levels."

"Sir, this place is huge. Do we even where to start looking?"

"We're in the right quarter."

"Sir - "

"Stow it, Lieutenant," Webb replied, swallowing another sweep of sickness which wasn't entirely to do with the atmosphere. "This is all we got. Just follow my lead."

Vergennes went back to concentrating on steering his bike, eventually having to drop back behind again as the way became narrower. Traffic peeled off on side-ways and ramps into the dark.

Webb's headlight suddenly lit up a dull smudge of fog. Before he could think they had plunged into it. A shudder passed through him. The fog pressed in on all sides, his headlight now only lighting a few feet in front of him. It felt cold and damp and smelled slightly salty. He shook away the confusing sense of being surrounded by sea air and concentrated on staying in his lane.

Finally, they descended to a place where there was more uniform lighting increasing the visibility. Snaking up on either side were guidance strips for what, one day, might be skyways for flyers and hover-vehicles, currently all empty and non-illuminated but Webb could tell that they were going to be big. Walls and columns rose up around them, all new-looking, all shining and lit with warm light from high-quality panels installed at regular intervals. There were wide entrances with plexiglass windows and doors, public information displays, currently dark, sitting areas and promenades as well as signage in English and Japanese directing the ways to the Conference Centre, New Civic Hall, iron farm rep offices, North-East ports and harbours, business centres and rec areas. Under these bright, electric signs, cruder printed signs were tied onto their columns pointing the way to the nearest boarding blocks, supply bunkers, repair workshops and an infirmary.

Webb pulled his bike over into a lay-by to take a moment to stare around. It would be beautiful one day, when the construction workers' signs and groundways were dissembled and whatever glitch in the environment controls that was generating the fog and dull air was fixed. As it was now, it felt like an abandoned city overtaken by the first homeless stragglers that had come along.

Vergennes had pulled in beside him, face blank behind his visor.

"What now, sir?"

Webb swallowed. There were people looking their way from the nearest promenade.

"Sir?"

Webb pulled his visor down to hang on its string around his neck and rubbed his eyes. "I'm fine, I'm thinking."

"This isn't like any of your other missions is it?" Vergennes asked, in a voice so low just his earbud picked it up.

"No," Webb said firmly, talking a breath of the damp, salty air. "But it's fine. I'll figure something - "

"Looking a little lost there, Captain Webb."

Webb spun around, tottering to keep his bike upright. A woman on an absolute monster of a two-wheeler was pulled up at the side of the groundway, heedless of the traffic that had to steer around her. She was in a stab-proof vest over a dark green shirt. She wore armoured elbow and knee pads, pistols at her belt and a knife sheath strapped to her leg. A black helmet and goggles hid most of her face. He thought he recognised the tilt of her smile and his heckles rose.

"Who are you?" he said, feeling like he was shouting to be

heard.

The woman pulled off the groundway and swung herself off her two-wheeler with practiced ease. She strode over to them, pulling off her gloves as she came. She walked perfectly steadily in the over-tuned gravity, using longer strides and planting her boots firmly with each step.

Webb reached for his gun and sensed Vergennes doing the same as she reached up to pull her helmet off. Dark hair tumbled out and her smile widened to reveal an ornamental silver tooth.

"You're that reporter," Webb stammered before pulling his gun and keeping it at his side. "Osgard. What are you doing here?"

"Come on, Captain. There's no need for that," she said, nodding at his gun. "And, please, call me Vee."

"You followed us?"

She raised her eyebrows. "Don't flatter yourself, Captain Webb. I'm here because Red Star are here."

"What do you know about Red Star?" Vergennes demanded.

Osgard heaved a sigh, tucking her helmet under her arm. "Look, boys. There's a lot we can do for each other. I tried to talk to you on Earth but you were having none of it. Now we're all out here together, and you look like you're well up the river without a paddle, why don't we put the toys away and speak like respectable adults?"

"I told you, lady," Webb said. "You want a press release, talk to the damn press office."

She smiled again, this time in a slightly pitying way. "You still think this is about news? I'm after much bigger fish here."

"Fish away," Webb said, starting his engine. "We're done here. Move that thing out of our way."

Osgard glanced back at her two-wheeler then looked back with another sigh. Her smile had gone and her eyes are hardened. She started to speak, but over the muted sound of Webb's engine it was only noise.

Webb shrugged and tapped his ear. "Can't hear ya, darling," he said then waved again at her machine. "Move, already."

Her face hardened and she came forward. Webb stiffened and his hand went for his gun again but she was too quick, grabbing a handful of his shirt with surprising strength and pulling him forward so she could speak directly in his ear.

"I can help you find Hugo."

Webb started, pulled back to look into her face. All her playful smiles were gone, leaving cold determination in their place.

"You need to back the hell away," he said, hating the smallness of his voice. "I don't know what you think you know, but forget it all. And quick."

"Don't be an idiot," she said, lip curling. "You're the one that knows nothing. And you're lost out here without the faintest clue what you're blundering around in. I found you pretty damn easy. If I did, others will too."

His belly went cold and he found himself glancing round. Construction worker visors and curious faces were still turning their way. Knots of people were pausing with their loads to stare and a few people were talking into wristpanels or comm links. There were some talking in Haven finger-speech and he caught the sign for *Service*. Vergennes was glancing between Osgard and himself and the surroundings with increasing levels of tension stiffening his frame.

"Shit," Webb cursed.

"You said it," Osgard said, straightening and letting go of his shirt. "Follow me. I know somewhere we can talk."

"How do we know we can trust you?" Vergennes called as she mounted her two-wheeler and pulled her helmet back on.

"You're just gonna have to, aren't you?" she said, twisting the starter. The machine growled, the tail engine glowing with power. "See if you can keep up."

She wheeled out into the traffic and Webb cursed, steering his bike out after her.

"Sir," Vergennes's protest came through his earbud.

"She knows, Vergennes," Webb replied, gunning his accelerator and keeping the glow of her engines in sight. "She wasn't just fishing on Earth. She knows why we're here. We have to find out how."

Vergennes gave up on arguing and Webb's visor showed the young man kept a close tail on him as they wove out into the traffic. Webb didn't like admitting he was grateful for the backup but couldn't deny it as Osgard led them deeper into the dark and tangled underbelly of the city. The fine promenades and well-lit thoroughfares disappeared. What rose in their place were clusters of pre-fabs made of plexiboard, concrete and screw-together metal frames. Hand-painted or cheap-cut plastic and metal signs over doorways were the only things to identify what they were.

There was no clear boundary between the road and the walkway, workers with lifters wove in and out of the bikes, scooters and two-wheelers with curses, gestures and shouts and rubbish was collected in drifts between the buildings.

The organic and sharp smells of too many humans living in close quarters overrode the salty tang of the fog. It may have been the poor quality of the light or his imagination, but even the mist looked dirtier here, darker and yellow-tinged.

The traffic slowed to a crawl between the crowds and the buildings. Finally, Osgard pulled her machine onto a side street and parked it up alongside a long rack of other mopeds and scooters. Webb and Vergennes pulled their bikes in beside hers and dismounted, staring around them. No one looked their way here. They were just three more bodies in the heaving sea of people.

"I hope you've got good locks," Osgard commented, pulling out a large polyfibre chain that had been looped at her belt and running it through the front wheel of her machine, locking the magnetic ends directly into the starter motor.

Webb blinked. "That could kill someone."

"Oh, I know," she said, straightening and tossing him a smile. Being unable to see her eyes behind her goggles, he couldn't tell if she was joking. "Come on. We don't want to hang round out here too long."

Webb tapped commands into the small panel behind the windscreen of his bike, ranking up the security settings. "Set your engine to Security Level 8, Vergennes."

"Yes sir," Vergennes readily agreed and Webb watched to make sure he had enabled all the protocols and synced the system to his wristpanel. Webb made sure his own was connected then hurried after Osgard towards the nearest doorway.

It stood open, spilling light and the smell of alcohol and overcooked food unto the rubbish-strewn ground. Webb's visor was scrolling all sorts of atmosphere readings and warnings again. He pulled it off, blinking in the gloom, squinting at the Japanese characters painted over the door.

"*Home From Home,*" he translated. "Cute."

"This way," Osgard said and they hurried after her into the barhouse. The air was thick with smoke, despite an atmosphere regulator that coughed and spluttered in the corner. The machine succeeded in adjusting the pressure to feel normal and his ears popped gratifyingly and he could hear properly for the first time in hours, but it didn't even make a dent in the smoke that was drifting from the hookah stands dotted around the room. It was like the Martian fog had penetrated the walls and thickened.

He'd been expecting an open room with scattered tables and a grimy bar, but instead the room was divided into a series of high-walled booths, some with a screen pulled over the doorway to shield the occupants completely. The sealed booths admitted strange noises and grunts. He could see the open booths held display tables that the patrons, some smoking hookahs, were using to order their drinks, food or watch movies, newsreels or…Webb rose his eyebrows.

Osgard grinned, seeing his reaction. "You're not prudish I hope, Captain."

"What is this place?"

"A place we won't be overheard."

She wove through the booths to find an unoccupied one at the back of the room. They all crammed in, Vergennes having to crush his long legs under the table. The display in the top went red the second they sat down and a 60-second countdown began.

"We need to order something before the countdown finishes or we get chucked out."

"If you order porn, I'm leaving," Webb growled.

Osgard laughed and swiped her hand across the display to reveal a block-texted menu and tapped an order in. "From what I've heard, I would never have pegged you for a shy one."

"Enough with the small-talk," Webb said. "What the hell's going on here? Who the hell exactly are you?"

Osgard put her head on one side and narrowed her dark blue eyes. "You really don't remember me?"

Webb felt heat ride into his face. "We've met?"

Her eyes narrowed further and she examined him a moment longer. The deep azure of her eyes stirred something in the back of his head, but it drifted away and dissipated like the mist in the streets before he could identify it. He sensed Vergennes glancing between them. Then she looked away with a shrug.

"It was a long time ago, when you were still with that pirate ship…what was it? The *Zero*?"

"Another lifetime," Webb muttered, keeping his face neutral.

"Feels like it sometimes," she said a little wistfully then straightened as a girl arrived at their table with a tray of screw-top flasks. Osgard opened her flask and took a long drink. Webb and Vergennes unscrewed their own and sniffed at the contents.

"Relax. It's beer."

Webb took a drink. It tasted better than he'd expected and was more welcome than he cared to admit. He downed half his flask and felt it settle in and steady him.

"Come on then, lady. Spill. Who are you?"

"I told you. Vee Osgard."

"The reporter, yes, I know that. But how did we meet…Osgard?" Webb repeated, realisation dawning as an answering smile spread over her face. "As in *Admiral* Osgard?"

"As in my dad. Correct."

Webb put his flask down on the table with a thunk. "You're his daughter?"

"Yes. Good lord, boy, do you need a diagram?"

"Wait," Webb kneaded his temples then stared hard at her, seeing the family resemblance at last. "So, you're in the Service?"

"I don't have a rank. But it's in my blood, Webb. That's more real than any pips on my collar."

"So you're telling me the daughter of Erica Hugo's second-in-command is a solarnet gossip columnist for the *Now* network site?"

Her silver tooth winked in the reflected light from the table display as she smiled again. "How do you think I get such good stories?"

Webb shook his head. "Unbelievable."

"It's no secret," she said with a shrug. "Any solarnet search of my name would tell you my connections."

"So why the journalist angle? Why aren't you commanding a Space Corps unit or something?"

She curled her lip. "My job is far more important than ferrying around the Service's gun-toters. I report what's really happening in the Orbit, to make people understand what the Service is doing for them and how it's protecting them."

"None of this explains why you're here," Vergennes put in, leaning forward. "Or why you approached us."

Her keen glance slid to him. "I'm doing Dad's work. The Service's work."

"What 'work'?"

She turned her cool eyes back to Webb. "You're here to retrieve the turncoat Hugo. So am I."

Webb stiffened. "How do you know that? Not even Admiral

Osgard knows that."

"My father knows everything, Webb. SC Hugo didn't tell him, no. But it doesn't take Dad's deductive powers to put two-and-two together when you have access to her procurement requests. When he saw she had scheduled an impromptu trip out to China where he knew your unit was stationed, and was commissioning a ship for an undisclosed mission, he sent me to investigate."

"Why didn't you mention any of this before, on Earth?"

"I still wasn't sure. The official report was you'd been taken off active duty for insubordination and that was believable enough. Besides, a good investigator doesn't reveal what they're really interested in until they're sure of their footing. And you surprised me when two of you turned up," she added, shooting another keen glance at Vergennes.

"What are you talking about?" Webb frowned, taking in the tightness of his lieutenant's expression.

"All the requisition orders were for a one-man mission. Dad was sure SC Hugo was sending you out alone. When you both turned up at the ship I wondered if we had got it wrong after all. But then I tracked the ship to the Sunside colony where Kaleb Hugo's sister's little underground enterprise is based, and was pretty sure you'd only be going to see her if you thought she knew something about her brother. Nice trick changing the ship registration, by the way. Nearly lost you there. But you should have done it before you left Earth. The Duty docked at Sunside 3 but didn't leave whereas *Job* left but never arrived. Sloppy."

"I didn't expect anyone would be keeping such a close watch from day one," Webb glared.

She smiled again. "'*Job*' huh? Cute. Is that how you feel, Webb?"

"Is what how I feel?"

She leant forward on her elbows, blue eyes examining his face. "Like *Job*? Like you've lost your faith? But faith in what, I wonder? The Service? Your Nova Catholica god? Or yourself?"

"Quit the psychoanalytical crap. You're telling us you did follow us after all?"

"More like I took an educated guess as to where you would end up and went on ahead to take a look around. And good thing I did too, since you seem to know next to nothing about this colony."

"You meant to team up with us all along?"

"Only if you proved you might actually be up to getting this job done. Since you've managed to get yourself this far, despite the worrying amount of cluelessness, I'm guessing SC Hugo and my father are right and you really are the best person to track down Kaleb Hugo, if anyone can."

"And what's in this for you and the good admiral?"

Her face hardened. "Damage control."

"Come again?"

"Cleaning up the mess Erica Hugo and her wretched family have made for the Service."

Vergennes stood, jostling the table, face red.

"Blaise, sit down," Webb warned when a few faces turned their way. Vergennes obeyed, though his jaw was bulging.

"Explain yourself," the younger man said.

Osgard took another swallow of her drink, watching the younger man over the rim of her flask. "Times are changing, boy. And they're only getting tougher. Using Eclipse intelligence and negotiations and promises of Mars VISAs to secure loyalty to the Service is weak. And stupid. The Service has survived for generations because it's a *military* organisation. Force is the only thing that can keep the Orbit in line, not deals and treaties."

"Oh yeah, that's worked out brilliantly," Webb drawled. "There have only been two tiny revolutions in my lifetime."

"There would have been a lot more than that if the Service was then what it's heading toward now. Now we have an atmosphere where a man like Arcadias Rose, touting the need for an Orbit Alliance, is in a position of power, gathering support all the time, while a serious threat like Red Star grows in strength under his banner. And all because of Erica Hugo."

"I don't follow," Webb said. "The Orbit is in a constant cycle of war, revolution and recovery. The Service slows it down, sure, but it doesn't stop it. Nothing has ever stopped it. That's humanity for you."

"The Service *could* stop it, if the Special Commander remembered she's a commander of an army and not a governor in a game of politics."

"And this is how daddy feels too, is it?"

She narrowed her eyes. "Not just my father. Many Service Commanders feel it's time for a new start. A new Special Commander, one that isn't scared to do what's needed to keep the peace."

"And what's that, exactly?"

"Root out and destroy Red Star, for one," Osgard said boldly, though she lowered her voice. "Toss Rose in a detention centre for mutiny and bring a full fleet of ships out to Mars with units of Ground Corps troops to take control of the population before the city is complete."

"Anything else?" Webb drawled.

"Re-introduce conscription," Osgard replied with a straight face. "Build troop numbers and increase the armed presence in the Lunar Strip, take back Lunar 1 and the remaining nations on Earth that aren't unionised."

Webb slumped in his seat, staring at her. "Nothing big, then?"

"Nothing big," she agreed. "Just what's necessary."

"This is why your old man is scuppering Eclipse missions left, right and centre, huh?" Webb said, voice hardening.

"He believes in a different way, Webb. Eclipse is underground, underhanded and ineffective in the long term. Dad believes in the direct way. The right way."

"This is beside the point," Vergennes said again. "This is politics. This is nothing to do with us, here, now. Why should we let you join us when we're here under SC Hugo's orders and you clearly have no loyalty to her?"

"I have loyalty to the Service," Osgard said fiercely. "And what's best for the Service is to retrieve Erica's wretched son, which her idiot of a husband still hasn't managed to do, even whilst out here virtually sitting in his lap."

"So you think Hugo's here in Schiaparelli City?" Webb said, ignoring the look on Vergennes's face which suggested he was ready to explode.

"I *know* he's here," she replied.

V

"We've had confirmation. Webb's here. In the city."

"No big surprise," the harsh voice drawled. "He may not be a threat, but he's not an idiot. Where is he?"

Hugo stared at the wall. It was made of red, sandy rock. There was a thin film of moisture on it. Sometimes the moisture gathered enough to form a drip that splashed onto the sandy floor. His breath misted out of his mouth to join with the thin strands of fog permanently wreathed in the air. The light from the single lighting pole made it look like ghosts drifting through the air.

"North East quarter," the woman's voice replied, "We've had visual confirmation of him poking about the foundation levels, then we lost him."

"Just have someone keep a tail. He's not our concern."

"You really think he's not a problem?" the lighter voice was slightly closer.

He dug his fingers into the rock beneath him. He'd long since worn his fingernails to next to nothing, but the feel of the nail roots scraping across the rock kept him anchored.

"Of course he's not," the harsh voice continued. "And for God's sake stop spouting off that you're worried whilst this one can hear you. I didn't spend all this time programming him only have to do it all again. Besides, I can't now. He needs to be able to stand upright. His moment is coming. Ain't that right, Kaleb?"

His view of the wall jerked away as someone took hold of his collar and spun him round. Now he was looking at a face. Blonde hair flopped into dark eyes, black as space, and faint, slightly red stubble scruffed his jaw.

"Got to be ready for the ball, haven't we? Answer me, soldier," he added with a shake when Hugo didn't respond. The motion sent lightning dancing through his head and his vision swam.

"Yes, sir." It was his voice, but he hadn't made it work. The answer must have pleased the man since the grip on his collar loosened and he was allowed to slump back against the rock.

"Finish your checks," the man snapped to the woman. "I've got more important things to be getting on with."

The woman mumbled agreements and then gloved and relatively gentle hands were on him, checking his pulse and shining a light in his eyes. He coiled himself away deep within the back of his mind, focussing on the scrape, scrape, scrape of his nail beds against the rock and not letting anything else in.

Δ

Webb took a moment just to breathe. Osgard's deep blue gaze was levelled at him, frank and challenging.

"*How* do you know he's here?"

"I know Red Star are here. And Hugo's with them. I know just as you know."

"I know shit," Webb said, wishing he was lying. "I'm following half a lead that might lead to half of another. And I got that from a very exclusive source. What led you here?"

"Such suspicion. Look, Webb." She shifted in her seat and put her hands over his. She'd pocketed her gloves and her skin was warm and smooth. "Stop questioning. I've given you my reasons, but they don't matter to you anyway. You want Hugo. I want Hugo. That's all that matters."

"What matters is that I'm out here on a whim and a prayer with next to no intel, and you seem to know everything already, aren't telling any of it and expect me to trust you."

"Lunar 1 screwed you up hugely, didn't it?" she said with an assessing look. Before Webb could form an answer, she let go of his hand and folded her arms over her stab-proof jacket. "Ok boys. I grow tired of justifying myself here. The bottom line is I know Silence City. I also know Red Star are here. I know all this but I can't get any further because people know my face. Now, you guys," she weighed them both up. "You could be made to blend in. But you've admitted yourself you don't know where to start. So what's it going to be? Spend the next few weeks floundering round the foundation levels hoping you don't get stabbed, poisoned or pushed off some scaffolding for being Service snoops, or do you shake my hand, take my info and guidance, and we all walk out of here with Kaleb Hugo safe and sound?"

Webb fidgeted. "It doesn't feel right."

He expected her to be scornful but she nodded. "I understand what it is to rely on your instincts. And I admit we got off on the wrong foot. But no matter how differently we think…Ezekiel…Blaise…" Webb swallowed and Vergennes went very still next to him. "I want to help you. We all want the same thing here."

"For different reasons."

"Does that matter?" she asked Vergennes, face now soft.

"You know my first name," Vergennes said. "You researched me?" There was a hint of colour riding in his face.

"I researched both of you," she said frankly.

"And what did you find?" Webb asked, hoping his returning fear wasn't evident in his voice.

She shrugged one shoulder. "Two men loyal to the same thing I am, in their own ways. Good soldiers. Efficient investigators. Obedient and dutiful…to a point," she added with an amused glance at Webb.

"Sir…"

"I…" Webb cut Vergennes off, pinched the bridge of his nose, then sighed heavily, swiping at the table top. "I need more beer. How the hell does this work?"

Osgard smiled faintly, batted his hand away and pressed a few commands. The young girl returned with more flasks, cleared up their empties and disappeared. Webb reached over and pulled the screen over. It clicked shut and Osgard raised her eyebrows.

"You realise people will be thinking we're sealing our deal in a very definite way now?"

"I don't care," Webb said, unscrewing his drink and taking a long swallow. "You reckon you can help us. Tell us how."

"Is that an agreement I hear?"

"Yes, dammit," Webb said before letting himself think. "We agree. Now what do you know about Hugo and Red Star."

Her smile returned, but it was brighter than before. Sharp. Eager. "I know that they're not only here, on Mars, but that their base and leaders are here too."

"How?" Vergennes demanded. "General Hugo has been investigating for weeks without coming up with any solid answers about where they're based."

She gave the lieutenant another long look. "I have my ways. And if we're going to work together on this I'd appreciate a little less suspicion."

"Vergennes," Webb said. The tall man was stiff with tension and Webb felt for him, but put a hand on the younger man's forearm. Vergennes swung a surprised look his way. "God help us, but she's right. We're feeling our way in the dark here. Let's see what she can give us, hey?"

He thought the lieutenant would protest, the lieutenant always protested, but instead he seemed to read Webb's face and nodded, then sat back in the booth cushions, back straight but arms folded.

"Go on," Webb said, leaning over the table.

"Red Star operates out of Silence City. They may have growing support all throughout the Orbit and rumour has it there are growing pockets of their armed forces gathering on Earth and in the Lunar Strip, but all orders come from here. The ringleaders are hiding out here. Somewhere."

"You don't know where?"

She shook her head. "They're too well hidden for anyone who's not in their inner circles to figure that out. There's a base somewhere in this half-built monstrosity, but their connections are utterly secret, wide and loose. And no one will talk. It's impossible to follow any trails. This place is a maze on top of a labyrinth buried under a construction site. There are official schematics of the city and plans of what they're building where, but over the last few years the constructors have made their own city down here. They have no maps, only places to sleep, eat, hide and…. you know," she added with a crooked smile and a glance around their booth. "And, besides, people know I'm either connected to the Service or news sites. Either way, not someone they want to talk to."

"Do you know where *House of Remus* is?" Webb asked, going out on a limb.

She hesitated a moment, glancing between them then a gratified smile spread over her face. "You have done your homework. My hope builds by the second."

"You know it?"

"Yeah, I know it," she said. "And I know it's rumoured to be somewhere Red Star sympathisers gather, and possibly Red Star themselves."

"That's where we need to go," Webb said, straightening and draining his drink. "Take us there. Now."

"Steady on, cowboy," Osgard said. "What, you think you can go park yourself in this bar and overhear someone spilling all the Red Star gossip? Nuh-uh. I'm telling you, these guys are underground. If they don't recognise you as one of their own, they won't talk. Believe me."

"What's the use of being a revolutionary if you're so damn secretive?" Webb growled, slumping back in his chair.

"Whoever their leader is, they know what they're doing," she said in a serious tone. "They're clever. They know about timing. Which is what makes them dangerous. They're not an organisation you're going to bring down by planting a couple of bombs or grabbing an informant or two and getting them to talk."

"I'm not after bringing them down, Osgard. I'm after Hugo. That is the extent of my entire involvement in this mess."

"Wise. So, we need a plan. Martians are prickly. They're a huge mix of people from all over the Orbit - Eurasia, South America, Old Europe and a bunch of born-and-bred Lunar colonists and a fair amount of Haven trash too."

"Steady," Webb warned.

She looked surprised, then she glanced at the Haven brand on his neck and smiled apologetically. "Sorry. Havenites, then. As I say, a real mix, but all with one thing in common: they all came here hoping for a new start, away from the Service. They believe they're building a better future for themselves."

"But you obviously don't believe that."

She sneered. "They've been brainwashed. The Service gave them the life they have, whatever it is. They won't survive without it, on Mars or anywhere else. But the bottom line is Martians are disparate in background, temperament and attitude but unified in purpose. Those that aren't active members of Red Star support them, or support Rose which is basically the same thing. They're developing their own culture and language and Rose is encouraging it all."

"So we need to be careful not to bad-mouth Mars. I get it. I could have figured out that much on my own."

"More than careful," she said earnestly. "Non-sympathisers disappear out here all the time with no chance of ever being found again. And we cannot afford for that to happen to us. We're the only ones with a ghost of a chance of succeeding."

"Fine. So take us to *House of Remus*, already. We're wasting time blowing air about in here."

"No one will talk, Webb. Haven't you been listening to what I've said?"

"We've got to start somewhere," Webb insisted, shifting in his seat with the frustration.

She chewed on her lip a moment, regarding him levelly. "Ok. I guess you're right. But I need you to know you just can't barge in, or sneak in even, and expect to hear anything. You need another plan. Be prepared."

"I *am* prepared. Good Christ. Now tell us where this place is."

She narrowed her eyes again, the hardness back in her expression. She drained her beer and stood, pushing back the screen. "This way."

She strode her way back across toward the door. Webb moved to follow but Vergennes grabbed his elbow to stop him.

"Sir, I don't think this is a good idea. I don't trust her."

Osgard was gesturing for them to hurry. Webb ground his teeth.

"I don't trust her either," he said. "But she already knows everything we wanted to hide. And we need her right now."

Vergennes didn't reply but he saw grudging agreement in the set of his face.

Osgard already had her helmet on and was unchaining her two-wheeler when they caught up with her outside.

"Follow me and stay close. We need to make a stop at my place."

"Your place?" Webb asked, using his wristpanel to disable the locks on his bike.

"It's not far. We need to make you look a little more Martian."

"How long have you been here?" Vergennes quizzed, adjusting his voice to carry now they were back out in the dull air. "We only left you at Headquarters a few days ago and it's the best part of a three-day cruise from there. How have you had time to find out so much?"

"Like I said," Osgard said, mounting her machine with a grin. "Research. And it helps I spent almost a year out here reporting for *Now* on Appollos Outreach. Now do you believe I know what I'm talking about?"

She didn't wait for an answer but fired up her two-wheeler, engine snarling and glowing to life, then backed out into the street, ignoring the yells of a moped driver that had to swerve around her. Webb shook his head in disbelief, scrambled onto his own bike and wheeled it round to follow. The journey was fits of break-neck speed interspersed with periods of crawling through choked up junctions.

It was noticeably darker now. Webb looked up into nothing but blackness punctuated with flecks of artificial light that spiralled up through the fog as far as the eye could see. He wondered what the Mars night looked like where you could actually see it, but then shook the fancy away as someone honked their horn to warn him he was about to plough into their trailer.

Thankfully, it wasn't long before the reporter pulled down a narrow side street, dismounted and wheeled her machine down a space between two buildings too narrow to drive down.

Webb and Vergennes climbed off and followed her. It was pitch black apart from what showed in their headlights. They came up against a sheet of corrugated iron blocking the way. It had been turned into a gate with the aid of some metal cable ties for hinges. Osgard keyed a combination into another polychain around the handle, unlocked it and pushed the gate open.

The space beyond was fractionally wider, though still dark. She parked her two-wheeler and secured it, then the gate behind them.

"What is this place?"

"My own home from home," she quipped then flicked on a len-slight. The floor was pocked tarmac. She went to a door, keyed a code into another lock then opened it up and went inside.

Beyond was a cramped space made from polyfibre boards that gave the impression of the space being walled off from a bigger space beyond.

"Used to be a storage cupboard for the supply bunker we're in," she explained, flicking on a switch. Lighting panels shimmered to life around the room. She pulled off her gloves and helmet and shrugged herself out of her stab-proof vest, but she did not take off her gun belt or knife sheath. "I bargained it off them and got it secured. We're safe here."

There was a bunk against one corner. It had thin, mass-produced bedding but was immaculately made up. The rest of the room was cramped but, again, ordered and neat. There was a pod containing a tiny washroom and a unit next to it with a battered but functional multi-purpose washer, microwave and workstation all stacked on top of each other to save space.

Osgard had opened a clothes locker and was rooting through it whilst Vergennes and Webb stood looking round.

She glanced back at them and sighed. "Come in, boys. I told you, it's safe."

Glancing at the wires that ran around the wall connected to small boxes with dull lights on them that looked to be an alarm system with cameras and gas canisters, Webb believed she was right.

"The supply bunker owners don't know who you are then?" Webb asked, sitting on a fold-out chair.

"They don't know or don't care," she said, dumping some clothes on the bed. "I looked round for a long time before I found someone who cared more about credit than who I was, though. This isn't the Lunar Strip, that's for sure. Now, let's see."

She turned and examined them with hands on hips. "Well, you both look a little too healthy to be Martians. But a few days breathing in their air might drain your colour a bit. I notice you've both managed to not walk like Service soldiers either, which is good."

"Hard to stand up straight in this gravity anyway," Webb muttered. "And give us some credit. We work for Eclipse, remember."

"Yes," she managed to not sneer this time, but only just. "Undercover and infiltration. You are made for this place, really. Just put these on instead." She tossed them a couple of beat-up jackets. They were worn and faded to grey where they had once been black, but were clean and had pockets on the inside as well as a thick insulating inner layer. The red disk patch he had seen on the arms of many of the Martians' clothes was stitched at the shoulder. "Apollos Outreach standard issue. They all wear them against the cold. And you'll need to get rid of that," she said, reaching out and pulling off Webb's cap.

"Hey," Webb protested as he tried to grab it back.

"Don't be an idiot," she said, tossing it on her bunk. "Anyone that has ever met you knows you wear one. It might not have mattered on other infiltration missions, but here everyone is looking out for anything new."

"I'm sure some Martians wear baseball caps, Osgard."

She shook her head. "Supply vessel space is at a premium. As is space on the immigration vessels. No one brings anything that isn't absolutely necessary."

"And the porn booths were necessary, huh?"

She quirked a smile. "Too right, they are. Here," she reached out and he flinched. "Don't be a baby. Sit still."

She moved behind him and scraped his hair back out of his eyes. He cursed, despite the fact that she was gentle. The top layer was just long enough to be tied back and she forced it into a tie.

"There. Workers don't wear hair in their eyes, for obvious reasons. You should have cut it."

"Pick on Vergennes now, will you?" Webb said, stepping back out of her reach. "He's the one that looks like Marcus Military."

She laughed and Vergennes frowned.

"Funnily enough, I think Blaise is fine as he is, now he has the clothes."

"Are you kidding? He looks like a spoiled rich kid. And French. No offence, bro," Webb added, seeing the young man flush. "But you know it's true."

"There are plenty of Old Europeans here. And he's got his hair sensible length and that observant, suspicious look. That's all that's needed since he's clever enough not to march like a soldier. Just change your shirt for this one," she said, handing Vergennes a loose shirt with long sleeves. "It'll hide your, ahem, athletic physique a little more."

She smiled in a predatory way and Vergennes glared though he was blushing fiercely. He flushed still deeper when she stood and watched him expectantly with her arms folded as he made a move to change.

"Osgard, give the kid a break."

She chuckled and turned her back and went to the cupboard. "I don't think there's anything wrong with appreciating the fine physical specimens a lifestyle in the Service turns out. But fine. I'll fix us something to eat and then you boys can settle in on the floor."

"What?" Webb said, standing. "Settle in? We're not going out now?"

"No, we're not going out now," she said coolly, placing tins and packs on the counter. "By the time we get there the bar will be closing."

"Bullshit, I've never known a bar that closes."

She looked angry for a minute. "For the last time I'm going to ask you to drop the attitude. We're on the same team now, remember? Yes, the bars close around here. This city depends on the health and wellbeing of the constructors to get built. There is a five hour curfew every night-cycle to ensure they all get some sleep."

"Construction stops at night?"

"Sure does," she said, emptying tins into containers and stacking them in the microwave. "This isn't Haven. Most people sleep at their worksites, there's too much traffic to get home to a boarding house every night, but sleep they do. And they work better for it, apparently."

The microwave hummed and the smell of savoury food filled the small room. Webb's stomach clenched, reminding him he'd had nothing but ship rations since HQ.

"Sir," Vergennes said. He'd changed his shirt and his new jacket was draped across the back of a chair. He was bending to pull off his boots. "We should practice again."

"What, here? There's no room."

"A contained environment also makes for good practice," the

younger man insisted, clearing the few chairs there were to the side of the room.

"Practice what?" Osgard asked as she laid trays out on the side.

"Vergennes insists we practice fighting every night," Webb said. "I've yet to fully understand why."

"You mean rounds of hand-to-hand?" Osgard said, and Webb thought he noted approval in her voice. "It's standard practice for students at the Academy. Eclipse probably don't bother, but most active Service units insist their troops practice regularly whilst out in the field, so you get to know your comrades' styles."

"Hugo never did," Webb grumbled.

"And look where he ended up."

Webb glared at the woman but she stared right back at him unapologetically. "Here we are Lieutenant," she said, coming forward to fold away a table. "This will give you more space."

"Stop encouraging him."

They ignored him, finished clearing the room then both looked at him expectantly. Webb rolled his eyes, muttered and pulled off his boots.

"Besides, a black eye and some bruises will help you to blend in even more."

"Why do you assume I'll be the one with the...Jesus," Webb jumped and stumbled as Vergennes swung for him without any further preamble. He just had time to take in the amused smirk on Osgard's face before he was fending off another of Vergennes's relentless barrages of swipes and slaps.

He was stiff and sore by the time Vergennes stepped back, declaring the bout over, but felt that he'd held his own better this time. He even earned a nod from his lieutenant, who was flushed and sweating and had a red mark swelling on one side of his jaw.

To his surprise, Vergennes and Osgard were the ones who made the tiny amount of small talk that was exchanged over their heated trays of protein mash and rice. Webb scowled, thinking how they must be bonding over their love of the more obscure and stupid Service regulations. He rubbed a sore spot on his shoulder and was secretly grateful they weren't going anywhere else that night.

After eating, Osgard cleared the trays into the washer whilst Vergennes folded the table and chairs back again without having to be asked. Osgard showed them where there were blankets in the cupboard then disappeared into the washroom and shut the door.

Webb stepped up to his lieutenant who was pulling out the blankets.

"So, what?" he said in a low voice, "You trust her now?"

"No," Vergennes replied softly, not looking at him. "But I feel I understand her."

He offered Webb one of the blankets. Webb muttered and took it.

She let them both use the washroom and then they all settled down to sleep. Webb took note that Osgard kept one of her guns with her as she climbed into her bunk. When she turned the lighting panels off the room was pitch black apart from the lights on her equipment. Above the gentle humming of her workstation and washer were the clanking and bangs of the supply bunker, but it was all muffled by the intervening walls and the dull air.

Webb lay on the floor staring up into the dark. His blanket was Apollos Outreach-issue insulated polyfibre but he still felt cold. He could hear Osgard's steady, even breathing and Vergennes was snoring softly. He closed his eyes and murmured a prayer under his breath, reaching up a hand and clutching a small silver crucifix at his neck. He wasn't sure what he believed about anything anymore, but this still comforted him in some small measure, though he wasn't sure why.

Δ

It was Osgard moving round the room that woke him. His sleep had been deep and, thankfully this time, dreamless. He checked his chrono and groaned.

"You let us sleep too long," he said, getting himself up on his elbows, then noted the lieutenant wasn't next to him and his blankets had been tidied away. "Hey, where's Vergennes?"

"Gone for a run," Osgard said then put a bottle down on the floor next to him. "Here, drink this."

"What is it?" he said, sitting up and eyeing the bottle warily.

"Vitamins, minerals, glucose. It'll keep you on top form."

"You Service types are all health freaks," he said, taking a mouthful and scowling. "Tastes like crap. And what? He's gone for a run? Around this neighbourhood?"

"He'll be fine. I gave him some worker-issue track gear. Plenty of Martians go running. You can't work if you're not fit."

Webb shook his head and got to his feet, cursing at his sore muscles, stiff from the bout, the crazy riding yesterday and the night on the hard floor.

"We're not as young as we were, huh?" Osgard said with a flash of a smile.

"Speak for yourself," Webb muttered bitterly before he could stop himself then froze, praying she hadn't heard.

But she had, turning and giving him an amused look. "That's true, that was one thing that came up in my research. Your date of birth. There isn't one."

"No, there's not," Webb responded, not looking at her as he reached for his own boots.

"You must have some idea when you were born," she pressed, eyes looking a little too keen. "Even Lunar 1 orphans from McCullough's Revolution have a vague idea from their youth units."

Every part of her sentence made him shudder. He didn't answer, just pulled on his boots and scowled at the floor.

"Fine, it's not important I suppose," she said and he again ignored the question in her words. The silence was threatening to stretch on to an uncomfortable length when Vergennes returned, sweating and flushed and looking altogether far too alert for Webb's liking. He accepted one of the vile drinks from Osgard with a nod and downed it in one go.

"Get a move on, Vergennes," Webb grumbled as he attempted some stretches to get rid of the worst of the aches. "We've wasted too much time already."

"Fix your hair," Osgard ordered.

"What?"

"It's come out of the tie. Here…"

"I'll do it," Webb snapped, suddenly reluctant to have her touch him again. She shrugged and turned away, tidying away the last of the ingredients she'd used to mix their drinks. She made him eat a Nutripak whilst Vergennes finished washing and dressing, despite his protests that we wasn't hungry. Which he wasn't. A knot had formed where his belly should have been. He was trying not to think about what would happen if they got to House of Remus and failed to find anything that might help them.

"Sir," Vergennes interrupted his thoughts. He was dressed, light hair tousled from the shower, but was looking at his wristpanel with a slight frown.

"What is it?"

"There's a message come through via *Job's* comm system."

Webb stood, scrabbling through his tech he'd shed on the floor for his own panel. "Finally. Is it General Hugo?"

"It's encrypted for you alone, sir," Vergennes said, just as Webb found his wristpanel and strapped it on. The comm light was blinking. He keyed in a code and the message scrawled across the display. His heart sank.

"Not General Hugo, sir?" Vergennes said, reading his face.

"No."

"You're trying to get a meeting with General Hugo?" Osgard frowned. "Why?"

"The man's been here for weeks," Webb said, swiping at the message to read the whole thing. "We thought it would be kinda useful to find out what he knows at some point."

"He knows nothing."

"How do you know that?"

Osgard raised a scornful eyebrow. "What did I say? Martians don't talk to the Service. Especially not the Special Commander's husband or his investigative unit. Rose is playing at good governor and entertaining him for PR purposes. But I can guarantee the general has found dick-all."

"We can't know that for sure unless we speak to him," Webb insisted.

"Well he'll be far too busy preparing for the ball, anyway," Osgard said, dismissively.

"What ball?" Webb said, frowning.

"The Commemoration Ball. It's ten years since construction began on Mars. They're having a huge, formal celebration at the New Civic Hall on Apollos Square. General Hugo is the guest of honour." She added the last in a tone that suggested exactly what she thought of the whole arrangement.

"Well it would still be useful if he took a break from brushing off his tux to fill us in."

"Who is the message from, sir?" Vergennes asked.

Webb sighed and deleted the message. "It's just something from Loade at Lunar Alpha following up on Nam's parole. Nothing useful." He saw Osgard making a mental note of the names, but at this point couldn't bring himself to care. "Can we get going then?"

"I'm ready when you are," Osgard replied.

Webb strapped on the rest of his tech and weapons, then they both followed Osgard back out to the bikes. Webb grabbed Vergennes's elbow and pulled him back whilst Osgard was unlocking her machine.

"You got your earbud in?"

"Yes, sir."

"Good," Webb said, turned on his own and wheeled his bike

out after Osgard. She must have had some sort of atmosphere filter in her room because Webb was hit again by the smell and vague saltiness of the air when they passed out into it. He pulled up his visor, not liking how exposed he felt without his cap, but was grateful for the warmth the jacket provided and fastened it right up to the neck before mounting his bike.

"*House of Remus* is on a lower foundation level. It's not far, but it will be busy and we'll need to take the main route. You'll have to stay close."

"We're ready," Webb replied and Osgard nodded, pulled up her goggles and fired her two-wheeler.

Webb managed to stick close to the reporter for most of the trip but there were a couple of times he lost sight of her and she had to slow down before they were in visual range again.

Eventually, they were on a wider groundway sloping down. A gap appeared between the towers and he saw, on the horizon high above, a jagged outcrop of rock, the colour of blood in the uncertain light. Perched on top like a figurehead on the prow of a ship was the half-built form of a huge, white building, grand and old-fashioned looking. He could see columns and an ornate balcony. But he could also, even at this distance, see into the interior like it had been sliced down the middle with a knife. There were three floors, dozens of rooms and one huge room on the bottom floor with tall, wide windows that flashed in the weak sunlight. It was at that point he noticed a tumble of white stone stacked against an exterior wall and realised it wasn't half-built, it was half-destroyed.

The groundway dipped still further and it was hidden from view.

"Hey Vergennes, did you see that?" Webb called.

"Yes, sir," the lieutenant's voice replied in his ear bud.

"What was it?"

"I don't know, sir."

"Hey, Osgard," he called, but she was too far ahead and didn't hear. He sped up and waved at her to pull over. She scowled, checked the surrounding traffic and pulled up against the thin railing.

"What is it?"

"What was that?" Webb called, gesturing back where they'd come.

"What was what?" she said, impatience clipping her words.

"That building, the big white one above everything, half-collapsed."

She craned her neck. "Back there on the cliff? That was the Civic Hall."

"What the hell happened to it?"

"Marsquake," Osgard said, edging her machine back toward the traffic. "One hit this area about four years ago. They never bothered finishing it. The ground up there is too unstable."

"I thought quakes happened only like once every million years."

"Apparently one was due. Can we get going now? We're gonna get mowed down if we stay here."

Webb blinked back toward the gap in buildings where he'd caught the glimpse of the Civic Hall, then swung his bike round and followed Osgard back onto the groundway. They went lower and lower. It became darker and darker. They came to a crossroads between the roots of four megablocks. Shouldered between the groundways and the buildings was another knot of pre-fab constructor dwellings as well as a space crowded with parked-up bikes, mopeds and two and four-wheelers. Osgard pulled into a space and waited for them to park up and shut down their engines. She came to stand between them, looking around her and not taking her helmet off.

"It's up there," she murmured, almost too quiet for the sound to reach Webb who leaned in closer for her to repeat it. She pointed at the third floor of one of the hastily put-together constructions propped against what Webb had to look twice at to realise was bare rock.

"Where exactly are we?"

"We're at the bottom of one of the natural crevasses in the planet surface. This foundation layer is at the lowest point of the valley that runs through the eastern side of the city. And that," she said, jabbing her finger at the top floor of the building again. "Is *House of Remus*."

Webb pulled off his visor and blinked at it. It looked no different from the dozens of other pre-fabs. But he didn't know what it was, it might have been Osgard's edgy demeanour or the depth of the darkness or the sight of the natural rock providing the backdrop to the metal and plastic, but something about it made goosebumps ripple over his skin.

"Ok," Webb said, pulling off his gloves and checking all his weapons were in place. "Guess we're going in."

Osgard pressed her lips together. "Just don't screw up, ok?"

"I never *plan* to screw up," Webb said, gesturing for Vergennes to follow him and made for the building.

"Stay sharp in there," she called after them. "I'm not hanging round here, so I hope you remember the way back."

She spun her two-wheeler and disappeared back into the traffic.

Webb swallowed, glanced around, then latched onto a group of workers skirting the parking pool. He followed them round, examining the building she'd indicated from all angles. Vergennes kept to his heels. They got closer, Webb watching out for anyone paying them too much attention. There were few windows in the structure, those there were dotted haphazardly and all different sizes. The ground floor windows all had blinds drawn across them. He checked no one was looking and pressed his face against one, peering round the edge of the blind and shining a lenslight into the dark interior.

"Sir - " Vergennes hissed.

"Boarding rooms," Webb said, switching off the light and stepping back. "Relax, Vergennes. Everyone's out at work."

Vergennes looked at the building doubtfully before following Webb as he paced the length of the building toward the rocky cliff at its rear. The dulled noise from the thoroughfare and construction sites faded. Webb's breathing was suddenly very loud in his own head. He stopped when they reached the rock. A tumble of stone was piled up against the wall and cliff face. He pulled out his lenslight again. It was rock was red, dark, gritty and when he put his hand to it, slightly moist.

Craning his neck up he saw the cliff disappeared into shadow above. Above that, the solid darkness of the rising spacescrapers than above that again a line of sky so thin it looked like a thread.

"We're real, real far down," Webb murmured. He took a breath to ground himself. "Right. I think I have an idea."

"Sir?" Vergennes looked dubious.

Webb rubbed his mouth. "Yeah. I think so. You go to the bar and order something."

"Alone?"

"Yes, alone."

"And what are you doing, sir?"

Webb looked up the cliff again. "Been a while since I did rock climbing. Hope I've still got the knack."

"Sir?"

"Like Osgard said, no one's talking to any new faces. But they might just say something if they don't realise anyone's listening. Go. Turn your transmitter up to full so I can hear what's happening."

Vergennes glanced up the rock fall and then the building and understanding smoothed his face.

When he was alone, Webb pulled on his gloves and clambered up onto the fall of stone. When he'd scrambled to the top of the rockfall, he got a grip on one of the shelves in the cliff face and hauled himself up. He kicked his boot into gap in the rock and pushed himself higher. It was slow going. It was dark and slippery and he was in the wrong sort of boots and gloves. But he trusted his body to do the work.

He kept as close to the side of the building as he dared, pausing just below one of the few lit windows. The light ebbed and strengthened as people moved about inside. He crept higher and peered in. The room was crowded with workstations, good ones too, with a worker at every one, scrolling through shift data, supply lists, deadline schedules and city maps. He was reminded of the Planning District on Haven. He skirted the edge of the light, making himself move painfully slowly so as not to be seen. He still didn't breathe until he'd left it behind.

Finally, he drew level with the roof of the pre-fab, collapsing to his knees on the flat surface to catch his breath. He scanned the roof space but saw nothing to break the flat surface but a couple of filter vents.

"Vergennes," he murmured. "I'm in position. Are you in the bar?"

"Yes, sir," Webb heard him murmur.

"What's it like?"

"Busy, sir," he said, then the general sounds of muffled conversation and the shuffling of people moving about filled his ear. He switched a couple of settings on his visor. The scan range was weak, but combining what it could detect with the location devices in his wristpanel, he was able to estimate the general layout of the rooms below him. The biggest space lay directly underneath him and was, he imagined, the main bar. There were a number of rooms off to the side, including one that registered hotter than the others which he assumed was a kitchen of some kind.

"I am being looked at."

"Just keep cool. Anyone doing anything more than just looking?"

"Not yet, sir."

"Meet people's eyes," Webb murmured, still examining the scans in his visor and working his way over the rooms, trying to get any detail that might be helpful. "Then tell me if anyone gets up and leaves and where they go."

There followed a long pause in which Webb just heard his own heart, then Vergennes murmured. "A group of three people have risen and are leaving the room, sir."

Webb's heart skipped. "Which way are they going?"

"Through one of the doors behind the bar."

"Which door? Which direction?"

"North, sir," Vergennes replied and Webb swore and scrambled to the north, closer to the cliff face. He pulled a small laser-cutter from his belt and made a hole, no bigger than the width of his thumb, in the polyfibre roof. The cheap material melted easily. When he was finished he paused to listen but there was no reaction from below.

"Ok, Lieutenant," he murmured. "Set your earbud to record and pray we got this right. Are you ready?"

"Yes sir."

"Stay where you are. I'm coming down. Out."

Webb plucked out his earbud and dropped it through the hole. He pressed his ear to the gap and could hear muffled voices, muted enough to convince him no one had noticed the earbud. He rushed back to the edge, swung himself back out onto the rock and scrambled down.

By the time he reached the bottom his heart was hammering and sweat stood out on his forehead. He pulled off his gloves and visor, tucking them into the pockets of his jacket. He paused to let his breath calm, before turning the corner and ambling through the front door.

There were people shambling up stairs and he followed them to the third floor, through an entryway into a large room. There were people clustered along the low benches that ran the length of the room. There were self-service food trays along one side and a bar along the other. It looked more like a cafeteria than a barhouse to Webb, but the lights were down very low and he noticed there were the black eyes of cameras dotted around the ceiling.

A few workers looked up at his entry but he kept his face blank and his stride shuffling as he looked around for Vergennes. The tall man was on a stool at the far end of the bar, hunched over a bowl of soup. Webb wove his way toward him, shoving his hands in his pockets and glancing around to try and spot if anyone was paying either of them more than reasonable attention.

But no one seemed overly interested in either of them. If it wasn't for that fact that next to no one seemed to be talking, Webb might have convinced himself there was nothing out of the ordinary here. It could easily be any feeding and watering hole on any one of a dozen colonies. Apart from the silence and the glances sliding to a heavy door at the north end of the room. Webb frowned at it. It wasn't polyfibre. It was steel and had both electronic and manual locks.

Webb let his glance slide off it as if disinterested then drew level with Vergennes. Only then did he notice the expression on the lieutenant's face. The young man's fine features were stricken. He wasn't even trying to hide it.

Webb felt his stomach drop and dug an elbow into the lieutenant's ribs, glancing round to see if anyone had noticed. "What is it?"

Vergennes blinked and visibly pulled himself together. His face smoothed but he was still pale. "We need to move, Captain. Now."

Webb coughed to try and loosen his throat, resisting the temptation to look around again. "Finish your soup, quick. It'll look weird if we do a bolt now."

With a tremendous effort of will, Webb made himself take the stool next to Vergennes who was stiffly scraping his soup bowl clean. A greasy barman wandered up his way, eyeing him a little too keenly.

"*Hai?*"

Webb eyed the list on the bar top. "*Koohii o onegaishimasu,*" he said.

The man eyed him a moment longer then bumbled over to the coffee maker and started spinning dials. What he brought was a close approximation to coffee, but Webb was too flustered to wonder whether it was his Japanese or the machine that was rusty. He took a few sips, waiting for Vergennes to finish and trying not to shift on his stool with impatience. Finally, Vergennes was standing and they made their way out.

"Don't rush," he hissed, glancing back up at the building as they left it. "Not yet."

Vergennes nodded, stiff and staring straight ahead until they reached the bikes. "We need to get further away, sir."

"What did you hear?" Webb said, searching the lieutenant's still-pale face. "Was it Red Star?"

"Further away first, sir," Vergennes insisted, mounting his bike. Webb took in his urgency and nodded, starting his engine. They left the crossroads, the cliffs and the House of Remus well behind them before Vergennes agreed to pull into a side street.

"Someone's going to kill General Hugo, sir," Vergennes said in a voice just above a whisper.

Webb froze. "You heard that?"

"Yes sir. At the ball tomorrow."

"You're sure?"

"Certain, sir."

Webb swore, heart racing, glancing around as if looking for proof. "How?"

"I don't know, sir. All I know was that I was listening to you on the earbud, then there was a crash and I was hearing voices in English. It was echoey. At first they were complaining about new faces in the bar, then they picked up what they'd been discussing before I came in."

"Were they Red Star?"

"They didn't say so," Vergennes said, a modicum of calm returning to him as he fell into reporting mode. "But one of them

was called Coale and they mentioned that everything was ready…
then there was a creaking noise and the voices stopped."

Webb slumped onto his bike. "They definitely said *General
Hugo*?" he asked, not sure what he wanted the answer to be.

"Yes, sir. Here, I recorded it all." Vergennes pulled out his earbud, pushed a couple of buttons with his thumbnail then handed
it over.

Webb put it in his ear. There was a muffled crashing which
must have been him dropping his own earbud through the roof
and then he could hear voices. One was harsh, demanding and
spoke quickly. There were two more, muttered and indistinct, but
the commanding one was clear as day.

"Everything's ready. The party kicks off at 20:00 hours. Let
Rose make his speech and he's insisted on a couple of dances. But
then the fireworks start."

Someone else mumbled something and he heard what could
have been the name 'Coale' but the first voice cut them off. "It
doesn't matter. The old man is ice." Another mumbled reply. "I
won't listen to any more backchat. General Hugo will not see another Mars dawn. It's time we let everyone know…"

The voice faded then there was a dull creak and a slam and
everything went silent. Webb stared at the floor. His hands and
feet tingled.

"We need to get to the general," he breathed.

Vergennes nodded and started his bike, face grim. Webb
whirled his own, tapping commands into the wristpanel and the
control panel on the bike, praying he could find directions to
Appollos Square. The navigation system knew the rough direction but didn't have any maps of the jumble of unofficial thoroughfares. Webb turned the bike up the first groundway that was
heading in the right direction and gunned the accelerator. He
cursed at every intersection and every time the traffic slowed, but
still managed to set a pace that had other pilots and drivers staring or yelling insults after them as they cut them up or cut them

off. He tried to use the comm on the bike and on his wristpanel to connect a call through to Hazuki, Lomax and even the general himself, but his calls went unanswered or were cut off.

"Damn all Hugos," he growled then turned them onto a ramp that brought them up out of the fog and blinked in the sudden light. The spread of activity around him was dizzying, but he kept focussed, following the directions on the inside of the bike's windscreen.

He swore loudly when they turned onto a route packed solid with unmoving traffic.

"Vergennes," he called over his shoulder, voice sounding like it fell dead when he left his mouth but the lieutenant must have heard and inched his bike up closer. "Have you tried hailing them?"

"Yes, sir. No response."

Webb swore again. "The idiots. The pig-headed idiots."

Vergennes looked like he agreed, though was too well trained to say so. Webb strained his neck to try and see a way through but an overturned lifter at the next junction appeared to be the problem and was going nowhere fast.

"Sir," Vergennes suddenly said, pointing. Webb followed his gesture and saw a glimpse of white walls between the intervening scaffolding.

"We must have turned off-course," he said, checking his map again and looking round. He wheeled his bike off the groundway onto the narrow lip between the road and its thin rail, and looked around. He spotted another directly below that snaked away in the right direction.

"Sir," Vergennes warned.

"I'm going ahead."

"Captain!"

Vergennes's shout died in the guttered growl of Webb's engine as he sped down the lip, pressing so close to the rail it nearly grazed his knee. He glanced down, took a breath, then pulled the bike over. It crashed through the rail like it was yarn. There was a rush of stale air and fierce grip on his belly as he fell through the air.

Too fast, too fast, he thought, feeling the over-tuned gravity get a fierce grip. Panic rode through him, but then his wheels were crashing into the solid surface of the other groundway. The bike tilted horribly but he kicked off the road-surface and sped on.

He turned around a bend and came to a ramp which snaked up towards clear sky. A plastic barrier with a *Restricted Access* sign blocked the way but he went at it at full speed and the bike smashed through. The impact caused him to skid but he righted, arms straining and heart hammering, and then he was zooming up, ignoring the shouts that followed him from work crews.

He ploughed through another barrier at the top of the ramp and out onto a wide open space that met his eyes almost blindingly white. He braked, skidding across the smooth surface and took a second to let his eyes adjust. His breathing was heavy. Sweat dripped in his eyes. He swiped at them impatiently and looked around.

Appollos Square was huge and airy, paved in red stone. Up close Webb could see the statues were all larger-than-life interpretations of the god Mars in his great, plumed helmet holding spear and shield. On one side rose the luxurious Conference Centre with hundreds of wide windows reflecting back the thin light. On the other the New Civic Hall stood, festooned with balconies and flagpoles. There were two intersecting guidance strips for skyways branching overhead along which a few expensive sport-model flyers cruised.

Webb took this all in at a glance, ignoring the shocked looks he was drawing from the well-dressed people strolling about. What he did take notice of were the official looking men heading toward him on speeders, masks amplifying their demands for him to freeze.

Webb swung the bike toward the Conference Centre. People

stumbled out his way as he wove round the statues. The building loomed above him. He passed the main entrance where people had frozen on the stairs to gawp. His pursuers were catching up as he made the corner but he swung round it, skidding around a patioed eating area where people stopped with forkfuls halfway to their mouths to stare, then raced on, following the tilt of the ground toward the supply and staff entrances of the building. He wove between tastefully-disguised trash skips and garbage disposals, startling hospitality staff who had snuck out for cigarettes. He pulled his bike over at a wide doorway where the rolling cover had been raised to allow a lifter full of crates access. He braked, dumped the bike, wincing as it crashed into the concrete ground and staggering as his legs suddenly took his weight, then pelted through the door, the whine of the security flyers growing louder and the yells of the disgruntled centre staff following him.

He was running through a storage basement, crates and racks of everything from crockery to cleaning equipment on one side and a doorway through to an industrial laundry on the other. It smelt of exhaust and soap. He shoved his way past a bewildered porter with a lifter and grabbed the swinging doors into the building before the closed.

The corridor beyond was empty apart from more startled staff. He pulled up the schematics of the building on his wrist panel, grateful the general's staff were staying in one of the few completed buildings with public plans. He ran toward some service lifts but staggered to a halt when he was faced with two guards with their weapons drawn. He swore and double backed, trying to lose them in the maze of service corridors. He ducked through the first doorway he found and was relieved to hear the security guards race past.

He leant against the wall, panting and tapping at his wristpanel.

"Sir?" Vergennes's voice coming through the panel's speakers sounding strained.

"Vergennes, do we know where the General's staying?"

"Conference Centre, sir."

"Yes, yes, where in the damn Conference Centre? This place is massive."

"Presidential Suite, sir. But - "

Webb cut the call. He pulled the door open and looked up and down the corridor, but it was empty. He ran back the way he'd come, noting the cameras at every corner and knowing he wouldn't have long. He took another glance at the building plans, ducked around a corner when he heard running, then found another swinging door that opened onto stairs.

"Finally," he said, then started racing up them. He'd almost reached the right floor when black spots started dancing in front of his eyes and pain like lightning in his skull crashed through his head. He staggered onto his hands and knees, sweat dripping off his face and breath hissing between his teeth.

"Not now," he prayed. "Please, not now."

He clenched his eyes shut, forced himself to breathe. The pain worked its fingers through the back of his head to the front and he slumped, nausea rolling through the agony. He forced his eyes open and made himself focus on the stair rail and the feel of the cold surface of the step pressing against his burning cheek. He dug his fingernails into his palms and took one breath after another.

Slowly, agonisingly slowly, the pain slunk away and his vision cleared. He got his feet under him, shaking and dizzy, grabbed the rail and pulled himself up. He made himself move.

He finally reached the right floor just as sounds of doors slamming and feet racing started echoing up the stairwell. There was a camera over the reinforced door and it was locked with an keypad. He wiped more sweat out of his eyes and pulled out his lenslight and switched the beam to UV. There were smudges from fingers on five of the numbers. As he went through combinations, he slowly felt the last remnants of the headache fade and his stomach settle. Left in its place was his racing heartbeat and straining chest.

There was a buzz and the door opened and he rushed through, clicking it shut behind him. He paused in the carpeted corridor beyond, staring about. There were numbered doors all around, tall windows at the far end, a deep carpet under his boots and fine digiprints on the walls. It was eerily quiet. He hurried along, finally seeing a sign for the presidential suit and followed it. He slowed when he heard the mumble of voices and the reply of comm speakers. Peering around the corner he saw a pair of double-doors guarded by three security guards as well as two fully-armed Servicemen.

"It's nothing to worry about," one of the centre security was explaining to a tall Service officer. "Some mad man's just run in of the street. He's on his own. Our team will have him in custody shortly."

"The general's security is the priority here," the tall woman in a Service uniform with close-cropped auburn hair said. "What does your Governor mean allowing maniacs to just run into his Conference Centre?"

"He's just a construction worker," the security man said. "Probably making a demonstration about pay or living conditions. He's not a threat. We'll have him soon enough."

Webb pulled back and breathed with his back against the wall, mind racing. He raised his wristpanel, hesitated, and sent a message to Lomax, this time with his location details attached to it. He stood there, breathing, the sweat cooling on his skin, then finally, the comm light blinked and the words *Incoming Call: Corporal Lomax* blinked on the screen.

Webb pressed the connect button. "About time," he hissed, edging a further back from the corner.

"Webb, what the hell are you doing out there?"

"Let me into the suite, Lomax. I need to speak to the general. We're seven classifications beyond urgent."

"This chaos outside, this is because of you?"

"No, this is because you pissing idiots refused to respond to my hails."

"We're on an official mission here, Captain. You are not."

"I damn well am, or did you not recognise Erica Hugo's seal?" There was a pause. "The general - "

"The general is in danger, Lomax. Are you hearing me?"

"What are you talking about?"

"Let me the hell in. I need to speak to him."

"For Christ's sake, Webb. You can't just crash into a restricted building, upset local security, spouting conspiracies - "

"It's not a damn conspiracy. I heard Red Star with my own ears - "

"Webb," Lomax's tone was sharpening.

"If you don't want me screaming this at whoever next comes round the corner," he said, "let me in to see the old man. You hear my voice? I am as far away from joking as I can be."

The connection cut and Webb cursed, but then he heard something change in the voices of the guards. Peering around again, he saw them being ordered to stand down by a thin man with mousey hair swept back from a high forehead wearing a grey-and-black Service uniform, boots polished to within an inch of their life and a stormy expression. After they'd obeyed, looking faintly bemused, the thin man stepped further into the corridor and glared in his direction.

"Well, Captain? Get your ass in here."

Webb hurried to him, earning shocked and then suspicious looks from the assembled security.

"Corporal Lomax - " the security guard began to protest, but the thin man held up a hand.

"Stand the alert down," he said, glaring at Webb. "He's one of ours. No threat, just a fool. Our apologies."

Lomax took a step back and opened the suite door. He politely rebuffed the remaining indignant protests from the centre's security man, ushering Webb through the door.

Webb hurried in and Lomax shut and locked the door behind him. They were in a beautifully furnished sitting area with a deep, red carpet, white walls and pristine soft furnishings in tasteful styles and colours. The digiprints on the walls displayed artful images of the Mars highlands. There were sliding plexiglass doors, beyond which was a wide balcony with a decorative rail, small statues and pots of plants. There was a table and chairs set up on the balcony with plates set for four.

There were two internal doors, both guarded by armed Servicemen and there were a half dozen more men and women stood or sat about the room, some in uniform, some not. The ones not in uniform wore tailored suits and dresses, with neat hair and expensive datapanels to hand and stylish wrist pieces. Webb felt every inch of his disheveled appearance as they all stared at him with a mixture of confused, wary or hostile expressions. General Hugo was not among them.

"Lomax?" A lean man with very black hair and eyes the colour of ice stood from the sofa, looking between them with a flinty expression. "What is all this?"

"Nothing for you to worry about, Councillor," Lomax said in a much nicer tone than he'd used with Webb. Webb recognised the suited man with a clench of the chest. "Webb, this way. Now," Lomax added, leading the way out onto the balcony. Webb hurried after the aide, waiting for him to shut the soundproof plexiglass before he started talking.

"What in the name of red hell is Councillor Pope doing here?"

"That is not even remotely your concern, Captain," Lomax replied coolly. "You should only be concerned about yourself. You're hanging by a thread. You better spit out what you came to say before I arrest you myself."

Webb glanced once more at the seated figure in the suit through the glass, his ebony hair neat, his smile wide and fake and reigned in his temper before forcing himself to focus on Lomax. "The general needs to get off this planet. Today."

"Back up," the aide said, face still hard. "Explain."

"Dammit, do I need to explain? Red Star are gonna kill him."

"Red Star do not exist, Captain," the aide said, acidly. "We've conducted a thorough investigation, with Governor Rose's full cooperation, and found nothing to suggest there is any armed force of any kind hiding out in the colony."

"Because you're asking *Martians*," Webb growled.

"Captain, I can assure you - "

"Lomax, I *heard* them."

"How?" he said, eyes narrowing. "And why are you even out here in the first place?"

"You would know that if you'd responded to our hails."

"Enough, I don't want to hear any more."

"God dammit, man," Webb said, grabbing hold of the corporal's neatly-pressed shirt. "Are you hearing me? They're going to kill the old man, tomorrow, at the ball."

Lomax slowly and deliberately peeled Webb's fingers back from his clothing and smoothed out the rumpled cloth. "Captain Webb. You may have always been one of the Hugos' pets, but all you really are is a born a troublemaker with delusions of grandeur. This is just another ridiculous stunt, no doubt to try and win you kudos with the general."

Webb sputtered, a thousand things rising to his mouth but nothing would align themselves into any useful order.

"Lomax?" A deep voice interrupted them. "What's happening out here?"

They both turned. A tall man with broad shoulders and an array of pips at his collar had stepped out of a door further down the balcony. His hair was dark, apart from a peppering of silver at the temples and his eyes were deep and the darkest brown this side of black. His heavily-lined brow was drawn down in a frown that only deepened when he recognised Webb.

"Webb? What's going on?"

"General," Webb came forward, ignoring Lomax's stammered apologies, saluted the older man then said, "You're in danger, sir. You need to leave."

"I apologise, sir," the corporal came forward, trying to step between them. "Please ignore him, I should never have let him in. The young man is misinformed - "

"Lomax." The general's voice wasn't loud, but it was firmer than steel. His eyes were hard as stones. The aide faltered into silence. "Get in here, soldier," the general said, opening the door further. "You too, Lomax."

Webb stepped into a large meeting room with a mock-marble table and chairs taking up most of the space. Some of the chairs had been pulled back from the table and there was a scatter of hand-held data-panels and styluses spread across its surface. A young Japanese woman in a suit stood behind one of the chairs, jotting notes, but looked up when the three men came into the room. Her eyes were quick and assessing, flicking over each of them in turn.

"Apologies, we'll have to finish the interview later," the general said.

The woman took in their expressions, nodded, gathered up a few more of the panels from the table and left through the interior door.

"Now, who's going to explain what's going on here?" the general said, heavy look sliding between them both.

"Sir," Lomax stepped forward. "This man is notorious for rabble-rousing. He's been trying to usurp your time here from the moment he landed. I strongly urge you to let me deal with him."

"He says I'm in danger. Is this true?"

"It is, sir," Webb said. "Your life is under threat."

"Sir - "

"Let him speak, Lomax. Webb. What makes you think this?"

Webb continued, keeping his voice level and calm. "I heard suspected members of Red Star discuss your assassination, sir.

And I have proof," he added, reaching up and removing Vergennes's earbud and holding it out.

Lomax's lips had gone white. Whether it was shock or anger, Webb couldn't tell. Hugo's father came forward and took the earbud, placed it in his ear and tapped it to play the recording. His only reaction when listening was to go still.

"Sir, I'm sure there's an explanation for this," the aide tried as the general removed the earbud again.

"Leave us, please, Corporal."

"Sir - "

"I understand you're concerned, Lomax," the general continued, voice becoming as heavy as his expression. "But I'm having to ask you for a second time now to leave. Don't make me ask a third."

Lomax's pallor deepened with a flush. "Yes, sir," he said, saluted and left with one last dangerous look flung Webb's way.

"How did you come by this recording, Captain?"

"I made it, sir."

"When?"

"Less than an hour ago, sir. I came straight to you. I tried to get official permission but - "

"Security is tight around my unit for a reason," General Hugo said, walking to a wall display and pressing commands into the controls at its corner. A list of names and ranks appeared on the screen. "I noticed you managed to get yourself and your lieutenant on the manifest, but that doesn't mean - "

"Sir, please," Webb cut in, temper flaring. "You have to take this seriously."

The general didn't immediately respond. He shut down the display then turned to face him, back straight, hands behind his back. Webb felt small and young under his sharp eye in a way he hadn't felt swearing his oath to this same man at his initiation seven years ago. "You've been trying to get in touch for several days now, Captain. Is that true?"

Webb blinked. "Yes, sir."

He paused again. "You used my wife's seal on the messages."

"Yes, sir."

General Hugo took a step forward. "I can guess why she sent you. She thinks I'm not up to retrieving Kaleb."

"No, sir," Webb said, flushing. "I mean…that's not - "

"My son is not here, Captain," the general said, the tiniest suggestion of emotion sharpening the edges of his words. "My unit has searched the entire colony from the foundations up. There is no sign anywhere of any armed organisation, or of Kaleb."

"Sir," Webb said, voice cracking. "You heard what they said."

"I'm not sure what I heard. But I thank you for bringing this to my attention. It will be looked into. But I must ask you and your lieutenant to take your ship and leave. Tonight."

Webb straightened, finding something hardening inside him. "I can't do that, sir."

"That's a direct order."

"I have my own orders, General," Webb said, pleased his voice stayed strong.

The older man eyed him for another long moment then pulled out a chair with a sigh. "Sit, Captain. Please."

Webb blinked, feeling uncertain about at the change in his tone, then pulled out a chair and perched on the edge, hands on his knees. General Hugo picked up one of the datapanels, glanced at the screen then replaced it and checked the next.

"Do you have any idea what a delicate stage of negotiation we're at here with the Martians, Webb?"

Webb shifted slightly in his seat. "I only know what's being said on the newsites, sir. But that's beside the point. You have to trust me."

"I do trust you. You were close to my family at one time, Webb. Very close." Images of Dana rose in his head and he felt his flush deepen, but held his tongue. "So, yes, I trust you. However this current situation is not within your area of expertise."

"Sir," Webb implored. "Red Star are real. And they're here. And they plan to kill you."

"Rose would never allow such a thing to happen," the general said. "Ignore everything you've read about the man. He is a man of principle. And honour. He may have outdated ideals, but he's not a man of war. Or of terror. He wants change, but not fighting. He has nothing to gain from hiding a secret army, or giving them orders to do me harm."

"But sir," Webb said, standing. "You heard what they said. There's a definite threat - "

"I am under threat all the time, Captain," the general said, standing also. "Everywhere I go there are revolutionists, separatists or maladjusted people desperate for validation who want to kill me. I have a hundred trained men and women around me at all times to make sure that no one gets close."

"Sir, if I managed to get this close to you - "

"But you didn't, did you, solider? Lomax let you in."

"I - "

"Not even your infiltration skills got you close enough to hurt me, Webb."

"If I'd had a bomb," Webb protested.

The general let out a laugh. "You're just clutching at straws now. Besides, all the corridors and stairwells here are fitted with scanners. If you'd been carrying a bomb, the doors would have locked down and your location would have been flooded with stun-gas. No, I promise you, I'm safe in this city. Even if some local malcontent wants to have a go at me at the ball, there is nothing to say they will succeed."

"Sir, I think your wife would like you to take this more seriously." Webb regretted the words the minute they lift his mouth. The general's face had gone still as rock.

"Close to my family or not, no one, and I mean no one, has the right to lecture me on what my wife or any of my family expect of me."

Webb's throat tightened. He tried to find something else to say, an apology, an angry outburst, anything to make the man listen to him, but his face was intractable, his eyes like onyx. He looked so much like his missing son at that moment that Webb choked and couldn't get any words out even if he'd been able to think of any.

His struggle must have showed on his face because the older man's face softened the tiniest amount.

"I appreciate your intentions. You might not believe me, but I do. I remember you as an earnest and honest young man, for all your insubordinate ways. I know Kaleb in particular trusted you with his life more than once. But you simply don't understand the nature of these circumstances. Lomax understands, though he's not always the best at expressing his views."

"Sir - " Webb tried again, but the general cut him off.

"I wish to return from this trip with Arcadius Rose's trust and cooperation. Both he and I want me to be able to tell the Orbit there is no Red Star base on Mars, that better times are coming and that Schiaparelli City truly represents the start of a new age for all humanity, with the Service working alongside its governor and electorate to achieve that. I simply cannot do that if anyone knew of a second, undercover investigation happening alongside our own, blowing up every workman's gripes into assassination threats and destroying the balance of trust. I know it's hard - " the man actually reached out and put a large hand on his shoulder. "But you also have to trust me. Go with my thanks and you won't be punished. But leave today. I will speak to Erica and explain."

Webb managed to straighten himself. "With respect, sir, my work is not done. I was sent here to find Kaleb."

The older man's face went grave again. "I will bring Kaleb home myself, Captain," he said, a slight catch in his voice. "But not from here. He is not here."

"I believe he is, sir."

"Are you telling me you think I'm ignorant? Or incompetent?"

"Neither, sir," Webb replied, keeping his resolved bolstered with an effort. "I just think there's more going on here than anyone has guessed at."

"I've heard enough." The general pushed a button on his highly-advanced wristpanel. "I appreciate your verve and dedication, Captain, but it is misplaced and also disruptive, maybe even dangerous, in a situation like this. If you don't agree to leave peacefully, I will have no choice but to have you arrested and removed by force."

"General, wait - " Webb said, looking up as Lomax came into the room, a slightly smug expression on his face, followed by two armed Servicemen.

"Captain Webb was just about to leave for his ship," the general said, striding away. "Kindly escort him safely there."

"This way, Captain," the first guard came forward but Webb stepped out of her reach.

"General Hugo, sir - "

"There's nothing left to say, Webb," Hugo said, pausing at the door. "And you're trying my patience. Don't take advantage of the last of my good feelings toward you."

"Sir - " Webb called, grabbing the general by the shoulder. The Service guards made another lunge for him and Lomax shouted orders, but the general was faster than all of them, spinning and pulling Webb's hand from him, slamming his wrist against the wall.

"Don't ever grab me in that manner again," the general said, face very close to Webb's own. Webb's heart hammered against the inside of his ribs. He couldn't speak.

"Go," the general said, releasing him. "You're creating a scene."

Webb looked through the open door to where the people in the sitting area were all staring.

Webb took a deep breath. "Yes, sir," he said. "I'll leave."

"Good," Hugo said, turning away.

"On one condition," he said, in a slightly louder voice. The Servicemen hovered.

Hugo grumbled, and turned on the threshold. "I'm sorry?"

Webb swallowed, mastered his voice. "Sir, I can go quietly, or I can go screaming and upsetting all these nice people, it's up to you."

Colour rode high in the general's face. He strode back into the room and slammed the door on the startled faces of the interviewer, Councillor Pope and new arrival with a uniform and badge that labelled him as head of Schiaparelli Security.

"This is the last warning you're going to get - " the general started.

"I'll leave, General," Webb repeated. "I'll go without a word and I'll go back to my unit on Earth and pretend this whole thing never happened. But I'll go after the ball."

"I beg your pardon?"

"I will do exactly as you've asked of me, without a fuss or any more backchat, I'll even talk nice to your wife about it all," Webb said, shrugging off the renewed hold of the now-hesitant guards. "But only if my lieutenant and I are allowed to attend the Commemoration Ball tomorrow as part of your security detail."

"Webb - "

"That's my last word, General," Webb said, voice raising. "You want me to understand your position. I understand it, believe me. I just don't give a rat's ass. I do, however, give a rat's ass about you surviving tomorrow night and stopping the inevitable Orbit-wide shitstorm that would follow if you didn't."

"I've already told you my security is more than adequate - "

"Then two more men won't make any difference," Webb insisted. "And if I'm wrong, I leave Mars behind and put the damn place out of my memory forever. You've got nothing to lose."

Hugo rubbed his jaw and examined him closely.

After a moment, Lomax managed to unstick his tongue. "Sir, the man is an outrage and an upstart, but he has a point." Webb stared at the other officer, but Lomax didn't meet his gaze, keeping his focus on the general. "He's got the potential to do us enormous damage. I still believe he should be arrested and disciplined for insubordination when we return, but if this is all he's wanting for in return for his cooperation right now, I think it's in everyone's best interests to do as he asks."

The general stared at the wall like it had done him personal wrong. Lomax watched him, looking tense. The Service guards had loosed their grip but Webb could feel them right behind him, ready to take hold again.

The general cleared his throat and looked Webb in the eye. "Fine. You have a deal. You and your lieutenant will be added to tomorrow's security detail and can attend the ball as part of my retinue, but I'm warning you, Webb," the man said, pointing a finger at him. "You are to leave the minute the ball concludes. I will authorise the launch window myself."

"Yes sir," Webb said, ducking his head.

"And if you or your partner do anything, *anything*, to show me up at this event, you will be wishing dearly that I had arrested and deported you tonight."

"Yes, sir. Thank you, sir," Webb said, grabbing a chair back, feeling weak with relief.

"Good. Now get him out of here. Find his lieutenant and get them a room here in the centre. I want them both close by so we can keep an eye on them. You better have taken a bath before tomorrow night, soldier," he added as he pulled the door open again, looking him up and down. "Gentlemen, my apologies," he said, addressing the people in the sitting room. "Something required my attention. I believe lunch is being served on the balcony."

The door shut and Webb was left with the uncertain guards and the livid Lomax.

"This way," Lomax said, opening another door. "And follow quietly, if you're capable."

VI

Webb stood at the window of the well-appointed bedroom, looking out over Appollos Square. The sun was setting, bleaching the sky dramatic ochres and oranges. He had washed and changed into some clean trackwear provided by the Conference Centres hospitality department. He felt warm, and clean and there was a hot meal waiting on the side. The building had top-grade atmosphere controls and his hearing was normal, as was the gravity. His body felt calm, but when he remembered the dense air, the smell, thickness, chill and darkness of the foundation levels, and the harsh voice with its harsh words, the comfort and normality felt disjointed and wrong.

He leant on the windowsill and pressed his forehead against the glass. All traces of the threatening headache from earlier had abated, but he felt drained, empty and bits of him ached that weren't physical. Hugo's father's words continued to loop in his head:

"I'll bring Kaleb home myself, Captain. But not from here. He's not here."

Webb tried to figure out whether he was hoping the general was wrong or not.

The sound of the door opening made him turn, but it was just Vergennes.

"Our motorcycles are secure, Captain," he reported. "They're in the staff parking pool."

"Good," was all Webb could manage, coming away from the window and shutting the blind. He contemplated having another go at hacking the electric lock on the minibar, but decided he didn't have the energy and slumped on his bed.

Vergennes hovered. "There's time - "

"No," Webb cut him off. "No more martial arts practice. I've been in the gym all evening, I'm not going back again. Especially now its shift-end and the practice mats will be crowded with people like you."

Vergennes looked stung. Webb regretted the outburst but was too tired to soothe the young man's ruffled feathers. He lay back on the bed, covering his eyes with his arm and willed his reeling mind to still. The workouts in the gym downstairs had managed to distract his racing thoughts for a while, but now they all crowded round his mind like impatient children, demanding attention.

"I think we should send a message to Vee Osgard, sir."

"Why?" Webb croaked, without lifting his arm.

"She helped us. I think it would only be fair to tell her what we've found out."

"We've got far bigger troubles on our hands now than keeping Osgard in the loop."

A long silence followed.

"You did the right thing, sir," Vergennes said softly.

Webb raised an arm to level a bleary eye at his lieutenant. "Come again?"

"The situation offered no compromise. If you hadn't forced the general to see you, we'd be on our way back to Earth and he wouldn't be prepared."

Webb humphed and covered his face with his hands. "I don't think the general is even remotely prepared," he mumbled into his palms.

"I think you should give him more credit, sir. He's served active duty for nearly fifty years, commanded field units for almost half that. Just because he didn't tell you everything he thought about what you said doesn't mean he didn't take you seriously."

Webb let his arms flop down on the bed at his sides. "Hugo's not here, Vergennes," Webb said softly.

"Sir?"

Webb stared at the ceiling. "Our Hugo. Kaleb. The Service unit have searched the city right down to the foundations. They've not had even a sniff. And neither have we. All we have is what Osgard told us. And what she had was just guesswork."

When Vergennes didn't answer, Webb propped himself up on his elbows. The younger man was stood at the window holding back the blind and looking out with a calm, collected look on his face, but his eyes were active.

"I have faith in the Service, sir," he said, eventually. "I have every confidence in General Hugo and his team."

Webb raised an eyebrow. "That almost sounds like there's a 'but' coming."

Vergennes dropped the blind and met his eyes. "But," he said slowly. "I think in this instance, guesswork or not, Osgard…and you…have a better understanding of the situation."

"Why do you think that?"

"What do your instincts tell you?"

Webb slumped on the bed again. "I don't know any more."

"I think you do," Vergennes said, moving to the side where the covered dishes were. "I think you've just let General Hugo shake your confidence."

"He'd shake yours too if you ever spoke to him."

"I don't doubt it," Vergennes said, lifting lids off the dishes and filling the room with the smell of cooked meat and rich sauces. "You should eat, sir."

"What's changed your tune, anyway?" Webb said, finally sitting up. "You all but hated me before today."

"I didn't hate you, sir," Vergennes said, mildly, picking up his own tray and sitting on his own bed to eat.

Webb laughed. "If you say so."

"I didn't," Vergennes insisted coolly, between mouthfuls of steak. "I would appreciate if you didn't assign such a base emotion to me."

Webb blinked in surprise. He stood and retrieved his own tray.

"Ok, then. You didn't hate me. But you damn sure didn't like me. And now you're telling me I've done the right thing and I should trust my instincts?"

Vergennes went on quietly eating. Webb sat cross-legged on

his own bed, cut the steak in half and lifted a piece in his fingers and took a bite. He chewed, watching Vergennes and waiting for an answer.

"Nothing's changed, sir," Vergennes said, and Webb wondered at the loaded emotion behind the words. "I just happen to think you're right this time."

Webb felt himself smile, despite everything, and dunked his steak in the root mash on his plate and took another bite. "Well ain't that a turn up for the books."

Vergennes looked up with a faint smile then noticed Webb's eating with his fingers, frowned and went back to his own food. Webb laughed again, licked his fingers and used the fork to shovel the mash into his mouth.

"So, if I'm right," he mumbled around his mouthful, "someone's gonna take a pop at the general tomorrow."

"Yes, sir."

Webb chewed meditatively for a moment. "Hopefully the old man's right and no one will get close enough to try, but we need to stick to him like glue in case someone does."

"Can I ask you something, sir?" Vergennes asked, pausing in his eating.

Webb took in the rather grave look on the lieutenant's face. "Shoot."

"Why?"

"Why what?"

He turned and looked him in the eye. "Why are you doing this?"

Webb frowned. "Why do you think, man? You know what would happen if the Special Command's husband was killed out here under Arcadius Rose's watch? War, that's what would happen. The Service would move in on Silence City and whilst they converged out here, the other arms of Red Star out in the Orbit would rise up to strike back while their back was turned. Chaos isn't the word."

"You're right," the younger man said. "But you've already said you don't care about the political ramifications of anything that's happening out here, war or not. So why are you putting yourself in the middle of the politics when you've spent the whole time we've been on this mission telling me it's nothing to do with you?"

Webb swallowed his mouthful and looked at his plate for a long moment. "Because I care about this," he said softly.

"Why?"

"Does it matter?"

"It does to me. I'm stepping into the firing line along with you, sir. I think it's only fair I get to understand why."

Webb raised his head.

"Because it's Hugo's dad," he said. "And Dana's dad. Because the man shook my hand at Hugo's wedding and told me I was a good man. He's a decent human being and he doesn't deserve to die because someone else thinks he can run the universe better."

Vergennes weighed him up and Webb felt he saw something in the younger man's eyes that, for once, wasn't scorn or disapproval.

"What are the timings for tomorrow?" Webb said, turning back to his food.

Vergennes finished eating and put the plate back on the tray. "The Commemorative Ball starts at eight. Guests will start arriving at the New Civic Hall half an hour before then. Security detail to be in place by 1900 hours."

"I want to go earlier," Webb said, finishing his own food. "We need to go over that ballroom with a fine toothed comb. The man on the recording said they're planning to strike a couple of dances after Rose's speech. I'll bet that means they're hoping to take their shot whilst the general's out on the dance floor somewhere." Webb shuddered, a memory of white velvet drapes, music, shadows and the feel of a rifle in his hands sweeping through him. "This kind of shindig is a sharp-shooter's dream."

Vergennes eyed him carefully and Webb turned away, putting his own plate back on the tray on the side.

"I don't think there are any balconies in this ballroom, sir," the younger man said, voice devoid of inflection. "And there's tighter security than at Tranquility Hall. Hopefully the general is right and it will be harder for Red Star than it was for you."

Webb winced. "You know a hell of a lot about me, kid."

Vergennes raised on pale eyebrow. "Attempting to kill your own CO doesn't get missed out of your public records, sir. But your pardon is almost as equally well cited."

"Yeah," Webb said, rubbing the back of his neck and looking at the wall. "I was lucky there."

"I'd say Colonel Luscombe was lucky one," Vergennes said, with a faint smile.

Webb blinked then smiled. "I like this side of you," he said climbing back on his bed. "But it was Hugo that saved the colonel that day, not me," Webb added softly, lying down and facing the wall. "He's always been there to kick my ass when I needed it."

Silence fell between them. After a pause, Webb heard the sounds of Vergennes getting into his own bed then the lights went out. Webb lay in the dark, breathing in the smell of the clean linen and let himself wonder for the first time whether he really would ever see Hugo again.

Δ

"Anything?"

"No, sir," Vergennes's reply came through in Webb's new ear-bud. "The corridors all around the ballroom are clear. There's a camera bank at both ends and security with scanners at the entrance."

Webb swore under his breath. "Do another sweep. They've found a way in, I know it."

"Yes, sir," Vergennes replied, voice a little strained.

Webb pulled his bike over as the general's flyer pulled up outside the front of the New Civic Hall. All security had insisted he ride the short distance over the square from the Conference Centre in an armoured vehicle. Webb had followed on his bike with the rest of the Service honour guard. Three men and two women in formal evening wear that tastefully hid their weapons and comm devices climbed out of the flyer and checked over the immediate area before opening the back door for the general.

Webb parked his bike up along with a string of others under the grand staircase to the main entrance, then hurried to return to the security team that surrounded the general and Corporal Lomax as they mounted the stairs. Webb was pleased to see the Servicemen go ahead and glance over the entrance before allowing General Hugo, resplendent in dress uniform, to pass ahead and through the scanners. Webb wondered if this security really had been all planned or if the general had actually listened to him.

He filtered toward the entrance scanners the Servicemen were passing through whilst having their weapons checked against their IDs. He chafed with impatience as the general drifted away across the entrance hall, talking to Lomax on one side and the young interviewer who had been in the meeting room the night before on the other. A surge of well-dressed people moved between him and the general and his heart began pounding.

"Vergennes," Webb said. "He's moving through into the ballroom. Get visual contact."

"Yes, sir."

Webb lifted his arms as the Martian security guard checked his guns against a swipe of his ID. He muttered curses when they made him pull up his sleeve to first show his wristpanel and then his trouser leg to show the knife sheath.

"The knife isn't permitted, sir."

"It's on my ID, man."

"It's policy, sir. None of your colleagues have knives."

"I'm special," Webb said, trying and shove past but the man stepped into his path, hand hovering over an alert button on the scanner's control panel. "We're all wanting a nice evening here, sir. Let's not have any difficulties."

"Fine, have the damn thing," Webb said, pulling out the knife and sticking it, point-first into the nearest table, making guests jump, then shouldered his way through and hurried across the entrance hall.

He caught up as General Hugo and his retinue passed through the tall doors into the ballroom. Webb and Vergennes had spent hours scouring the vaulted space earlier in the day, but it still felt like he was stepping into another world now it was lit only with rolling projections of evening skies on the walls and strings of LEDs around the stage and seating areas. There were a thousand shadows to hide in and easily half a thousand people milling about the room. His ears popped and he noticed the other guests subtly touching their ears or pinching their noses.

"They've activated an atmosphere controller somewhere, Vergennes," Webb murmured. "See if you can find it. Make sure it's not been tampered with."

"Yes, sir. I think it's behind the stage."

"Where are you?"

"At your two o'clock sir," Vergennes replied.

"Check out that generator than do another sweep."

The lieutenant acknowledged and Webb drifted onto the dance floor after the general. His other bodyguards were spacing out, mumbling instructions and confirmations into their comm devices, watching the whole room with keen eyes, but Webb's gut would not settle. The harsh voice from the recording, so full of deadly certainty, echoed in his ears.

He hovered a few paces behind General Hugo whilst he and Lomax talked to one of the many finely dressed couples that had stepped up to meet them. Music drifted from invisible speakers and there was the clinking of champagne glasses all around. Webb turned full circle, taking in every person in sight, but couldn't see anyone acting strangely.

The general moved on and was intercepted by the tall man with black hair Webb recognised from the night before. He wore his dinner jacket and white tie like he had been born to them, shoulders square and proud, but his piercing eyes were cold, even as he smiled and shook the general's hand. A telltale thinness of frame was the only thing that betrayed his colony upbringing.

"General Hugo is with Councillor Pope," Webb murmured and drifted around them, trying to get close enough to hear the conversation.

"Lunar 1's Councillor Pope?" Vergennes's reply was surprised.

"Yeah. He was hanging about the suite last night. Must be here for the shindig. Have you found the atmosphere generator?"

"Yes sir. It checks out normal. It's being guarded too."

Webb ground his teeth. "Why is it that every time we fail to find something going wrong, I feel more nervous?"

"I'm coming out again now, sir."

"Do another search of the corridors," Webb ordered, shifting from one foot to another and looking intently at every person that drifted near. "Service access too."

"Yes, sir," Vergennes said, not quite exasperated but as close as could be, and the connection cut.

"I see you're being well looked after tonight, General," said a supercilious voice, pitched to carry. Webb turned and saw Pope looking right at him. The general glanced back, pausing as if surprised to find Webb right behind him.

"Governor Rose was accommodating enough to allow the usual Service standard security detail," the general said in a neutral voice.

"And rightly so," Pope commented. His voice was smooth, like rich velvet. Webb found himself pinned to the spot by the unnervingly keen glance. "I think I recognise this intense young man. He was in the suite last night, yes?"

"Yes, that's right," General Hugo replied just as smoothly. "Webb's been a loyal commander for many years. He was good enough to drop in on me yesterday to bring me some family news."

"Nothing bad, I hope?"

"Not at all. Something minor, nothing of consequence," said the older man, turning a black look on Webb.

"You said 'Webb' yes?" Pope said again, this time taking a step toward him.

"That's right," the general replied. Webb felt his skin crawling under the man's scrutiny. "Captain Ezekiel Webb."

"Captain," the councillor said with enough admiration for it to ring false. "And one of our own Webbs from Lunar 1?"

Webb stiffened. "Yes…sir," he remembered to add just in time.

"You smarten up nicely, young man," the man said, with a glance at Webb's dinner suit. Webb fidgeted as the general began to drift away but Pope had shifted close enough to block his path. "Forgive me, but it always gratifies me to see the victims of your generation making their way in the world," the man was saying, with a smile like a shark's.

Webb kept his face neutral with an effort. "I'm not a victim, sir," Webb said and found he believed it.

"Of course not. Apologies," the councillor said with a duck of the head. "Forgive me for distracting you from your duties. I've just met so many orphans of McCullough's Revolution with not even a name to call their own. Too many of them became lost or rudderless over the years. It's good to meet one with a direction."

"I'm not like the others," Webb said and the man smiled.

"You're not, are you? In fact, I feel I know you from somewhere."

"We met last night…sir," Webb said, keeping his tone respectful with an effort.

"No, from longer ago," the man mused. "I have met and worked with many of our colony's prominent personages over the years. Perhaps you were an associate of Chancellor Ling? Or Councillor Vincent Marlowe?"

Webb struggled to hide the sudden feeling of having ice dumped down his neck showing on his face.

"It came to light that the councilor was involved in some rather unfortunate business in the end," Pope said, eyes sharp and a little too knowing as they pinned him in place. "But he did a lot of good for the colony in his time. And I know he worked a lot with the youth units."

"I've never met the man, sir," Webb bit out, knowing it was truth but wishing it felt more like it.

"No?" Pope continued, head on one side, eyes roving over him, lingering on the scars on his neck and the Haven brand just above his collar. "You've clearly had a colourful life, either way. Glad to know you've found yourself a future along the way."

"Thank you, Councillor. Can you excuse me?"

"Of course," Pope said and raised his glass. "A pleasant evening to you, Captain Webb. Do visit Lunar 1 if you get the chance. We've made some impressive changes."

Webb hurried away, scanning the room until he spotted the general further ahead, near the stage. He spotted three bodyguards stationed at points around the floor, but also saw at least four blind spots they'd left open. He rushed over, eyeing the nearest tables, the stage where the orchestra was assembling and the nearest alcoves, but still found everything clear.

The pre-recorded music drifted to a close as Webb took up position between General Hugo and the nearest door. The stage started to glow. A spotlight centred on an elegant plexiglass lectern at the front of the stage and a hush fell. An invisible announcer requested everyone to welcome Schiaparelli City's Governor Arcadius Rose to the stage.

A round of applause gained volume as a man with dark red hair and finely tailored dinner jacket mounted the stage, waving a hand and smiling warmly. His face was fine and clean-shaven, his smile almost too easy. Webb glanced about for Vergennes and spotted him covering one of the blind spots by the main entrance.

He shifted closer to the general stood near the stage, applauding with everyone else.

"Thank you, thank you," the red-haired man said, voice artificially amplified to fill the hall by some invisible pick-ups in the lectern. "And thank you, everyone, for coming. Today marks ten years exactly since work began on our very own Schiaparelli City and I'm here not as your governor, but as one of you, to celebrate and thank everyone that has helped us build our lives here."

Rose has a nice voice. It was warm, with the softest lilt that betrayed an Old Europe background, but was so faint it could easily have been picked up from one of European-populated Lunar Colonies as on Earth. He held everyone's attention, apart from Webb's, who was using the opportunity to scout out anyone who wasn't watching the stage. Pope was stood off to the side, pointedly looking in the other direction and talking in the ear of an attractive young woman who was hiding her smile behind her champagne glass. Webb let his attention move on, taking slow steps around the immediate area, scanning the skylights above, but they were all still shut and locked.

"Vergennes," Webb murmured. "You confirmed the skylights were bulletproof, didn't you?"

"Yes sir," came the inevitable reply and Webb swallowed, feeling his palms prickle.

"There must be something…or someone here…something we've missed…" Webb muttered. He noticed a figure moving quickly in the general's direction and moved forward. Two other security officers had noticed him too and had moved to intercept, only for all three of them to fall back when the man changed direction towards his partner on the other side of the room.

"And in that spirit," Rose continued, "we must welcome out guest of honour, General Seamus Hugo, who has granted us the great privilege of his presence here tonight."

A small smattering of polite applause went through the crowd and the general inclined his head. Webb watched Rose's face intently, wondering if his glance lingered just a little too long on the Service general.

"We should be proud he is here. I know I am," the man continued, warm gaze sweeping the throng like a family man might look over his children. "But we should also be proud of what we are and never forget we are something different. I want to take this opportunity, with General Hugo and his people from the Service here to witness, to state again that Schiaparelli City, called Silence City by some, will be silent no longer. We are ten years old, with a population of over seven hundred thousand and growing. Seven hundred thousand souls building their own world from the rock up."

Enthusiastic clapping went round the room.

"We are not of the Orbit," Rose spoke on, voice gaining volume. "The Orbit is what we have left behind. It is Earth, a war-torn and overpopulated planet. It is her Lunar colonies which are poverty-stricken and decrepit. It is also the cities on the moon that are one weak governor away from another revolution and the five Sunside colonies that grow fat and lazy on the Service's credit and good favour."

Murmurs rippled around the chamber. Guests were looking General Hugo's way for a reaction and a fair few at Councillor Pope too. The general looked calm and collected, however, listening politely with a carefully blank expression. Councillor Pope's smile had gone but he drank deeply from his glass, giving the appearance of nonchalance at least.

"We are Martians," Rose said with pride and finality. "We are the future."

The greatest cheer of all rose from the guests, ringing off the walls and high ceiling. General Hugo clapped politely, as did Pope.

"Tonight marks the first ten years of life on Mars. But this is only the beginning. Here's looking forward to the next ten and the ten after that. Enjoy your evening with this in mind, everyone. Enjoy your evening in this grand hall built with our own hands on our new planet and dream of what is to come."

He ducked his head to more applause and left the stage where he was immediately accosted by a host of guests wanting to shake his hand. The spotlight widened to illuminate the stage and the invisible panel lighting around the rest of the ball room dimmed. The orchestra struck up the opening bars of a piece of upbeat music and Webb felt a ripple along his spine.

"Get ready, Vergennes. Two dances, that's what they said."

"Yes, sir," his lieutenant replied.

Webb took up position where he could see the whole of the dance floor, watching every movement and scanning every face. Still nothing looked out of the ordinary and he began to dare hope that maybe the general had been right. Maybe he had mis-interpreted what he'd heard. Or maybe what they heard wasn't Red Star and perhaps some rag-tag wannabe terrorist was at this moment being pinned to the floor in the parking pool by Martian security.

He didn't let himself believe it, though he sorely wanted to. The music played on. Couples swung around the dance floor in perfect time, women smiling, men bowing. More couples hung around the edges or sat at the scattering of velvet-draped tables, sipping champagne, watching the dancers. Waiters and waitress-es with trays full of brimming flutes wove between them all, smil-ing and doling out glasses. Arcadius Rose had just asked a hand-some woman to dance and was leading her through the twirling couples, politely nodding to everyone who called out greetings to him.

The general wasn't dancing. He was stood at the side, Lomax talking in his ear. Webb looked around again and strode over to him just as the music ended and more clapping went round the room. Webb reached the general just the Japanese interviewer reached him and held out her hand.

"Sir," he said urgently. "Don't take this dance."

Lomax looked anxious but the general only smiled. "And turn down this young lady's invitation?"

The young woman beamed, eyes shining.

"Sir, dance the next one, just not this one."

The music started and he took the girl's hand. "Have you seen anything untoward so far, Captain?"

"No, sir."

"Has any of the rest of my security detail?"

"No, sir. But - "

"Then I suggest you relax, Captain Webb. Have a dance yourself," the older man said, allowing the girl to lead him out onto the dance floor. "We're guests here, after all. Wouldn't do to be rude."

Webb's muscles tensed as the music gained pace and the older man swung through the steps of the dance with his young partner. He stood next to Lomax, noticing an expression on the corporal's face that he was sure mirrored his own.

"You feel it, don't you?" Webb said in a low voice. "Something's wrong."

Lomax's thin face turned his way, lines of concern etched into his high forehead. He looked back at the general and raised his wristpanel to his mouth. "All units be on the alert. Repeat, keep alert."

Webb looked around the room again, heart pounding, then looked up. "No," he whispered to himself, voice sounding far away in his own ears. "Jesus. Lomax, up there."

"What?" Lomax followed Webb's look up to the ceiling. "I don't see anything."

"There's someone up there," he said. "At the skylight."

"Roof detail, come in," Lomax barked into his comm, following Webb as he hurried across the dance floor. "Do you see anything?"

"Negative, sir," came the reply. "Roof is clear. All skylights secure."

"They've missed something," Webb said, already running. "I'm telling you there's someone up there." He increased his speed and ignored Lomax calling him back.

"Sir, what's happening?"

Webb ignored Vergennes's urgent query in his ear and ran, only glancing back once to confirm Lomax was heading straight to the general with the bodyguards at his heels. He skidded into a service corridor and flung himself up the first set of stairs he came to. Lomax, the other security guards and Vergennes were all yammering through his wrist comm or in his ear, insisting the roof was clear and that he should halt and return, but he ignored them. He'd seen that skylight move. He was *sure* he'd seen it move.

He could hear the orchestra reaching a crescendo through the vents in the stairwell just as he slammed open an access door to the roof, sending alarms blaring. He stumbled as the gravity changed and he nearly went over, but righted himself and panted, looking round.

"Sir, you can't be up here." A Serviceman who had been guarding the door had caught up with him and grabbed his elbow. "Please, return below."

Webb didn't stop to explain but tore his elbow free. The man was fast, but thanks to his practice with Vergennes, he knew which way the Serviceman would grab and ducked out of the way, staggered out of reach and ran, ignoring the curses of the other man as he tripped in the uncertain gravity.

This section of the roof was wide, flat and shadowy. Stars glinted overhead and light bled up from Appollos Square, but not enough to disband the darkness. He made out three glowing points of wristpanels from the remaining roof detail stationed at the far corners as they moved in the dark…wait, three?

"There are only four security guys up here," Webb panted, hoping Vergennes was still listening. "Aren't there supposed to be five? Christ," he swore, seeing starlight glint off an angle of a plexiglass skylight that lay out of line with the others. "There," he cried. "There's someone there!"

He heard the guards call out and start running, but they were all too far away. Even the guard from the door hadn't caught him up. The music ended. Webb ran toward the open skylight. He made out the outline of a figure hunched against the light from the room below when there was the unmistakable sound of a gunshot. And then another.

There were shouts from the security around him and from the ballroom. Shouts turned to screams. The dark figure dropped a long-range rifle with a metallic clatter and ran. Webb pelted after them.

The beams of lenslights from the confused guards swept through the darkness, glancing off the running figure. Commands to freeze were shouted as weapons were drawn, but the sniper was fast drawing a handgun. Servicemen went down. The remaining guards kept going, barking reports into comms. More shots were fired, but it was too dark and the shooter was too fast.

Webb just ran. The gunman was heading for the edge of the building. Webb didn't stop. The shooter reached the edge and grabbed a cable that was clipped onto the lip of the ledge, swinging over into nothing. Webb skidded up to the ledge and drew his gun.

"Freeze," he yelled. "I will shoot you, I swear to God."

The figure looked up. A vapour mask and goggles completely covered the face. He stopped long enough to hurl something onto the roof. Webb swore and grabbed the cable, swinging off the roof just as the grenade went off. The noise left his ears ringing. Bits of masonry rained down on him and the inside of his eyelids glowed red. He felt the heat of fire and the cable shuddered. He looked down. The gunman had reached a balcony halfway down the hall's facade and was climbing onto another cable secured around its rail.

"Vergennes," Webb yelled and slid down the cable just as the ledge crumbled away above. He dropped the last few feet onto the balcony, dodging more raining brick and metal. "Vergennes," he called again, but there was no answer in his ear. He pulled out his earbud, fried by the grenade blast, and threw it away. He pushed a button on his wristpanel before clambering down the gunman's second cable just as the figure below reached the ground. Webb fired off a couple of shots but the man already had too much distance.

"Sir," Vergennes's voice sounded urgently from his wristpanel. "There was an explosion - "

"I'm in pursuit," Webb panted, landing heavily on the ground. "He's heading to the north side of the building. We need to intercept him before he reaches the parking pool."

"Yes, sir," Vergennes replied. A pause. "He's dead, sir."

"What?" Webb snapped, stumbling.

"The general's dead sir. Shot."

Webb's gut heaved. His head emptied of thought. "Get security to the north, Vergennes," he managed. "Out."

Webb willed his legs to move faster. He'd cursed the restrictive dinner suit a thousand times by the time he reached corner of the building. He skidded round then jumped over the crumpled forms of two more security guards, groaning and bleeding on the floor. He kept running, heart fit to burst, but was knocked off his feet by the force of another explosion.

The starry sky danced in front of his eyes and his ears were ringing. He got to his feet and kept moving. The warm stickiness of blood and burns covered his hands and face. Confused noises, human voices, alarms and the distant roar and crackle of flames reached him through the ringing in his ears. He blinked, staggering to a halt. An entire quarter of the New Civic Hall's parking pool was a smoking mess. Flyers, bikes and luxury four-wheelers were scattered from their berths with fire streaming from fuel tanks and upholstery, chassis bent and broken.

Webb stood panting. The amplified voices of security evacuating the hall could be heard above the clamour, but over on his left he heard the sound of a single engine roaring to life. He ran toward it around the flames, ignoring the heat that caused sweat to stand out on every inch of his body and sear at his skin. He caught the glint of firelight flashing off metal and the glow of a two-wheeler engine before it disappeared into the shadows towards a bank of darkened shuttle rails.

Webb elbowed through the confused stream of people pouring down the stairs from hall. He used his wristpanel to activate his bike before he reached it.

Shouts echoed after him as he sped out from under the stairs across the square. Security on flyers tried to wave him away from the blast site, but he ploughed through the burning edges of the debris and turned toward the shuttle rails. He coaxed more speed from the bike, leaning low and weaving between ruined vehicles. He left the heat and light behind and plunged into darkness and chill. His headlight lit up shuttle rails ahead. The windscreen display picked up nothing in immediate scan range but in the eerie quiet he heard the sound of an engine growing faint in the distance.

Webb gunned the engine, racing the bike onto the rails. The space between the metal rails was narrow, but solid with connector panels so the machine barely juddered. He followed the rails west, his headlight shining off the unused metal. His speed pushed the digital needle on his display into the red. At the next bend he caught sight of a two-wheeler riding the rails far ahead.

Webb clenched his teeth and willed more speed out of his machine. Fog rose and wrapped around him, obscuring his view. He cursed, turned off his headlight and picked out the gunman's vehicle by the glow of its engine. His two-wheeler's tyres were wider and had a better purchase on the uneven surface, but it also meant his turns had to be slower. Webb began to gain.

His quarry slowed so suddenly Webb's heart leapt into his mouth. The two-wheeler swung hard left, juddering over the shuttle rails and launching into the air.

"Two can do that trick," Webb snarled. His bones rattled as he went over the rails but he refused to slow, speeding into the air. The two-wheeler thudded onto an empty walkway and Webb landed, wheels screaming, right behind him. Webb cursed. Ornamental pillars narrowed the way to the width of a hallway. The man ahead was gaining distance again.

Webb dared more speed, not looking at how close his knees were to the pillars and turning off the warning systems blaring red on his display. He sped on, gaining and losing distance, getting close but never close enough. The man dropped another grenade as they skidded from the walkway onto a foundation level promenade. Webb just made it past before the blast rocked the ground under him and sent his bike swerving. Debris struck his back and scattered ahead, causing him to duck and weave through broken building blocks and twisted metal.

The two-wheeler turned under a dark archway in the foundations of a spacescraper. Webb followed into the pitch blackness, keeping the his quarry's engine glow in visual range. The smooth surface gave way to something uneven and his bike shuddered.

He thought he was finally about to catch up when the rider made a sharp turn and then they weren't under a spacescraper anymore. It was dark, damp and smelt somehow familiar. Webb's heart pounded and he switched his headlight back on. The light died a few feet from his bike, washing to nothing in fog. He only just had time to realise that they were biking down a narrow strip of bumpy rock that bridged a vast cavern, when there was a blinding flash and ear-splitting blast as the man ahead dropped another grenade.

The narrow rock bridge shuddered and crumbled. Webb put on a burst of speed that carried him off the collapsing rock to a skidding landing on the rock platform beyond. His teeth rattled in his head and his bones knocked against each other. His quarry had paused to watch him fall, but when he hadn't gone down had spun his machine to continue his escape, but the pause had cost him. Webb was right behind him.

The man turned down a narrow tunnel, but by then he was in range. Webb drew his gun and fired. He missed the man but hit the wheeler's back tyre which exploded and sent the machine skidding sideways, flinging its rider. Webb braked hard but had to jump free before his own bike crashed into the wreckage of the other vehicle. He hit the rocky ground with a roll, felt something crack but used the momentum to fling himself at the other figure who was just staggering to his feet.

He caught the gunman off balance and brought him to the ground. He tried to immobilse him, but the man was strong and elbowed back Webb's grip and drew a gun. Webb had kept a grip of his own and tried to bring it round but the man landed a dizzying blow on his temple with the butt of his own weapon. Webb's skull pounded, but he grabbed out, fire crackling through him.

His hand fastened on fabric and he heaved the other man over, trying to put as much force as possible into slamming him into the ground. The man gasped but managed to bring up a leg and pin Webb's gun arm to his side. Webb lashed out with his free hand, landing a glancing blow on the side of the man's head. He aimed another, hoping to stun him enough to wrestle his weapon from him, but the man turned his head and Webb missed, knocking the man's mask and goggles off.

Webb froze, fist frozen in the air. His heart had clambered into his throat. His skin flushed cold and his bones turned to water.

"Hugo?"

The hesitation was all the other man needed. An iron grip fasted itself onto Webb's jacket and he was slammed over, knocking the air from his lungs. Hugo grabbed his right wrist and smashed it into the rock floor. Webb yelled as the bones broke and he dropped his gun. He rode the pain, blinded by it, and struck out with his left arm. His fist connected with the hardness of an armoured vest and then another blow across his face sent his senses swirling.

"Hugo!" he called. "Hugo, *stop.*"

But he didn't stop. His former captain pinned him to the ground and rained blow after blow down on his face. Webb yelled and struggled, but the blows kept coming. He was blinded by blood. He gave up trying to land strikes of his own and shielded his head with his arms but the other man knocked them away and kept hitting.

Webb took a huge breath, coughed on blood and pulled himself together enough to get an elbow down and heave himself up. His head connected with something hard and there was a grunt of pain. The weight on him wavered and he bucked the other man off and scrambled back, turning and desperately trying to crawl back to his bike. He spat out teeth as he went, flailing and going over as he tried to put weight on his broken wrist.

He heard Hugo get to his feet behind him, his breathing rasping in the close air. Webb looked back, peering through blood and matted hair, saw the gun levelled and the blackness in Hugo's eyes. The gunshot cracked off the rock walls and everything went black.

Δ

Awareness came and went in red flashes. With it, beakers of pain. When he stayed conscious long enough to focus, Webb felt himself being jolted and jostled and could see a rocky path and someone's heels below him. They were lit by the bobbing beams of lenslights. He watched drops of his own blood splash on the rust-coloured rock. Every jerk sent flashes of pain from ripped flesh and broken bones pulsing along his nerves. Everything felt hot and strained and sticky. There was acid in his mouth and a white, blinding pulse of agony was spreading from his right shoulder up his neck and down his back.

The person who had him slung over their shoulder was complaining about his weight and also that this was bad. Real bad.

The boss wouldn't be pleased. There was never a reply.

His vision went grey and he slipped away again.

The shock of being dumped onto hard, cold ground jerked Webb from oblivion. He lay sprawled on his back, head spinning. He managed to roll over, shoulder and ribs screaming, before he vomited. He hadn't eaten in hours so it just came up acid and blood. He tried to spit out the foulness, heaving breath into his broken ribcage and choking.

"Jesus Christ, he's dying. You *idiot*, Hugo. Where the hell is Miki?"

"I'm here, Hans," a lighter voice, panting, vaguely familiar and the sound of boots on rock. "What's going on here?"

"Hugo's only nearly gone and killed that Webb guy."

"What?" the lighter voice replied and then the boots came close. All Webb could do was try and get breath into his body. "I thought Hugo was completing the mission."

"The damn idiot let this prat chase him down into the caves then damn well shot him."

"This is him?"

"What's left of him. Jesus, Miki, tell me you can fix him up? The boss'll spit nails if he croaks."

Hands were on him, gentle but firm. They turned him over onto his back and he heard himself cry out as weight shifted on his shoulder.

"It's not good," the lighter voice, Miki, said as hands probed the gunshot wound in his shoulder. "He's lost a lot of blood."

"This is bad."

"We need to get him to the infirmary."

"We can't take him to the infirmary," the male, Hans, argued. "He's Service!"

"It's not like he's in any condition to do any spying."

"You don't understand," Hans replied, coming closer and lowering his tone. "There's special orders out for this one. He's out of bounds and a lot of the guys aren't happy about it. They see him spark-out in the infirmary with all those lovely needles lying about." He made a slicing noise and Webb imagined someone drawing a thumb across their throat. "And then it would be our hides."

All this time, Webb was aware of a third person nearby, stood still, not speaking.

"Hugo," he tried, but the word choked off in more blood.

"Well, I'll do my best," Miki said, "but no promises. You better tell Coale."

"You, come with me," Hans barked and two sets of footsteps faded away, echoing.

There were hands on him again, prodding at his face, his shoulder, his wrist and his ribs. Every touch sent fire burning through him. He heard himself gasp and whimper but couldn't make himself stop. He could hardly see. One eye didn't open and the other was sticky with blood. He could just make out artificial light reflecting off damp rock and was aware of the smell of iron and something else, but all that mattered was the pain.

The woman, Miki, pulled off his tie and undid his shirt, pulling it back and doing more prodding, poking and splashed stuff that stung on him, but didn't speak. At last, when he flinched and cried out again there was the prick of a needle in his neck and it all went blessedly dark.

Δ

Webb began to make out a wet, wheezing sound. It rattled. He couldn't measure time except with the repeating, laboured noise. Gradually, senses connected in his brain and told him it was his breathing. As soon as he became aware of that, a violent trembling took hold of him. His right shoulder pulsed heat with every convulsion. He tried twitching his fingers and discovered his right arm was secured to his chest. His head pounded, his face blazed with pain and his mouth felt swollen and tasted foul. He tried slowing his breathing, hoping to still the shaking. It calmed but didn't stop. Cold had sunk into his bones and injuries like cement, solidifying and sharpening the pain.

He tried to open his eyes but only one obeyed. He was on his back. There was a rocky ceiling above, shining with moisture. The air was damp and tasted salty. His breath misted above him. He tried moving his left arm. Slowly, he lifted his hand and felt his face. There was bandaging over one eye. His lips were split and scabbing. His free eye socket felt bruised. His tongue probed his mouth and found that two teeth in his bottom jaw were missing. When he tried to swallow, his throat was raw and the hinge of his jaw throbbed.

He took a few deep, shaking breaths to try and steady himself and shifted up onto his free elbow. The effort left him dizzy and blind, flashes riding up and down his ribs. The trembling came back full force and for a minute he thought he was going to be sick again, but the feeling passed. He blinked around him.

He was still in his dinner suit. It was filthy, rimed with dark rock dust, dirty water and soaked with old blood beginning to turn the same rust colour as the rock around him. Someone had lain him on a blanket and thrown another over him but it did little to stop his shivering. His right arm was strapped across his chest with bandaging with his dinner jacket pulled over the top. His belt and tie were missing, as were his wrist panel and all his weapons.

He was in a small cave, roughly rounded, and, by the look of the laser-cutter marks, man-made. It was lit by a single lighting panel that was screwed into the rock above. The ground was relatively level, but pitted and gritty. There were puddles in the dips. The only narrow opening had been fitted with bars. Beyond the bars all he could see was a rocky passageway, lit by some unseen source. It was utterly quiet, apart from the echo of dripping water.

A plastic bucket had been placed near the wall. An unpleasant smell coming from it told him he'd already been sick more than once. A tray with a flask of water, another of some sort of vitamin drink and some Nutripaks was on the other side.

He gathered himself and sat. When the dizziness passed again, he tried calling out, but his voice cracked and died. He winced, shuffled onto his knees and crawled, one-handed, to the tray and took a long drink of the water. His mouth, throat and ribs all stung with the effort and the water tasted coppery through his broken gums, but when he'd swallowed half the container he was able to unstick his voice.

"Hugo," he called. "Hey, Hugo." His throat grated. It hurt. But he kept calling. "Kaleb Hugo you unutterable bastard. I know you're out there. You get here and face me. Now!"

The echoing sound of his own voice and water dripping was the only answer. He cursed and wrestled his legs under him. Leaning heavily on the cave wall, he managed to get to his feet and shuffled to the bars. He called again, voice gaining volume and strength as his anger burned hotter. But there was still no answer.

A wordless cry ripped out of him and he kicked the bars. The shock rode up his body and made his shoulder scream and his knees buckled. He hung his head, breathing through his teeth until he could see again.

When the sound of his own heartbeat had quieted in his ears, he heard footsteps and low voices nearby.

"Hey," he cried. "Who's there?"

"Quiet your mouth," the man's voice he recognised as Hans's from earlier barked down the passage and then the man stepped into view. He was older, face dark with beard and there was a roughness and slight thinness to his features that Webb recognised as belonging someone who has worked too hard on too little food for too long. He was accompanied by a shorter, Japanese woman with sharp eyes, black hair scraped back into a long tail down her back. They both wore nondescript dark clothing, belts with guns and knives and armoured vests with the insulated Martian worker jackets open over the top.

"He's awake. And standing. That's gotta be good," the man said.

The woman nodded, giving Webb an assessing look. "He made it through the night," she said, and he recognised her voice. Miki, the prodding and efficient hands from earlier. "I'd say he'll be ok, if he doesn't catch pneumonia from this cell."

"Who the hell are you?" Webb said. "Where am I? And where's that bastard Hugo?"

"We should tell Coale," the woman said and turned to leave.

"Holy Christ," Webb said, recognition hitting him like another of Hugo's bullets. "It's you. You were the interviewer in the general's suite…and at the ball…you danced with him."

The woman didn't react, she just turned her back and strode away. The man turned to follow without a word. Webb's knees went and he slid to the ground. He rested his forehead on the bars. Confusion marred with pain swirled through him, tangling his thoughts with his feelings and leaving everything indistinct, heated, pained and without answers or sense.

He must have passed out again because someone kicking the bars of his cell jerked him awake so violently he swayed and nearly toppled over.

"You're sure he's ok?" a harsh voice said. "He don't look too good."

"He was standing before, sir." Miki's voice.

"And mouthing off," came Hans's voice. "You. Webb. Stand up and say something." A boot kicked the bars again.

Webb blinked and peered up. When he managed to focus he saw Miki and Hans stood behind another, taller man. He got his feet under him and struggled upright, trying not to let the pain show in his face. The taller man had fair hair, long and tucked behind his ears with a scrub of reddish stubble. A chunk of one of his ears was missing and there was a heavy scar across his forehead. His eyes were a dark, reddish brown and sharper than steel.

"You really Ezekiel Webb?" he said. Webb recognised the harsh voice from his earbud recording.

"You're Christof Coale," he croaked.

The man's face shifted, he glared at Hans. "How does he know me?"

"Beats me, sir," Hans replied. "Someone musta told him."

"Are you going to speak to me?" Webb growled, trying to draw himself up. "Where the fuck am I?"

"Shut your hole," Coale growled, looking at Webb like he was something he'd found on the sole of his shoe. "Well this is a fuck-ing balls-up. How did this even happen?"

"He followed Hugo, sir," Hans said. "I heard it all happen through Hugo's comm and got to them just as Hugo was about to put a bullet in his head."

Webb's stomach lurched. His head span.

"Jesus, what a mess," Coale said, glaring at Webb.

"At least the mission is complete, sir," Miki said.

"Of course it is. But the old man's been a pain in the backside about this plan from the start. It's done, but now I have to tell him about *this*." He gestured at Webb, a disgusted look on his face. "I'll have that Hugo's guts for this."

"Hey," Webb croaked. "Where's Hugo? Is the slime ball too scared to come look me in the eye?"

"You mean the one you've got left?" Coale sneered. "You're lucky to have that, by the look of you. How bad is he, Miki?"

"Hugo shot him in the shoulder. There was a lot of blood loss. He really went to town on his face and ribs too, but he should live."

"That's something," Coal's black look never shifted. "We knew he was going to be at that damn ball. I'm the one that told the old man that no one, not even Webb, could chase Hugo down. This was the whole point in using a damn Serviceman for this mission in the first place."

"Webb's more reckless than we thought," Miki said.

"More suicidal more like," Hans muttered. "There's three gre-nade blast holes in between us and the New Civic Hall. And two wrecked bikes."

Coale swore bitterly. The two Martians flinched and looked like they were fighting the urge to step back.

"Well, I better go face the music," Coale growled. "Like I have time for any of this right now. At least I can tell him he's alive."

"Hey," Webb called again, voice cracking. "You're Red Star?"

Coale turned back with a measuring look. "At least your brain seems to still be working."

"You killed General Hugo," Webb rasped.

A corner of a smile turned up Coale's face. "He had to go. It's time for something new. Something…better."

"You've started a war," Webb said, feeling his knees threaten to give again but he made himself stand. "Millions could die."

"My dear, short-sighted friend," Coale said, reaching through the bars and grabbing Webb by the jaw. Webb hissed as the man tilted his head to look him in the eye. "That's the entire point. Miki, Hans. This way."

"Hey, wait," Webb called after them, grabbing onto the bars. "Where's Hugo? Send me Hugo, God dammit!"

Their voices and footsteps faded away. Webb sunk to the floor.

There was no way to measure time. The light never changed, the air never changed. No one came by. Very occasionally, he heard footsteps or voices from somewhere down the passage, but they never came close enough for him to make out what they were saying. He examined his cell without much, finding there was no lock mechanism he could see and the controls were somewhere out of reach and out of sight. He finished the water and the vitamin drink but didn't have the stomach for the paste in the Nutri-paks. On one level he was grateful as it meant not having to use the bucket.

He wrapped himself in the blankets when his shivering increased and curled again against the bars, listening out for any familiar voice. He slept and woke, stiff and sore. More time passed. Still no one came.

He tried shouting again but no one responded. At some point someone came by and gave him a new bucket and a fresh tray of water and vitamin drink. His injuries faded from flashing pain to dull aches as they knitted in the cold air. Every muscle hurt so he stayed curled against the bars, drifting in and out of wakefulness.

When he slept he dreamt about what might be happening on the planet's surface, or out in the Orbit. Sometimes it was visions of outraged protests, angry politicians and Service commanders on newsreels. He saw Erica Hugo's ashen face, orders to strike coming robotically from her mouth. He saw Vergennes standing on a front line in a desert somewhere, following an order to advance and running straight into a hail of bullets. Sometimes it was just explosions, blood and gunfire.

Once he dreamt of the Service storming the Martian caves. He saw the bodies of Hans and Miki and Coale and a thousand more faceless Red Star soldiers, broken and bloodstained, strewn over red rocks like so much discarded rubbish. He was the one standing over the blind and staring body of Kaleb Hugo, gun smoking in his hand and the tastes of burning and death were heavy in his throat.

He woke with a start, panting and sweating. The chill settled into his flesh again and chased the last remnants of the dream away. But the smell of combat didn't leave. He grasped the bars, shifted closer and took a deep breath. He could still smell it: coppery, sharp. His thick pulse slugged in his ears and throat and he curled back into his blankets, mind swimming with what he might or might not be sensing.

He was somewhere between sleeping and waking when the sound of steps pulled him to reality. He blinked his free eye, shifting closer to the bars and heard voices getting closer.

"I hope you've at least been checking on him," came Coale's gruff voice. "I've got enough to do without having to remember to keep him alive."

"Miki's been checking him," came Hans's reply. "He's sleeping a lot. She still thinks he needs to be moved somewhere warmer."

"That's up to the old man," Coale said and stepped into sight. His eyes found Webb on the floor and his lip curled. "Good lord, what a state."

"You sure this is a good idea, boss?" Hans was at his side working at some unseen locking mechanism in the rock near the bars.

"He wants to see how Hugo acts around him."

"Isn't the fact that he tried to kill him proof enough that he'll do anything we say?" Hans asked. Something clicked and he pulled back a door in the bars.

"He wants to see how he acts now there's no adrenaline flying. Get him up."

Hans hoisted Webb to his feet. "Come on, you lanky sack of bones. You're the one that wanted to see Hugo so bad."

Webb tried to speak, but every inch of him ached for being curled on the floor for what might have been days and he couldn't find the energy. His healing injuries pulled and protested and the thin warmth that had been afforded by the blankets was stripped away, leaving him shuddering with chill again.

"We should have thought to get him changed or something. He looks half-dead."

"He is half-dead," Coale said, with a baleful look. "But he'll have to do. Come on, I want this over with."

"Walk, will you?" Hans grumbled as Webb staggered. He got his shoulder up under Webb's good arm, pulling it over his shoulders and pulled him upright. "Get the lead out, already."

Webb groaned and put one foot in front of the other. A couple of steps down the corridor and his legs seemed to loosen. Hugo's name had lit a fire in his belly that was now gaining heat. He made himself move faster, even though it meant stumbling and leaning on the other man.

Webb found the strength from somewhere to lift his head. They were moving down a passage with barred cells like his on either side. Most of them contained crates or boxes of supplies.

Some were filled with ammunition and weapons.

They moved into a wider passage. The rock arced above and over in smooth, rounded arches. Lighting panels were installed at regular intervals, washing the space a rusty orange. There were tunnels branching off and natural fissures opening up into other spaces above and below. People in dark clothes and jackets wearing gloves and scarves, breath misting in front of them, thronged the space. All wore weapons and were mostly young, twenties through to late thirties. The general air was of grim excitement.

They gained momentum as Webb's legs strengthened and his blood warmed. Coale got wide-eyed looks, nods and salutes off everyone they passed. Webb drew confused, wary or hostile ones. The sharp, coppery smell strengthened and the hair on the back of Webb's neck rose as he finally recognised it.

He dug his heels in. Hans cursed as Webb strained to see down into one of the caves below. It was brightly lit, with rows and rows of benches with workers in face masks, gloves and tunics bent over them. They all had large melting pots, burners, crucibles and industrial mixing pans to hand and were syphoning, melting, mixing and moulding hundreds of cubes of a pinkish, gelatinous material onto wire ignition cages. Vats of bloodgrease stood open between the benches, tubes pumping the red liquid into the mixing pans. The blood-like smell was like a solid thing even in the cold air.

"Red cement?" Webb gasped. "You're making red cement?"

Hans only grunted wrestled him along. Webb's mind whirled as he was dragged along through more tunnels and caves. Pockets of fog wreathed through the wider spaces. Finally, they turned down a narrower, quieter tunnel. There were doors built into the walls instead of just hap-hazard openings in the rock.

Coale stopped at one that had a guard outside it. The guard saluted and Coale tapped at a keypad next to the door. It clicked then hissed open.

Coale took a hold of Webb's elbow. Webb suppressed a hiss

when it pulled on his injured shoulder. "I'll take it from here. You get back to work."

"Yes sir," Hans said, sounding grateful to shift Webb's weight over to Coale and left before Coale manhandled him through the door.

The warmth of the room beyond wrapped him like a blanket. His muscles went slack and it soothed some of the aches but caused all the cuts and bruises to pulse angrily. He was dropped into a chair. He sat waiting for everything to stop spinning.

"Alright, here he is," Coale announced to the room.

Webb raised his head. The room had polyfibre walls, keeping the conditioned air warm and dry. There were more doors leading into other rooms, shut and key-coded. There was a deactivated display on the opposite wall and the black eyes of camera domes in the corners of the ceiling.

There was only one other person in the room. Hugo sat in a chair against the wall, his back stiff and straight with his hands resting on his knees. He wore plain, sturdy trousers and boots in dark colours and a long, Martian jacket. He was a lot thinner than Webb remembered, his cheek bones, scuffed with stubble, sharp angles in his wasted face. There were shadows under his eyes and Webb could make out the bones of his eye sockets. His hair was cropped so close to his head there was barely any of it left. One eye was blackened and there was tack-tape over his nose, probably from where Webb had head-butted him. There were also old puckered scars on his temples and down his jaw that looked raw.

His eyes were black, empty and staring. They were locked on Webb.

"Hugo?"

Hugo didn't respond.

"What's happened to you?" Webb croaked, the emptiness of the man's black eyes making his skin crawl.

"He's seen the light, Captain Webb," Coale said. He was stood with his arms folded, looking over at Hugo with something like pride.

"Hugo," Webb tried again, attempting to stand. He steadied himself on the back of his chair. Hugo's unblinking eyes followed him. "What's going on?"

Hugo just continued looking at him without interest or recognition.

"You killed him." Webb said, the words sticking in his mouth. "You killed your father." Hugo's gaze didn't waver and his face didn't move. Webb felt cold, despite the heat of the room. "You really got nothing to say?"

Hugo looked on, unmoving.

"What have you done to him?" Webb turned on Coale.

Coale smiled. His teeth were very white and sharp-looking. "Convinced him, that's all. He understands now that the Service's rule is outdated and inhumane. We are the new start. Your old CO gets that."

"Hugo, think about this," Webb said, staggering forward. He thought Coale would stop him, but if anything his smile encouraged him. "These people want to wipe the Service out. Millions could buy it."

"He has thought about it," Coale said. "He still believes."

"That's your brothers, Hugo," Webb said, stepping still closer to the man in the chair. "Your mother. Your *kids*."

The only reaction from his former commander was a slight flaring of his nostrils. It was like Webb was approaching an animal rather than a former crewmate.

"Kaleb," Webb said, voice growing thin. "Do you even know who I am?"

"He knows," Coale drawled.

"I want to hear it from him," Webb snapped. Hugo had stood and taken a step back, now eyeing Webb like he was a poisonous bug he was considering stepping on. "Well? Do you know me?"

"Yes." His voice was low. Expressionless.

"You've done something to him. Drugged him or something.

This isn't him."

"Tell yourself what you want," Coale said, checking the time on his wristpanel. "He's Red Star now."

"I don't believe it," Webb said, unable to stop his face twisting which woke pain in the cuts and scrapes. "I don't believe any of this. Hugo wouldn't do this. He wouldn't shoot his own dad."

"Oh no?" Coale said, in a bored voice. "Hugo. Kill this man."

Webb stumbling back as Hugo pulled a gun and levelled it at his face.

"Stop," Coale called just as his finger started to squeeze the trigger.

Hugo holstered the gun and sat back down, hands on knees and resumed staring into space.

"See?" Coale said, but he wasn't addressing Webb. He was looking up at one of the cameras. "All is as I said. Our only mistake was assuming this mentalist wouldn't chase Hugo. But we can deal with it. All can go on as planned."

Coale looked from one camera to another, putting a finger in his ear to listen to something coming through an earpiece. Webb slumped in his chair, his heartbeat slowing to a thick punch in his chest.

"Hugo," he murmured, his voice catching. The man looked his way. The empty coldness in the look hurt more than if he'd shot him again.

Coale was fidgeting and looking impatiently around the cameras. "Yes, exactly," he said. "Like I said. Is this settled now? Can we get on with the next stage? Our timing right now is integral."

A pause. Coale's look slid from the cameras to Webb.

"He's not as bad as he looks. I've had a medic see to him. Yes, she wants him kept somewhere warmer but I don't see…" Coale's face darkened. "But…" Coale slumped a little, rubbed his eyes. "Yes, alright, alright. I just want it noted I think it's a bad idea. The living quarters aren't as secure…" Coale was cut off again, face reddening. "Fine. I'll see to it."

Coale went to the door and called for someone. Webb barely noticed when another Red Star soldier came into the room and followed Coale's instructions to hoist him out of his chair. He let himself be dragged away. The door closed between him and Hugo with a click.

He didn't come back to himself until they'd stopped outside another door with another keypad. The man holding him keyed a code but Webb was too sore, tired and sick with despair to memorise what he pressed. The door slid open and they stepped forward into a sparse cabin-like room. There was a bunk, wash stand and small workstation wired into the corner. The air was warm and dry and blessedly didn't smell of bloodgrease. Webb stood swaying on his feet for a long time after he'd been locked in as the warmth slowly sunk into his flesh, stilling the shivering that had returned, but he still didn't move. Outside, everything was raw, ripped and aching. Inside, everything was numb and empty.

Because he didn't have anything left with which to do, think or feel anything, he shambled to the bank, lay down and let go.

The woman, Miki, came. She changed his dressings and left him with clean clothes, Nutripaks and instructions to wash and eat. After she left, he lay back down and stared at the polyfibre wall until it blurred and he blundered into his dreams again.

Δ

"Still no direct response?" the older man with snow-white hair said in his soft but firm voice.

"No, sir. The Service are broadcasting a general call for us to disarm and surrender but are not responding to any demands."

"What about Rose's statement?"

"Our long-range pickups are showing its doing the rounds on the solarnet. There's a lot of activity on news and network sites, plenty of civilians have something to say, but the Service haven't responded."

The discussion fluttered around the edges of Hugo's consciousness like moths around a lighting pole. His hands were hitting keys, his eyes skimming text. He watched everything from the back of his own mind, where it was quiet and dark.

"Hugo," the older man said, coming forward. "Have you found anything?"

"A Service fleet has been dispatched for Mars," Hugo replied.

"Have they identified where our Earth bases are?"

"No, sir."

A pause. "And no one in your family has tried to contact you about this?"

"No, sir," Hugo said.

He felt the man looking at him again. He lifted his eyes from the screen and let the man examine his face. He had very pale blue eyes, like Earth sky after a rainfall. Hugo knew them well. They reminded him of another pair just like them. But the recognition was from a part of him that wasn't real any more. He let it drift away, holding the man's gaze, waiting to be told what to do.

The older man turned away and addressed the other people in the room. They were busy at workstations or tapping datapanels. Talk ebbed and flowed about troop movements, supply caches, unit numbers, strike times and positioning. Hugo let his hands fold in his lap, waiting to be assigned another task.

The conversation rose then quieted and then the older man was stood at his side.

"Hugo, follow me," he said.

Hugo got up and followed the grey-haired man toward the Operation Room door.

"Wait," Coale stood from his workstation and hurried after them. "We still need - "

"You're in charge, Coale. I want reports on all positions by midnight Martian time."

"Fine," Caole said, not quite hiding his disapproval before sliding a warning look to Hugo. Coale's eyes were ruddy brown, but looked almost red in the underground light. Hugo knew them even better than the old man's. He could always feel when they were on him. They produced the sensation of electricity firing through his skin.

He firmly clamped down on his thoughts and trailed after the older man. They stepped out into the chill and the damp of the caves. They passed through the red cement processing labs, hot and steamy and then again out into more cold corridors. The older man was stopped several times by people wanting to show him things on datapanels, receive instruction or just salute and demonstrate allegiance. He acknowledged and dealt with each and every one, but did so in a curt, hurried manner that told Hugo where they were going was more important to him than where they were.

"In here, Hugo," the man said as a young guard stepped aside to allow the older man to unlock a door. Hugo stepped through into living quarters like his own, but the workstation was off, the lights were on full and there was someone in the bunk.

The door hissed shut behind them and there was a clunk of the lock. The older man stood in the middle of the room, look-ing down at the man on the bunk with strain visible in his face. The prone figure shifted stiffly into a sitting position. He was in a plain t-shirt and loose track trousers. His feet were bare. The flesh on his arms and face was pale apart from the livid purple and red of healing cuts and bruises. One arm was tied flat across his chest and there was bandaging tacked over one of his eyes.

It was the man from a few days before. He'd asked Hugo if he knew who he was. Hugo knew. He just didn't care.

The scabs and bruises on the younger man's lips and face stood out all the more when what little colour that had been in his face drained as he took in his company.

"I don't understand," the younger man eventually said. His voice was small.

"I'm sorry, lad," the older man said. "I truly am."

The other got shakily to his feet. "Red Star is you?" he, Webb was the name Hugo remembered, said, face still pale.

"Not all me. We are in the thousands."

"Mac," Webb said. His voice broke with a choking sound. "I don't understand," he said again, putting out a hand to steady himself on the wall.

"Sit down, lad," Mac said, stepping forward to take hold of his arm.

"Don't," Webb cried, pulling his arm out of reach. "Don't touch me."

Hugo stepped back. Webb looked at him as if only just noticing he was there.

"I get that you don't understand yet, lad," the older man said. His face looked pained. Hugo found it vaguely interesting. A memory of another time he had met this man tickled at him, when they'd both been different people, but he crushed it before it formed. "I tried to keep you out of it. I really did."

"You tried to *what*?" Webb's bruised face contorted.

Mac sighed and ran a strong, gnarled hand through his white hair. When he looked back up he had all emotion once more under control. "You were not meant to be involved. Not yet."

"Not yet?"

"No. You have a place in our plans, Ezekiel. But not at this stage."

"I have a place in your plans for Orbit Domination, do I?"

Mac didn't react. "Not domination, lad. Liberation."

"You bastard," Webb said, voice loaded with venom. "You arrogant, ignorant bastard."

"I know you're angry - "

"Angry?" Webb's voice rose. "I'm not angry. There isn't a big enough word for what I am."

"Son," Mac said in a firm voice. Webb flinched. "I'm not going to try and talk you round. I knew you would never agree with the process. But believe me, the result, the future Red Star can give us all, will be worth the sacrifice."

"Sweet Jesus in heaven. I can't believe this. I just can't. Have you not learned anything? All you are doing is killing people, Mac. Again. Dress it up any way you like, you're still just a terrorist."

"You're too young. Too idealistic. This world has lived too long staring down the barrels of Service cannons." Something flickered in Mac's eyes. "I tried to gain freedom for the Lunar Strip when I was their governor. I failed. I got scared. I hid. Then you came along. My poor murdered boy, brought back from the dead by a mother who was supposed to love him." Mac took a breath. His eyes were bright. Muscles stood out on Webb's neck as he clenched his jaw shut.

"All that mattered then was you," Mac continued, voice softer. "You were something I could finally be proud of. Protect. So I left Earth to find you on Haven to help you. But then I was on the run." His eyes went far away. "And I saw it. I saw it all over again. I saw what Councillor Pope was doing with Lunar 1. I saw the cities on Earth at the edge of the fallout zones, their residents dying of radiation poisoning because nowhere else will take them. I saw people attending balls in Tranquility Hall while men, women and children in the same city lived in slums along its groundways, begging for scraps. This is the world the Service had given us, lad. This is the world that needs saving. And I realised I can't just care about you alone. I have to care about everyone. It's who I was born to be."

Webb was shaking. "Duran McCullough returns from the dead to save the world? It's a nice fairytale, Mac. You left out the part where millions of people die."

Mac sighed and looked at the ground, rubbing his neck. "You weren't supposed to know. Not yet. You were supposed to stay assigned to Eclipse, out of harm's way, until all this was over. Then I was going to claim you as my heir and offer you a new and better world to inherit."

Webb shook his head. "I can't even begin to unravel your crazy. If you really thought I would want any part of any of this, you're beyond mad."

A charged silence descended. Hugo flexed his fingers, feeling the ragged remains of his fingernails scrape against his palms. A faint hope he'd be sent away started to uncoil in his chest, but he quashed it. He knew what would happen if he dared hope for things. He looked between the two men who he knew as father and son, but refused to think about what that meant.

"Red Star are more powerful than anyone knows," Mac said gently. "We have forces everywhere, ready to move. What I want more than anything is a peaceful transition. But we can only be certain to secure that with enough force to make the Service stop and think. It's been years in the making, but we're almost ready to show our hand."

"Then what? You take Erica Hugo's top office at Headquarters? Because, you know, she would have probably just given it to you if you gave her son back."

Hugo's face twitched.

"I take nothing," Mac said, "from anyone. Rose will take power to begin with, and oversee Orbit-wide elections. We will have a democratic Orbit Alliance, with people in charge who everyone wants to give that power too. Then more construction on Mars, making more space for people ready to live somewhere new with no fear of having to run to or from the legacy of the Service."

"So this is all Rose, then?" Webb said. "This is his idea?"

"It's all our idea." Mac looked almost pitying. "Don't you get it, lad? This isn't ego. And it isn't arrogance. This is what people want."

"And the red cement?" his son bit out. "I've seen enough here to blow this colony into a smoking crater ten times over. Are you telling me the people want that too?"

"It's not your concern," Mac said, lifting his chin.

"And General Hugo?" Webb countered, voice cracking. The

words sent something rippling through Hugo and he sunk mental claws deep into himself to keep himself focused.

"My Military Commander's plan," Mac said.

"Coale?"

Mac nodded. "A warning shot. To prompt discussion."

"And I bet Special Commander Hugo's been very forthcoming with negotiations since you murdered her husband."

"Lad, I came down here so you'd know about me. I couldn't decide what was best, but then I saw that I need to get this all straight with you now you're here. This is not your vision, I get that. You want nothing to do with it right now, that's fine too."

"Never."

Mac's face darkened. "We'll see what the future brings. But I wanted you to know the whole story. And know that I tried to keep you out of this. But Vergennes and I never guessed - "

"Vergennes?" Webb's face slackened. "What's he got to do with anything?"

"He's my agent," Mac said, taking a tentative step forward, pressing his hands together. "Don't get me wrong, he's a sworn Service officer. He doesn't know I'm anything to do with Red Star. But I got to know him when he was training at the Academy. I helped him out on one of the survival exercises when he'd got turned around in a storm. I saved him, like I did you. And he was grateful. He used to visit me. After a while, he figured who I was. Bright lad. Knows his modern history. But he kept my secret and became my connection to the outside. When he graduated, he transferred into Eclipse at my request. I was on the run by then, but we kept in touch. I asked him to watch out for you, and keep me posted about you."

Webb's jaw was tight. His visible eye was pained. "He knows about me? What I am?"

The lines in Mac's face deepened. "He, does son. He also knows how much I care about you."

"He lied to me. You all lied to me."

"For your own good, lad. Always for your own good."

Webb looked like he was either about to faint, lash out or be sick. He suddenly turned his face to Hugo. It was taut with emotion. He straightened up from where he'd been leaning against the wall with a wince and came forward. Hugo tried to step back but found himself against the door. Webb came close enough so Hugo could feel his body heat and smell the antiseptic from his dressings.

"Hugo?" he said, searching his face. "I know you're in there somewhere. Are you going to look me in the eye and tell me you're really a part of this?"

"Yes." Hugo let the word come out, knowing it was the answer he was supposed to give. He wasn't really sure what it meant, or why it caused the stricken look on the younger man's face. Hugo saw the cuts in his lips and the missing teeth and remembered what it felt like when his fist had crunched them out. His gut tightened but he kept his face blank.

"Why did you bring him with you?" Webb hissed at Mac. "To rub my face in it? Or to scare me?"

"Neither," Mac replied. "So you can see he's ok."

"You call this ok?" Webb waved a hand in front of Hugo's face. "What the hell have you done to him, Mac?"

"Not me. Coale."

"Coale?"

Mac nodded. "Coale turned him to our cause. He's the most recognisable of Erica Hugo's sons. He's an important card to play later in the game."

"And that was that Coale's idea too, was it?"

"We all agreed. We're a team, Rose, Coale and I. Coale's the tactician. Rose is the political face."

"And what are you? The has-been revolutionary mentor?"

"I'm the heart of this all," Mac said gravely. "I'm its soul. And its knowledge."

"You're its asshole." Webb's face flushed. "Spitting out its shit."

Mac moved fast. Hugo watched him grab his son by a handful of his shirt and slam him against the wall. Webb grunted and his face went grey, but he glared with his good eye, daring the older man to take his best shot.

"You're on thin ice," Mac growled. "I love ya, but push me too far, I will hand you your arse, get it?"

"Would you kill me?" he said softly, nastily. "If it came to it, would you kill me as well?"

Mac released him. "Yes. I'd do everything possible to make sure it didn't come to that. But if you were between me and success… yes. I would, lad."

"Then you might as well do it now, because I'll make it my entire business to be between you and your success."

"You're just angry now. And misguided. I don't blame you for either. You've had a hell of a life. But I promise, lad, in time, you'll understand. And you'll want to be part of it."

"Well, if you won't do it. Hugo? Kill me."

Mac sighed. "He won't obey you, Ezekiel. Hugo is our man."

"Dammit, Hugo. Shoot me. Do it now." Hugo's spine stiffened. Webb looked in his eyes, his gaze intense. "You nearly did it before. Finish the job, already."

When Hugo glanced to Mac for guidance, Webb lunged for his gun. Hugo grabbed his wrist. They struggled, the younger man making frustrated noises. It was easy for Hugo to hold back the injured man but he'd already managed to grab the gun.

"Hugo," Mac warned, just as he got a grip on Webb's injured shoulder. "Don't hurt him."

But Hugo was riding instinct. He squeezed, feeling the torn flesh give. Webb yelped, buckled and went to his knee. He pulled Hugo's gun, hand and all, round and pressed it against his forehead. He looked up at him through tangled hair and angry tears.

"Shoot me, Hugo. Do it now. If you're in there anywhere, get me out of this. Please."

He was breathing through his teeth, clutching the metal barrel against his forehead hard enough to bruise. Hugo stared at him. A similar image of holding another gun to this same man's head in another place and time rose before his eyes, giving him double vision. It threatened to engulf him. He felt the blackness yawning and his hand start to shake.

"Hugo." The older man's voice slammed into him. He twitched, wrenched the gun away, holstered it and took a step back.

Webb buckled over on the floor, sniffed and shook.

"Stand up, you great jessy," Mac sneered. "I should have known better than to let you be brought up by Americans. Your melodramatics are shameful."

Webb glared, swiping at his eyes and got to his feet. "So is you're pride."

"Ezekiel, for God's sake, don't you see? This is bigger than you. It's bigger than me or your friend here. It's bigger and more important than his family or mine."

Webb's face was set, but he found nothing more to say.

Mac moved to the door and knocked. The guard opened it. Mac turned in the doorway. "You'll be kept here until everything's over."

"I'll be *what*?"

"It might be months. It might be years," Mac said. "Change doesn't happen quickly. But it will be worth it. You can have access to the solarnet to watch what's happening, though I warn you not to try anything funny. Maybe seeing it happen will help you understand. Either way, you'll be kept safe down here out of the way until the time is right."

"When will that be?"

"When everyone knows I'm alive, remembers my name and knows what I've given them," Mac said. "The name McCullough will mean something great again. Then people will know it's your name too and that you are here to follow after me."

"It's not my name," Webb said, eye flashing blue lighting.

"Yes it is," Mac said. His face had softened. He reached out and put a gloved hand to his son's face. Hugo expected the younger man to flinch or pull away but he did neither. He just stood looking all of a sudden lost and scared. "I'd named you, you know. When I first knew you existed. Your mother knew that name too, though she never told you."

"I'm Ezekiel," Webb said. His words were thick. "Ezekiel Webb."

"That's the name of a Lunar 1 orphan raised by youth unit nuns. That's not who you are. Your real name is Errol. Errol Mc-Cullough." Mac let his hand drop. Webb's mouth trembled. "I never told you before because it didn't matter then. But that's the name people will come to know. I want the world to know you're my boy."

"That's not me," Webb choked, finally letting the angry tears fall. "Your son's dead."

Mac went very still. There were hundreds of things going through Webb's eyes, a hundred things that part of Hugo understood and felt as his own.

"Hugo," Mac barked and Hugo flinched. "We're leaving."

Hugo followed the older man from the room. Webb stared after him until the door shut between them, a lifetime of hurt heavy in his face.

They went back the way they'd come. Mac ordered Hugo back to the Operation Room and he went, glad to feel safe again. Coale was directing operations when he arrived. Hugo took his usual seat at his usual workstation, loading up his usual searches and checks to monitor Service communication and tracking channels, looking for something Coale or Mac might need.

As the streams of text and figures scrolled by on the screen, he felt his heart calm. He felt his peace and silence return. He felt everything become easy again and was happy to sink into it and leave his reactions unacknowledged.

VII

Webb was never able to decide which was the worst part of the days that followed. And he spent a lot of time considering it, as there was nothing else to do. The slow healing of his injuries provided a backdrop of pain to every waking moment. Harried Red Star medics only checked on him sporadically. He was sure his ribs were healing crooked. He was scolded when he unwrapped the bandages binding his wrist to his chest, but wouldn't let them tie if back up. He was fed up with fumbling round one-handed.

One of the medics dug up a wrist brace and made him wear it. The extra weight pulled on the gunshot wound in his shoulder which made his neck, back and head ache like a network of hot wires had been strung through his flesh. When the bandaging was finally removed from his eye, his vision in it was blurry. The medic who shined a lenslight in it didn't say anything but when days rolled by and it didn't get any better Webb wondered if it was damaged for good.

Behind the physical discomfort pulsed the mental, like a grey wash of dirty water swilling around under his skin. Faces rose in front of his eyes whether he was asleep and awake: Hugo, Mac, Vergennes. Even his mother, Admiral Pharos, who he hadn't let himself think about in years, was suddenly clear as day in front him. He remembered her iron-grey hair, her hard sneer and her eyes, needle-sharp and resolute. He remembered what they looked like when they stared up at him, blank and empty, after he'd killed her.

Mac's voice would then swamp everything and make him feel like kicking, screaming, crying and hysterically laughing all at once. He blamed himself for ever daring to think he was happy or trusted people. Then he cursed himself for being melodramatic just as the old man had said and poked at the gap in his teeth with his tongue to distract himself with pain.

He refused to eat until Miki came by one day with two large Red Star soldiers who held him down whilst she force-fed him through a tube. After that, he always finished everything brought to him, but it didn't stop him throwing the empty containers at the walls until they stained and dented the polyfibre.

He refused to touch the workstation, solarnet connection or not, out of sheer bloody-minded stubbornness. He told himself he didn't care what people thought had happened to him or what might be going on in the wake of the general's assassination. He told himself he didn't care that Hugo had turned his coat, killed his own father and ushered in another age of fighting and fear. It hurt too much to care anymore.

After they'd pumped his stomach of an entire bottle of pain-killer tablets that had been left on the side, he wasn't even allowed to administer his own medicine. He succeeded in hacking the lock on his door, making a mad dash and being brought down three times before they changed it to a manual door on hinges and fixed an iron bar over the outside that could only be removed with a key.

Every Red Star soldier that entered his cell to bring him food or replace the cameras he routinely smashed, gave him disdainful or disgusted looks if they gave him any attention at all. Clearly these weren't people that thought you were entitled to respect just because of who you were born to. Webb didn't care. He didn't want their respect.

Mac didn't come to see him again.

Days rolled on. The chrono on the workstation marked off the hours but he gave up looking at it. In the end he gave up moving altogether and lay on the bunk, face turned to the wall and let the despair drown him in grey and black waves.

One day he woke up from a fitful sleep, sat up sweating. As the violent dream faded, leaving just his shuddering heart and damp skin in its wake, he finally looked over at the workstation. He chewed on his lip, wondering whether anything that was really happening out in the world could possibly be as bad as what was going on in his head. He hesitated, then got up, his still-healing body creaking and sore, swallowed some water to wash away the last taste of the nightmare and hobbled over to the workstation.

It booted up quickly and was smooth and responsive, made of barely-used components. The long-distance connection to the solarnet took a while to activate, but once it had, the connection was good and the static feedback minimal. It didn't take long to find that his access had been greatly restricted. He could read reports, reel newsfeeds, check real-time updates, but he couldn't send anything, access any sort of communication or messaging software or alter any content. He spent a fruitless hour trying all the tricks in his repertoire to get around the restrictions, but as his access was blocked over and over, his faint hope of getting in touch with Service HQ was crushed.

Instead, he started reading. It had been just over a fortnight since General Hugo's shooting. Webb felt like he'd spent months underground in the dark with his nightmares. The Orbit was in uproar. Red Star, through Arcadius Rose, had gone public. They had claimed responsibility for the assassination and declared ownership of dozens of outposts in the most densely populated areas on Earth and in the colonies and stated that they were armed and ready to strike back should any violence be unleashed against their people.

The responses were myriad and impassioned. Some people were clamouring for revenge, some people were cheering on Red Star. Some were just begging various authorities to not let it go any further. As for official responses or statements from the Service or from Erica Hugo, there were none.

Webb went cold. Mars was under a supply boycott from Earth. A fleet of Service ships under the flagship Perseverance had been dispatched and Martian newsboards reported that it was stationed in orbit over Schiaparelli City. Webb was unsurprised to learn the fleet was under the command of Admiral Myles Osgard. There were many video clips of the man stating that the situation was under control, but when asked why the fleet had done nothing further than attempt to land and been denied by the colonists, he didn't elaborate. Webb could see his contained passion and thwarted rage in the set of his jaw and was reminded of his daughter.

The only thing being reported more than the presence of the Service fleet was the details of an upcoming Schiaparelli City rally, gathering everyone from the city together to show the Service ships and the whole Orbit just how strong and united Martians were. Sound bites of Rose were on every news network, encouraging everyone to watch the live feed if unable to attend themselves. It would give them hope and strength in the new future that Mars promised to provide for everyone.

Webb felt sick. Sick and tired. So tired. The physical and emotional exhaustion was enough to pull him back to his bunk, curl in a ball, pull the blankets over his head and decide to wait for it to all be over.

And so it was one day that he drifted awake to again be slammed with disappointment to find himself still alive, only to become slowly aware that there was someone in the cell with him. He shifted and reached for the light command by the bunk.

Hugo didn't blink when the light came on. He was stood near the door, dark, empty eyes on Webb.

"Good Christ," Webb swore. "How long have you been there?"

"Not long."

Webb scrubbed his face, wincing as he pressed on still-healing bruises and sat up. "What do you want?"

Hugo carried on looking at him. Webb felt a chill go through him and dropped his eyes. He hated seeing the face that was all at once painfully familiar and yet completely unknown to him.

"Are you here to put that bullet in me finally?"

"No," he said, voice low and sounding rusty, like he was unused to using it. "McCullough won't have you harmed."

"That's what you call him? He's not General or Governor or Our Glorious Saviour?"

"There are no titles here," Hugo said. His voice came easier but was flat and completely devoid of expression. "No ranks. We are all equal parts in the same whole."

"Christ in Heaven, Hugo. Is that really you?"

"Yes."

"I don't believe you."

"It's me, Webb."

"So you do know who I am? Really?"

"Yes."

"Who am I, then? To you?" Webb tried, with a narrow look.

"You are a former crewmate."

"That's it?"

A hint of uncertainty crept into Hugo's face before being swept away. "You are also Errol McCullough, Duran McCullough's son and heir, who must be protected until the time comes for him to take up his role."

"Protected? You shot me, you asshole."

"I was on a mission," Hugo stated. "You interfered."

"I don't understand," Webb said, wondering if he'd ever be able to stop saying it. "The Hugo I knew would never be part of something like this."

"I'm not the Hugo you knew," Hugo returned after a pause.

Webb got to his feet, slowly and carefully, not taking his eyes from the other man's. "What did they do, Hugo?" he asked indicating the ageing burn scars at his temples and along his jaw.

Hugo went still. His eyes revealed a flash of deep, dark pain, then closed up again. "Coale helped me understand."

"How?" Webb asked softly.

He said nothing and remained still as stone.

"Ok, ok. You won't answer me that. So what are you doing here, then? Did the old man send you?"

"No. Everyone's asleep."

"What do you want?"

"It's useless to resist, Webb. You're part of a plan bigger than yourself. Accept it and play your role."

"This is something they sent you to tell me?"

"No," Hugo said. "Though I know they will be pleased I did."

"And this just occurred to you now?"

"Yes. I was sleeping. I had a dream…" his face tightened a moment.

Webb clutched at a chair with his good hand to steady himself and took a step closer. "A dream?" he promoted carefully, chasing the flash of emotion he saw in the other man's face.

"Yes. It was of a time from before. We were on a bridge of a flagship. It was crashing."

"The *Resolution*?"

Hugo nodded stiffly. "It reminded me that you always do the right thing…but that sometimes need to be told what that is."

Webb winced. "What's the right thing, Hugo?"

"Follow Duran McCullough's dream. Do as Christof Coale says. Follow Arcadius Rose's instructions. Obey the commands of those who can change the future for everyone and be grateful for being a part of it."

Webb aching jaw tightened. "You really think all that?"

"I do."

Webb glanced up at the cameras around the room. "They will know you're here, you know. They'll know you're talking to me."

"They will be pleased with what I'm saying."

"You've been gone a long time," Webb said softly. "Have you been here this whole time?"

"No. I was moved around before being stationed here."

"Africa? The moon?"

"Among others," Hugo replied, showing no reaction. "But Mars is our base. When we had this secured, I came here."

"Do you remember what happened?" Webb asked, eyeing the camera. "Do you remember leaving home?"

Hugo's face tightened again. Webb watched him fight another battle then calm. "I came to be with them."

"Of your own free will?"

"I came to be part of Red Star," Hugo said.

"Kaleb," Webb tried, taking another step. The other man tensed but Webb put a hand on his shoulder to keep him where he was. He was shocked to feel the hardness of bone and sinew through the man's shirt. The thick jackets had concealed how thin he was. Tendons stood out on his neck like ropes. He could see the shape of his jaw under his skin. His eyes, this close, were all at once blank and haunted. "Kaleb," he repeated. "Do you remember Becca and Amye?"

"My daughters."

Webb swallowed. "And Marilyn? Do you remember Marilyn?"

"My wife."

Webb searched his face, disbelief like a stone in his stomach. "Your mom sent me to get you. To take you home to them. Don't you want to go home?"

His eyes hardened. "I am home."

Webb let his hand fall and Hugo turned to leave.

"Hugo," he said. The man paused. "I'm sorry."

Hugo looked confused.

"I'm sorry," Webb repeated. "For not being there."

"I don't understand."

Webb felt a sob climb up his throat and swallowed it. "If we hadn't fought…if I'd been around…I'd have never have let this happen."

A faint frown of bewilderment pulled Hugo's brows together. "It wouldn't have made a difference."

"Oh, it would. I would have locked you in a closet rather than let you walk out that door."

Hugo looked at him, perplexed.

"I just wanted it said. If there's any part of the real you left in there, I want him to know."

"This is the real me, Webb. I stand with the people now. You should too. You are an asset. You should be honoured to take your place at McCullough's side."

Webb closed his eyes, unable to look at him anymore.

"You've always tried to stand on your own," Hugo added softly. "Why not be part of something?"

"I don't believe in it," he whispered. "I don't believe killing people helps them." There was a long pause. Webb opened his eyes. Hugo was looking at the wall with a thoughtful expression on his face.

"You should come to the rally," Hugo said, as if deciding something.

"Come again?"

"You should be there to listen to Rose speak. You should see it. It would convince you."

"My old man would never allow it," Webb said carefully.

"Coale would. He would believe it would be good for you to see."

Webb didn't say anything, feeling everything balance on a knife point. He waited.

"Yes," Hugo said, turning back to the door. "You should attend the rally. I will talk to Coale."

Hugo left. Webb stood in the middle of the room with his mind starting to tick. He made himself go back to his bunk, lie back down and turn the lights off. He closed his eyes but didn't fall back asleep, thoughts whirling and hope quickening his pulse.

Δ

Webb had to fight to act normal as one day rolled into the next. He sat at the workstation just to watch the hours slip by on the chrono. He paced, forming and then rejecting one escape plan after another. He read everything he could find on the solarnet about the rally. It was written about widely on newsites, some articles factual, some fearful, some angry. Reports of General Hugo's death still took precedent. Webb skipped over those posts with a tight chest.

The *Now* network site had a rather conspicuous nothing posted by Vee Osgard on anything. Webb chewed on that a moment but put the matter aside when he couldn't decide if it was significant or not.

The rally day approached and still no one came to confirm if he would attend. The little flare of hope that had been kindled in him was snuffed. Unable to contain the claustrophobic frustration any longer, he tried a desperate hack attempt around the workstation's restrictions, not caring to keep his processes subtle, to blast an SOS message out to the Service or to anyone that might be listening. But before he came close to breaching the safeguards, his door was slammed open and three soldiers barrelled in to haul him from the workstation. A technician scurried in and permanently disconnected the machine's networks and wiped its processors.

They left him with renewed pain in his ribs and shoulder and a disconnected and useless workstation.

Time lost all meaning. He stayed in the dark, letting himself drift between wakefulness and oblivion like he were going up different levels of a spacescraper in an express left. He couldn't bring himself to care which state he was in from one moment to the next.

And that was how they found him when his door was opened, the light was turned on and in walked Hugo with two large Red Star foot soldiers.

"It's time," Hugo said.

Any regenerated hope fled when the two men came forward carrying binders and a vapour mask. Webb cursed and tried to scramble away but he was weakened from injury and the forced inactivity and they subdued him easily. He could not stop crying out as they manhandled the broken wrist into the binders and pulled on his wounded shoulder. They fitted the vapour mask over his nose and mouth and fastened it on cruelly tight.

Webb swore and struggled but then one of them flicked a release on the side of the mask and Webb's nose and mouth filled with a cool, dizzying smell. He coughed then swayed, his vision swimming. When he came back to himself, a scarf had been wrapped round his neck and a coat had been flung over his shoulders and fastened at the front, hiding his bound arms. Hugo was stood by watching.

"It has five doses in it," one of the soldiers said to Hugo, gesturing at the mask. "Just flick the release if he tries anything. The dose will build up in his system so you can knock him right out if you need to."

Hugo nodded and came forward. Webb tried to speak but the mask muffled his speech and his tongue felt swollen and wouldn't obey. His head spun. Hugo had to lift him from the bunk and then march him from the room.

"Coale says this is on you, Hugo," one of the men muttered as they marched. "He disrupts anything, Coale will take it out of both of your necks."

"I understand," Hugo responded in a monotone. He reached up and pulled Webb's hood up over his head and then pulled up his own and put on a visor to cover his eyes. Then they were joining a stream of foot traffic flooding through a wide, rough-honed passage.

Webb blinked about him, vision and head still swirling. It could have been the drugs or it could have been the light, but to Webb all the Red Star foot soldiers looked the same. They were all in black, all had close-cut hair, marched at the same speed and all had the same set, confident expression with an edge of fierce joy. Many of them had their hoods up and visors on so they looked like an army of mass-produced robots. Or clones.

He shuddered inside.

Far ahead, he spotted the yellow-haired head of Christof Coale above all the others. He was surrounded by a cluster of foot soldiers vying for his attention. He spoke with all of them, patting shoulders and smiling his shark-like smile. He hadn't donned a hood or visor and his reddish eyes glowed.

Just as Webb's head started to clear, the traffic slowed and then stopped, queuing for hole cut in the rock, beyond which he could make out stairs, up which the crowd was swarming. He opened his mouth to try and speak again, but still couldn't make himself sound clear through the mask.

"Quiet," Hugo commanded as they edged forward.

Webb was trying to pull together enough focus to form a plan when the crowd parted and Coale's tall form headed straight toward them.

"Over here," the man said in a low voice and wove his way out of the flow of people. Hugo dragged Webb along to join him.

"He's secure?" Coale asked, eyeing Webb like a grenade with the pin pulled out.

"Yes, sir," Hugo responded.

Coale leaned forward, lifting Webb's hood to look into his face then dropped it again. "Well the mask should stop anyone from recognising him. This is not the time to make this move."

"We're not making any moves, sir," Hugo continued. "No one will see him. This is just to show him as you showed me."

Coale's eyes narrowed a fraction, looking hard into Hugo's face. "I'm trusting you here, Hugo. You'd better not let me down."

"I'm honoured to have your trust, sir," Hugo intoned. Coale's look lingered a moment long enough to suggest he wasn't convinced.

"That's good." Coale put his hand on Hugo's shoulder and squeezed. "You know I don't tolerate failure."

"No, sir," Hugo said. His voice remained steady but his lips had gone white. Coale's hand lingered on his shoulder a moment longer, then his gaze swung Webb's way so he didn't see Hugo start to shake.

"Listen and watch, Errol McCullough," Coale said, looking him right in the eye. "This is your future, one way or another."

Webb scowled but then someone further up the crowd called Coale's name and he disappeared back into the throng. Hugo's hand had stopped trembling on Webb's elbow but his grip was uncomfortably tight. Webb jostled him and he blinked and appeared to come back to himself. Webb gave him a questioning look but Hugo didn't look at him before pulling him back toward the stairs.

The stairs were darker than the cavern they left behind. Clouds of fog drifted past them and the sound of dozens of people in boots climbing in the confined space sounded like a waterfall in Webb's ears. He blinked in the sudden light as they passed through an opening into a small pre-fab room with crates and barrels against the wall and then through another, heavier door into a wide, open room. The benches had been all pushed against the wall and all the lights were on full but Webb recognised it as the *House of Remus*.

His mind continued to reel as Hugo marched them with the crowds out into the foundation levels of the city. Crowds of constructors had gathered to watch them pass, large numbers following them to the crossroads. The press of people got bigger and bigger as more and more constructors and labourers, men, women and children joined their march. They cheered and called and waved red flags.

The general chatter amongst the civilians was like a dull hum in the thick air, but quiet had fallen along the column of Red Star foot soldiers. They reached a groundway. All the vehicles pulled over to let them pass. The way tilted up and they moved up towards thin, yellow daylight.

Webb looked around but the solid press of people revealed no chances to run for it. He tried pulling at Hugo's hold anyway, resulting in the man tightening his grip and pulling him in closer. Webb swore to himself, the curses gaining colour and flavour as the stun vapour faded out of his system. His muscles were stiff with frustration, his insides rolling with adrenaline.

It took over two hours for the Red Star contingent to march to Appollos Square. Webb was panting with the strain to his healing body, his limbs shaking. Hugo hadn't even broken a sweat. Nor had he so much as looked at his former crewmate once. The square was already half-full with Red Star soldiers and chattering, excited civilians. Everyone made room for the foot soldiers to file down to the front directly before the main entrance of the New Civic Hall. All the hall's windows and doors were flung open and black banners, each adorned with a single red star, hung from the roof. A lectern was set at the top of the entrance stairs and ranks of soldiers lined the steps, faceless in visors and hoods, standing to rigid attention. Webb could see Coale behind the lectern, taller by half a head than all those gathered around him, his blonde hair standing out against the sea of black. Webb could read the grim satisfaction on his face even from this distance.

Hugo wrestled them forward through the tighter and tighter press of people.

"I can see just fine from here," Webb grumbled as Hugo dragged him toward the stairs, but Hugo didn't respond. They took up position behind Coale's left shoulder. The fair-haired man looked back at them, gave Hugo a narrow glance, loaded with warning, then turned back to face the front.

As he took in the square, now a solid mass of black jackets and eyeless, visored faces, a shudder went up Webb's spine. Civilians pressed in around the edges and had taken up position at the windows and on the roofs of all the surrounding buildings. Children had climbed up onto the bases of the statues. The nearby groundways were crowded, vehicles gridlocked and abandoned as their owners strained against the rails to try and see. The noise of thousands of people talking in the weakly-pressured air was like a powerful engine deep in the belly of a monstrous ship.

Red Star, by contrast, were lined up in silent rows, shoulder to shoulder. Their set faces were all turned up toward the lectern. Every public information display in view was showing a red star on a black background and the local time with minutes ticking toward midday.

Webb blinked to try and clear his head, knowing it was no longer the drug that was making him dizzy.

Hugo stood still as the statues with his face turned toward the crowd. Webb glanced up into the yellow sky, knowing there was a Service fleet orbiting out of sight, but it felt like they might as well be a million miles away for any chance he had of reaching them.

Midday flashed up on the surrounding displays and all noise fell away into an expectant hush. A small group of people came out of the open hall doors behind him. The trim figure of Arcadius Rose was at the head of the party. His bronze hair, neatly combed back, shone in the washed-out sunlight. Red Star soldiers parted to let him pass. Those accompanying him took up position with the other soldiers and the man walked up to the lectern alone. A roar of applause surged through the still air as he stepped up to the podium. The only people who weren't clapping or shouting were the soldiers standing motionless on all around him.

Rose waved and the noise swelled.

"My friends," he said, voice warm, friendly, like it had been when he addressed the guests at the ball that to Webb already felt like a lifetime ago. "My comrades. My people."

More roaring. Webb looked around, praying that some of the soldiers around him might be distracted, but they were all rigid and watchful.

"I can't tell you what the sight of you gathered here today does to my heart," Rose continued, voice ringing around the square through speakers. "It both warms and stills it with pride and joy. We have come so far together and I'm privileged to be the person you continue look to usher us along our path. Especially now we have finally struck our first blow and announced to the whole Orbit that the time for change is here."

Roses's well-formed, passionate and persuasive statements continued. Webb's shoulder and wrist pulsed from restriction of the binders. His head pounded. He grew weak, weak with hunger, weak with the drugs in his system, the pain of his battered body and the feeling of being so utterly lost and alone he wasn't even sure how to think. Everyone around him was united, driven and uniform in purpose and desire. He felt like he stood at the top of a precipice, watching water crash past him and plunge down somewhere dark, taking his resistance with it.

Webb looked at his boots as Rose's words rang in his ears, momentarily overwhelmed by a recollection he knew wasn't his but saw so clearly it was like it was tattooed into his memory. He was a child. He was hungry and tired and cold. He'd reached an age at which he had a vague understanding of what was about to happen, but still thought anything was worth not having to spend another day hungry.

He'd let them take him off the street to someone's apartment. He remembered taking a deep breath and stepping into a room where a tall man was waiting for him. A man with a fine suit and cruel, strong hands but with credit. Lots of it. A man called Vincent Marlowe who had cut-glass eyes that sliced through his skin as surely as a scalpel.

Webb had stepped through that doorway and into another world, one that he had previously never known existed but from which he would never be able to escape.

He felt like that again now. Being here at this moment amongst these people, listening to another man in a fine suit make different but just as weighty promises, he was in a new world he never dreamed could be real, but now that he'd stepped into the surging tide, no matter where he ran, he'd still be caught in the flow.

The thoughts melted into a dull fog. He stared at the steps under his boots, vision blurring. Rose's voice, punctuated by occasional cheers, talked on.

It was only when movement out of the corner of his eye caught his attention that he was able to drag his focus back from the shadows inside his mind. He glanced down the steps to where some civilians had crowded and noticed one had elbowed her way right to the front and was staring up at him. She wore a helmet with the visor up, dark blue eyes fixed on him and on Hugo at his side. When she saw that he'd seen her she smiled, showing a silver incisor, then let her gaze slide away to Rose.

Webb jolted, looked around to see if anyone had noticed her, but everyone else was fixated on the governor. When he looked back, Osgard was still looking away. It was only when he looked at her hands, held out of sight down by her thigh, that he saw she was talking in Haven finger-speech.

Get down here. Bring Hugo.

Webb stiffened, looked around, but still no one looked her way. Again, Osgard signed. *Get Hugo and get down here. I'll take care of the rest.*

Webb pulled at his binders and shrugged at her, trying to make her understand.

Do something. We're running out of time, she signed, giving him an earnest look.

A surge of applause louder than any so far filled the air. Even the honour-guard around him took a step forward to applaud their leader. Hugo's hold on him wavered as they were jostled forward. Webb didn't think but flung himself sideways, breaking Hugo's grip and running. The noise and excitement were enough to give him a few seconds before anyone had realised what had happened, but Hugo was already after him. He reached the bottom of the stairs just as soldiers turned to see what the commotion was. Hugo grabbed him from behind, slammed him against the wall and was smacking his face to activate the mask. Webb's head pulsed and his knees buckled. The nearest Red Star soldiers started hurrying toward them.

A blast erupted somewhere nearby that Webb felt rather than heard. Hugo staggered. They tangled together, falling to the ground as people around them dropped to their knees or crumpled to the floor, covering bleeding ears.

A helmeted head leaned over him, then Osgard had a strong grip was on his collar and was hauling him to his feet.

"Run," she said right in his ear, the word deadened by the ringing from her stun grenade, but he didn't need to be told twice. He got his legs under him and ran. He was deaf and almost blind but something had burst inside him and he didn't stop.

He was brought up short by someone grabbing him and yanking off the jacket. He blinked as his vision began to steady and then the vapour mask was ripped off his face. He took a deep breath and staggered as oxygen flooded his addled system. There was a click and the binders fell away. He yelped as the tensed and damaged muscles and bones were released and then something cold and metal was being pressed into his good hand.

"Take this," Osgard's voice in his ear again. "Keep running."

He obeyed, senses gradually returning. He was pelting down the side of the square, Osgard at his side, skirting the stunned crowds. The reporter was pulling along a dazed-looking Hugo who was staggering and fumbling for his gun. His visor had fallen off and his eyes were wide and crazed. Behind them was the noise of Red Star regaining their senses and starting pursuit. Bullets whizzed through the air around them.

Webb called a warning just as Hugo managed to pull his gun but Osgard was already moving, pulling her own and firing. Hugo yelled, a terrible, strangled sound of a man still partially deaf crying out into the thick air. He dropped his gun and blood gushed from his hand.

"There," Osgard shouted, pointing to a flyer pulled up ahead, its cockpit open and the console inside already alight and active.

Hugo momentarily rallied, halting and pulling back on Osgard who staggered.

Webb dashed over, transferring his gun to his weak hand, gritting his teeth as the muscles tried to grip over the broken bones, and grabbed Hugo's sleeve in his good hand. The last effects of the stun grenade combined with the pain from his wound meant Hugo was no match for both Webb and Osgard as they both laid hands on him and heaved him to the flyer, dumping him in the back seat. Osgard climbed into the pilot seat and Webb scrambled in next to her, just as the fastest of the recovered Red Star troops caught up to them. There was a barked order from somewhere behind to stop shooting. The men made a grab for them but Osgard fired the flyer's engines and they rocketed upwards before the cockpit even closed, leaving injured and yelling soldiers below them.

Osgard swung the stick over, ending their climb and turning them away from the square. Webb swallowed rising bile, seeing the square and the crowds drop away into a blur of black uniforms. Rose was still on the podium, watching them zoom away and fading to a smudge against the white of the New Civic Hall steps.

"Here, put these on him, quick," Osgard ordered and dumped Webb's binders and vapour mask in his lap. "Stroke of luck you had them."

"I didn't *have* them. They - "

"Quick," Osgard snapped as Hugo groaned and shifted.

Webb clambered into the back, making a grab for Hugo's wrists. The man struck out but was still half-dazed and the punch lacked power. Webb gritted his teeth and forced first one wrist and then another into the binders. Hugo growled and struggled. His right hand was limp and slick with blood. Webb wrestled the vapour mask over his face and activated it. Hugo took a deep breath, eyes widening and then he slumped down, eyes fluttering and closing.

"You shot him," Webb said. He turned Hugo's hand over, saw a ragged wound through the palm, blood gushing and bone jutting. Webb flinched and pulled off his scarf, wrapping it tightly around the hand.

"What was I supposed to do?" Osgard asked matter-of-factly.

"He's no good to anyone dead," Webb growled, shifting Hugo to sit upright and propping up his bound hands against his chest, hoping to slow the bleeding. "Where are we going?"

"Harbour," Osgard said, steering them around the jutting spines of spacescraper scaffolds. "We need to get him off this rock as quickly as possible."

"How did you know we were going to be there?"

"I didn't," Osgard said, checking her instruments and increasing their speed. "I thought you were dead."

"What?"

"In the explosions at the Commemorative Ball. That's what was being said."

"What's been happening?"

"What happened to *you*?" Osgard shot back, looking at him in the rear-view display. "I left you at *House of Remus* and never saw you again. We were supposed to be working together. Where the hell have you been?"

Webb rubbed his eyes, thoughts sluicing around his head like oil draining down a pipe. "I heard their plans for the assassination and went to try and stop the general attending the ball."

"Good job on that."

"I tried my best," Webb protested. "The man is…was…as stubborn as an ox." Webb's throat tightened. "I chased down Hugo after he'd taken the shot."

It took a second for Osgard to process that. "Wait, what? *Hugo* shot the general?"

Webb nodded, glancing at his former captain. Hugo's head was lolling on one side. With his eyes shut and the lines of stress and pain etched deep in his forehead, he looked all at once a lot older and younger then he truly was.

"I heard rumours," Osgard went on, shaking her glance and shooting Hugo looks in the rear-view. "But I didn't believe them. I didn't think even he could…" She shook her head again then straightened herself. "So you went after him and they got you?"

Webb nodded again, closing his eyes.

"Where have you been?"

"There are caves under the city. Miles of them. And they're full of Red Star soldiers and supplies."

"Yes," Osgard gritted. "Seems even *I* underestimated their numbers."

"It's insane," Webb said faintly, shaking his head and remembering the ocean of black coats and the thunder of countless marching boots. "There's…so many of them."

"The Service will soon fix that."

Webb shuddered again. "You didn't know I was going to be at the rally?"

"No. I had the flyer ready in case they brought Hugo with them, though I didn't know how I'd get to him even if they did. I just hoped a solution would present itself. And then there you were. Would take more than a mask and a hood to hide you from me, Captain."

"Where did you get the flyer?"

"I borrowed it. Relax, Webb. It's all over. I'll get you out of here." She arced the flyer's course downwards. "My ship will get us out of the city to up the fleet."

Webb looked at the hunched and frail-seeming form of Hugo. His dark eyelashes rested on the bruised hollows of his eye sockets and the burn scars across his temples now pulsed red against the pain-paled skin.

The flyer dipped as Osgard descended into a familiar harbour. The few customs officials who were left to guard the gate had black visors turned their way and were pointing.

"We need to be quick," Osgard said as she applied the air-brakes. "Can you lift him?"

"Yeah," Webb said, heart speeding up. "I think so."

She hit the cockpit release and the roof slid back. She was out before he'd managed to get his arm under Hugo.

"Come on," she snapped, reaching in to help Webb manhandle

Hugo's prone form out of the flyer.

"That's mine," Osgard said as they dragged Hugo along, nodding towards a sleek space yacht two berths down. "I've opened the starboard hatch already…"

Webb hoisted Hugo higher up onto his good shoulder and increased his pace. His pulse thundered in his throat. They were going to make it.

"Shit," Webb froze.

Osgard swore, tugging at Hugo from the other side. "Webb, come on. They're coming."

"*Job*," Webb said, staring at his ship still in its berth across from Osgard's yacht. "She's still here."

Osgard's face flattened. "Leave it. We don't have time."

Webb looked over at the fierce look on her face and the possessive grip she had of Hugo.

"*Job*'s faster," he said. "And I can get her into Sydney HQ, no messing."

"You're not taking him to HQ," Osgard snapped, throwing a glance over her shoulder at the approaching guards, who were now drawing weapons. "Dad's waiting in orbit for him."

Webb's grip on Hugo tightened. "I'm taking him back to the special commander."

"No," Osgard growled, trying to wrestle Hugo out of Webb's hold. "He's being taken back to Command. He needs to be interrogated - "

Webb felt a rush go through him. He wrenched Hugo from Osgard's grip. Hugo twitched and got his feet under him.

"Hugo, run," Webb hissed in the other man's ear and ripped off the vapour mask. There was a mumbled reply and Hugo's eyes flickered open and then they were running. Hugo staggered then straightened, shambling with him so as not to fall. Osgard cursed and ran after them.

Webb sweated and strained. Every inch of his body screamed in protest. Hugo was keeping pace but clumsily. The gate guards were almost on them and Osgard was forced to abandon her chase to make for her own ship before they caught up. Bullets were flying by the time Webb was forcing Hugo up *Job*'s boarding ladder.

"Climb, Hugo, damn you."

Hugo clambered awkwardly with his bound and injured hands. Webb scrambled up next to him, slamming the hatch release as a shot buried itself in the hull inches from his head. He shoved Hugo through the hatch before it was fully open, scrambled in after him and slammed the hatch lock. Heart pounding, he stepped over the dazed Hugo and ran for the command deck.

He skidded to a halt on the threshold, staring at Vergennes who'd risen from the workstation, eyes wide. Webb drew the gun he still had from Osgard, levelling it with the younger man's face.

"Get back," he ordered.

Vergennes eyes widened further but he didn't move.

"I said get *back*," Webb barked, taking a step closer.

Vergennes rose his hands and stepped away from the controls. There was the sound of more shots thudding into the hull and the hail lights on the command panel were all flashing, but Webb ignored them, advancing on Vergennes.

"I thought you were dead," Vergennes said, still staring at him.

"Liar," Webb hissed, reaching out and relieving the younger man of his own weapon. He tucked it into his waistband clumsily with his bad hand then gestured at the access corridor. "Go lock yourself in your cabin. Now. Or I swear to God, I will ventilate you."

Vergennes must have read the certainty in Webb's face because he disappeared toward the cabins without another word. Webb sat at the control panel, saw by the readings that Vergennes was indeed in the crew cabin, then activated a ship-wide lock. Then he cursed as he attempted to fire the engines and get everything online with one hand.

Job lifted from its berth just as Osgard's yacht lifted into the air almost directly ahead. Webb powered the engines to full and they blasted away from the dock. The ship's alarms blared from the heat of the blowback of firing up to full so close to the ground. The hull held, however, and the ship zipped right over Osgard's yacht and out towards the sky.

The hail lights faded away to leave just one blinking on a short-range frequency. He opened the channel.

"I'm sorry, Vee," he said, cutting across the stream of curses spouting from the comm. "But I have my own orders."

"I saved your skin, damn you," she barked.

"I know. I'm sorry."

"Webb, you ten-levelled idiot. My father needs what he knows. And what you know too."

"I can't hand him over."

"You ignorant waster," she cursed again. "You have no idea - "

Webb cut the channel. He watched the grids, spires and scaffolds of Schiaparelli City fall away until they dissolved into nothing more than lines and shapes in his scopes. He gritted his teeth as his readings showed Osgard's yacht gaining and then there was a flash as she fired her guns across *Job*'s stern.

He cursed as the ship shuddered. She was going for his engines. The yellow sky faded to black around him and stars came into view. Just as he made out the bullet-shaped form of Service flagship *Perseverance* dead ahead, he was steering desperately to port as a wall of Service fighters bore down on him.

"Dammit, Osgard," he cursed, opening the channel again. "Tell them to back off if you don't want our intel splattered through drift with our brains."

"They're not under my command, Webb," came Osgard's cold response. "Dad will see you both blasted to pieces before he lets you take the traitor back to his traitor mother."

Webb swore and put aside everything apart from trying to dodge the fighters' fire. The throb of his protesting wrist faded into the back of his awareness as his piloting instincts took control. The interior lights dimmed as he redirected all available power to the engines and the ship lurched forward. The fighters were good, all Service pilots were good, but Webb knew their style too well to let them land more than a token blow once he fell into the rhythm of battle. They came within his targeting scopes again and again but he couldn't bring himself to fire, wondering which amongst them he'd had drinks with at HQ or attended training exercises with.

His entire command panel flashed red as the Perseverance's weaponry locked on.

"Jesus, Mary and Joseph," Webb breathed, slamming his palm down on the acceleration controls as he pulled the ship into neck-breaking nose-dive. He could almost feel the laser-cannon blast's burn as it skimmed past his bow.

"Come on, come on," he muttered, trying to stay on top of analysing the patterns of the pursuing fighters and the angle of the flagship's cannons and coax yet more speed from the sloop.

It felt like it had taken half his life, but he finally was gaining precious distance. Laser fire faded as he slipped out of range. The ships all fell back. Webb let himself breathe again, but knew he couldn't relax yet. Even now, Admiral Osgard would be putting the call through to his units in the Orbit to intercept him.

He kept the ship's speed up and racked his brain for what to do.

"Fuck this radio silence," he muttered and slammed numbers into the comm. It buzzed and flashed, flickering to try and make the long-distance connection but eventually the lights turned green and a voice came from the speaker.

"Sydney HQ receiving. Please identify."

"Put me through to the Special Commander," Webb said, voice strained. "Red-level urgency."

"Please identify yourself."

"Fuck that, just put me through."

"Please identify yourself, long-range vessel."

"I've got the seal, damn you!" Webb said, sending it via a ping.

"Put me through!"

There was a long silence. He took his eye off the heading long enough see some warning codes scrolling across the comm display, swore again and cut the connection. He paused then typed in a different comm number. He swiped stinging sweat out of his eyes and watched the connecting light blink on the comm.

"Long range vessel, please identify yourself."

"Damn is that you again? Where's Analyst Rami? This is her private comm!"

"Long range vessel…"

The warning codes indicating another digital probing of his systems reappeared and he again cut the call. He scrubbed his good hand over his face and made himself take one long breath. But when he opened his eyes he was still barreling full-speed on a nowhere-heading in deep space with a Service fleet right behind him and God knew how many ahead and nothing but the blackness of vacuum on either side.

He clenched and unclenched his good hand then programmed in the only course he could, though it almost physically hurt to do so.

The scraping noise of a boot on the deck behind him was all the warning he got. He turned just in time so that Hugo's swing grazed his shoulder rather than pounding into his temple like it was meant to. He scrambling away, swearing, as Hugo lunged again. The older man's face was a twisted mask of outrage and anger, the kind of anger that's brutal enough to drive you without you even knowing why.

Webb tried to yell at him to stop but the man didn't give him time to draw breath. He was still unsteady, but that just served to make his attack more frenzied and unpredictable. Webb batted another strike at his head away but Hugo countered with an elbow into his belly. Webb staggered, pulling his gun, but Hugo sent it flying with a back-hander.

Webb ducked and managed to get a firm enough footing to

kick out Hugo's legs. The other man went down but seized Webb as he fell and they tangled together on the deck.

Hugo was stronger and Webb, especially in his current state, but Hugo's drug-induced unsteadiness meant Webb was able to roll the other man under him. He wrestled his forearm in the wrist brace across the other man's neck and pressed all his weight into it.

Hugo growled and thrashed but gradually he stilled and his eyes widened and he scrabbled at Webb's arm.

"I'll let you up if you calm the hell down."

Hugo stared at him, red-eyed and wild, but stilled. Webb eased back. He should have known that would be all Hugo would need. The older man hurled himself up, flattened Webb and grabbed fistfuls of his shirt, slamming him into the deck over and over.

"Take me back," he yelled, almost screaming. "Take me back now!"

"Like hell," Webb shouted as he tried to wrest Hugo's hands off him.

Hugo howled, a terrifying sound, purely animal and packed with despair. Webb took advantage of the opening and scrambled away. He grabbed the gun from the deck and stood panting over Hugo. The other man was slumped on the deck, breathing heavily, arms over his head, rocking back and forth.

"Get up, Hugo. I don't want to hurt you, but God help me my patience has been ground wafer fucking thin."

Hugo didn't move. He was making a choking sound. Webb hesitated, then shoved the gun in his waistband and limped forward to crouch next to him.

"Hey, Hugo," he said, trying to look into his face. "It's ok. I'm taking you home."

"I don't belong there," Hugo said, voice flat and dead. He raised his head. His face was strained, his mouth a thin line. His eyes were red-rimmed and sore-looking. Whilst Webb was searching for words, Hugo lunged for the ship's console. Webb lurched after him, grabbed him by his jacket and wrenched him back. Hugo made angry, sorrowful, wordless noises and struggled but was now so exhausted Webb was able to take control. Getting a firmer grip, he succeeded in dragging Hugo all the way to the cabins.

"I'm sorry about this, Hugo. I really am."

Webb typed his override code into the door lock and it hissed open. Vergennes stood from one of the crew bunks, the fine lines of his face deepened by bewilderment, but Webb didn't give him time to speak. He bundled Hugo in and locked the door. The metal cut off the sounds of Hugo's shouts and Webb collapsed against the bulkhead, chest heaving, body shaking.

He only got three paces back toward the command deck before dizziness swirled through his head, black dots danced in his vision and pain like thunder rolled up his body and burst through his head. He staggered, fell to his knees and didn't even have time to make noise before it all went dark.

Δ

Usually it took Webb a few minutes on waking from a blackout to figure out where he was. This time, even before he opened his eyes, everything rushed back like a tidal wave. He felt the bullet go through his shoulder again. He felt teeth crunch out of his mouth as Hugo's fist connected. He smelt the cold, coppery air of the caves and heard Hugo's desperate howls echoing in his ears.

He opened his eyes to the dimmed lights of his cabin, knowing exactly where he was and what he'd done, but under the dull ache of his battered body and the throbbing of the fading headache, he only knew a great, swallowing greyness.

It was then he registered that he hadn't blacked out in his cabin, and yet now was on his bunk. His boots were on the deck and his wrist brace had been adjusted so it gripped his arm tighter. He sat up, rubbing at his face to try and chase away the lingering bleariness. The chrono told him he'd been out for a couple of hours. He pulled himself upright, groaning. Everything hurt. He pushed it all aside with an effort and stumbled to his cabin display and punched in commands with his left hand.

Their course was still as he'd programmed. He frowned, strapped on a wristpanel from the locker and padded barefoot as quickly as his messed up body could manage up to the command deck. Vergennes rose from the pilot chair as he stepped through the hatch. Webb fumbled for the gun that was no longer in his waistband.

"Get back from there," Webb growled, hurrying forward.

Vergennes stepped back and Webb pushed past him and dropped into the chair.

"I haven't changed anything," Vergennes said. His face was calm, his voice level. "I couldn't even if I wanted to. Your ship-wide lock is still on. But, sir, why are we heading to Lunar 1?"

"It's the only damn place we can go where we stand a chance of not being shot out of the sky on sight," Webb muttered, checking all the readings to make sure they were all still locked before turning on the younger man. "How did you get out of the cabin?"

"The door lock was easier to hack than the controls."

"When I put you in there, you were to damn well stay in there."

"You didn't look well, sir," Vergennes said mildly. "And I heard you collapse. I thought it best I check on you and the ship."

"What in the name of seven hells were you still doing on Mars anyway?"

"Gathering as much intelligence as I could, sir. After the shooting at the Civic Hall, the remaining Servicemen were forced out or made prisoners of war. I saw myself as the only one still available to keep track of operations on the ground."

"Yeah, you're a real patriot," he snarled. "Where's Hugo?"

"He's still in the cabin, sir," Vergennes replied, confusion clear in his eyes. "I dressed his hand and gave him a sedative. He's sleeping."

Webb stood, trying not to lean too heavily on the chair. "Get back in there. I won't have you wandering round my ship."

Vergennes's brow creased further. "I don't understand, sir. I thought you were dead. Where have you been? What's happened?"

"You've been spying on me, that's what's happened."

Vergennes's face flattened. "Sir?"

"Don't play dumb. I know everything. In fact, hand over your wristpanel and any other comm links you have," Webb ordered holding out his hand.

Vergennes didn't move. "I've not been spying on you, sir."

"Bullshit. Mac told me everything."

Vergennes's blue eyes widened a fraction. "Governor McCullough? You've spoken to him? When?"

"On Mars, dumbass," Webb growled, coming forward and grabbing at Vergennes's arm. The man was limp as Webb pulled off his wristpanel. "Who do you think's the ringmaster of that psycho-circus?"

"No," Vergennes breathed, not reacting to Webb searching his pockets and belt for any more comm links or weapons. "No, that can't be."

"Can't it?"

Colour rode high Vergennes's cheeks. "Duran McCullough is a great man. A peaceful man. He wouldn't - "

"Wake the fuck up. Red Star is *him*. The asshole wants to take over the universe. Again. And he doesn't give a rat's ass if he blows half of it up in the process."

"No," Vergennes said again, voice firmer. "You're wrong."

"Vergennes, he told me."

"I don't understand…"

Webb narrowed his look. "You really didn't know? All your little cosy chats about me and he never once told you about Red Star?"

Vergennes's face was tight. He didn't speak.

"They have a nice little war nest in the caves under the city.

Mac was there. He told me everything."

Vergennes put out a hand and steadied himself on the co-pilot chair.

"Sucks being lied to, huh?"

"Sir," Vergennes said. "I never meant to - "

"Then what did you mean to do, Lieutenant? You were slipping confidential information to a terrorist."

"No," Vergennes protested. "No, sir. I wasn't providing any information on the Service. He knew I would never do that and he never asked me to. It was just you he was interested in. He just wanted to know you were safe."

"What a load of crap. He could have got me on the comm any time himself."

Vergennes shook his head. "After he left you on Haven, he was a fugitive. He couldn't risk - "

"So you were ok communicating with this fugitive then? Pretty slippery moral compass you've got there, Vergennes. What exactly did you think you were doing?"

"I was honouring a friend," Vergennes said, straightening his back.

"A *friend*?"

"That man saved me. And not just my life. He helped me understand how meaningful it is to serve something greater than yourself."

"He shafted you, my friend. Just like me. He used us both."

"That's not true. He loves you, sir."

Webb let out a laugh with no trace of humour. "I'd like to see how he treats someone he hates."

"It's true, sir. You're his son. He would do anything to protect you." His face tightened, his eyes sharpening. "The fact that he never wavers, despite you constantly demonstrating yourself not worthy of his consideration only makes me admire him more."

Webb sneered. "I'm not good enough to be his son, huh? And, what? You are?"

Vergennes eyes, usually so calm, flashed blue fire. "I honour and respect him. I know him well and he knows me. He knows I would obey him without question. He relies on me in a way he never could rely on you."

"Blaise, get your head out of your ass. The man's a *genocidal maniac.*"

Vergennes drew himself up. "McCullough believed in something great. But it cost him too dearly. I know would never contemplate inciting revolution again, not after last time."

"Jesus, pal, he sure pulled one over on you. But then, he's had a lot of practice."

"I don't believe you," Vergennes said again, a detectible shake in his voice.

"Have you not seen that human wreckage in the cabin?" Webb said with an angry gesture toward the access corridor. "That was part of his plans. He broke Hugo to the point where he shot his own dad, and was happy to do it."

"I can't believe this, sir. Duran McCullough is a peaceful man. He's my saviour. I would die for him."

"Yeah, well that might happen sooner than you think since the war of his dreams should be breaking out any day now."

Vergennes shook his head again. "It can't be - "

"Wake up and smell the bloodgrease, Vergennes. The man's got enough red cement stuffed in those caves to blow the Earth out of orbit."

Vergennes went pale.

"*Now* you get it. Now get the hell out of my sight."

"Sir - "

"Stow it," Webb glared. "All I care about now is getting Hugo home. What's left of him, anyway."

Vergennes winced, glancing back toward the cabins.

"Oh, more good news. Vee Osgard and her damn father are on the hunt for him too and they've got the whole Service out after our asses. That's on top of Red Star out for our blood too. The entire Orbit is queuing up to blast us into drift and you and your shitfuckery is right up at the top of the list I don't have time for."

"Sir - "

"Consider yourself under arrest. Get yourself to the cabin and stay there."

Vergennes clenched his fists. His face had gone still. "Sir, I don't think - "

"Vergennes," Webb cut in, voice low. "If you're not off this command deck in the next five seconds, no amount of practice with the fight stick will prepare you for what I'll do."

Vergennes paused, body stiff and face aflame. Then he turned on his heel and marched off. Webb waited until the ship's scanners showed the lieutenant entering the crew cabin again then reactivated the door lock, taking a moment to overlay three different overrides.

"Try hacking through that one, you stiff-necked son of a bitch."

He lowered himself again into the pilot's chair, all his energy fleeing with his anger. He checked over the controls but Vergennes had been telling the truth. His course was still laid in and everything was locked. He spent some time going through various readings and scans, even though they were hours into space by then and nothing registered on either the short or long-range scopes. He should have been relieved but he didn't have enough resources left to feel anything.

Δ

The cycles seemed to crawl by, but when they were finally approaching the Lunar Strip, Webb felt it had gone all too quickly. He'd spent some of the time at the workstation, searching for news. No movement had been made on any side but the newsreels, wherever their sympathies lay, were unanimous in their prediction of untold violence to come.

Martian footage of Rose's speech at the rally was doing the

rounds on the vid sites. He noticed the commotion that he and Osgard had caused had been mostly edited out or covered up, though a few sites discussed the potential reasons behind the pause Rose made toward the end of his speech and some apparent disruption in the background. Nothing even hinted at his or Mac's involvement, Red Star hadn't yet shown their full hand, but more and more sources were picking up the rumour that Hugo had been the gunman in his own father's assassination.

Webb tried again to get messages through to HQ, but every time he attempted to connect anyone in the Service, digital probes were pinging back, searching his systems for his location or issuing him with orders to return to Command willingly or face further reprisals.

He cut off all the ship's comms and severed the connection to the solarnet to be safe, just as they entered Service-controlled space. The regular patrols were easy to dodge and *Job* was small and quick enough to slip away when he came within anyone's scan-range, but it didn't stop his skin constantly crawling with the feeling like he was a mouse trying to slip through a room full of sleeping cats.

He had been so preoccupied with getting through undetected, that when Lunar 1 appeared on his scopes it caught him by surprise. His palms dampened as he gazed at the colony hanging against the dark backdrop of space like a giant piece of debris. He found he still knew the patched hull and busy space lanes all too well.

When he got close enough for Harbour Control to contact him, he almost turned aside. But he drew a breath and re-activated the comm.

"Hey, Control," he said, keeping his voice light and thickening up his Lunar 1 accent. "Any chance of a quiet berth somewhere?"

"*Job*, your ship is on the inter-Orbit Offence registers," came the reply.

"Yeah, it's a funny story that…" .

"I'm sending out Security Skiffs. They'll escort you in. Co-operate and there won't be no trouble from us."

"See, thing is, Control," Webb said as he saw two small blips making straight for him on his scanners. "This is all just a big misunderstanding. The Service have their panties in a bind over nothing. I'm gonna sort it, I am, I just need somewhere to lay low while I get my shit together."

"Sorry, *Job*," the voice responded. "Rules is rules."

"Look, man," Webb said, having no trouble in letting a little desperation bleed into his voice. "I swear I ain't looking for trouble. Just let me land somewhere quiet, I won't be around long enough to put anyone's noses out of joint. I just need some breathing space. Come on, man. You've been here, ain't ya?"

"I hear ya, *Job*," the man replied. "But I got a boss too, you know."

"Look, I'm sure we can work something out," Webb said.

The pause that followed was long enough to make Webb wrestle between thinking it was working and thinking he'd just sealed his fate. Finally, the comm flickered to life.

"Well, *Job*, I could be convinced that you're just having a rough time right now. Lord knows you wouldn't be hitting this dump if you weren't desperate. I'll set you up with an unregulated private berth along the rim in Sector 3, ok?"

"Bless you, man," Webb said. "You've saved my ass."

"These unregulated berths aren't cheap, *Job*," the reply came with an edge.

"Hearing ya, Control," Webb said, keying in more commands. "Give me the numbers for the payment transfer and I can get that sorted right away."

As Webb transferred a handsome amount of credit to the account the control officer specified, the two approaching Security Skiffs, now in visual range, peeled off in another direction. Control transmitted the details of his berth and signed off.

"God bless Lunar 1," he muttered under his breath as he joined a space lane heading to Sector 3.

The berth was even worse than he expected - cramped, dirty and the lights didn't work. But the fact that it was just big enough to fit *Job* gave him reassurance that he wasn't going to be getting any nosey neighbours. He got up stiffly and went to the hold to arm himself from the weapons locker before returning to the locked crew cabin.

Vergennes stood up from his bunk when the door opened. Hugo was curled on the other with his back to the room.

"Come on," Webb ordered, gesturing with his gun. "We're leaving."

"Where are we going?" Vergennes asked.

"I don't know yet. Be we need to get away from this ship."

"We aren't secure?"

"From now on always assume we're not secure, Vergennes. Come on. And don't try anything funny."

A flicker of offence went over the young man's face but then he stepped out of the cabin as directed.

"Hugo," Webb said. "Get up. We're going."

Hugo didn't move.

Webb made an impatient noise and shook him by the shoulder. "Get up, already."

The man flinched and curled into a tighter ball. "You have no idea what you've done," he said in a voice so quiet Webb almost didn't hear him.

"We don't have time for this right now," Webb said, tugging at Hugo's jacket. "If I've been able to bribe Control to let us land, someone else will be able to bribe them to tell them where we are. We have to get into the colony."

Hugo remained unresponsive. He started to shudder.

"Hugo, get up now or I'll give you a bullet hole to match mine."

"Sir," Vergennes said, stepping up. "May I?"

"May you what?"

Vergennes nodded at Hugo. Webb stepped back with a skeptical look and the younger man knelt by the bunk.

"Vice-Admiral Hugo, sir?" he said softly but firmly. "It's time to go. We're in danger here."

Webb grumbled but Vergennes held up a hand. Webb flushed with anger but Vergennes cut off anything he was about to say by putting a hand on Hugo's shoulder.

"Sir, nothing's being asked of you right now. But you are very important to a lot of people. You need to be kept safe so we can make sure other people are also kept safe. Do you understand?"

"He's not a baby, Lieutenant," Webb snapped.

Vergennes gave him a cool look. "He's hurt, sir. He doesn't understand what's happening."

"He sure as hell does," Webb said, ignoring the stab of guilt that pierced him when Hugo flinched.

"Sir," Vergennes said, turning back to Hugo. "If we get you somewhere safe now, it will mean we can talk more about what's happening. I know you want to explain to Captain Webb what you need, don't you?"

Hugo very slowly sat up. Webb took in the look on his thin and bruised face and felt like he'd been punched in the gut. He'd recognise Hugo angry, determined, commanding or ready to kill. This look he didn't recognise. He looked scared. Lost.

"I'll make you understand," Hugo murmured, staring right at him, black eyes bottomless. "Then you'll take me back."

"Fine," Webb said, looking away. "But we need to get the hell out of here first."

Hugo stood sluggishly, like he was moving through zero-g. Vergennes stepped back to give him room. Webb suddenly felt wrong to be holding a gun on both of them, but pushed the feeling aside.

"Come on. You two go in front. And be quick."

VIII

Hugo put one foot in front of the other and followed the blonde Service officer because he knew it was all he could do right now. Webb was close behind him. He could feel his eyes on him as easily as he felt the presence of the gun in his belt that he kept his hand rested on, but he didn't look at either.

He followed the tall blonde man along a busy groundway. There were sights and smells of a colony around him. It smelt of people, exhaust, cooking food, oil and old air. The walkway was crowded with industrial workers and the buildings around them were tall and busy, with lights on in every level. Lifters, cranes, flyers and shuttles on rails crowded into the spaces between them. High above them, the hull of the colony curved over them like a sky made of metal. The track-lights were turned up to full for the day-cycle and he could see the huge sector numbers marked between them as well as areas of discolouration and patches of mismatched materials that told of hull-breach repairs. The shut-off layer in his mind told him this was a familiar place, but he cut off the thought before it formed and followed the blonde man as he turned another corner.

"Jesus," Webb muttered as they passed a site where a huge building was being torn down. Ragged children were darting in and out of the rubble, even as the machines were tearing down the walls, grabbing abandoned fixtures, broken panels and boxes of old ration bars, anything they could seize before it was destroyed. A couple of harried-looking Enforcers were attempting to chase them off with stunners and nightsticks.

Further on they passed a a group of five children, all on their knees in a line along the walkway, hands held up, begging for food or credit. Webb hurried past, even when the blonde man stopped to stare. Webb harried them on, muttering threats. Hugo could see there was a riot of emotion being contained behind the rigid mask of his face.

Hugo followed them, fog thick in his brain, telling himself he just had to wait. Wait for his chance.

Twice they stopped on an intersection and Webb looked around with a bewildered air. The blonde man asked him questions but Webb didn't answer. He closed his eyes once. Hugo considering running but before he could decide, the younger man had grabbed him and was dragging him along again.

They avoided clusters of dark-suited Enforcers that were gathered at most street corners. Some patrolled the groundways on two-wheelers. At one crossway, Hugo saw an Enforcer chase down and grab a girl in her early teens. There were screams and tears, she said she wouldn't go back. The noise went right through him, freezing him to the spot.

"I can't go back!"

The noise only silenced when she was shut in the back of a patrol flyer and carted off. Hugo's mind reeled through the same three thoughts: *I can't go back, but I have to go back, I need to go back.* They gave every step purpose.

He blinked when they stopped at a large metal gate, razor-wire and security orbs mounted on top. What he could see of the building beyond was solid, square and imposing. The few windows there were were barred. The walls were solid concrete and dotted with cameras. The only thing that told Hugo is was a church was the tall iron spire, set off to one side of the intimidating facade, and the white cross painted on the front of the building.

Webb stood, staring up at it. He was clutching something on a chain around his neck and looking uncertain. Hugo almost took the opportunity to slip away again but then Webb was pushing a buzzer in a comm unit set in the gate. After a moment there was an answer. Webb and the person on the comm spoke for several minutes. The grip he had on Hugo's wrist tightened and Hugo winced as it ground the bones against old bruises and pulled on the angry flesh of his injured palm.

Finally there was the sound of metal protesting and the gate lumbered open. Webb hustled them through. They passed through a deserted yard, dusty and cluttered. There was an ancient swing set and a slide with steps missing on their left. On their right was a bank of half-wrecked flyers and an ancient emergency generator. The building itself loomed above in a mass of grey concrete with wide stairs leading up to an armoured front door. It creaked open just as they reached it. A middle-aged man with greying hair was gesturing them in.

It was dim inside. Hugo got a hazy impression of the man's dark clothes, sleeves rolled back to reveal powerful, scarred forearms with an intricate crucifix tattooed onto the thick skin above a basic wristcomm. There were guns at his belt and knives strapped to his legs. Hugo took all this in before looking away when he caught sight of the man's green, green eyes. They threatened to bring the memory of someone else's green eyes to the surface and he skittered away from it as he would from touching an electric fence.

He gazed at the cracked tiles in the floor as they were hurried through chilly, dim hallways. There were turns and more heavy doors and then a large, vaulted space, dark as the caves. It smelt cold, of old incense and blown-out candles, then they were going down more steps and it was getting colder and darker. Hugo blinked, breathing quickening.

He registered that they'd stopped at a small room and were waiting for him to go in. The old priest reached inside and turned the light on, saying something, but the words meant nothing.

"Hugo," Webb's voice penetrated the fog in his mind. "Get in."

Hugo stared at the cell containing a cot, a corner water closet and a sink. No window and blank walls made of concrete blocks. His breathing sped up further and his blood pounded in his ears.

"Don't lock me in," he heard a voice, his own, murmur. "Please don't lock me in."

There was a sharp reply and then a moment's pause before he

took a step back, but hands took hold of him. He felt his chest burst with terror. He kicked and bit and punched but it was no use. Webb was injured but the stranger was strong and the tall blonde man stood behind them to block his escape. He was forced through the door, pressed to the bed and then someone was pulling one hand over his head and cold metal clasped against his wrist.

He heard the voices, the curses, heard the deadness of it in the enclosed space and then the slamming of the door. When he heard bolts snap home he arched his head back and screamed until he could taste blood.

Δ

"Sir, please. This really isn't necessary."

"Don't you start," Webb growled, holding another cell door open for Vergennes, but even he could hear the shakiness in his own voice. Hugo's screams, getting gradually hoarser, could still be heard and each one made Webb want to collapse into a heap on the cold floor and sob. But he didn't. He held the handle of the door of the next cell with a white-knuckled grip. "Get the hell in, Vergennes."

The younger man glanced back at Hugo's cell just as he screamed again, then looked back to him. Webb was damned if he couldn't see a flicker of sympathy in the younger man's look. It made his blood boil. Webb shoved Vergennes into the cell and slammed the door on his mild, accepting expression. He activated the locks himself and leant against the door, covering his face with his good hand.

"You look like you could use some rest yourself," the priest said.

Webb tried to respond, but Hugo's shouts were all he could focus on.

"I've got to get going, but there're a couple of spare cells on the next level down, if you need some peace," the man continued.

Webb nodded his gratitude. "Thank you, Father Marcus."

The priest shrugged, giving Hugo's cell a wary look. "You're in a hell of a hole here, son. I hope you're doing the right thing."

"Me too."

The priest's gaze lingered on him a moment longer. Webb searched desperately through his mind for any clear recollections of him. The man knew his voice on the comm and knew his name when he spoke it. But the only thing Webb remembered about him was the green of his eyes and the vague feeling of reassurance he projected. Webb prayed it wasn't misplaced.

"Alright, lad. I told you you'd always find safety here if you needed it and I meant it. I just hope you don't need it for too long. These aren't exactly ideal times to be hiding political runaways."

"I know. Thank you."

Marcus searched his face a moment longer but Webb couldn't tell what he was hoping to find. With one last wary glance towards Hugo's cell, he left him. Webb took a breath, rubbed his face again then straightened and made himself leave the cells behind.

He found his way down to the next level and stepped into the first empty cell he found. It was clean, empty apart from the basic furniture and blessedly silent. He collapsed on the cot, ignoring the shoots of pain that went through his injured shoulder and wrist and pulled the thin pillow over his head.

He didn't know it would have been at all possible to sleep with the volume in his head turned up to maximum and every inch of his body and soul feeling like it had been through a meat grinder, but none the less, Webb found himself slowly waking some hours later. His body was calmer, his breathing steadier. There was no longer screaming in his ears or flashing in his mind and no tell-tale throbbing ache that was the hangover of a blackout. He groped after any feeling whatsoever and shuddered inwardly to come back with only emptiness.

"Pull yourself together," he grumbled, words muffled against a soft, clean sheet. He heaved himself up and limped to the sink to splash some cold water on his face. He dared a look at his reflection in the looking glass. His chin-length hair stuck out in all directions, his skin was fish-belly pale and the bruises and cuts from his time in the caves were fading to a hideous array of purples and yellows. His lips were cracked and his eyes bloodshot. He looked worse than when he'd come round from overdosing on Haven. He shuddered at the memory and left the room

He kneaded his temples, knowing he had to face Hugo, but found it hard to make himself move. He spent a moment looking around and breathing in the still, quiet corridor. The smell of stone and cool air went some way to soothing his ragged nerves and he gathered himself and climbed the stairs.

All the doors were shut on the next level and it was quiet as a tomb. He was almost at Hugo's cell when the door opened and out walked another priest with a heavily lined face and bushy grey eyebrows. He was carrying a small case.

"What were you doing in there?" Webb snapped.

The man blinked at the sharpness of his response, then recovered and frowned darkly. "You the guy that brought him here?"

"I told Father Marcus he needs to be left alone."

"The man's a state. You all are," he said, with an up and down look at Webb's stooping posture, bruised face and filthy wrist brace. "And he was screaming the place down. I've patched him up and sedated him. Marcus may have agreed to your sanctuary, but we don't want to have to explain any Servicemen corpses to the patrols, thanks very much."

Webb leant against the wall, panic leaving him so suddenly he felt drained. "Sorry. Thanks. Is he sleeping?"

The man shook his head and hitched his case higher on shoulder. "Not right now."

"Thanks," Webb said again.

"Whatever. I gotta go. My street patrol starts soon."

Webb nodded and the man left, calling over his shoulder, "Kitchen's open all night. If you don't want your friends to be wandering about, you'll have to bring them food yourself. None of us have time to look after you."

He was gone before Webb could thank him again. He stood staring at the cell door, feeling the beat of his heart painfully hard against his ribs, then pulled back the bolt and went in.

Hugo was flat on the bunk, staring at the ceiling. Webb winced when he saw the bandages around the wrist and wondered how hard he'd struggled against the cuffs. The gunshot wound in his hand had been bound tight. The fingers were white and bloodless. His eyes were open, dark and blank. The greyness under his eyes was even more pronounced now that he was white from fatigue, the bruises and cuts on his face standing out like paint. His eyes and cheeks were sunken and he looked thinner than ever.

"Hugo?"

He didn't move or speak. He didn't even blink.

Webb took a step closer, pulling up a stool and sat down just out of reach. "Hugo, can you hear me?"

The other man took a deep breath. He finally blinked, then said something low and choked.

"What?"

Hugo took another breath then said again, "Please open the door."

"Not a chance, buddy," Webb said, trying to keep his voice light.

"I can't go anywhere," Hugo murmured, rattling his cuff against the cot's metal frame. "Please. Just open it a little. I can't breathe."

Webb frowned. Hugo was staring like a blind man. His jaw was tight. His fists were clenched. Webb got up and opened the door just a crack. Hugo closed his eyes, rigid body finally going limp.

Webb went back to his stool. "I don't get it. I locked you up on the ship and you didn't freak out."

"That was a ship," Hugo croaked. "Not a cave."

"We're not in a cave. We're in a church."

"We're…underground…"

"We're on a colony. There's no ground to be under."

"We're below street level...there's no windows...the walls are stone...I can't..."

Webb's mouth was dry. "What exactly did they do to you?"

Hugo didn't answer immediately. When he did, it was another creaking whisper that Webb had to get him to repeat.

"Let me go. Please let me go," he said.

"What, so you can pound on me some more? Or so you can run back to your revolutionary buddies?"

"You don't understand."

"Help me understand," Webb tried desperately, pulling his stool a little closer. "Hugo, what's going on with you? Are you in there at all?"

Hugo blinked his eyes open but didn't speak.

"Do you understand what you've done?"

Hugo's head lolled to the side and he finally looked at him. His eyes were heavy with pain. "I understand."

"You shot your dad, Hugo. He's dead. You killed him."

Hugo's eyes swam. He blinked, blearily. "You must let me go," he whispered.

Webb looked away, fists clenching and and fingernails digging into palms. He only spoke again when he felt he could trust his voice. "I'm taking you home, Hugo. I want you to want to come with me. But I'll drag you there kicking and screaming if I have to. There's no way I'm letting you go back to Mars."

Hugo sat up. He did it slowly and it was horrible watching the sluggish, halting movement of his drugged and battered body, whilst the deep, black eyes never shifted away from him.

"Webb," he breathed and for a split second, Webb saw his old friend looking back at him. "Please."

"*Why?*"

"I have a role."

"Fuck your *role*." The words came out harsh. "You left your family. You left your mom and your wife and kids. You left them all behind and now you killed your dad. For what?"

"If you take me back to Earth now," Hugo said. He was starting to tremble. "It will all have been for nothing."

Webb stared. Anger made the skin of his face hot. "What did they do to you, Hugo?"

Hugo didn't answer.

"They tortured you, right? How?"

Hugo shivered but still didn't speak.

"Well whatever they did, they did a fucking top-notch job," Webb growled. "You would've killed me, wouldn't you? If they hadn't stopped you, you would have killed me in the caves, right? Speak, dammit."

"I don't know what you want me to say."

"Anything," Webb said, jerking to his feet and knocking the stool over. The clattering made Hugo wince. "Say fucking *anything*. Give me a sign I've actually found you and not just your breathing corpse."

Hugo blinked at the wall past Webb's hip.

"Ok, you don't care about me, I can live with that. We haven't exactly been good to each other and you were pretty damn pissed at me. Maybe you still are. But what about Harvey, Hugo? What about Becca and Ayme?"

Hugo's eyelids flickered.

"You can't sit there and tell me you want to help start a war that could get them killed."

Hugo's face screwed up. Webb thought he was going to start screaming again but he just bent over and shuddered in horrible silence.

Webb took a tentative step closer. Then another. He hesitated a second more then put his hand on Hugo's shoulder. "I'm sorry," Webb choked. "I just…I don't know what to do."

Slowly, Hugo stilled. "Just please let me out. I can't stay in this room."

"I'm not - "

"Just don't lock me in again," Hugo said, voice shredded. "Lock the building, I don't care. I'll stay in the building, for now. Just please don't keep me in here. Shoot me, stab me, kill me, but don't keep me locked in this room any more. Please."

He tugged feebly at the binder cuffing him to the cot frame, eyes huge and lips parted.

Webb swore then pulled the release fob from his pocket, swiped it over the cuffs' panel then keyed in the release code. It snapped open and Hugo pulled his wrist free, then stumbled to the door.

Webb jumped after him, but the other man just swung it wide and slumped against the frame, clutching at the doorjamb like a drowning man to a life preserver. Webb stood back, unable to move. Eventually, Hugo seemed to calm. He pushed the door open as wide as it would go then stepped back and lowered himself to sit on the edge of the cot.

"Thank you," he said.

Webb's strength fled. He wobbled to the cot and sat next to him. Even without touching him, and even with the door open, Webb could sense the tension still strung through his old friend like wire.

"Do you want to sleep? I won't shut the door."

Hugo lifted his head. For a horrible second, Webb could see him trying to remember who he was, but then his face softened and his eyes drooped again. He nodded, blinking blearily. He checked the door again, then lay down without a word. Webb shifted to give him room.

"A priest said he'd looked at you. Did he patch you up ok?"

Hugo nodded, eyes closing.

"Just so you know, I still don't trust you not to bolt, so I'm sitting right here while you sleep."

"Just don't shut the door," Hugo murmured.

"Ok," Webb said. He reached out a hand again, hovered it over Hugo's arm, then withdrew it and picked up the stool and sat on it.

He thought Hugo had fallen asleep but then he mumbled.

"Where are we?"

"St Giles' Church, Sector 4, Lunar 1. We're safe here."

"They just took us in?"

"Webb used to live here," he said, feeling something with claws stir in his belly. "At least, I think he did. They seem to remember me, anyway."

"You don't remember?" Hugo said.

"It was a long time ago. Just go to sleep."

"Why are we here?"

"Jesus, aren't you chatty all of a sudden?"

Hugo didn't answer. Webb sighed.

"We're here because we've got half the Service after our necks and the other half I don't trust not to tell the first half where we are. Then the rest of the Orbit is crawling with Red Star or their sympathisers. So I figured it best to hide away somewhere close to neutral until I can figure out what the hell I'm going to do to get us back to Sydney."

"I can't go there, Webb," Hugo said after another long silence.

"Well you're gonna."

He glared at the back of Hugo's head but he didn't move or speak again. His breathing levelled and calmed. When Webb checked him, his eyes were shut, his mouth open and he was sleeping deeply. He looked calmer than Webb had seen him since he'd found him.

Webb slumped on the hard floor, leant against the wall, covered his face with his hands. He drifted in and out of his own exhausted stupor, jerking himself awake every time he caught himself slipping away. But Hugo didn't move. He slept the sleep of the deadly tired. Webb pulled his knees up to his chest, cradling his broken wrist in his lap. Emotional and physical chaos warred for dominance inside him, but the patches of exhaustion between were swelling like fog.

Time crawled on and Hugo didn't stir. Webb finally stood, unable to bear it any longer. He left the cell but paused before shutting the door. His instinct was telling him to bolt it with every bolt available. But he remembered Hugo's face and tortured plea and couldn't bring himself to do it. He pushed it to, turned out the light and left. He paused outside Vergennes's cell and stopped himself with his hand on the handle. The urge to talk to him, anyone, was almost overwhelming, but he pulled back, reminding himself the man wasn't his friend.

Unable to think what else he could do, he left the sleeping cells. On the next level up he could smell the kitchen nearby but the thought of food made him sick. He slipped through the back of the church hall - there was a night service going on and several priests and novices were bent in silent prayer - and found his way back to the front entrance. He keyed in the code Father Marcus had given him and slipped out into the street.

It was cold. He ached. He was so tired he couldn't even remember when he'd felt more ragged. He ducked into shadows whenever patrols of Enforcers went by. They were all armed and traveling in twos or threes or in Jeeps or low-flyers, moving through the streets and skyways with painful regularity. Webb wondered where on earth Pope got the man power for so much security.

But the patrol would pass and he'd move on, not sure where he was going but feeling something inside tugging him onwards. It was only when he was stood at the top of a flight of stairs leading down to a basement door at the back of an old, crumbling building he realised where he'd been heading. His jaw clenched. His heart skipped about. He hadn't realised he even remembered where it was.

He remembered the last time he'd seen Doll. It was his own memory, therefore all too clear. He remembered her face, angry and betrayed and impossibly sad all at once. It made him clench the railing like he'd wrench it off and he had to remind himself he didn't actually know her. What memories he had of McCullough's wife belonged to another life that wasn't his. But the feelings of comfort and need they generated were too real.

He stumbled down the steps. He just needed to see her. Even if she shouted, even if she pulled another gun on him, she was someone who had cared. He just needed one moment away from everything else. He needed a moment in his old life to pretend it really was his, to pretend he really did have memories of a time when he'd been happy.

The door stood open and the space beyond was dark. He hesitated, then pushed through. It smelt damp. With a sinking heart he paced down the passage to the inner door to the basement apartment. It was closed but not locked. It opened with a shove, stiff on unused hinges. The small room beyond was barely lit by the one window at street level that was even more grimed with muck than he remembered. It allowed a shallow bleed of streetlight to illuminate the empty room. It smelt of dust, damp and chill. There wasn't a single piece of furniture left, though marks on the floor showed where objects had been dragged away. Even the shelves were gone.

Webb almost convinced himself he must have the wrong place, apart from the trailing wires from where a workstation had been ripped out of the wall were exactly where he had a memory of sitting and scrolling through local rumour boards for mentions of the Splinters. He stumbled down to the next level. It was pitch black and he fumbled out a lenslight. All the tiles in the bathroom and kitchen unit had gone. Even the plastic flooring had been taken. He leant against the wall in the stairwell, breathing heavily, then ran back up the stairs, through the dusty room and out again into the alley.

He stood panting, then ran to the nearest street and took a turn and then another. He purposely didn't look at the numerous derelict lots and the gaps where buildings had gone. He ignored the patrols of Enforcers with their floodlights sweeping the street, stopping people at junctions to find out why they weren't in work or at home past curfew. He was able to slide past them all without notice, old instincts serving him well, until he came up to the gates of humming, clanking building with the huge scroll-ing door ratcheted up, spilling heat and light out onto a pitted concrete yard. The relief he felt at finding the meltworks still in operation was palpable.

He hurried through the open gates, weaving through a line of workers coming to start the night shift. He looked at every face, trying to spot Doll.

"Hey, kid," someone shouted and he saw a large, bald man with a panel frowning at him. "What are you doing?"

Webb hurried forward. "I need to speak to Doll. Donatella. Is she working tonight?"

The man frowned. "Donatella who?"

"McCullough."

The man frowned, checked his panel then shook his head. "Don't know anyone of that name. You got the wrong place."

"She worked here. It was a few years ago but it was definitely here. Do you know if she transferred somewhere else?"

"I'm just starting up a shift here, kid. Move on, will ya?"

"Hey," a woman had broken away from the line of people fil-ing into the meltworks. Her hair was cut short like all the other welders and her face was lined with age and pitted up one side with spill scars. He didn't recognise her, but there was something familiar about her voice. "Did you say you were looking for Doll McCullough?"

Webb nodded eagerly. "Do you know where she's gone? Did she retire?"

The welder glanced at the man with the panel and took Webb by the elbow, leading him away from the entrance.

"Donatella, right?" she said.

"Yeah," Webb said. "Do you know her?"

"My name's Phoebe," the woman said. "I used to work the same shift as her. Who are you, then?"

"I'm...sort of an old friend."

The woman's scarred face shifted. Her lips pressed together.

"Jeez lad. Sorry to have to tell you this…"

"What?" Webb breathed as cold tendrils snaked up his throat.

"She passed away. About four years ago." The woman put a hand on his shoulder. "I'm sorry."

Webb's belly flipped. "What happened?"

The woman winced. "An accident," she said. "A nasty accident."

"What accident?"

"It was here," she said, nodding at the meltworks. "Just as Pope took over as Councillor. We were understaffed but the quotas had gone up. We were all working double shifts…someone didn't check a pressure regulator on one of the tuns and it went up. Took five welders with it. Doll was one of them." Her face creased as she saw his reaction. "I'm sorry, lad. Really am. You were one of her kids, huh? From the youth unit she worked at back in the day?"

Webb choked. "I wanted to be."

Phoebe's brow clouded a little but she said, "Sorry, lad. She was a good woman. I liked her a lot. But I gotta go now. You be ok?"

Webb didn't answer. He fled into the streets that were all at once so familiar and completely alien. Twice he passed entrances to the maintenance ways but turned away. With his mind the mess it was, he didn't trust himself to not get lost forever in the colony's metal innards. Not that he was any longer certain that wouldn't be better than going back.

Day-cycle was dawning by the time he found his way back to St Giles. He passed a pair of priests, recognisable by their high-collared long-coats with white crosses sewn on their arms, heading out on patrol. He ducked into the shadow of a trash skip, not wanting to answer anyone's questions.

He shut the front door firmly behind him, hoping it would shut away everything that had chased him all the way back from the meltworks, but it didn't.

He drifted to the church hall. The last of the congregation was filing out from a morning service. The smell of snuffed candles wreathed in the air with the tendrils of their smoke. Light from the arched window, split into bars by the protective iron rails, fell across the bare, concrete floor and the high, white-washed walls. The half-dozen rows of polyfibre pews took up all the available room. The alter was just a table covered in a white cloth. The simple metal cross placed in its centre stood out a stark black against the slanting light.

Webb's steps were loud in the stillness. He willed the peacefulness to sink through his skin and calm the tumult in his heart. He sat and clutched his hands together on the back of the pew in front and bent his head onto his fists, ignoring the pounding from the injured wrist.

Eventually, his shaking stilled and he was left feeling rung out. Empty.

"How long have been there, Hugo?" he asked without raising his head.

"I'm not sure." The other man's voice was quiet and still hoarse.

Webb slumped back on the pew. His eyes felt grimy. His chest ached. Hugo sat next to him with unnatural stillness.

"Doll's dead," Webb said.

Silence, heavier now he wasn't alone, filled the chamber like gas. Webb stared at the brightening light from the window. In the levels below their feet something crashed then was quiet again.

"I'm sorry."

"What?"

"I'm sorry," Hugo said again, a little louder.

"Which particular part of this five-star crap storm are you sorry for?" Webb's exhaustion sucked all the sting from the words.

"About Doll," Hugo murmured after a long pause. The man's eyes still held their unfamiliar darkness, but now they were full instead of empty. Too full.

Webb couldn't think of anything to say. He rose stiffly from the pew and moved to the alter. He leant on the rail, bowing his head. "It doesn't matter. None of it matters now."

"It doesn't?"

"No. Everyone's dead. Even you." Webb glanced back. Hugo hadn't moved. In the splintered light he looked like a ghoul, staring at him with tortured eyes like something brought up from hell to judge him. "You must be dead," he heard himself saying. "Kaleb Hugo would never have done the things you've done. He's gone. Doll's gone. The man I thought was my dad never even existed. What's the point?"

He slumped onto the alter steps. His vision swam and his breath caught but he said no more. There were no more words in him.

He heard Hugo move. He approached slowly then lowered down next to him. Webb drew his breath in and out with aching ribs, unable to decide if he want to hit Hugo or grab onto him so hard it hurt.

"This is a nice place," Hugo murmured. "I like it here. You lived here?"

"Webb did," Webb said, flexing the fingers on his injured hand. "The real Webb. When he was a kid."

"For how long?"

Webb winced. "I don't know. I can't remember."

A different sort of pause. "I would have thought he would have remembered this place."

"He did," Webb softly. "I remember…him remembering. But it's not clear."

"I don't understand."

"It doesn't matter."

"It sounds like it matters."

Webb looked up. He couldn't decide whether seeing more of someone he recognised looking out of Hugo's eyes was making him feel better or worse. He looked away, picked at the straying threads on his sleeve. His mouth was dry. "I've been getting headaches. Sometimes nightmares too. And blackouts."

"Blackouts?"

Webb nodded. "They started when I was still with Dana. They

were just once or twice a year then. Now it's…more often."

"Have you seen a medic?"

"No," Webb said, pulling his knees up to his chest. "It would mean having to explain everything."

"What do you mean?"

Webb let out a shaking breath. He closed his eyes and let himself say it. "Every time I wake up…something more…of *him*…is gone."

Hugo was quiet. He sensed the question hanging in the air.

"I'm losing his memories. I know we never understood how I even had them. Even Yoshida was never able to figure that out. But now…they're fading. Everything from waking up at the Medic Centre is clear. Too damn clear. I wish some of that would fade away. But before then…there's gaps. And they're getting bigger."

Webb looked at his hands. The fingernails were blunt and broken, rimed with dirt. The knuckles and palms were callused. The marks, scars and tattoos were all his but they felt wrong, at odds with what he felt he should be remembering. Webb's hands hadn't looked like this…but he was struggling to remember what they had looked like. He blinked, admitting to himself for the first time how used he'd become to having the double-vision of his own life refracted through that of his predecessor. And how lost he was feeling now it was leaving him.

"I'm losing everything," he breathed.

"Will it all…go?" Hugo asked quietly.

"I don't know. Maybe. Probably." Webb heard himself continuing to speak, his voice and mind detached, tired. "Sometimes I dream of the memories I'm losing before they go. Sometimes I relive bits of his life like they were happening now." He shivered. "I hate it. But I know as soon as it stops…there'll be nothing left. And then…Jesus, I have no idea what then."

Hugo shifted.

"You don't have to say anything," Webb said in a low voice. "There's nothing to say anyway."

"That man is gone," Hugo said, after a very long pause. "He's been gone a long time now. Maybe it's best his memories go too."

Webb pressed his forehead against the alter rail, squeezing his eyes shut. "Go away, Hugo. I don't care anymore. Just go. Go back to Red Star, if that's what you want. It's over. I'm done."

"What do you plan to do?"

"I don't know. It doesn't matter."

Webb waited for him to leave, but he didn't.

"I didn't kill him."

"What?"

"I didn't kill my father."

Webb snorted. "I saw you do it."

Hugo shook his head. "They didn't trust me to go through with it, so they had a Plan B."

"What are you gibbering about?"

Hugo's face was tight, his eyes wide like those of a cornered animal. "There was another gunman, Webb. He was stationed in the ballroom. I was supposed to shoot by a given time. When that didn't happen, the other gunman was under orders…"

Webb's chest clenched. He swallowed, throat dry. "You ain't shitting me, are you?"

Hugo shook his head. "I was going to do it. I went there planning to. I'd done everything else they'd told me. But when I was on the roof…I couldn't."

"Hugo…"

Hugo screwed his face up, closed his eyes and leaned in and buried his face in Webb's shoulder. Webb froze. His former captain shook. Something crumbled away inside Webb and he put his arms around Hugo and just held him. The broken man clung to his clothing and Webb let him. They sat there, clinging to each other and not speaking, shaking and clutching like they would drown in their own emotion if they let go of each other. Webb felt a rush that was all heat and fire and anger and sorrow, but it still felt good just to feel again.

He didn't let Hugo go until he straightened up on his own. He peeled himself away from Webb slowly, and stood, staring at the door to the entrance hall. His face was red, the dirt on it smudged with moisture and his jaw was clenched.

"Are you going back?" Webb forced the question out.

"I have to."

"You don't, Hugo," Webb said, scrambling up. "You really, really don't."

"Yes I do. You don't understand."

"I do," Webb cried. "You're scared, aren't you? Really scared. They've tortured you into it. I know what it's like to be that scared of someone. But I promise, Hugo, your mom can help. She can protect you. Come back with me. Please."

Hugo shook his head and ground the heels of his palms into his eyes. "I can't."

"Do you mean to tell me you actually *want* to go back?"

Hugo stood there, breathing heavily, keeping his eyes covered. "No," he said. The word was loaded.

Webb's heart jumped. "Then don't. Whatever shit is going down, it doesn't have to be anything to do with us. You didn't kill General Hugo. You're still you. Get away somewhere safe, then let everyone else deal - "

"No," Hugo, dropped his hands. His voice was forceful again. "It's not that simple."

"*Why*?" Webb said, taking a handful of the man's shirt and spinning him to face him. "Tell me, Hugo. I can't help if you won't tell me."

"You can't help. You should never have been involved. No one wanted you involved, Webb. Not McCullough. Not me."

"That's bullshit," he growled. "I had some big glorious role, same as you. You told me yourself."

"Not yet. Maybe not for years yet. But those are their words. For the last year I've been unable to say anything but their words. Now I'm here," he looked around the wide room and up at the cross and the window. The light shone on his grimed and bruised face, the burns on his temples and the close-cropped hair like that of a prisoner or a plague victim and Webb could suddenly see every moment of pain and terror that had brought him to where he was written into it. "Now I'm away from those caves I can finally know which are their words and which are mine. But I still have to go back."

"Why?" Webb breathed again, every ounce of desperation coursing through him poured into the one word.

Hugo stared over his shoulder for the longest time. Webb had almost convinced himself he wasn't going to answer, but then the other man's gaze moved to his, slowly, like it took an almost physical effort. He swallowed, opened his mouth, shut it again.

"Tell me, Hugo."

Hugo's eyes widened. Fear paled his face. "They've got them."

"Who?" Webb said, shaking him slightly. "Who's got who?"

"Red Star," Hugo said, starting to tremble. "They've got my children."

Δ

"Webb. Webb, stop."

"Like hell."

"Webb, *please*," Hugo grabbed Webb's elbow and clung on, stopping his head-long rush down the corridor.

"Hugo, what's the matter with you? We've gotta tell someone."

"You can't."

"Like fuck on a Sunday morning I can't," Webb's face was red. His pale eyes burned.

"I told you, any hint that I've told anyone about them, they'll be killed. If you start sending messages out about this, Red Star will find out - "

"What about Harvey?" Webb said. "Does she know?"

"Marilyn knows. They've got her under surveillance too," Hugo said. The words felt alien in his mouth. The conditioning in his brain was firing warning shots across his synapses. He almost felt the electricity coursing through him again, but he closed his eyes against it and forced the words out. "She's risked enough just by letting mother send you after me. Red Star must not have realised she had or Becca and Ayme would be dead already."

Webb's face had a grey tinge.

"Please, Webb," Hugo said, voice cracking. "Let me go. I have to go back to Mars before - "

"No. No way."

"Webb," Hugo pleaded.

"This is not a negotiation," Webb growled. "If Red Star have your kids, we're getting them the hell back. But we're gonna need help."

"You *can't* - "

"She sat there," Webb said, face stricken, "Harvey sat across the table from me and didn't say anything about this. She didn't tell me..."

"She couldn't," Hugo insisted. "Don't you understand? These people are everywhere, Webb. They've got spies in every level of the Service. They might not have found out about you coming after me, or if they did they didn't think you'd succeed, but if Marilyn went to anyone for help about our children, or Red Star got any hint that we were trying to track them down, they'd be killed on the spot."

"You have no idea at all where they are?"

Hugo shook his head. "They were taken from their dorms at the Academy. No one heard anything and the security had all been bypassed. Red Star loaded fake Leave Passes into the school's databases and no one even knew anything was wrong until…"

Hugo saw the horror that had haunted him every hour of his life since that day painted clearly on Webb's face.

"So Red Star tried to recruit you for months, threatening and blackmailing and when you didn't buckle, they took your kids?"

Hugo shuddered, closing his eyes. "It's my fault. It's all my fault."

"Shut your hole," Webb growled, stabbing a finger in his chest. "This isn't your mess, Hugo. It's *them*. Coale and Rose and god-damned *Mac*. Those self-righteous sons of bitches, declaring and promising new and better lives to people when all the while they're murdering, blackmailing and snatching kids right from their beds. Why the hell you didn't tell me at the time?"

"I couldn't," Hugo said again. "Nothing I did or said would have got by them. And besides..." Hugo trailed off, blinking at Webb whose face fell then he looked away.

"Yeah, yeah," he muttered. "We haven't exactly been best buds of late, huh? But, Christ in Heaven, Hugo. You could have come to me with *this*."

Hugo stared at the floor. His vision blurred. "I couldn't think straight. I didn't know what to do. They took my children and the next night Coale came for me and I went. I didn't even wake Marilyn to say goodbye..."

Hugo's stomach heaved. He hadn't thought of that night for over a year. That night and his life before it had been buried under a layer of protective concrete in his mind but now it was cracking.

"So they took you away and tortured you?"

Hugo swallowed. "Coale locked me in a room with no light. When I wouldn't say what they wanted me to say, they shocked me with electricity. I just wanted my children back," he breathed. "I begged them just to let me see them. But they wouldn't even answer my questions. Coale told me I had to understand, first. He told me I would believe...I *had* to *believe*, Webb. I had to obey."

"It's ok, Hugo," Webb's voice sounded from somewhere far away, beyond the rushing in his ears. "It's ok. We'll get the girls back. I promise."

Hugo didn't move. His breathing hitched in his chest. "You don't understand," he repeated, painfully slowly, each word hurting him. "Don't you think I've thought of everything? Don't you think I've tried?"

"You've just told me you *didn't* try."

Hugo's shivering took on a violent edge. His teeth chattered trying to get the words out. "I did everything, *everything* to track Red Star down when they first contacted me. But they were buried too deep. Even Rami couldn't track the communications channels they were using."

"Rami knew?" Webb said.

Hugo shook his head. "Not the details. I just sent the comm codes her way to look at."

"Why didn't you tell anyone else?"

"Because I knew right away, Webb," he snapped, looking up finally. The man's face was blurring in front of his eyes. Every darkening bruise and scrape on his face, the gap in his teeth. Hugo knew now, and understood, that he'd put those marks there and looked away. "I could tell from the very first communication that Red Star were…dangerous. We all know investigating intel like that has to be need-to-know. The only thing getting more people involved would achieve would be tipping their hand. I thought I could track them down before they could do any harm. I was wrong."

Webb visibly ground his teeth and Hugo knew he was stopping himself saying he was damn right about that.

"Red Star will destroy the Service. With me on their force for propaganda they can do whatever they want."

"Why you? Your mom's got six kids. Your brothers are higher up the chain. Why did they take you?"

Hugo trembled. "I don't know."

"I know why," Webb said darkly. "It's because you're the only one with your own brain. You're the only one that questions anything. They thought…Mac thought…you'd *want* to join."

Hugo closed his eyes. "I don't care. I don't care about any of that. I just care about my daughters."

"I told you, we'll get them back."

"No, you won't. With me as their man, these people can do anything."

"You're not their man anymore."

"Yes I am," Hugo said quietly. "You can't get Becca and Ayme back, Webb. They will only be safe if I go back to Mars and play my part."

"And you believe that do you?" Webb snapped. "After everything else they've done, do you really think they'll keep your kids safe if you go back and play good solider for them?"

"I told you this because I thought you'd trust me. I told you because I thought you'd help."

"I *will* help," Webb said, spinning on his heel and marching away.

Hugo hurried after him, telling him to stop, voice gaining volume.

"You either leave me to deal with this," Webb snapped as he pushed open a door onto a wider, brighter corridor. "Or I lock you in your cell again. Your choice."

Hugo balked, lightning going through his head and flesh seizing. "No, you can't."

"I can and I will," Webb growled.

Hugo froze, trembling all over, clenching his eyes shut as electricity forked through his brain. He clenched his fists tight. Coale's voice rang in his ears like he was stood next to him.

"You will be a great man one day, Kaleb Hugo. Your daughters will grow up proud of you. You know you understand."

He collapsed against the wall, shuddering.

"Hugo?"

Webb's voice somehow cut through it all and he blinked. He was on the floor with his back against the wall and arms wrapped around his knees. Webb knelt in front of him. His face was tight with concern.

"I can help, you know I can. Now pull yourself together. There are workstations in the library we can use."

"You can't tell anyone, Webb. I don't know how to tell you again. Coale will find out and he will kill them."

"Hugo," Webb said in a firm voice, leaning in to make Hugo looked into his pale eyes. "You have been tortured and frightened into believing things you know, deep down, are bullshit. I am getting on the comm and I'm getting a message to someone we trust. And I'm doing it even though you've asked me not to because if you really, really believed I was only putting your kids in more danger, you'd have killed me rather than letting me get this far."

Hugo swallowed. His throat was tight and dry. His breathing was harsh in his own ears. Webb's face looked calm, but the intensity in his eyes was hot.

"What are you going to do?"

Webb stood, pulling Hugo up with him. "We need to talk to Rami."

"Anita Rami can't - "

"Anita Rami," Webb cut him off, pulling him down the corridor, "can do anything. And you know it. Now come on."

He followed Webb in a sort of dream. He knew he should stop Webb in any way possible rather than let him do what he was about to do. Voices were in his head and the smell and chill of a tiny, dark, underground room was in his nose and against his skin. But Webb's words and tone, and his hand on his arm, were also there. Beneath the layer of pain and darkness that had been his whole world for months, a small flame was now burning. He nursed it cautiously.

Webb pushed open a large door and they both blinked as they stepped into a much brighter room. There were shelves along the walls all holding hard-copy books. Hugo had never seen so many gathered in one place. There was a bank of workstations against one wall. A scattering of people looked up from desks and shelves as they came in, giving them wary looks. There were both men and women, all strongly built and in mismatched civilian clothing but all with the same worldly look about them. They sat at desks amongst piles of books, working on panels or on the work-stations. A beat-up display hung on the wall with a Lunar 1 news channel on mute, subtitles spelling out the report on a worker riot in another sector.

Webb gave the people a nod and went straight to a workstation. Hugo followed in a daze.

"What is this place?" he heard himself asking in the quietness as the last of the room's occupants went back to their work.

"It's a church, Hugo."

"What do they do here?"

"The priests live here," Webb said, as he booted up the workstation. "And learn about medicine, mechanics, systems, you name it. Anything to help the community. In my day they ran a youth unit too. Nowadays is seems the nuns and priests are more like a private army again, trying to keep the authority's stranglehold in check like they did when the colony first was built. In those days the authority was the precursor to the Service. These days, it's Councillor Pope. Seems history's come full circle. Again."

One of the women got up and went out, eyeing them cautiously the whole way.

"Are we welcome here?"

"They've given us sanctuary," Webb said. "Being welcome is another matter."

Hugo swallowed.

Webb was already typing. Hugo watched command windows opening up on the workstation's display with a sick feeling in his stomach. He couldn't follow all that Webb was doing to establish a secure connection but it still felt like it wouldn't be enough.

"What are you doing?"

"I have to try and get through to Rami's personal comm on a back channel on the under web," Webb said, face a mask of concentration. "The Service blocked all my attempts to communicate with anyone from my ship. They must have logged the ship's comm ID. Hopefully, they won't recognise the one from this machine."

"Will the Service units not register someone trying to get through on a back channel?"

"I don't know," Webb said dully. "They're on the alert for us. They are probably monitoring all my contacts' comms. But Rami's an Analyst now. And hates my guts, so hopefully they won't think to monitor hers."

"Rami doesn't hate your guts."

Webb gave him a baleful look then carried on typing. The minutes stretched on. The codes Webb inputted got longer and more complicated. Hugo gave up trying to follow them. He also gave up trying to bank down the rising sense of fear that was building in his chest.

Finally, a window opened up on the screen and the word *Connecting* appeared in red. Webb glanced around the room and Hugo followed his look. The priests were all still buried in their work. Webb grabbed a headset from a hook next to the display and put it on, putting the mic near his mouth as his eyes stared unblinking at the screen.

The word *Connecting* vanished but no video appeared. A steady green light flashed on Webb's headset.

"Rami," Webb asked in a low voice. "Is that you?"

Silence. Hugo tried to stop himself twitching as Webb listened to whatever was happening in the headset.

"It's me. Yes. Webb. No, it really is, I swear. Rami, calm down."

Hugo tried to read Webb's face but he'd closed his eyes.

"Do I sound dead to you? No, we can't do visual, it's too risky. Oh, Jesus and Mary, it's me dammit."

More silence as Webb listened. Hugo fidgeted as Webb's face went slack.

"Shit, really?" he said, glancing at Hugo. "Listen, Rami. I've got Hugo. *Kaleb* Hugo. Yes. He's right here."

More quiet. Webb shifted in his seat. "I can't tell you. Don't trace this channel, it's too dangerous. Listen, this is important.

You need to get to Harvey. You need to get to her and make sure she's somewhere safe. Red Star have her daughters and we - " he cut off again. He looked up at Hugo, mouth open. "When?" he breathed. Hugo felt a his stomach clench. He gripped the back of Webb's chair, his knuckles standing out white. "Ok. I understand. No, I haven't heard anything. We're stuck where we are and all my own comms are being monitored. I don't know." He lowered his voice even further. "Ok. Yes, I'll leave it to you. I - " he stopped, blinking, then pulled off the head set. "She's gone."

"What's happened?" Hugo forced the question out.

Webb swallowed, staring at the blank screen. "Harvey's missing."

Hugo felt his knees threaten to give and clutched the chair tighter. "What?"

Webb looked around and stood. "Come on, we need to talk away from here."

Hugo followed Webb back down to their cells in a daze. He felt sick and dizzy. He had to will himself to keep breathing. They got to Hugo's cell and he followed Webb in. Webb didn't shut the door entirely, watching Hugo carefully, but he did push it to.

"Sit down before you keel over."

"No, tell me what's going on."

Webb scrubbed a hand over his face. "She's gone. She disappeared just after I left Earth."

Hugo felt like he'd been kicked in the stomach by someone in steel toe-capped boots. "What happened? Have there been any demands?"

"You don't understand," Webb said gently. "She wasn't taken, Hugo. She waited until I was launched on my own mission to find you, then she left and swore Rami to silence. Officially, she's on a field mission for Eclipse. She had Rami program all the details into the mission roster. This is how Admiral Osgard managed to take control of Eclipse's missions. Hudson's a force to be reckoned with, but without Harvey or me there to represent you and the

Hugos, Hudson's only as powerful as her rank."

"She's gone to find Becca and Ayme," Hugo breathed, mind reeling. "She's gone off on her own."

"It looks that way. Don't panic, Hugo. This could be for the best."

"How could she..." Hugo said.

"Harvey can hold her own," Webb insisted. "She's timed this exactly right. Red Star have their hands full right now. She stands the best chance - "

"They were watching her," Hugo cried. "They will know."

"Hugo, you're panicking," Webb said, standing and coming forward. "Just breathe, ok?"

"I don't need to breathe," Hugo said. "I need to go."

"Snap the hell out of it." Webb, for the first time, sounded genuinely angry. "Wake up, already. Trust your wife."

Hugo staggered and sat on the cot. His blood pulsed through his head. His skin along the scars on his face tingled.

Webb took a breath of his own, visibly calming himself. "Now listen. Rami says entire fleets and divisions of the Service Ground Corps have turned their coats. Their numbers are becoming obvious and the Service is like a dog backed into a corner. To top that, there's division in the Service between those that want to follow your mom and those that want to follow Admiral Osgard. The man's made a bid to replace your mom as Special Commander and execute his insane plan to blow everything close to or around the rebels to oblivion. Rami said he's been hiring mercenary armies and made deals with every underground force from here to Sunside to strengthen his cause. He even has Service ambassadors in his pocket to do the negotiating for him." Webb's jaw clenched. "I saw one of the bastards sneaking about meeting a guerrilla army on the Chinese boarder. Now I know what he was doing there, and why that asshole Major Tremaine didn't want me reporting it. Tremaine is exactly the sort to rally to a man like Osgard. Don't you see? Everyone is arming up and ready to fight.

And all of them, *all of them*, are on the lookout for you and me because they think we know too much."

"So what do we do?" Hugo asked.

Webb threw his hands in the air. "You tell me. *Do* you know anything? Do you know what Red Star will do next?"

The threat of static rippled through him but he found himself nodding. His jaw felt slack, his heart empty.

"Well in that case, it's back to plan A. We get you back to your mom. She's the only one in this assembled army of nut bars that has a hope of doing anything useful with the info."

"How do we get back?"

"I haven't the faintest clue. But we better think of something fast."

Hugo stared at the wall. His palms were damp.

"Hugo," Webb said quietly. "Harvey is safe. And she'll get the girls back. You know she will."

"I don't know anything anymore."

"You know me," Webb said. "And you know you can trust me. Right?"

Hugo blinked at him. "I shot you," he breathed.

A corner of Webb's mouth turned up in a wry grin. "I know."

"I nearly killed you."

"Again, I know. I remember. Vividly."

"Why are you helping me?"

"Do you even have to ask that?"

Hugo swallowed.

Webb searched his face and sighed. "Well, one reason is that you're the only sorry son of a bitch available to help the Service find a chink in Red Star's armour. But also because…well…I give a shit, don't I?"

"About me?"

"About all you wretched Hugos," Webb said, face animated. "I owe you all too much. Even if you can be the most pig-headed, bloody-minded and stubborn bunch of morons I've ever come across. But if it makes you feel any better, you're the worst of the lot."

"But before…in the church. You said it was over. You said you'd given up."

He looked uncomfortable for a moment. "I know I did."

"So what changed?"

"You came back from the dead." Webb's smile was crooked.

Hugo stared at him. His light blue eyes were tired, but warm. Hugo's own mind was a sorry mess but the fire was burning brighter in his belly. He took a deep breath, closed his eyes and let himself breathe.

"I'm hungry," he heard himself say.

Webb let out a soft laugh. "That can only be a good sign. Stay here. I'll get us some food. I'm guessing the universe will survive a couple more days while we rest up and come up with some kind of plan. And I guess I better check on Vergennes too."

"Vergennes?" Hugo reached for the word's meaning.Webb nodded at the wall.

"My lieutenant. He's locked in the cell next to yours."

"Why?"

"Because he's in deep shit, that's why. But I guess I shouldn't let him starve."

Hugo searched for words to express what he was feeling but they didn't come before Webb had left the room.

Δ

Webb paused once on the way to the kitchens try and process everything. When no solutions presented themselves, but he found that he was, for the first time in weeks, relatively calm, he decided not to push it and hurried up the stairs.

His indistinct memories of the church were less than useless but he kept moving and could eventually smell the kitchen again. When he found it, he ventured in and got a grunted greeting from an older woman who was layering up trays of protein noodles in a hatch that opened onto a dining room. She barely looked at him. He guessed either word had already spread about their presence or she was used to having waifs and strays wandering into their kitchen. He loaded up three trays with the hot noodles and packs of vitamin paste from the cupboard, thanked the woman and left.

He balanced the trays awkwardly as he went back down to the cells. When he arrived at Hugo's he was asleep again, head pillowed on his arm. His mouth was open and he was breathing softly. He looked more peaceful than before, like he was dreaming something nice at least or nothing at all, rather than sunk so far down into the depths of exhaustion that he might never come back. Webb laid the tray on the floor and backed out of the room.

He steeled himself and pulled back the bolts on the next cell. Vergennes stood to attention when he stepped into the room. His face was still blank as ever but Webb thought it looked strained.

"Food," Webb said and dropped the tray on the bed.

"Thank you, sir. Sir?" Vergennes added as Webb moved to leave. Webb tried to make himself walk out but stopped. Vergennes was looking at him like he was searching for words.

"What?"

"Do you know what's happening? Out there I mean," the younger man said, nodding vaguely through the doorway.

"Looming disaster," Webb said. "What else is new? Now, eat. I don't want to have to drag you back out of here unconscious."

"I'll eat, sir," Vergennes said. "But first, can you let me talk?"

"About what?"

"About everything."

"There's nothing to say," Webb said, moving to the door again but Vergennes grabbed his elbow.

"Sir, please. I think I deserve - "

"Vergennes," Webb snapped, juggling his tray. "You're a mutineer. You spied on me. I don't hold much truck with Service codes and rules but I damn well stand by the rules of a ship. Ten years ago and another life and I would have shot you and be over it by now."

"But you haven't shot me," Vergennes said.

"There's still time."

"Sir, you haven't shot me because I don't think you really think I did anything wrong."

"That just shows how little you know me. And my quota on feeling sorry for brainwash victims has been all used up today."

"Sir," Vergennes tried again, grip tightening on his elbow.

"You're going back to Earth for a hearing. That's it."

"You don't even believe in hearings and court-martials."

"No," Webb said with a narrow look. "But you do. Behave yourself until we get back to Earth and I won't deliver judgement myself, clear?"

Webb pulled his elbow free. Vergennes stood ram-rod straight with his arms at his sides. There was a dark look in his eyes that was almost a glare but didn't carry quite enough emotion.

"You wouldn't be reacting this strongly if you felt nothing for him like you pretend," the younger man said.

"You need to watch your mouth."

"You need to admit that you love your father."

Webb slammed the door and threw the bolts home. He took a moment to marshal himself, then returned to Hugo's room to eat, unable to shake the fear of his former captain again waking up a stranger.

IX

Hugo stayed in the cell for the next couple of days. He wandered up to the church hall one more time, but the people milling around and looking at him unnerved him. The fact that it felt safe felt wrong when he knew what must be unfolding beyond the hull of Lunar 1. But, with Webb's insistence ringing in his mind, he allowed himself to let it go, at least for now, and concentrate on letting his body recover whilst Webb endeavoured to plan. The gunshot wound in his hand was knitting quickly with the dose of the healing-acceleration drug the priest had given him and everything finally felt on the mend now he was allowed to be still and rest. Webb saw this progress and nodded his approval.

The younger man didn't have to say out loud that he hoped Hugo's mind would continue to recover in this safe, quiet place along with his body. It was clear in the way he looked at him.

Hugo felt the stirrings of gratitude for Webb's consideration but he knew, even though his mind was quieter than it had been in months, it wasn't something that would just leave him. It was all still there, the fear, the darkness, the whispered words in Coale's grating voice, like a monster under the floor in his mind.

But for now, he let himself ignore it. He ate, he slept, he washed in the communal shower room and put on clean clothes donated by the priests and just let himself be quiet.

But despite the uneasy peace that had begun to steal into him, he couldn't help but notice Webb getting more and more tense. The younger man had scrounged a panel from somewhere and spent hours bent over it, not speaking and never admitting to having come up with any reliable way of getting them to Earth without being stopped or shot into drift by any one of the warring factions desperate for their heads…and what was in their heads.

Hugo tried to help but he couldn't make his mind strategise. Whenever Webb tried to discuss anything, the information just slid off his bruised mind. He felt like he may finally be able to follow Webb's instructions rather than the ones echoing in his head, but trying to decide what he thought himself was still too muddled.

"At least the ship's still where I left her," Webb said one evening as the sounds of the priests leaving a service echoed down through the ceiling. He sat on the floor of Hugo's cell, glaring at the panel, swiping at something on the screen. "Though I'm half afraid firing her up might be like lighting a beacon."

"Are your ribs still hurting?" Hugo asked softly, seeing Webb wince as he shifted on the floor.

"I'm fine," he grumbled.

Hugo lapsed into silence, staring at the covering on his cot. Webb swore and tossed the tablet aside.

"It's hopeless. They've tripled the defences around Sydney. We haven't a paper piss-cup's chance in hell of getting into HQ."

"Would that be so bad? If it's the Service that pick us up?"

"I've told you, Hugo. The Service is divided. Osgard could start his hostile takeover any day now and having you in his hands would be the last weapon his arsenal would need. There's no way to know who are his men and who are your mom's."

"Have you tried to contact Mother direct?"

"Her comms are being monitored." Webb mumbled, voice muffled by his hands covering his face.

Something flipped inside him and he heard himself saying: "Have you tried asking Dana to help?"

Webb dropped his hands and blinked at him. "Dana? Why?"

"She has connections with Lunar 1," Hugo said, still staring at the blanket. "She might be able to get us out."

Webb made an impatient noise and brought his knees up to his chest, winced and lowered them again. "Sorry to break this to you, but Dana has taken time to remind me recently that she is less than usually inclined to help me with anything, and I've already pushed my limit with her."

"Even if she knows I'm with you?"

Webb chewed his lip, thinking. "I don't know that she wouldn't just want to keep you to herself."

"It doesn't sound like you're talking about my sister." Hugo said, quietly.

Webb frowned at him. "Are you being deliberately obtuse? Or deliberately naive? She stopped talking to all of your family forever ago."

Hugo felt an unfamiliar heat flush his face. "Not me."

"Yeah, and what good did that do you?"

"She's not a monster."

"I didn't say she was a monster. Just mercenary."

The heat in Hugo's chest gathered power. "You're in no position to be judging her."

Webb looked dumbstruck, then anger crept into his face. "Say again, Vice-Admiral?"

"I remember now. I remember why we stopped talking."

"Because you were an asshole."

"I seem to recall you were the asshole."

"Jesus wept," Webb cried, colouring. "Is this really what you want to talk about right now?"

"I want to understand," Hugo said. "I thought I knew you. I want to trust you. But I remember what you did and it wasn't an act of someone who cares about my family."

"I didn't do *anything*, Hugo. How many times do I have to say this before people believe me?"

Hugo just looked at him.

"I don't know how else you want me to explain it," Webb said. "I didn't cheat on your sister. I just fucking didn't. That woman was a contact. A baranium dealer that I was getting info from for an Eclipse mission. Dana found out about the meeting and... took it the wrong way. And she wouldn't listen."

"Dana never thought you cheated on her," Hugo said, remembering her stony face that she'd frozen solid to stop herself from crying whilst she told him everything.

Webb's face went blank. "Huh?"

"Dana never thought you'd cheated on her, Webb," Hugo said, watching the other man's face. "She knew that woman was one of your points. But she also found out that you'd given her information on some of Dana's baranium traders."

Webb blinked slowly. He looked confused, then stricken, then angry.

"It's true, isn't it?" Hugo said. "I know it's true. I checked your mission reports."

Webb flushed red. "Those traders of hers were scum. They were bottom-feeders, smuggling dirty intel and weapons as well as baranium."

"They were contracted by Dana to feed her information from Lunar 1."

"I don't care," Webb said. "They were dangerous. And they were using her. I gave their names to that dealer because I needed her cooperation and she needed a way to strengthen her connection with Lunar 1. So, yeah, I gave her the traders' names and the name of their fence."

"Knowing she'd have them arrested, or get them killed to clear her own way into the colony."

"Yes," Webb said, smacking the floor with his palm. "They were criminals. The Orbit was better off without them."

"We're all criminals." Hugo felt his heart speed up. "What was the difference between those men you sold out and the crew of the *Zero*?"

"The *Zero* was commissioned for the Service. Whatever it did, it worked to keep the peace."

"You don't believe that. You may have lost some of his memories, but you remember what Webb and his crew thought of their lot. They worked the missions and did the job because it kept them in regular food, credit and protection. If any of them could get that reliably from anywhere else, they'd have left in a heartbeat."

"That's not true."

"Webb most of all," Hugo pushed further. "If Red Star had been around then, he would have joined in ten seconds flat."

"That's not true," Webb said again, going red. "It was different. *I* am different. Those smugglers of Dana's were bad news. The Service couldn't get enough evidence to arrest them and they were getting their claws into your sister."

"They were Dana's people and you sold them out. Dana lost her connection with Lunar 1. She had to find other ways of keeping her intelligence stream up. Including making deals with Councillor Pope."

Webb's fists were balled and his jaw tight. "Are you seriously sitting there and telling me that you and she were angry with me because I got rid of her pet smugglers?"

"You went behind her back," Hugo said, unable to stop. "And insulted her by assuming you knew what was best without even speaking to her."

"Have you ever tried speaking to Dana about something like that?"

"I know better than to assume I'm entitled to make decisions for her."

"I don't believe you. Ok, I can get her pride was bruised, but you, Hugo? For real? You're pissed with me for ridding your sister of a group of underworld parasites that could have turned on her at any moment?"

"I'm pissed at you for hurting my sister. And for not trusting her."

Webb stared at him, aghast.

"Dana may not have chosen the path any of us wanted for her. But at least we respected her enough to make her own choices. Interfering with her life like that…it was *worse* than if you had cheated on her."

Webb had gone limp. The colour had drained from his face. He looked shocked. Hugo's anger was as fresh as it was the day he'd been told about it.

Webb shifted, crossed his legs and stared at his boots.

"Well," Hugo said. "Say something."

"Like what?" Webb snapped. "Sorry? I won't because I'm not. And if Dana honestly expected me to marry her and not watch out for her then clearly we were never meant to be together anyway."

"Speak of the devil," came a quiet voice from the doorway.

"Dana," Webb and Hugo said at the same time and scrambled to their feet.

"What the Christ?" Webb said. "What are you doing here?"

Dana let her cold smile slip and straightened up from where she'd been leaning on the doorframe. Hugo felt his heart skip about. She looked completely different and yet exactly the same. Her eyes were hard but clear. Her stance was balanced and her decorative hairstyle had been tied out of her face. She wore spacer boots, cargo trousers shirt and gloves, a weapons belt slung low on her hips and a cropped jacket over it all so the guns were to hand. He knew her well enough to recognise the flicker of pain in her eyes when she looked at Webb and wondered whether his former commander could see it too. Then her gaze landed on him and she visibly swallowed.

"Hey Kale," she said. "Or what's left of you."

"Dana," Webb snapped. "What the hell - "

"Stow it, Captain," Dana said, flicking Webb a dark look. "Since you're clearly looking up at me from the bottom of a well full of shit, I'd appreciate you keeping a civil tongue in your head."

Webb flushed but Hugo was gratified to see him swallow his response.

"Dana," Hugo said, taking a tentative step closer. She looked at him again and her face softened. "Dana," he said again and his anger at Webb, his fear for his family, his loathing of himself and his shame at everything combusted into a burst of emotion and he staggered forward. She caught him in her arms. She started off stiff but he buried his face in her hair and held on tight and he felt her loosen.

"Marilyn's gone," he whispered in a hoarse voice. "Becca and Ayme are gone."

"I know," she murmured softly and he felt her gloved hand take a warm grip on the back of his neck. "I've spoken to Rami."

"Rami sent you?" Webb said.

"No one *sent* me. Rami told me what was happening and I came, since you are clearly incapable of getting from point A to point B without everyone in the Orbit trying to kill you."

Hugo raised his head. He felt his eyes sting and his throat close. "Father dying…I didn't…"

Dana's brow clouded. Her eyes were hard as she watched him look for words.

"I didn't kill him, Dana," Hugo groped for her hand and she let him take it, though she didn't squeeze back. "You mustn't believe it."

Dana's face twisted before she managed to hide her thoughts. "People are saying - "

"People are wrong," Webb said softly. He was leaning against the wall, arms crossed, face carefully blank. "He came close… damn close. But he didn't go through with it. There was another gunman. Everything else is just spin for the newsreels."

"Red Star say you're one of them," Dana said. "They've said you're their man and you killed Father to prove it."

Hugo hesitated. He looked at Webb who was giving him an assessing look. Hugo tried to find words.

"He's clearly not," Webb put in finally, earning a sharp look from Dana. "He's here, isn't he?"

"It doesn't look like either of you got out easy," she said looking them both up and down, gaze lingering on Webb's wrist brace and both their bruised faces.

She pressed her lips together a moment, then stepped back out of Hugo's hold. "So. If all that's true, I guess you're needing a berth back to Earth?"

"Your mom is the only one we think can stop this before it gets any shittier," Webb said.

"Mother's got half her own soldiers petitioning to replace her," Dana said, looking grave. "You really think she's in a position to do anything?"

"The Service can still stop this," Webb said. "With the right intel it can beat these bastards. Kaleb is the only way of getting a jump on their plans."

"So why are you hiding here? The Service has all its fleets in drift, on the ready. You could have got to any of them with this."

"If Admiral Osgard gets his hands on Hugo first, he'll use him and his info to gather more support. And then it's game over for your mom."

"How do you know that's not for the best?"

Webb flushed. "If the Service declares war on itself, what resources will it have left to stop Red Star? Besides, SC Hugo tasked me with a mission and I'm not backing off until I've brought your brother home to her like she damn well asked me to. Oh, and since you've butted in and managed to see him now for yourself and can ask him anything you like, I'll consider our own contract fulfilled."

Their heated words passed back and forth like sparks in a generator. Hugo listened, but couldn't respond. He watched his sister's face and fought the urge to grab onto her again. Dana's gaze flicked between them, considering. Then she shrugged.

"Actually," she said. "Having seen the way this is going, what intel Kale has is probably too hot for me to handle. And however the Orbit decides to blow itself up and how you plan to stop it is really no skin off my nose. But if Kale wants to go home," Dana's dark eyes softened, "I'll help him get home."

Hugo wished she'd used any other word. 'Home' conjured images of his apartment with Harvey, of their daughters playing on the living area rug. He smelt the minty soap in their hair as they hugged him goodnight. But on the heels of such memories came others programmed to follow. Darkness. Pain. A promise to keep, if he only did as he was told.

He knew they were both watching him. He felt the sweat stand out on his forehead and, hoped they couldn't tell what was going on in his head. "How can you get us...back?" he eventually forced out.

Dana glanced over her shoulder and took a step further into the room, lowering her voice. "I've got the *Thorn* with me. She's registered for Lunar 1 hauls. No one will think twice about her coming and going. If Rami really is right and no one has realised you're here, no one will suspect."

"How did Rami know where we were?" Webb asked.

"How do you think?"

"She tracked the signal?" Webb said. "I specifically told her that was too risky."

"Seriously, Webb," Dana said, raising an eyebrow. "You think Rami doesn't know about risk?"

"That's not it. I just - "

"She's forgotten more about systems than you'll ever know," Dana replied. "She tracked it securely, believe me. Seriously, she's wasted as an Analyst."

"Is my hearing all bust up or did I just hear you compliment a Service officer?"

"Don't let it go to your head," Dana retorted.

"And how did you even get in here?" Webb pressed.

"That wasn't easy," Dana said. "Gotta hand it to these priests, they run a tight ship. But when I promised to get you out from under their feet, they seemed more willing to be persuaded." She looked at her wrist panel. "Well, this revolution of yours isn't getting any younger. But I need to leave *Thorn* in dock long enough for it to look like a legit deal's going down. We'll ship out first hour of the next day-cycle."

"And you can really get us out without the Service ships spotting us?" Hugo asked.

"Of course. What do you think I've been practicing all these years? In the meantime, who do I have to bribe to get some food around here?"

Δ

Webb stared into the mirror over the washbasin in his cell for a long time. He was trying his best not to figure out how he felt but the sound of Dana's voice was fresh in his ears and the sight of her still made his belly stir. He closed his eyes, pressing his knuckles against his forehead.

He shook his head and forcing himself to assess his injuries. Everything appeared to be slowly healing, but he still ached everywhere and couldn't seem to get warm. He'd been shivery for days. He didn't let the thought of what might be wrong form, but instead pulled his lip back to look at the gap in his teeth. The lip and gum round it were still red and sore to touch. Both his eyes were blackened, the left one was still blurry and its pupil was enlarged. The bruising along his cheek bones was fading to an ugly yellow. He winced and pulled off his shirt. His skin was paler than normal and he didn't like how grey it was. He took the wrist brace off and tried flexing his hand, cursed, and clutched his wrist. When the pain subsided he tentatively unwound the loosened binding across his ribs one-handed. He swore as the pressure changed and shocks rode up his side and spine. He clutched at the basin to stay upright.

"That doesn't look good."

Webb craned his neck and glared. "You need to stop sneaking into guys' doorways."

Dana came forward, looking him up and down as he slowly unwound the last of the binding. "I'm telling you, that doesn't look right."

"It's about right for any sort of mission with your brother involved."

"Stand here," she ordered, pulling him forward then raising his arm up and down, watching his torso. He swore and pulled back. She muttered and ran a hand over his ribs.

Webb shivered. "Hey now, I'm not really in the mood you know."

She ignored him, digging her fingers, now without their gloves, warm and strong, into his side. He cursed again.

"They're cracked and not healing straight."

"Joy."

She lifted his right arm gently by the elbow and probed the swollen wrist. He bit down his protests and grunts of pain and let her work. "Same with this. They not have a medic here?"

"One of the priests fixed up your brother, but they're busy enough without me whining."

"What exactly happened?" Her voice sounded different. She was still examining his wrist and didn't meet his eyes.

"Your brother happened."

Now she looked up. "Kale did all this?"

He shrugged. "Let's just say he couldn't be immediately persuaded to cooperate. Did you want something?"

She held his gaze a minute longer then stepped back, letting his arm drop. "I came to speak about Kale. I'm worried."

"He's been through a lot," Webb said, turning back to the basin and running the hot water.

"He doesn't seem himself."

Webb snorted.

"Are you going to talk or just make stupid sounds at me?"

"I don't know what you want me to say," Webb said, splashing his face. "You're brother's been fucked up by Red Star. They beat and brainwashed him. It can take a guy a while to get over that sort of thing."

"You speaking from your experience, or Webb's?"

He turned on her. "Does it matter? Look, Dana, I'm tired. I know you're still mad at me and if we're in a sharing mood, I'm happy to tell you I'm still mad too. But can we leave off poking each other with sticks for five minutes while I try and get my head together?"

Her jaw tightened and fire danced in her eyes. He braced himself for another assault but she just turned on her heel and left. Webb sat on the bunk, feeling deflated. He clutched at his ribs, closed his eyes and just tried to breathe. He was so tired. He knew he should sleep but doubted he could.

When Dana returned carrying the priest's medic case and shut the door, he couldn't deny the flush of happiness, but carefully schooled his face.

"Stand up," she ordered.

He did as he was told, sensing a fragile peace in the air and, for once, reluctant to break it. She opened the case, fished through it and brought out some clean binding.

"Everything has already started to heal crooked. That's why it's still hurting. You'll probably need corrective surgery at some point. But this will help for now. Arms up."

Webb lifted his arms as Dana started to bind his ribs.

"This may hurt. Try and stay still."

She tightened the bandages and he gasped. He thought he sensed hesitancy in her touch but then she continued, strapping the binding up over his good shoulder to hold it in place. He kept his eyes closed and just focused on her efficient but gentle touch. His mind floated back to a dark chamber in the Haven between-ways, when she'd first touched him like this and that stirring in his belly returned. He opened his eyes to watch her work, drinking in the sight of concentration on her face, rather than hard and defiant look he'd seen on it most in the last few years.

Once she was done with the wrist he found he could use the hand a little more. Then she was peeling back the old dressing on his gunshot wound. The look on her face produced a chill.

"What is it?"

She looked up at him, raised a hand and put her hand to his forehead. It was cool and more soothing than he liked to admit. "Are you hot?"

He shook his head. "No. Cold."

She pursed her lips and ripped open a new pack of steriwipes from the case and cleaned the entry and exit wound. His whole arm was pulsing.

"What's wrong?"

Dana was behind him, running the hot tap. He felt a warm, wet rag dab at the exit wound and winced. "It looks angry," she said.

"What does that mean?"

"Could be infected," she said, voice clipped. "How old is this one?"

Webb closed his eyes. "I dunno. A few weeks? What's the date?"

"The 13th."

Webb counted back. "They kept me in the caves for about two weeks, maybe three. This was just before that."

"Caves?"

He shook his head. "Long story."

"And it didn't occur to you to get someone to look at this once you got out?"

He was too weary to snap back. He just shrugged.

"There are no antibiotics in here," Dana said, rifling through the medic case. "I'll go see if they have any."

"No," Webb put a hand on her arm to stop her.

"Webb, that is not a good wound."

"Is there such a thing?"

"I'm serious."

"So am I," he said, summoning some determination from somewhere. "Do you have any idea how much medical supplies cost around here?"

She folded her arms. "So you're happy to develop sepsis?"

"No," Webb countered. "But thanks to your friend Pope, there are people on this colony needing these things way more than me."

Her face flushed. "My *'friend'*, Pope?"

"Let's not start," Webb said, wearily, lowering himself onto the bunk.

"You honestly think I like the man?"

"I was clinging to the fact that you had more sense than that," Webb said, meeting her hard gaze. "I met the man on Mars. A charmer, sure, but not your usual type."

Dana put her hands on the bed either side of him and leaned into his face. Her eyes were black fire. "If you honestly think I have anything to do with him other than out of lack of choice then I'm even more ashamed of you than I was before."

"Hey, I'm not the one who makes deals with the guy."

"The man governs Lunar 1," she snapped back. "I make deals with him and get the legit runs to this damn colony or I sneak round him and get my ships blasted out of drift on approach. How do you think places like this even get their medical supplies?"

He blinked at her, face inches from his own. He swallowed. "You run meds?"

"Oh and little things like food. Tech parts. Straight to the markets, too. Not to Pope."

Webb narrowed his eyes. "He lets you sell directly to the colonists?"

She straightened and folded her arms again. "Like I said, I have a deal. Now I'm through justifying myself to you. Are you going to take the antibiotics or lay down and rot away from the inside? I'm honestly happy either way, just tell me so I can go to bed."

He looked at the floor, throat tight. "Do you have antibiotics on the *Thorn*?"

"Yes."

"Well I'll take those. I'm not taking anything more off the priests."

"Fine," she said, storming to the door. "I trust you have enough credit to cover them."

She left before he could respond and he lay down on the cot and stared at the ceiling, hurt and shame coursing through him with equal strength.

Δ

Dana had to wake Webb when the time came for them to leave. Her face was once again closed but her gaze lingered on him as he painfully eased himself up from the cot. Their exchanges were clipped and perfunctory. Webb let them be, knowing the continued coolness was mostly his fault.

She told him to meet her at the entrance in an hour and left. Webb washed his face, swallowed some water, dressed then made his way up to the main level of the church. Priests milled about in the corridors, but he didn't spot Father Marcus. He eventually tracked him down in a store room, sleeves rolled up to reveal his forearms banded in muscle and inked with Nova Catholica tattoos, loading boxes onto a lifter.

When he saw Webb in the doorway he paused and dusted off his hands.

"You're off then?"

Webb nodded. He opened his mouth, searched for words. "Father…"

"No need to thank us, sonny," Marcus said, coming closer and giving him a good look up and down. "Just be careful out there."

"I will," Webb ducked his head.

"It's good to see you again, Ezekiel," the older man said after a long pause. "I know you weren't with us long but I remember you were a stubborn and flighty sod. Too clever by half. But I also remember thinking that there was a lad who would get what he wanted from life. I hope you have."

"I'm alive, I guess," was all he managed.

"And that's more than some could say," the priest said with a heavy look. "So, what's next? You taking your friends home?"

"Friends," Webb muttered to himself with a shake of his head. "Yeah, that's right. Something like that."

The older man nodded. "I'm not as up to date with Orbit politics as I could be. I know something is happening here, but I think we'll both agree I'm better off not knowing any details relating to you, so I won't ask."

"I appreciate it."

"Just remember one thing, Ezekiel: the Orbit is just debris in drift. All of it. Your place in it is no more or less important than what you make it. Try not to get sucked into the vacuum, ok?"

"I think you probably know more than you're letting on," Webb returned with a wry smile.

"We hear some things, even here," Marcus said, turning back to his boxes of stores. "And anyone who thinks the tides of change won't eventually reach them is a fool. But at the same time, remember you're just one man. And you ultimately have a choice about what your role should be in the whole sordid mess."

Webb paused at the door. "I know you told me not to, but I do thank you, Father Marcus. I don't remember much of being a kid here…it feels like another life…" He fought to keep his face blank. "But these last few days here have been the first time I've felt…safe…for a long time."

"Glad to hear it," Marcus said. "Now go on back to your big, important calling, whatever it is. And I'll get on with forgetting you were ever here in case Councillor Pope comes asking."

Webb made his way down to the cells slowly. He shook his head and firmly shelved the doubts raised by the priest's words. They weren't back on Earth yet and he had enough to do without worrying about what would come after they did. He pushed Hugo's cell door open. His former captain was sat on his cot, bolt upright, staring at the wall.

"Ready to go, Hugo?" Hugo didn't answer or move. Webb felt a finger of concern work its way up his spine. "Come on, man. It's time to go. Dana's waiting."

Hugo nodded and stood. Webb held the door open and Hugo left the cell, face blank and eyes glazed. Webb bit the inside of his cheek and told himself the man was just tired. He took a deep breath and unlocked Vergennes's cell door, resting a hand on his gun.

The young man was stood by his cot, spine straight and expression blank.

"We're leaving," Webb said, waving him out. "Come with us and don't make any trouble."

"I have no intention of making trouble," Vergennes replied coolly, and stepped out. Webb gestured them both to go ahead of him up the stairs. Webb kept a close eye on both of them, but they climbed up without a word.

Dana was waiting at the front entrance. Webb keyed the codes for them to get out and she lead them down the concrete stairs to a flyer parked up beside the abandoned play equipment. Webb ordered Hugo to climb into the front next to Dana whilst he and Vergennes took the back. Webb still watched them both closely but Vergennes did as he was told and Hugo seemed barely awake. As Dana took them out the gate and up onto the nearest skyway, he saw her give her brother a wary glance.

It didn't take them long to reach the private dock where Dana had moored the *Thorn*. She dropped the flyer off with a generous tip to the rental company near the entrance and lead them through the busy harbour area.

They came within sight of the berths, still not having exchanged a word and Webb watched her walk ahead of him, back straight and eyes fixed in front and felt a surge he couldn't this time suppress. He took her by the elbow, gesturing for Hugo and Vergennes to go on ahead.

"What's the hell?" Dana growled, lowering her voice and glancing round. "What's wrong?"

Webb chewed on his lip for a long moment as two sides of himself battled in his head, then found himself opening his mouth.

"I…"

"Yes?" she prompted with a glance at the other two men who stood just out of earshot.

Webb swallowed. "I…don't know…it's just…"

"Dammit Webb, of all the times for you to be lost for words, this is not the best time you could have chosen. What is it, already?"

He hadn't let go of her elbow. He looked at his hand on her arm and felt the warmth of her through the sleeve. His throat closed. He made himself look up and meet her eyes. "I'm sorry."

She raised her eyebrows. "Come again?"

Webb looked at Hugo, who didn't look back, but he made himself speak. "Your brother and I…had a chat."

"A chat?"

"Well…a discussion. Of the heated variety."

"About what?"

"About you."

Her face fell. "Oh?"

Webb let his hand drop. When he met her gaze, her face had a look somewhere between warning and expectancy.

"It appears I had the wrong idea about why you made me leave."

"*Made* you?" she said, words loaded.

Webb shook his head. "Ok, let's not not get caught up in the semantics right now…"

"I'd rather not."

"But," Webb continued, forcing his tone to remain reasonable. "Either way. I'm sorry. Not for what I did…particularly," he said and continued quickly, seeing her eyes flare, "but for not realising what would come of it. And for not talking to you about it. Like…ever."

She narrowed her eyes slightly. "You know that's not really an apology, right?"

He swallowed the exasperated noise before it escaped his mouth. "Well maybe I'm not as sorry as I should be. Your brother certainly doesn't think so. But either way…I wanted you to know I've realised we…" he rubbed the back of his neck and looked at her boots. "*I messed up. Messed us up. And, well…it was a dick move.*"

She folded her arms and huffed but when he finally looked at her face some of the habitual hardness was missing from her expression. "You're telling me. Is that all?"

"Truce?" he ventured and couldn't deny the fluttering in his gut when her smile warmed to something more genuine.

"We'll see about that, Captain. Come on, we're wasting time."

They strode to catch up with Vergennes and Hugo, who both eyed them with equally different but equally unreadable expressions. Dana strode past them toward one of the private berths and Webb followed, unable to deny the new lightness in his heart that went some way to rebuilding some of his fractured hope.

"Sir, what about *Job*?" Vergennes asked as Dana used a swipe card to get them into the dry dock.

"If the Service want her back bad enough they can come get her themselves," Webb muttered, following Dana, Hugo and Vergennes into the single-berth dock.

Webb felt a jolt as he took in the *Thorn*. He'd forgotten how familiar she was. She was small for a trading vessel, though still bigger than a runner like *Job*. Dana had had her sprayed matte black since he'd last seen her. She looked like space. Her engines were small to allow for the large hold but she was still sleek with clean lines, a large cockpit viewscreen high up on her front and visible weaponry so impressive he knew it was only just legal.

"Ulster not with you?" Webb asked, asking after Dana's pilot.

"I told her I'd do this run alone," she said, approaching the ship and tapping some commands into her wrist panel. Her hatch opened and a ladder descended. "No one can know I was involved in this. I have a reputation to maintain, you know."

Webb stopped the crack that rose to his lips and instead murmured, "Thank you, Dana."

She turned and gave him a level look. She was about to speak but then her eyes widened and he saw her about to call a warning. Webb moved, but Hugo was too close and too fast. The next thing he knew the older man had wrestled Webb's gun from his belt and had levelled it at them.

"Step back from the ship," he said, voice unnervingly dull.

"Hugo - "

"I said, *step back*," Hugo repeated gesturing to the side with the gun.

"Do as he says," Dana said after a heavy pause, holding her hands out to the sides as she stepped away from the ship's hatch.

"Hugo, what's going on?" Webb asked as he raised his own hands and followed Vergennes and Dana towards the wall.

"I'm taking her," Hugo said, approaching the ladder. "I'm sorry," he added, but his voice was without emotion. "I have to go back."

"No you don't. We talked about this."

"I'm not talking about it anymore," Hugo said, reaching the ladder, gun still trained.

"Kaleb," Webb pleaded. "This is not the way to save your family."

"You don't understand," Hugo said. "Red Star have already won. The Service just doesn't know it yet."

"How do you reckon this?" Webb said, trying to keep his voice calm

Hugo hesitated, staring at them with fever in his eyes. "You don't know what they're planning."

Webb felt himself go cold. "What are they planning?"

Webb could see the lines on Hugo's brow deepen and the gun shook slightly with the tightness of his grip. "Red cement."

"What about it?"

"They've been shipping it all over the Orbit for months. They've got caches stored under hundreds of major Service outposts and holdings. Including Sydney HQ."

Webb's mouth went dry. He felt Dana go very still at his side and a glance at Vergennes showed the younger man's face had fallen from its disciplined lines.

"It's only a matter of time before they reveal they have the Service at their mercy," Hugo murmured. "They can't be stopped, Webb. They have the means to halve the Service's numbers and resources in a matter of minutes. Then they'll have no trouble wiping out what's left and taking control. It could happen anytime. They only reason they've held off this far is because they're watching their timing. They're still hoping to invoke a surrender. But I know the Service. They won't surrender and neither will they abandon their outposts. The red cement will be detonated and there will be destruction on a scale we've never imagined before. Red Star will seize the Orbit in the chaos. It's going to happen. It's years too late to stop it. All I can do is make sure my family makes it through alive."

"We have to warn your mom," Webb forced the words out his tight throat.

Hugo shook his head. "She can't do anything. It's too late."

A shot rent the air and Webb tensed, but it was Hugo who cried out. Webb dove for cover behind some crates, Dana and Vergennes scrambling after him.

"What's the hell?" Webb cried, peering out. Hugo was on the deck, hand clutched to his leg, blood oozing between his fingers.

"Come out," a familiar voice called from near the entrance. "Let's end this quick and clean, shall we?"

"Osgard," Webb cursed as the woman stepped into view, gun ready. "What the hell are you doing here?"

"Finishing a job. Now come out, Webb. I'll let the sister live if you and Kaleb Hugo both give yourselves up without any more trouble."

Hugo had got to his knees and was trying to crawl for cover. Osgard aimed but Dana shouted and pulled her own weapon and fired. Osgard swore and ducked behind the *Thorn*. Dana ran to her brother and started dragging him back towards the cover of the crates. Osgard leant around the ship and fired again. Webb ran to help Dana with Hugo, grabbing his gun off the deck in the process. There were more shots and Dana grunted in pain. Webb's blood surged through him. He pulled them both the last few feet to the relative shelter. He could smell blood.

"Jesus," he said softly, helping Dana get to her knees. She was clutching at her belly. Darkness soaked the front of her clothes. "Dana, no."

"Come out," Osgard's bellowed command was fierce. "Face me like men."

"Dana," Webb said, clutching at her hand, slick with blood. Her breathing was ragged. Hugo sat against the crates, eyes wide and staring.

"Return fire, idiot," Dana said, thrusting her gun at him.

"Hugo, help her," Webb said, easing Dana into a sitting position. "Hugo," Webb snapped when her brother continued to sit motionless. He blinked and crawled over, helping her sit up. She gasped and started to sweat.

"Here, make yourself useful," Webb snapped, shoving Dana's gun into Vergennes's hands. The man took it without question and took up position, aiming towards Osgard's hiding place.

"Show yourself," Webb called, anger coursing through him like fire. "This ends now."

"You're right," Osgard's voice echoed around the dock. "Enough is enough. I tried to help you. My father would have helped you. But you have proven you are every bit the piece of murdering, lying scum your father is."

"What?" Webb said, a jolt like a kick in his stomach.

"Oh, it's all come out now," Osgard hissed. "Duran McCullough back from the dead to lead the Orbit in another revolution and his son a high-ranking Service officer appearing at Rose's side during his rally."

"I was a prisoner, you moron," Webb cried out. "You were there."

"So you would have us believe. All I can believe now is you, Kaleb Hugo and his sister are all mutineer trash and better off dead."

"And how do you think things will sit with SC Hugo if you ice two of her kids, huh?" Webb hissed.

"Erica Hugo's time is over," Osgard said and he heard her footstep and readied his gun. "My father will lead the Service to victory, but we will not tolerate the likes of you wearing the uniform any more. Have some dignity and come out and take it standing up. Although I'm quite happy to kill you on your knees like the cowards you are."

Several shots buried themselves into the crates. Webb and Vergennes ducked just in time.

"Sir, if I approach from the other side I can cut her off..."

Webb looked at Vergennes. His expression was controlled, his cobalt eyes intense.

"Go," Webb said, burying his reservations, and Vergennes hurried away, staying close to the bulkhead. His boots made next to no noise. Webb risked a glance down at Dana, saw her trying to get to her knees. Hugo had moved back to give her room. His face was again an unrecognisable, blank mask. His leg was bleeding.

Webb scanned for any sign of Osgard's position, straining his ears for any sound of movement.

"Get ready to make a move for the hatch," Webb said in a low voice. He heard the scuff of a boot and then ducked as the crates splintered with a shot from his other side. He swung round and shot blindly toward the ship's stern just as Osgard fell back out of sight. There followed the sound of a shot from elsewhere, then Osgard cursing loudly.

"Go, sir," came Vergennes's voice from around the ship. "I've got her covered."

"Come on," Webb said, not waiting to rethink. He got his arms under Dana and lifted her off the floor.

"Put me down," she growled, though her body was limp as a doll. "I can walk."

"Hugo," Webb barked and the man looked up, startled. "Come on."

Webb hurried to the *Thorn's* boarding ladder, Dana protesting the whole way. Helping her climb up was painfully slow. Their blood-smeared hands slipped on the rungs. Hugo followed robotically. When they reached the hatch Webb ordered Hugo to take his sister. Dana limped on board in her brother's arms.

"Vergennes," Webb called. There was an eerie silence in the dock. "Come on, time to blow."

Still no reply. Webb called the lieutenant's name again and finally the man stepped into sight. He was holding the gun at his side.

"What happened?"

"Osgard's gone," Vergennes said, with a glance toward the exit.

"What do you mean?"

"I let her go."

"You *what*?"

"She agreed to let the ship leave if I let her go. She had grenades. She was going to blow the dock if you made it on board. It's important you get Vice-Admiral Hugo back to the Special Commander, sir. He needs to tell her everything."

"Fine, I guess. Get your ass up here. We need to shift before the local Enforcers get here."

Vergennes hesitated, glancing toward the exit again.

"Lieutenant. Come on."

"I'm sorry, sir. No."

"'No'?"

Vergennes took a step back. "I won't go back to be branded a traitor, sir."

"Blaise," Webb began, either anger or desperation bleeding into his tone, even he couldn't tell which.

"No, sir. I'm sorry. I am. Whatever I thought about you before this mission…you've changed it. You're brave. And loyal, in your own way."

"There's no time for this, Lieutenant," Webb barked. "You're a man of honour, right? Get your ass back to HQ and accept your punishment. I can't let it go, but they might. It's too dangerous out there and they need every Serviceman they've got - "

"No, sir," Vergennes said again, backing toward the exit. His eyes were bright. "I have something I must do. The Service had been my whole life. But now…" he shook his head. "I have something I must do. I wish you luck."

He turned and ran for the exit. Webb called after him but the man hit the door release and was gone. Webb stood frozen but then a voice came through on the dock's loud speakers.

"Merchant Vessel *Thorn* and crew, please remain where you are. You are under arrest."

The automated voice repeated itself as Webb swore and skidded up into the spacious command deck. He fired up the ship's engines and the ship lifted and steadied. He backed it out of the dock, sending up prayers of thanks that Dana had splashed out on a berth with a vacuum shield and not a hatch.

The vast blackness of stars and space suddenly surrounded them. He turned the ship, put Lunar 1 to her stern and fired the engines. Two patrol ships were heading their way but they were too far away. Webb brought the *Thorn* up to full speed quicker than was probably safe and set her course toward Earth, praying they got a decent lead on Osgard. He watched the colony fall away on the scopes and his breathing calmed.

Once they were safely in a long-distance space-lane and no one had caught up to them, Webb called Hugo and Dana on the ship-wide comm. No answer. He cursed and went in search of them, finding them in one of the cabins. Hugo was knelt on the floor, elbows on the bunk with his face hidden in his arms.

Dana was on the bunk, staring up at the ceiling. Blood soaked the sheets, her shirt and jacket. Webb stood rooted to the deck, stomach heaving and veins running cold.

"Dana?"

Hugo flinched but didn't raise his head. Webb took a heavy step forward, then another. He reached out a hand. Dana didn't move or blink. He touched her face. Her mouth was slightly open and her eyes hooded like she was thinking about falling asleep. Her cheek was soft under his fingers. Her black eyes were clear. Calm. Empty.

"Dana. No…"

Δ

Hugo heard Webb's voice. He registered the feeling in it but didn't hear the words. He clung on to the bunk's blood-soaked sheets with his breath rattling in and out of him, seeing nothing but darkness and feeling nothing but coldness.

"You."

Hugo understood this word but couldn't conjure up a reaction. The next thing he knew the other man was hauling him to his feet and slamming him against the bulkhead.

"You bastard. You ten-sided bastard. *Christ*, Hugo. Are you happy now? She's dead. She's fucking *dead.*"

Hugo stared into Webb's face. It was creased with fury. The eyes burned blue fire. The sight blurred and cleared as his own eyes filled and overflowed. The cabin lurched around him. He felt sick.

"Fucking *say* something." Webb shook him.

"Let me go," he choked out, clawing at Webb's hold.

"You son of a bitch," Webb snarled, stepping back like he couldn't bear to be near him. "You human shitbag. You…you…" He let out an inarticulate yell and kicked the bunk. "If you hadn't tried to take the damn ship, none of this would have happened."

Hugo swayed. He couldn't look away from Dana. Her face was turned slightly away like even now she couldn't look at him.

"I can't..." Webb was muttering, staring at the deck like he could set it alight with his eyes. "Everything's fucked. I can't..."

"Don't you *dare* make this about you." Hugo only heard his own words a beat after he'd said them, but felt the rush of anger that had generated them clearly as a brand across the skin.

Webb's face flushed. "I *loved* her, dammit. I fucking *loved her.* You don't even know what that means."

"You've only loved her since she put her hands on you on Haven. I've loved her her whole life."

"Well you damn sure didn't act like it."

"You think you know so much."

"I know when someone's treats their sister like a child. I know when someone's screwed up family drives them off because they don't feel good enough for them. Or when their arrogant asshole of a brother starts the mess that gets her killed."

Fire rode through Hugo, burning away everything and making him move without thinking. He shouldered Webb against the locker and grabbed his bad wrist before he could swing a punch. He slammed the limb against the locker over his head and the man yelped. He pinned the other wrist to the bulkhead, leaning his whole weight into holding the clone still.

"Don't you ever, ever accuse me of not loving my family," he snarled. "Ever. Again."

Webb's face was slack, his mouth parted. His cheeks had paled, but whether it was with shock or pain Hugo couldn't tell. He squeezed the broken wrist hard enough to see Webb flinch then loosed his grip and stepped back, staggering, feeling like he'd shed all his strength. His knees gave and he sat heavily on the deck. Webb slid down the locker and bowed his head, his whole body shaking. Silence filled the cabin.

"Hugo, I..."

Hugo looked at Webb. His eyes were red. The younger man cast a look at Dana. His face crumbled and he put the back of his hand to his mouth. He looked so vulnerable for a second Hugo could almost swear it was a man he'd never met before.

Hugo wanted to move closer to his sister, to take her hand or to gather her to him. But he couldn't move. They sat without speaking, the ship thrumming around them and the smell of tears and blood in the air.

"Can we clean her?"

"What?" Hugo croaked.

"There's so much blood," Webb said, voice high. "She doesn't like mess…"

It was too much. Hugo left the cabin. He made it into the head, locking the door behind him. He sunk to the floor, pressing his forehead to the deck and clenched his fists so hard the tendons ached and the remains of his fingernails cut splits in his palms. He stayed there, no longer caring where they were going or what was going to happen next. He allowed himself to be one with the pain.

When Webb finally came to find him, banging on the door until he opened it, he felt dried out and brittle. Webb's face was ashen and his eyes looked bruised but they were hard. He stood straighter than before.

"Here's the deal. We make it up to her."

"What?"

"This isn't over. We can't let it be over. We owe her that."

"How?"

"We get back to Earth. We warn the Service about the red cement. We give the generals enough information to stop that bastard Osgard gathering any more support so there can be a united Service strike against Red Star. And we take Dana home to her mother."

Hugo didn't think there was anything left in him to break but he felt yet more of himself tear to pieces with these words.

"You know," Webb said with a sharp look. "You know it's what you have to do."

"My…children…" Hugo said feebly, but the fire that had fuelled him in the Lunar 1 dock had long since been damped to steam.

"Marilyn will find your girls," Webb insisted. "She knows what she's doing."

Hugo knew it was just words. He knew Webb was just saying this to help himself believe it. The truth was his daughters were either already dead or soon would be. With that thought a sweep of numbness carried away the last of anything real in him. His throat closed up. He blinked sore eyes and straightened his back.

"Yes. You're right. I will talk to Mother."

Webb nodded. He, too, looked numb. Whereas earlier he had looked younger than Hugo had ever seen him, now he looked older. For a second it looked like he was going to say something more but he didn't. Hugo sense that a gulf now stood between them, cold, wide and dark as the distance between them and Earth.

"Sort your leg. Then come up to the command deck," Webb said, then left.

Hugo glanced down, blinking at his stained trouser leg and only now feeling the dull throb of the injury. He removed his trousers and washed it mechanically. Once it was clean it turned out to be little more than a graze. Already the bleeding had slowed. He had no doubt that Vee Osgard had intended to kill them, but this first shot had just been to distract. He found some gauze in the cabinet over the sink and bound it then limped up to the command deck.

Webb had taken the pilot's seat. Hugo took the co-pilot chair, though he could do little more than glance at the blinking controls. It was a beautiful system, slick and responsive and top-of-the line. But it was also too Dana. He clutched his hands together in his lap and stared out the viewscreen.

"How long until we land?"

"Three hours. Maybe more. Depends how many ships we have to skirt round in between here and Sydney."

Hugo didn't know what to feel about that so he didn't try and feel anything. He just stared at the blackness outside the ship that didn't look as dark or empty as the inside of his head.

"Still nothing on the scopes," Webb said, voice mechanical. "We might just have got away after all. Hey, Hugo." Hugo blinked up. Webb didn't look at him. "Do something useful, will you?"

"Like what?"

"Oh, I don't know. How about check the solarnet for what's going on out there, what our positions are in all this, check if an alert's been put out for the *Thorn*?"

Hugo swung his chair round to face the info station and started typing. He read the text, processed the information, but nothing penetrated any deeper than his skin.

"We've both been declared fugitives by the Service," he said. "Our photos and profiles are being circulated."

"Just like old times," Webb said, though there was no humour in his tone. "What charge?"

"You: suspected insurrection. Me…mutiny and murder. The reg details of *Job* are being circulated too."

"Has anyone started blowing anyone else up yet?"

Hugo kept searching. "A number of small breakouts of violence on the moon and some small scale strikes on minor Service outposts. Red Star testing the water. Arcadius Rose is insisting the Service submit to the election of a democratic Orbit Alliance to have power over them. The Service has cut Mars off from supplies and are demanding a complete surrender."

"Silence City can't wait out forever."

"They don't intend to."

Webb looked at him then looked away. "Have they told anyone that they have half the Orbit wired up with red cement?"

"No."

"Great. Anything else?"

"Yes," Hugo said, enlarging a news article from the *Now* network site. "McCullough has come forward, revealed his identity and announced his allegiance to Red Star."

Webb's face hardened. "So everyone knows."

"It was always his plan to reveal himself at this stage. It's supposed to bring the population of the moon and Lunar Strip to side with Red Star."

"Has it worked?"

Hugo tapped a few more commands. "Hard to tell. There are conflicting reports on the moon's official standpoint. Their governor has yet to make a statement."

There was a pause. "I'm trying to decide which I find worse, you as an emotional volcano or you as a robot."

Hugo just looked at him. Webb didn't look back.

"Speaking of the moon..." Webb's attempts to pretend the chasm between by forcing a casual tone only made it seem wider. "Why did you bad mouth me to Jaeger?"

"Jaeger?" Hugo frowned, chasing memories.

"*Sturm Hafen* landlord. My name was mud when I saw him. And he knew who I was...*what* I was. He said you'd told him. There're also articles floating about outing me as bad blood. It hadn't filtered up to Service Command at the time, but enough to cause stirrings on the ground. What was that in aid of? Doesn't seem fitting with Mac's master plan."

Hugo blinked. Something uncurled at the back of the cave of darkness in his mind. He unstuck his tongue with an effort. "That was before...before they'd completely..." Hugo rubbed his temples, feeling the memory of electricity start to fizz there again. "Before they completely..."

"Broke you?"

Hugo swallowed then took a deep breath. "I still remembered things then. I still cared. I was scared for my daughters but I wasn't Red Star's slave. Yet. Coale sent me on small intel missions to test me. I started to plant information when I knew it was safe, hoping it would be enough to upset the balance."

"Why?" Webb asked, unable to hide the incomprehension. "You wanted me shot or something?"

"No," Hugo snapped, balling his fists. "No. I was hoping…I don't even know now what I was hoping."

"Don't give me that. Tell me why you shafted me."

"I hoped you'd be discharged," Hugo said quietly. "I hoped that if the Service kicked you out, you'd cut all ties with us. With my family. You and I had already fallen out. You'd split up with Dana…" Hugo's voice caught. But the words were coming now and he forced them to carry on. "I hoped if you lost your position and reputation and relationship to my family, it would lessen your value as a bargaining chip in Red Star's game and you might be left alone."

Webb went stiff. "Well that plan sure went to shit."

"I've underestimated many things." Hugo stated, staring out at the stars.

"Go and get some rest," Webb said impatiently. "*Thorn* will get us to Earth. There's nothing I need from you now."

Hugo swallowed. He waited for Webb to look at him but he didn't. He found an empty cabin, but paused in the doorway, then returned to Dana. Webb had changed her clothes and cleaned away most of the blood. He could almost believe she was sleeping. He sat on the deck next to her bunk and stared into the middle distance, the ship's hum around him and silence in his heart.

Δ

It was the ship juddering as it broke atmosphere that jerked Hugo back to the present. He hadn't been asleep, but he hadn't stayed in the room. He shifted, wincing at the stiffness in his limbs. He noticed the aches of healing bruises waking up and paused just to let himself feel them a moment. It occurred to him it had been a long time since physical discomfort had been important enough to notice.

Then his eyes landed on Dana and all thoughts of himself fled. He'd seen bodies before. Many times. More times than he liked to think. But this was his sister. Except…it wasn't. Not anymore. His chest clenched and his stomach rolled. His eyes stung as he pulled the sheets up over her grey face.

He heard boots approaching and then Webb was in the doorway.

"We're here."

"Where?"

"Sydney," Webb said, glancing once at the bundle on the bunk then turning back down the passageway.

"They let you land?" Hugo asked, following him.

"It's Dana's ship," Webb said, words clipped. "But we need to hurry. It's only a matter of time before someone figures out who we are."

"What about…" Hugo said, looking back towards the cabin.

"We leave her here."

Hugo couldn't look at Webb as he opened the exit hatch.

"She'll be safe. Come on."

It was night but the Australian wind was balmy with midsummer heat and salt. Hugo paused on the top rung of the ladder, letting it fill him with a hundred memories he thought he'd lost.

Webb was already on the ground and moving. Hugo blinked around him, trying to get his bearings. They were on a landing platform jutting from a megablock. The structure towered up on his left, miles of lights and neon signs that faded to a glowing blur in the night sky above him. Their platform was deserted. There were no flood lights and no other ships.

"Where are we?" he asked as he hurried to catch up.

"Trader Town, North of Lavender Bay."

"I don't recognise it," Hugo murmured, looking round.

"When was the last time you ventured into Trader Town?"

Webb said, without stopping, and Hugo couldn't decide if his tone was judgmental.

"My parents' apartment is in Lavender Bay," Hugo breathed, still staring round. "How could I not recognise this place?"

"Dana chose it carefully."

"What?"

"This is Dana's private landing platform."

"It's *what*?" Hugo asked, glancing round the stretch of dark polyfibre. There was just one door and Webb was heading right for it.

"I found it logged in the *Thorn's* location preferences. Appears she had it built about a year ago, but she's never used it."

"She was going to come back to Sydney?" Hugo mused, pausing at the door to look back at the *Thorn*, a black, silent shape against the neon city backdrop.

"I guess we'll never know," Webb said bitterly, then started tapping keys on a keypad by the door. He tried a number of times but every time a red light flashed. "Dammit."

"What is it?"

"I've cracked the code but the lock's DNA restricted. You try."

Hugo input the code Webb gave him and the light flashed green and the door opened into a deserted access corridor.

"Where are we going?" Hugo asked as they hurried down the corridor.

"We need to get to your mom."

"Where is she?"

Webb swallowed but didn't look at him. "At a service for your dad at the Memorial Music Hall."

Hugo stopped in his tracks. "No. We can't go there. If any of Osgard's staff are there…"

"I'm not talking about storming the stage," Webb snapped. Hugo didn't remember ever seeing him so fragile. "We pull her aside, get her some place quiet."

"No," Hugo said firmly. "It's too risky. And anyway…" he

paused, looking at the floor. "It wouldn't be right."

"Right?"

"She's saying goodbye," Hugo said softly. "I won't take that away from her too."

The mask of Webb's face slipped. "What do we do then?"

Hugo thought for a moment then set off again. "Follow me."

It was a surreal experience for Hugo to find a way to their destination without being seen. He knew how to duck and hide, avoid surveillance and guards well enough to do it in his sleep, but to do it here, in a place he used to walk openly through the groundways with his family or co-workers, summon transport with a tap on his wrist panel or attend functions at which he was the centre of attention, felt all wrong. Thankfully, Webb just followed his lead and didn't make it any more difficult than it already was.

By the time they were stood outside a large set of doors on the penthouse level of the secure megablock, his heart had slowed and his breathing was shallow. He stared at the familiar doors, unable to untangle what he was feeling.

"Well," Webb prompted, looking up and down the plush, carpeted hallway nervously. "Come on then. There are cameras here."

Hugo clenched and released his fists, then finally put his eye to the tiny scanner set in the doorjamb. He saw capillaries flash up like live wires across his vision as the light scanned his retina. There was a pause in which Hugo worried they had revoked his security but then there was a quiet bleep and the doors clicked and slid open. They hurried in but Hugo stopped Webb before he reached for the light switch.

"There might be people watching the windows," Hugo said. "This way."

Hugo led Webb down the hallway. The carpet was soft under his boots. Again, he smelled the citrus carpet cleaner his mother still favoured in memory of his eldest sister Catherine, and felt the close, soft, warm air of the perfectly balanced environmental controls.

"They don't have any alarms set?" Webb asked in a low voice. "No security?"

"They would only be triggered by an anomalous retina scan," Hugo replied as he stepped down a level into the wide living area. The blinds were down and the room dark as pitch. Webb cursed as he bumped into something.

"Over here," Hugo said, finding a sofa and sitting down. He sat bolt upright. It felt wrong sitting at all but he was too tired to stand. He heard Webb mutter then felt the sofa shift as he sat next to him. A soft light washed into existence as Webb checked his wristpanel. It illuminated his drawn face for a moment before he pulled his sleeve over at and they were in darkness again.

"The service should be over now," he said. "Hopefully she won't be long. Never felt like I'm on borrowed time more than now. And that's saying something."

Hugo didn't answer.

"You grew up here?" Webb asked after a moment.

Hugo placed his hands on his knees, looking around at the shapes of familiar sofas, shelves and wall displays in the dimness. "Academy Training starts at age six."

"I know," Webb said, tone desultory. "But you were kids here? All of you? Hard to imagine."

"You must have been here before."

"Nuh-uh. Not even when Dana and I were…no. I never came here."

"Why not?"

"I was never asked. I don't think your mom likes me very much."

"You've got a good commission, Webb."

"I'm not talking professionally," Webb said. "I'm a good fighter. And a good sneak. She's smart enough to know the Service needs that. But…personally? As someone close to her family? Nah," Hugo sensed him shaking his head. "Don't think she's ever been keen on that idea."

"You don't know her as well as you think you do."

"Are you sure you do?"

Before Hugo could reply he heard the front door open and the hall light came on. They stood. There were male voices in the hall. The lights went on in the living area and Hugo took a step back.

"Good God, the scan was right. It is him." Riley stood in the doorway, face taut.

"Kaleb?" Giles appeared at his older brother's shoulder and blinked, then took in Webb. "And Webb too? What the hell's going on here?"

"We need to talk to Mother. Where is she?"

"Kaleb," Giles said again, disbelief, confusion and some hurt evident on his uncharacteristically open face. "Is that really you?"

Hugo lifted his chin. He made himself stand tall. The action made Giles stop where he was but he saw derision curl the lip of Riley.

"Giles, we should call security," their older brother said.

"Hang on," Webb started as Giles said, "No." Then Giles closed the gap between them and stared at Hugo's face, eyes raking the scars, bruises and burns. "What's happened? How did you get here?"

"Where's Mother?"

Giles's brow furrowed. "She's not here. I am. Talk to me."

"It has to be her."

"Webb," Giles ordered "You explain."

"I'd love to Giles old buddy," Webb said, narrow glance still fixed on Riley and hand resting on his gun. "But I'm afraid that's what they call a long story. Too long a one to tell you when Hugo number three over there seems so twitchy."

Riley bristled.

"He won't hurt you," Giles said firmly.

"They're fugitives," Riley growled, stepping into the room finally, dark eyes shooting daggers at all of them. "This one's a known menace," he said pointing at Webb. "And Kaleb killed Father." For the first time in memory Hugo saw one of brothers look like he was about to lose control. "I'll need a bloody good reason not to put a bullet in both of them right now, Giles."

"By asking that question I know you want there to be one," Giles said, voice deliberately slow. "So how about this? He's our brother."

Riley seemed lost for words but his face was red with everything he wasn't saying.

"Where's Mother, Giles?" Hugo asked again, looking his closest brother in the eye. The older man seemed tired. His black suit was pristine but slightly loose on him. His eyes looked sunken and his shoulders had a slump to them. Riley showed no signs of physical deterioration but the ferocity of the emotion contained in his eyes was unchecked and would have been alien on any of them.

"I've put you through a lot," he heard himself say. "I have explanations for some of it. Not all. But there's more to come that we need to prepare for. Much more. We need to inform Mother."

"She doesn't want to see you," Riley said, stabbing a finger into Hugo's chest. "It would have been better if you'd never come back."

"Kaleb?"

All the men froze. Special Commander Hugo stood in the living room doorway. Hugo felt his throat close up. Like Giles, his mother looked like she'd aged more than was fair for the year they'd lost. But she still stood tall with her shoulders square. She was in a formal black suit like her sons, with a sapphire brooch on her lapel. Hugo remembered it was one their father had given her as an anniversary present. There was more silver in her hair than he remembered. She wore it scraped back from her face which was pale, her dark eyes wide open and heavy. Her lips were white.

Hugo took a step forward then stopped. The thousand things he wanted to and had to say crowded into his mouth but he only managed one word. "Mother."

She didn't look at anyone else in the room. Her arms were

straight at her sides. Her look held him in place and he was so riveted by it he was able to see the exact moment when she attempted to close herself up.

"My bodyguards are at the apartment door," she intoned. "You have exactly twenty seconds before I call them in to arrest you."

"Mother..." Hugo said again, choking on the only thing that suddenly seemed important. "Dana's dead."

It was like the room had been filled with water. The air was thick and cold. His brothers wore identical expressions of weary pain. Webb looked like he was holding his mouth shut as tight as possible to stop himself from speaking. His mother was searching his face, hoping for a lie. She'd rather her son was torturing her than telling her the truth. The thought kicked Hugo in the stomach.

"How?" she eventually said.

"Admiral Osgard sent his daughter to kill me. Dana tried to save me and got shot."

It sounded so simple when he said it like that. Just words. Words can't gouge chucks out of you like a knife, but he saw his mother feel every one like a blow.

"We've brought her home," he continued. "She's nearby."

SC Hugo took a deep breath. Her eyes were bright with moisture but she blinked it away, nodded and then went to the drinks cabinet in the corner and uncorked a bottle of red wine.

Everyone started talking at once. Riley was yelling, Giles was flinging questions at him, Hugo was trying to answer them. Only Webb hadn't moved.

His mother clunked the wine bottle down on the cabinet with a bang. The brothers quieted. She drained the glass in one go then poured another before turning to them. Her eyes were now dry but her face was strained.

"Your twenty seconds are up, Kaleb," she said in a low voice. "Riley. Go and get the guards."

Hugo sagged against the sofa. Giles protested.

"You don't want to do that, ma'am." Webb pitched his words to carry.

"Captain Webb, your position has never been more precarious. Telling me what I do or do not want to do is really not in your best interests."

"Riley, friend, stop where you are," Webb said and pulled his gun. The man froze in the doorway, staring at the gun, face flushing puce.

"Captain Webb - " SC Hugo began, voice deadly cold.

"It's kinda fun being this far up shit creek," Webb replied, though his voice and face held no humour. "It's the far end of nothing left to lose. I think you've lost enough family for one year haven't you, Erica? How's about you shut up and listen?"

His mother's fingers around the wine glass had gone white. Hugo wished he could move, speak, do anything, but every inch of him burned with taught nerves too charged to function.

"Very well," she eventually replied, taking another sip of her wine and taking a seat on the edge of the sofa with painful slowness. "Go ahead, Captain Webb. I just got back from my husband's funeral which has been delayed weeks because terrorists initially refused to hand over his body. He is dead because our son assassinated him. This event has caused fractures through the entire fabric of the Orbit. Many have died already, but that's nothing compared to what's to come. That same son has now broken into my apartment with the help of a deserter to tell me my daughter has also been killed because of him. You have words to fix this situation, Webb? Because, on second thought, I do believe I would like to hear them."

Sparks flew in the air. Webb's body was rigid. The hand that held the gun aimed at Riley's head was steady as a rock but Hugo could see the tendons standing out in his wrist. Under the bruises and cuts and the mop of dishevelled black hair, Webb's face was set. Every last vestige of his humour, irony and hope had been chased from away to leave only a white-hot resolve.

"You charged me with a mission," he said, slowly. "You told me to bring your son home. I have. Don't tell me you only wanted him home to blame him for everything because I don't believe you."

"*Wanting* to blame him and being faced with the truth are two very different things."

"He didn't kill your husband," Webb said. "And he didn't kill Dana. Red Star killed General Hugo. Admiral Osgard's daughter killed Dana. So, right now, I'd say neither side is one you should be hurrying to exonerate."

"Why should I believe any of this?" SC Hugo said, but the slight catch in her voice told Hugo she desperately wanted to. "After everything you've done, how can I trust anything you say?"

"Because you have to," Webb said. "I did those things because you asked me to. Actually, no, if I remember rightly, you ordered me to. You know the way I work and you knew it was the only way to find him. You also knew I wouldn't want to, so you made me."

Hugo looked at his mother, feeling a cold gather under his belly. The slight frown line between her brows had deepened.

"Where I come from," Webb continued. "It's a pretty bad commander that has to threaten their troops to make them follow their orders."

Riley and Giles both spouted protests but their mother silenced them with a raised hand. "Where you come from, Captain Webb? You don't come from anywhere."

"That's - "

"Let's think about this," SC Hugo continued, standing. "Who really are you? Why are you in my presence, yet again, amongst my family, snarling like an animal about matters too important for you to understand?"

"Because he's my friend," Hugo said. All eyes turned his way like they'd forgotten he was there. "He's the only one who..." Hugo paused, gathered himself and carried on. "Under duress or not, he's the only one that came after me."

For once, his mother didn't seem to be able to think of anything to say.

"Too much has happened," Hugo went on, keeping his voice level and formal. "I don't know if I'll ever be able to accurately report it all. Or justify it. But the reason I'm here is because Webb did his job. And because we knew that telling you what Red Star have planned is more important than anything else."

"You'll understand if we're a little reluctant to move on any intel a traitor provides, Kaleb," Riley said.

"Riley, Giles," SC Hugo had set her glass aside and stood. "Leave us."

"Mother," Riley protested. "We can't leave you alone with these two - "

"Riley," she cut him off. "Leave us alone. I will call if I need you."

Riley muttered but left, followed by Giles who let his glance linger on Hugo before leaving. Hugo tried to read what his brother was trying to convey but failed.

"You too, Captain Webb."

"Me?" Webb said.

"Yes," she replied. "Please." She added. "I think I'm owed a few minutes alone with my son, aren't I?"

Webb grumbled, holstering his gun and looking around the room suspiciously.

"Webb," Hugo said quietly. "Please go."

"Where?" Webb stalled.

"Anywhere. Just a few minutes. Please."

Webb glared at nothing then left, glancing back at the door then turning the opposite way down the hallway to the one the brothers had taken.

Hugo looked back at his mother. She was stood with her fingertips pressed together. She was looking at the wall and not at him. Hugo stood motionless, waiting for her to speak.

"She's really dead?"

Hugo stiffened then nodded.

"Where is she?" she asked, raising her eyes to meet his.

"In her ship. She has…had…a private landing platform on one of the megablocks in Trader Town."

His mother put a knuckle to her mouth.

"Mother," Hugo tried a step forward. She took a step back, out of his reach.

"No," she said, shaking her head. "I can't."

"You can't?"

She looked at him. She was unmasked, tired, and unutterably sad. Her eyes traced the burn marks at his temples, his shorn head, his sunken cheeks and thin body. Hugo sensed she was looking at him properly for the first time.

"I wanted it to be you, you know," she said. "I wanted you to have shot your father. I wanted you be Red Star's rising star. And now Dana's dead and I wanted that to be your fault too. I needed it to be you. Do you know why?"

Hugo shook his head, hurting all over.

Her eyes were dry but naked and raw. "Because, deep down, I knew that if you hadn't done it all, the reality was that my son had been blackmailed, kidnapped and tortured, my husband assassinated and my daughter murdered, and for what? I couldn't face that reality. I still can't."

"I'm sorry," Hugo murmured.

"You're sorry?" she said, staring at him.

"There're no words big enough for this."

"You're right. There aren't." She went to the cabinet and poured herself another glass of wine but then just set it on the side and looked at it.

"Mother," Hugo said after the silence stretched on, trying to make his voice firm. "She died to get me back. Please listen to what I have to say."

"Yes," she said, voice empty. "Go ahead. Report."

Hugo steeled himself. "Red Star have caves under Schiaparelli City which they have used to plan their moves, stockpile their stores and manufacture tonnes of red cement."

She didn't look up but her shoulders tensed.

"They have been smuggling it into the Orbit for months. They have it laid in strategic places around the Earth and on the moon and in the colonies."

"Where?" she asked.

"I don't know the full list," Hugo said. "I know Service HQ in Tranquility, Glasgow, Washington and Johannesburg were on the list."

"What about Sydney?" she asked.

Hugo ducked his head. "Here too. I don't have everything. I can give you what I know. But either way it's too late to try and save these places."

"Why is that?" she said, finally looking up. He felt a flicker of reassurance that she appeared more like herself, her face calm as she took control.

"I escaped…" Hugo stopped, started again. "Webb extricated me from Mars some time ago. I'm not sure exactly how long, my mind's…not been clear. They know I've been loose with this information for days. The leaders trusted I had been too well programmed to reveal anything and that I would make my way back to them. I nearly did." Her eyes flickered, but she kept quiet. "But if Osgard tracked us down to Lunar 1 and saw us escape in Dana's ship, Red Star agents will have picked up on that by now too. McCullough, Rose and Coale are not the sort to act rashly, but knowing that I am probably here giving you this information may be enough to force their hand."

"What options do we have?"

"Evacuation."

"You're talking about hundreds of locations potentially containing hundreds and thousands…millions…of people," SC Hugo said. "It's not logistically possible…" she faded off, looking at the wall.

"Red Star think the same thing. They're counting on it. But we're on borrowed time," Hugo said. "Whatever happens with the rest of this fight, if it starts with a loss like this, the Service may never gain the foothold to strike back."

"Fuck the rest of the fight," his mother said, draining her second glass of wine. "Admiral Osgard's so damn keen to on it, let him do it."

"Mother?"

She turned to him, fists clenched. "The commanders aren't my commanders any more. They all think I'm weak. Osgard is gathering them to his side. He's welcome to them. I'll let him take the helm and see how well he does sailing direct into a hurricane. I'm stepping down. But I'll be damned if I let half my own people be killed before I do. Giles! Riley!"

Riley was there in seconds and Giles wasn't far behind him.

"We have an emergency on our hands. I want you to contact your brothers. Get them to HQ immediately."

"Mother," Riley started, looking confused.

"We've got no time for questions, Major," SC Hugo commanded, striding past them. "Use my workstation, it's secure. Mention nothing, not Kaleb, not Dana, not anything. Just say they need to be at Sydney HQ in the next twenty minutes and we'll meet them in the Command Comm room. Then come yourself."

"Yes, ma'am," Riley replied, hurrying to the workstation in the corner. "Giles, go ahead of us to HQ. Get to the comm room and clear it."

"Clear it?" Giles frowned.

"I won't have panic. No explanations. Just order everyone from the room and your brothers will meet us there."

"There are several streams of reports coming from the Lunar Strip and Mars's orbit that need close monitoring from that facility, ma'am," Giles started

"You have your orders."

Giles looked nervously between them for a second, took in the set look on his mother's face, saluted and left. Hugo followed his mother down the hallway.

"Get Captain Webb, Kaleb," she ordered over her shoulder. "We may need him again before this is over. We usually do, it seems."

She disappeared into her private quarters and he heard her un-latching her weapons locker.

Hugo looked everywhere for Webb. When he found the sliding door onto one of the balconies open his stomach gave a hitch. He rushed out into the warm night air, but Webb was just leaning on the railing, gazing over the bay. He looked up as Hugo came hurrying out.

"What, did you think I'd done a bunk? Or jumped?"

Hugo took a breath. "I've told her everything."

"And she believes you?"

"Yes."

"I owe myself a beer," he muttered.

"We've got to get to HQ."

"What the hell do you want me for?"

"What do you mean?"

Webb straightened, brushing off his clothes in an affection of nonchalance. "My mission's complete."

"What?"

"I was ordered to bring you back. I did it. It cost me broken bones, blood-loss and more emotional trauma than I care to think about, but this is where I get off. If your mother really is smart enough to be making the move I think she's making, you've not more need of me."

Hugo took a step closer. "Don't pretend this doesn't matter to you. You can't make me believe that you only came after me be-cause she told you to."

He hesitated then shrugged. "Sorry, Hugo. I am. But she threat-ened to discharge me unless I did as she said. That was it."

"We've had this fight before," Hugo said into the darkness when neither of them had spoken again.

"This one in particular? So we've had that many that we've gone full circle?"

"We always fight about whether you care or not," Hugo countered. "You like to pretend you don't. You think it protects you. But I *know* you, Webb. You can't ever pretend to me that you don't care."

"You're right," Webb said coolly. "We have had this fight before. Because this is where I tell you I'm not the man you think I am. It's not even certain I am a man. Your mom was right. I don't come from anywhere. I'm a no-one. Webb's memories made me into something close to human for a while, but they're gone. They were never mine to begin with, even though you tried to convince me they were. I had another blackout on the *Thorn*, by the way..."

Hugo swallowed, the breeze suddenly chill against his skin.

"I don't know which memory I lost. But it was the worst pain yet, so bet it was something big. So, what, Hugo? You gonna carry on kidding yourself I am who you want me to be? Cos I ain't falling for it anymore."

"Then why?" Hugo managed. "Why put yourself through everything you have for me, if you really think you're not part of this?"

Webb hesitated just long enough to make Hugo hope he'd hit a nerve. Then the clone laughed.

"Dana had me figured," he said. "She had me pegged from the start. Don't you get it? I'm a Service Captain because it absolved me from all responsibility for myself. I could kick and bitch about the Service all I wanted, but ultimately I stayed in because nothing was my decision and I liked it that way. After trying to get over the reality that I'm not even meant to be alive, all I could do was at least make my life someone else's problem."

Hugo felt colder and colder by the minute.

"When your mom threatened to kick me out, I panicked. I knew I'd be out in the Orbit again on my own, trying to decide what the hell I was. I couldn't face it. There'd be no crash land on Haven this time with Jazz waiting to piece me back together. Heck, I thought that if did a decent job maybe your old lady might move me up the chain, give me more security. Of course, that was before I realised that thanks to Red Star the Service might not last out the year."

"I don't believe you."

"If only Dana were here. She'd tell you. As it stands now, I guess I'll have to find a hole to bury myself in until the Orbit is done tearing itself apart. After that…I don't know."

"Captain Webb. Vice-Admiral Hugo." SC Hugo was stood in the doorway. She'd taken the time to change into her uniform, complete with stab-proof vest and weapons belt. Hugo couldn't tell how much of the conversation she'd heard. "We need to move quickly. My flyer is waiting."

Webb waved a lazy hand, a wry smile on his face that was almost a sneer. "Have fun, Hugos all. Good luck with this one. I can tell it's going to be a hum-dinger."

"Captain Webb, you have not been dismissed."

Webb shrugged. "Sorry, doll. I've completed my mission. The rest of this is on you."

"Webb - " Hugo started but his mother cut him off.

"Captain Webb. My only care right now is to warn my people that they are in danger, but considering your personal importance to Red Star, I'm afraid I can't allow you out on your own until my task is completed."

Webb was bristling. "You really think I'm gonna have anything to do with that bunch of - "

"I am confident you wouldn't join them willingly. But they have proved that you don't need to be willing for them to use you." Her eyes landed on Hugo. "So, kindly accompany us to HQ. Once I've done what I need to do, I would appreciate you and Kaleb reporting all you know to the Analysts. After that," she drew herself up looking keenly at both of them. "You are at liberty to decide your own future."

Webb blanched. Hugo wasn't sure which part of the statement had affected him more.

"Don't make me call security after all," SC Hugo said when they still hadn't moved.

Webb swore then scrubbed his hand over his face. "Fine. Let's get this done with. But I want it noted," Webb began as he strode after the special commander, "I'm only doing this only because I can hear Dana's voice in my head telling me not to be an asshole."

Neither Hugo or his mother responded to this. SC Hugo strode through the apartment without a word. Her face was set in familiar, controlled lines. Hugo didn't like to admit that it comforted him, but it did.

Her two large guards followed them from the front door to her private flyer pool. A uniformed pilot was waiting but she dismissed him and took the controls herself. Every few minutes her wristpanel bleeped with messages and she answered the calls with clipped words and succinct orders. Hugo caught the names and ranks of all his brothers in the spoken communications. He and Webb sat in the back seat. Webb was slouched with his arms crossed, glaring out the window as they flew over Sydney at speed. Their angry words still sounded in Hugo's ears, but he pushed them aside, knowing there were more important things at hand. He only wished he could stop wondering about what would really happen next.

He steered away from that thought because behind it lurked a black pit of fear. He shook his head, rubbed his temples. He couldn't think about that right now. He couldn't.

He caught Webb's gaze on him but the younger man quickly looked away.

"What is the plan anyway?" Webb said. "Is there one?"

"There's only one thing I can do at this stage if what Kaleb said is accurate," SC Hugo replied, fielding messages on the control display as she piloted the flyer.

"I'm surprised there's even one," Webb muttered.

"It's not…ideal," she said. "Strategically, it's the last thing we should be doing. But it's all there is."

"Mother…" The air in the flyer changed. Hugo made himself say the words. "Red Star have Ayme and Becca."

His mother's hands tightened on the controls then he saw her deliberately loosen them. "I know, son," she said softly.

"You know?"

She tilted the flyer down as she made the final approach to the sprawling complex of Service HQ. The lights from the dozens of approaching skyways and thousands of lighted windows washed over her still face.

"I surmised," she continued. "I suspected…long ago…but the Academy's official line was that Marilyn had applied for a year's absence for them both. We…your father and I…knew it would be dangerous to chase it." She turned to look at him over her shoulder. "But we have, son. How do you think your wife was able to cover her absence so well?"

"I thought Rami was the only one that knew…" Hugo said breathlessly.

"It was too risky to speak of it. To anyone, even your brothers. You know how delicate an operation their retrieval will be. Especially now."

Hugo felt his heart climb up a rung. He didn't ask what she knew, whether she'd heard from Harvey or knew anything he didn't. He didn't dare. But for the first time, he no longer felt alone.

When he looked across Webb wasn't exactly smiling but the angry lines in his face had eased.

They landed. The parking pool held a collection of waiting aides being waved back by Giles.

They climbed out into the warm night and SC Hugo made for the entrance.

"It's done, Special Commander," Giles reported, referring to a hand-held computer panel. The aides scurried after them, holding panels of their own and calling for SC Hugo's attention. "The Command Comm room is clear. Your aides have had messages from Command demanding we explain what's going on."

"Tell them they will all get their explanation soon enough," the older woman said, loud enough to carry to everyone. The aides fell back as she entered the building. Hugo followed his mother and brother to an express lift, Webb slouching along behind them. When the lift opened SC Hugo turned and put a hand on Giles's shoulder before he could follow her.

"I need you to do one more thing for me." She didn't say the words as a commander to her officer and Giles answered in the same way.

"Anything."

Their mother paused and Hugo saw her fingers tighten on Giles's shoulder. "Go get Dana," she said.

Giles's eyes flickered. He nodded. "Yes, Ma'am," he looked at Hugo. "Where?"

Hugo took Giles's panel from his hand. He booted up a map of Sydney and put a pin in the location of Dana's private landing platform.

"She's on the *Thorn*," Hugo said. "The platform is DNA-locked but I was able to open it. You should too."

Giles's dark eyes held him still for a long moment. "Thanks, both of you," he said, looking at both him and Webb who shifted uncomfortably, "for bringing her home."

"Go," his mother said, voice hard again as she stepped into the lift.

X

Webb leant against the wall of the lift with his arms folded, glaring at the floor and chewing on his lip. Hugo couldn't think of anything to say to him. His mother strode out of the lift the second the doors opened. Service officers, admin workers, technicians and typists still with their headsets on were hovering in the corridor. Their frenzied chatter ceased when SC Hugo came in sight. Hugo and Webb, still scruffy and dirty from their escape from Lunar 1, drew curious or uncertain glances.

SC Hugo strode through the assembled comm workers, ignoring all questions, until she reached the doors at which point she turned and said in a voice loud enough to carry: "I'm about to order an evacuation of this building. Please make your way quickly but calmly out of HQ. Do so now."

There was a moment of silence when everyone looked at each other.

"You heard the Special Commander," shouted the nearest officer, a lieutenant by her pips, "Everyone out. Calmly."

There were murmurs of acknowledgment and then everyone in earshot turned and was filtering down the corridor.

"You haven't lost your touch then," Webb said as they both followed SC Hugo into the Comm room. Displays of every shape and size hung on the walls and were wired to the rows of workstations taking up the entire floorspace of the large room. The desks were hastily abandoned, headsets left on keyboards and chairs, command panels blinking questions, dozens of communications channels open with either confused voices trying to hail a response or text prompts scrolling on the screens.

SC Hugo made directly for the largest setup at the far end of the room. The desktop control panel was big enough for three comms officers to work at at once and the display took up the entire wall space above it. The keys and controls flashed and the display showed several windows of data and reports streaming in from various sources.

SC Hugo sat in the middle chair and began executing commands with fluid movements of her hands that cleared one screen after another.

"Special Commander!"

They all turned as Hugo's two eldest brothers, Verne and Francis, entered the room at the same time. They were still in their black suit jackets from the memorial service. They were panting like they'd been running, their dark hair dishevelled.

"Kaleb," Verne's eyes widened. Both men froze near the door, staring at him. "Mother, what's going on?"

The door opened again and Riley entered, fierce face set.

"Riley?" Francis promoted. "What is this? Why has the Comm room been cleared?"

"Approach, everyone, please," SC Hugo commanded.

The men all glanced at their youngest brother as they stepped up and their mother continued to input commands in the control panel.

"I'm going to need you to stay calm," SC Hugo finally said, clicking one final key on the panel. A demand for identification flashed up on the screen and the handprint scanner in the controls illuminated. She stood and turned to her sons with her hands behind her back. Hugo saw all his brother's backs straighten. Hugo swallowed and dtepped in line with his family.

Their mother met their eyes each in turn as she began to speak. "Your brother has returned to me at some considerable cost to report that the terrorist group Red Star's intention is to hold the Service hostage by means of explosives planted at a number of strategic points throughout the Orbit."

"They what?" Riley bristled. "They can't."

"It appears they can," the mother continued smoothly. "There's no time to explain details. We don't even have much detail. And what I am about to do may very well force them into action early so I want everyone prepared."

The men all glanced over her shoulder at the display.

"Mother..."

"Admiral," she cut off Verne and he silenced and straightened again. "I have explained there is no time. We all know my position as leader of the Service is...precarious...at this time, a time when the last thing we need is instability. I have called you all here because you are the only officers I can trust. The next 24 hours will be the biggest challenge of all our careers. But you've all proved to me you're up to the challenge more than once." Hugo wondered if he imagined her look lingering on him. "Come in please, Giles."

Everyone turned. Giles was lingering in the doorway. At her command he came forward and took his place in line.

"Russian," Webb suddenly laughed. Everyone startled and looked his way like suddenly realising he was there. He pointed along their line and back again. "Been bugging me forever. Russian Dolls. That's what you look all like."

"Captain Webb." Their mother didn't need to say anything more. Webb resumed his position leaning against the wall. Hugo was sure they could all read the derision in the younger man's expression as well as he could. How much Webb's attitude mattered to him at a moment like this surprised him.

"As I was saying, this is not going to be easy. I'm shortly about to activate the Emergency Broadcast System and order an evacuation of all Service-held bases, stations and strongholds that hold more than one hundred people, including HQ here in Sydney."

"Special Commander - " Hugo wasn't sure which brother had spoken, his own head was rushing, but he wasn't allowed to voice his protest.

"Commanders..." their mother's voice had raised slightly. "Take your fastest ships and rendezvous with officers whom you trust. And I mean really trust. Involve as few people as you can, but get yourselves and your officers to places where you can coordinate this evacuation. I want someone in the Western Hemisphere, someone in the Orient, and one of you in drift. HQ here and the Command Space Station I imagine are at highest risk, but we have no way of knowing exactly what Red Star's response to the evac will be. The priority is to get people out of these buildings. All of them."

"Special Commander, if I may," Verne dropped his salute and stepped forward. His face was grave. "I'm never one to question your orders - "

"Then why are you starting now?"

Verne winced. "I wouldn't be doing my duty if I didn't point out that by abandoning all our strategic outposts in one go, we are not only risking mass panic but we will also be weakening our position on every front and leaving ourselves open - "

"I am aware - "

"They could take the Service down without a fight," Verne continued, looking his mother in the face with a defiance that Hugo momentarily envied. "This could be the end of everything."

"If we don't evac," his mother replied patiently, "who can tell how many lives will be lost before the same outcome is reached?"

"You can't..." Riley was flushed with heat. "You can't be meaning to just run away, Mother."

SC Hugo stood still, hand on the back of her chair. Hugo saw her eyes flicker and wondered which members of their lost family she was wishing were there to help her. Probably all of them.

"There's nothing can be done," Hugo said. His brothers all looked at him. Webb too. "Christof Coale will stop at nothing. He will pull the trigger. I'm only surprised he hasn't already."

"Coale," Riley sneered. "Mother, our intelligence says he's number 3 in their pecking order, if that. Arcadius Rose is a loud talker but he's a politician. And McCullough's an idealist. None of them would dare to do what you're saying. Threaten it, maybe. But to actually push the button?"

"Your intelligence is wrong."

Riley huffed at Hugo. "We're supposed to trust you?"

"As the only one of us who's actually been inside their organisation I'd say we have to," SC Hugo put in coolly.

"Mother, he - "

"If you're about to accuse your brother of killing your father then you are also about to prove to me that you, too, are more easily swayed by propaganda than by your own instincts. And I will have none of my children admit to such a claim in my presence."

Riley flushed from his white collar to the roots of his dark hair. Giles was silent and assessing. Verne and Francis's heavy looks was directed straight at Hugo. He met his brothers' gazes with a frank one of his own.

"Mother's right," Verne said and Riley made an inarticulate noise but was silenced by Giles's hand on his shoulder. "You're scared," Verne continued. Hugo realised how much their eldest brother looked like their father and looked away. "We're all scared, Riley. But we've been scared before. We do now as we did then. We follow our orders."

"For the record," Webb put in, raising his hand. "You're all certifiable. But, unfortunately, you're all out of choices. Having been privileged enough to have met Coale, I can attest that Kaleb's right in saying the man would happily blow his own mother up if he thought it would give him the tactical advantage. And if you underestimate his position in Red Star, you underestimate everything."

SC Hugo gave Webb a nod and there was no mistaking the look of satisfaction on her face.

"But after this evacuation, what are we supposed to - " Riley started.

"There is no after," SC Hugo said, sitting back at the control panel. "Not for me. This is my last act as Special Commander." All four older brothers surged forward but she held up a hand. "Our only concern is not letting Red Star destroy countless numbers of our people just to make a point. They can make all the points they want in discussion with my successor. We pull this off, we save everyone's lives and, who knows, we might just prompt some real discussion and not just a deadly pissing contest." She turned in her chair and looked at all her sons and Webb in turn. "You know Rose is not alone in his desire for an Orbit Alliance. The likes of Osgard can think what they like, but the Orbit is tired of military rule. It was necessary, for a long time. But whether it still is or not, its time in its current incarnation is done. People have lived through too much."

No one said anything.

"And so have we, don't you think?" she added, face softening.

The men shifted and glanced at each other. Webb turned his face to the wall. Hugo searched his mother's dark eyes and found defeat and strength in equal measure.

"You have your orders, commanders," she said, turning back to the control panel and placing her hand on the hand scanner. "Go."

They all looked to Verne who nodded after a pause, his firm face grim. They all acknowledged and started to leave. As they moved for the door each brother gave Hugo looks that ranged from wary to sorrowful. It was the most emotion he'd ever seen on them and he knew then that everything as they knew it was surely ending.

Webb looked like he was about to make a comment but stopped when every display in the room went black before displaying the image of SC Hugo's face. She straightened in her seat and started talking.

She spoke calmly but firmly, listing her rank and position. She ordered everyone to stay calm, then went on to issue a blanket order that every official Service stronghold, outpost or command station that contained more than a hundred people was to be evacuated as quickly as possible. Her voice was level, her commands clear. Hugo felt the hair rise on the back of his neck as her voice, magnified by the dozens of speakers in the room as well as the speaker system in the rest of the building, explained they were under immediate terrorist threat and they should all come together to aid the evacuation. Hugo followed Webb's gaze out the window to see the advertising billboards over the skyways and on the walls of the megablocks displaying his mother's video feed.

"That's quite a system," Webb murmured. Hugo continued to hold his breath.

"I will finish by saying this." His mother paused a moment. Already the sound of rising activity could be heard in the rooms around them. On the dozens of screens, Erica Hugo blinked and took a breath. "This is my last order as Special Commander of the Service. I hereby tender my resignation, effective immediately. I hope this move will prompt more forthright discussion between the Service and Red Star and not more violence. I invite Red Star's leaders to approach my successor with a view to finding a peaceful compromise to serve the Orbit and not fracture it further. Both sides should understand that I say from experience that bloodshed does not lay reliable foundations of a newer, better era."

SC Hugo finished with a salute and shut down the system. The displays fizzed and defaulted to start-up screens. The noise of raised voices and hurrying feet began to grow from the hall.

"We should go," Webb said, wiping his palms on his trousers.

"Stay calm, Captain," SC Hugo said, standing from her chair. "We have effectively declawed the beast."

"You know what a declawed beast does?" Webb said, making for the door. "It uses its teeth. Come on."

SC Hugo tapped one final command into the control panel which prompted the building's speaker system to start repeating an evacuation order and then they were heading for the door.

"Do you think it will work?"

Hugo paused at the door, blinking at his mother, surprised by the question. "You're asking me?"

"You know their leaders. You know their plans. Do you think they really meant to commit mass murder or just hold us hostage?"

"Does it really make a difference right now?" Webb snapped as he gestured toward the door.

"Yes it does," SC Hugo said. "Because either we've just saved everyone or forced their hand."

"Either way," Webb said before Hugo could speak. "We should get our asses out of here."

"Webb's right," Hugo said. "I can't say what they'll do now. Coale is…unpredictable."

"Very well. Let's move."

"*Thank you*," Webb said and activated the door control. The corridor beyond was heaving with people heading to the flyer pool, express lifts and stairways. Webb glanced round at the Servicemen suspiciously but, bar a questioning glance or two, the HQ staff and officers were more intent on getting out and away then by wondering about their presence.

People chattered and the corridors and access halls were filled with the sounds of feet, personal comms going off and the automated warning system, but Hugo was relieved to see no one shouting, no one pushing and everyone heading in the right direction for their nearest exit. For one unsettling moment he was back on the *Resolution*, slipping through Admiral Pharos's flagship crew as they calmly and efficiently carried out her orders, unaware or uncaring that she was steering them right into disaster and death.

But he shook his head to clear the sensation. This wasn't Pharos. As he saw the concerned but relatively calm faces around him and the higher ranking officers directing people at corners, he appreciated perhaps for the first time what his mother had built.

"This way," she directed them, taking them back towards her private flyer pool. She was fielding messages on her wristpanel and stopping to answer questions with clipped, precise instructions and Hugo listened to her issuing orders to her sons and her generals as they reported in. He also saw her cut off a call from Admiral Osgard with an impatient swipe of the reject command.

The sky was noticeably lighter when they reached the flyer pool. All other flyers apart from Hugo's mother's were gone and the floodlights were off.

"Giles," she said, into her comm as she hurried to her own flyer, "I'm getting Kaleb and Captain Webb away from HQ. I want the city governor to issue an evacuation order for a square mile around HQ. As soon as all sites are reported clear we are to organise bomb disposal crews - " She halted, tapping her wrist panel and frowning.

"What is it?"

"It's dead," she said, swiping at the blank screen.

Webb pulled back his sleeve to check his own. "Mine too. This can't be good."

They reached the flyer and SC Hugo opened the door to find the controls dark. She leaned in, jerked at the steering and start-up levers but nothing happened.

"Step away from the vehicle, Special Commander."

Hugo felt like ice had been tipped down his neck. He turned to see a tall man with pale hair and a scruff of reddish facial hair step out of the shadows of the HQ building. The sight of him sent ripples of electricity across his temples and down his spine. His fists clenched. Sweat sprung out on his face.

"Kaleb Hugo. I'm very, very disappointed in you."

"Coale," Webb swore. "You cockroach. How did you - "

Coale pulled a gun and fired. Webb swore and ducked for the shelter of the flyer. Hugo couldn't move. His mother had to drag him out of harm's way.

"You've lost," Coale called. Hugo heard his boots approaching. Webb and his mother were drawing and checking their own weapons but all he could do was stare at the sky, breathing choked and muscles unresponsive. "It's already over. Come out and face your end with some dignity at least."

"I'd say the conclusion wasn't all that certain if you've made the effort to come yourself, Coale," Webb called.

"I wanted this," Coale barked. There was an edge in his voice. Not many people had heard him speak like that. Hugo had. "I came to have this moment for my own. The Service will fall and it's only right SC Hugo be the first to go down with her ship."

"The whole damn place could be dust any second, you maniac," Webb called. "And you with it."

"SC Hugo dies by my hand," Coale shouted louder. "Then Service HQ will be destroyed. I will secure Red Star's victory. Then Rose and McCullough will see. Then everyone will see."

Hugo was sweating. The harsh voice wrapped around his brain and pierced his heart. He blinked when his mother put a hand on his. Her look was questioning. Hugo shook his head to try and clear it of the ghost of pain and fumbled for his gun.

"Kaleb," Coale's voice was different again. Hard. Certain. "Bring SC Hugo to me. And McCullough's meddlesome bastard too while you're at it. I will show everyone what a clean start really is."

Hugo clenched his eyes shut. His knuckles ached with his grip on his gun. There was noise wafting on the air, the booming evacuation command from external speakers, flyers launching and thrum of a spacescraper full of alarms under him clamouring in his blood. But all he could hear was that hard, insistent voice.

"Hugo!" Webb and Coale both shouted at the same time as he started to stand up. Hugo shook his head. Black stars flashed across his vision and he heard his own screams but didn't know if they were real or remembered. He smelt the red cement and damp caves, felt the hard rock against his skin, but then a hand squeezed his hard enough to hurt. His mother's voice was stronger than everyone else's as she commanded him to get down.

He dropped to his knees as his mother rose to her feet, aimed and fired her gun. There was the noise of returning fire. Hugo heaved in a deep breath of Sydney's morning air, the breeze off the bay bringing the scents of water, exhaust and sun-warmed metal and used it to ground himself. He was moving before he knew it, running out of cover and pulling his gun. Coale was concentrating on getting out of his mother's line of fire whilst still trying to return fire and couldn't dodge the shots Hugo sent his way. He yelled and stumbled before flinging himself behind an electrical relay shed.

Hugo, his mother and Webb edged towards the shed, weapons drawn.

"You're outnumbered, asshole," Webb called.

Something sailed through the air and rattled to a stop, bumping against Hugo's boot.

"Stun grenade," Hugo shouted. They flung themselves on the ground and covered their ears. But nothing happened. Surreal, quiet seconds ticked by before Webb got to his knees and tentatively scooped up the grenade.

"It's dead," he frowned at the metal casing, all its lights and commands dark.

Coale bellowed a curse from behind the relay shed and began firing from his cover.

"If Coale didn't knock out the electrics up here, who did?" Hugo said as ducked from Coale's line of sight, guns ready, glancing around.

A burst of automatic gunfire had all of them, including Coale, flinging themselves to the floor. There was a rush of air and the whine of flyer engines. Hugo crawled toward the cover of their own flyer as a sleek two-man craft came to a halt over the flyer pool. Out jumped a tall figure head-to-toe in body armour, rifle blasting the air apart.

Hugo added a curse of his own to Webb's startled outburst as they crushed themselves against the stern of his mother's flyer, desperately trying to stay out of the newcomer's rifle sights. Metal and glass rained down on them as the bullets tore through the flyer's air rudder.

"Perfect," Webb cursed. "Fucking perfect."

"Who's that?" his mother growled as she ducked under more fire.

"Vee Osgard," Hugo replied, shuffling them sideways as the other woman circled round towards them, still firing. He could see the flashing control at her belt for a heavy-duty electric damper but couldn't see the actual damper anywhere.

"Osgard?" his mother's face was stony.

"Do we let them draw straws or something?" Webb growled as they continued to crawl, keeping the flyer between them and Osgard without coming within sight of Coale. The firing stopped.

"Everyone come out," Osgard called over the noise of her hovering flyer. "There's nowhere to run."

"You'll have to join the queue, Osgard," Webb called. "Coale is first in line. And just for the record, this whole building could be blown into orbit any second."

"Coale?" Osgard barked. There was movement behind the relay shed. "Red Star traitor. Show your face."

"Service scum," Coale yelled. The edge was back in his voice. "Time for your reckoning!"

Osgard took another step closer. A grim smile pulled her mouth up at the corners. "When my father takes the Service in hand your people will understand what the true meaning of power is. I'm just sorry you won't live to see your plans fall in blood and fire."

Hugo breathed in the warm air. His mother's face had turned to stone.

"Mother?"

She turned hard eyes on him. "This is the woman that killed Dana?"

Hugo nodded.

"Captain Webb," she continued in a low voice as Osgard and

Coale continued to exchange angry insults and the occasional burst of gunfire. "You and Kaleb navigate round to the right to take out Coale. I will take care of Osgard."

"Mother, we're out-gunned. Osgard's weapon - "

"We move quick," she said, checking her ammunition. "Whilst they're distracting each other."

"She's right, Hugo," Webb said, craning his neck and surveying Osgard as she approached the flyer and the relay shed. "The clock is ticking here."

"They won't blow the building whilst their military commander is here," SC Hugo said, looking towards where Coale's voice rung out from behind the shed.

"Only if they know he's here," Hugo said in a low voice.

"Enough talk. Move."

Hugo closed his eyes for a second and willed his pulse to slow. He was moving before his eyes had opened again, close on Webb's heels as he raced, bent low, towards Coale's shed. An expletive and gunfire from Osgard tore the air apart. Hugo and Webb flung themselves to the side. Bullets roared over their heads. Hugo came up shooting, chunks of the metal relay shed shattering with the impact.

Coale had ducked away from them, but was now exposed to Osgard on his left. But Osgard wasn't shooting any more. Her voice was raised in angry shouts, and there was the sound of an automatic rifle fired at close range into concrete. Hugo skimmed round Webb's defensive position, back flat against the shed and threw himself around to face Coale.

Webb yelled a warning but Coale was still recovering from ducking a volley from the other combatants and Hugo landed shots before the blonde man could reposition. There was a cry and a spray of hot blood across Hugo's face. Coale staggered, left arm hanging limp at his side, but brought his weapon to bear. For a split second Hugo took in his frozen mask of a face, red with rage with every last scrap of the control he'd managed to hang onto melting away. He was seeing Coale's real face for the first time and it froze him to the spot.

Hugo pulled himself together with less than a second to spare, rolling under the shots Coale squeezed off at his head, but was at too close range for Coale to miss entirely. Hugo felt a line of fire blaze across his shoulder blade, but snapped back to his knees and fired. He didn't stop shooting until his gun was empty. His heart thundered behind his ribs and the taste of copper and gunfire was thick in his throat.

"He's dead, Hugo," Webb was saying at his side. "Let it go. You got him, pal."

The mist cleared from Hugo's eyes. Coale's corpse stared up at him, eyes wide, mouth open in a last yell of fury. His armoured vest had stopped some of the fire, but hadn't stopped the shots that had found his neck, head and legs. Hugo's gun felt hot in his hands. He had imagined killing this man every waking moment he'd been in his own mind in the caves. This man that had taken his children then caused him to retreat to a place in his own mind where he hadn't even cared.

The shooting had been too good for him. Hugo tasted sourness on his tongue.

A high-pitched cry snapped him back to reality. Another thunder of automatic rifle fire into metal. Osgard's flyer whined and pitched.

"Shit," Webb cried and they ran toward where Erica Hugo was on top of Osgard, wrestling the rifle from the younger woman's grip. The concrete around them was shattered by close-range fire. Blood soaked SC Hugo's uniform and slicked Osgard's armour, but Hugo couldn't tell whose it was.

They reached the women just as Osgard's flyer impacted with the wall over their heads, downed by the last stray volley from the rifle. Osgard was younger and taller than SC Hugo but his mother was having no trouble pinning the enraged gunwoman in place. Her face was a cold mask whereas what he could see of

Osgard's under its visor was contorted and enraged.

Webb and Hugo reached them just as his mother managed to tear Osgard's weapon away. SC Hugo stood, aiming the weapon at the downed figure. Hugo and Webb halted. The younger woman lay on her back with her hands up, breathing hard, mouth scowling.

"Even now you can't do what's necessary," Osgard said. "And you call yourself Special Commander."

Hugo's mother was quiet, but her eyes screamed. "Admiral Osgard is welcome to the title. Good luck to him. But *you*. You killed my daughter."

Osgard pushed her visor back and sat up, looking the SC Hugo right in the eye. "Unlike you, old woman, I'm prepared to do anything necessary."

Hugo's skin went cold. His mother raised the rifle. The younger woman lifted her chin, glaring.

"No," SC Hugo said after a pause, lowering the gun again. "I want you to live long enough to understand. You need to watch your own friends and family die in the name of your cause before you'll really understand. Believe me, it will happen. And when it does, you'll think of me and my daughter. Captain Webb?"

"Ma'am?"

"Relieve Miss Osgard of the damper control."

"With pleasure." Webb strode forward with his own gun ready at his side. Osgard glared at him as he bent and pulled the flashing damper control off her belt. Webb flicked the switch and lights came on around the flyer pool. SC Hugo kept Osgard covered as they backed towards her flyer.

Hugo climbed into the pilot seat and began punching commands into the now-responsive panel. Webb climbed in behind. SC Hugo lingered, watching Osgard get to her feet. Nothing more was said but the set of his mother's face told Hugo she was rethinking her decision.

"We need to go, Mother."

Her finger trembled on the trigger. Osgard's eyes flicked to it and she hardened her glare. SC Hugo muttered something, tears standing in her dark eyes. She let out an impatient noise and climbed in next to Hugo. He pulled the stick up and blasted the engines. The disgusted look on Osgard's face lingered in the rear-view monitor. The flyer shook, the damaged air rudder struggling to steer and Hugo fought for control.

"Shit," Webb swore. "Hugo, gun it. Coale's still moving down there."

Hugo looked again at the rear view display. He just made out that the broken and bloodied figure of Coale was now propped up against the relay shed. Osgard had noticed him too and was running. They saw him lift his hand. It held something that blinked.

Hugo's blood pounded. He flung the accelerator forward with enough force to send a twinge through his healing hand. The flyer sped upwards, the chassis rattling with the speed. He saw the sun rising in the east before the explosion blotted out everything.

The roar punched into his ears. The controls of the flyer were yanked out of his grip as it was tossed on the shockwaves. He struggled, blinded and deafened, for control. His mother's warning finally penetrated and he pulled the controls up and around, narrowly missing a comm pylon. They clattered off the aerials, the hideous sound of metal scraping on metal overlaying the screaming of the flyer engines and the rumbling of the collapsing building behind them.

"Auxiliary, Hugo," Webb was yelling. "Engage the auxiliary."

Hugo stabbed at the controls as his mother did something with quick, efficient hands on her half of the control panel. He finally felt the craft start to respond and applied the air brakes. Their crazy tail spin levelled.

"Keep going," his mother ordered.

Hugo blinked the sweat out of his eyes and concentrated on swerving amongst the buildings and erratic air traffic.

All three of them were panting. Hugo could smell their sweat and the blood on his mother's uniform. He braced himself and glanced at their rear view display. Even with the intervening chaos, he was able to see the remaining levels of the Service Headquarters collapse in plumes of smoke and wreckage. Debris flew and spirals of flame belched higher than anything else on the skyline. Civilian flyers were accelerating away as fast as their engines would take them. There were collisions and panic. The buildings kept crumbling. The noise, even with the growing distance, was deafening.

His mother was staring straight ahead, face white. Webb was twisted in the back seat, staring out the rear view.

"Do you think everyone got out?" Webb queried into the silence.

No one answered directly, but SC Hugo was swiping through incoming messages and calls on her wristpanel with a grim expression.

"Your brothers are accounted for," she said, with a perceptible shake in her voice. "They can take over matters from here." She straightened in her seat, wincing.

"You're hurt."

"It's not important, Kaleb. Get us away from here. The less air traffic in the area the better."

"Mother..."

"Just fly, Kaleb. Get us somewhere safe, somewhere away from the city so I can regroup."

He did as he was told. His stomach felt like a cold stone, heavy in his abdomen. When he blinked he saw flames against the inside of his eyelids. He wove his way along the crowded and chaotic skyways, heading for the first route out of the city centre.

"There's a lot of folk want to talk to you, Special Commander," Webb murmured. Hugo craned his neck and saw Webb's own wristpanel was flashing with incoming calls. "I have no idea where they got the number for this comm. I don't know it myself. But they're all hoping I'm with you."

"Don't respond," she replied. "They have my orders."

Webb shook his head, eyes flashing with the reflected light from his wristpanel. "HQ is utterly destroyed. And looks like Red Star have blown some other places too. The New Tokyo Commissioning Offices and…shit…."

"What?" Hugo snapped.

"The Academy." Webb's face was pale. "The shit's hit the fan and all asking for you, lady."

Every channel on the flyer's comm unit was now flashing. SC Hugo visibly swallowed. "It's not my fight any more."

"I've got at least three generals trying to crawl up my ass here," Webb thrust his arm into the front of the vehicle to show her the panel. "Osgard's support must not be as extensive as we thought. Now the chips are down, they all want you."

His mother didn't look at Webb's wristpanel or at her own. She stared, unblinking, out the windscreen. Hugo snuck her sidelong glances, trying to read her face.

"With respect, ma'am," Hugo ventured. "I don't think your part is over. Not yet."

"I think he's right," Webb said. "The Service is only going to get everyone out of Red Star's way if they work together. They will only do that if someone they trust is calling the shots."

SC Hugo lifted her arm and skimmed the messages scrolling across her wristpanel, face still grim. Hugo steered the craft downwards. The daylight had continued to grow and the noise calm as they left the chaos of central Sydney behind them. The proximity sensors blinked as he neared the earth. He landed, took a breath and opened the door, stepping out onto sand.

The air was fresh and cool. A gentle breeze licked at the sweat on his face. It was laced with the smell of water and smoke. The rising sun caught the tops of the ripples on the lake. Hugo blinked out across the water to the shifting shadows of the cliffs and trees on the far side, just starting to be touched by the warm glow of the early morning. Beyond that, the neon jungle of Sydney rose up against the purple skyline. Even at this distance, they could still see the flames from the destroyed Service Headquarters. Floodlight beams washed holes in the dawn dimness as emergency crew freighters and flyers skimmed around the site, pouring out water and flame-retardant chemicals. Every light in the sky indicating a flyer or vehicle either seemed to be heading directly to or away from the carnage.

Webb, who'd come up beside him, breathed a curse. The orange flickers of the distant fires shimmered over his face. SC Hugo stepped up on his other side.

"I always thought that humanity had finally got through the worst of itself," she said softly. "But it keeps proving me wrong."

"We're only a few thousand years removed from animals," Webb muttered. "What do we really expect?"

"Animals don't do this," Hugo said as the last supporting frames in the biggest HQ buildings collapsed in a shower of sparks.

"It's true the view from here on your wedding day was considerably better," Webb said.

Hugo looked up at the last of the stars, wondering where Harvey was now.

"I've sent a message to Captain Harvey," his mother said, as if reading his mind. "I've told her you're back. Go to your apartment, Kaleb. Wait for her. You've done enough."

"You've spoken with her?" Hugo said, heart jerking.

"No. But I know she's safe."

"Ayme and Becca," Hugo choked, "does she have them? Has she found them?"

"I don't know," his mother replied, putting a hand on his shoulder. "Not yet. But you married a capable woman, son. And Red Star finally have larger problems on their hands than you. Go home and wait for her to come to you."

"What if she hasn't found them?" Hugo whispered.

His mother straightened. "Then come to me. All cards are on the table now. You will be given anything you need to retrieve my grandchildren."

"What does this mean?" Hugo said, raising his head. "You're not resigning?"

She looked back toward Sydney. "No, I am. I'm a soldier. It's all I know. But that's not what's needed anymore. However, you were right. My duties as a leader are not complete. At least…not yet." She began typing commands into her wristpanel. "I will be picked up here. You get somewhere else. Somewhere safe."

"There's nowhere safe," Hugo replied.

"Kaleb. I'm not ordering you. I'm asking you. Please, go home."

Hugo swallowed. It might have been the light but her face looked different. The word 'home' curled around his mind. He could feel Harvey's arms around him and smell her hair. He shut his eyes, feeling heat flare behind them.

"Give me the flyer and I'll get him home," Webb said.

She raised her head, examining the clone in the dim light. "I'm not sure about that. What do you propose to do after?"

Webb let out an impatient noise. "Listen, lady, if this whole fiasco has proved anything, it's that all I want is out. So badly it hurts. Just let me the hell go already. Haven't I already done enough?"

"It's true, Mother," Hugo murmured. "He's done everything we've asked of him. He always has."

Webb snorted. "Well, that's pushing it a little."

"No, he's right," SC Hugo replied in a meditative tone. "You've got a loud mouth and an even louder attitude, Captain Webb, but you've always done your duty…if sometimes inventively."

"Well as much as it makes me glow with warm fuzziness to hear you admit that," Webb retorted with a mock bow, "I would like to leave now. What with everything, I doubt anyone will miss me."

"Not immediately, no," SC Hugo conceded. "After it's all settled I think everyone would like to know what happened to Mc-Cullough's Service-officer son. But, thankfully, that won't be my problem."

There was a roaring whine and the beach around them was flooded with light. The gust of engine exhaust rushed around them and blasted sand against their ankles as a large copter with a two-flyer escort set down near the tree line. The doors opened before it had finished landing and out jumped three men in Service uniforms, a myriad of pips flashing at their shoulders and matching expressions of urgency mixed with relief when they spotted the special commander. The fourth person to climb out was Division Commander Hudson. Hugo's heart clenched. It had been so long since he'd seen his CO's face, the sudden appearance of it made his chest tighten.

"Special Commander," one of the men said, saluting as he joined them. Hudson's eyes widened as she took in Hugo's and Webb's presence but the man was talking again. "We've established an emergency control centre in the Operations Barracks. We need you there urgently."

"I am aware of the situation," SC Hugo replied. "What of Admiral Osgard?"

The man's face tightened. "I don't know, ma'am. He has refused to acknowledge the call for aid to assist in evacuations. And now we've lost communication with his fleet. His remaining units here in the Orbit are looking to you for guidance. Ma'am, you're injured?" The man took in her blooded uniform and limp arm.

"It's not bad. Lead the way."

The man nodded, turned on his heel and strode away, chattering into a comm link, ordering medics to be ready at the Operations Barracks. The other men followed, conferring as they went, urgency still in their voices and stances but there was no mistaking the renewed hope in their faces.

"Kaleb. I won't ask you again."

Hugo swallowed, taking in his mother's earnest face. Some of her hair had worked itself free from its knot. Her face was grimed with sweat and dirt. But the command in her eyes, stronger than he'd seen it since arriving back, was unmistakable.

"Yes, ma'am," Hugo heard himself say in a small voice. "I'll go home."

She surprised him by putting a hand on his face. Her hand was warm.

"I'm glad you're back, son," she said, then strode to the copter, the waiting officers hovering like expectant children. Hugo watched her go, trying to understand the swirling mix of emotion in a part of his mind that had for so long been empty.

"Had I all the time in the world, which I don't, it still wouldn't be enough to give you two the ass-kicking you have earned," Hudson said, startling Hugo from his thoughts, "but either way, it's bloody good to see you both. Please tell me you have a plan."

"We have our orders," Hugo replied.

Hudson snorted, glancing over her shoulder as she was called from the copter. "You're not paying attention to orders, right?" She looked at Webb. "Right, Zeek?"

Webb gave a shrug. "I don't know what anyone else's plans are, Cheryl," he said with a crooked smile. "But I'm out of here first chance I get."

A knowing smile warmed Hudson's face. "That's what I thought." She leant forward and whispered: "Good luck," then hurried away.

Hugo frowned at him. "What is she talking about?"

"I have absolutely no idea," Webb said airily, turning back to the flyer.

"Webb," Hugo shouted over the blast of copter engines. "What's going on? What are you really doing?"

"Like I said," he replied climbing into the pilot seat of the flyer. "Getting the hell out of dodge. Need a lift?"

Hugo craned his neck to watch the copter lift off into the lightening sky. He climbed into the passenger seat.

"Tell me what Hudson meant. No playing around."

"'No playing around'?" Webb said, starting the engines and

launching from the beach. "When have I ever agreed to such a ridiculous idea?"

"Webb," Hugo growled. "If you're planning what I think you're planning, tell me."

"Will you leave off? I'm too exhausted for plans, or games either for that matter. Aren't you?"

"Fine," Hugo relented. "Let's go to my apartment."

Webb raised an eyebrow. "What exactly are you suggesting?."

"I'm suggesting regrouping, restocking. Washing." He drew in a deep breath and then let it shudder out of him, feeling every muscle in him slump. "We need to just…stop…for a minute. Before we do anything else."

"What 'anything else'?" Webb replied softly, after a moment.

"I'm coming with you."

"Coming where?" Webb asked warily.

"Back to Mars."

Webb blinked. "Excuse me?"

"I'm not letting you do this alone."

"Do what, exactly?"

"Hudson's right. You're not one to sit by and watch this all unfold without doing anything any more than I am."

"You've got the star chart upside down again," he said, but he wasn't looking at him as he steered the flyer back towards the city. The skyways had been cleared. Red warning lights were flashing at every junction telling people to land. Webb steered through them. The orange glow coming from the remains of HQ flickered in their external displays and through the rear windscreen.

"You're the last card to be played," Hugo murmured. "There may still a chance to stop this."

"By going to Mars?"

Hugo looked at him. "You're playing dumb. Coale is gone. Whatever happens now is down to Mac. And he'll listen to you."

Webb ground his teeth.

"It's fine if you're still angry with me," Hugo ventured. "I'm still angry with me too." Dana's face threatened to rise in his mind and closed his eyes against it before it could form too clearly. "But I won't let you fight on alone. Not again. I owe Dana that much. And you, too."

Webb slid him a look. Hugo saw wariness in it, but also a cautious flicker of hope.

"You don't need to say anything," Hugo said. "Just take me home. Then we'll go from there."

Webb still didn't answer. Hugo noted their course was taking them towards his apartment and said no more.

It took almost more strength than Hugo had left to overcome the choking emotions that threatened to take him down when he stepped through his own front door. It was dark, quiet and cold. The low sun was bleeding through the large windows, but he still turned on all the lights and wall displays, trying to fill the emptiness. The displays were all tuned to news channels. Reports and footage of explosions, burning buildings and assembling lines of Service soldiers filled every screen. Webb paused to watch the one in the hall, his face fixed.

Hugo found himself in front of the main comm station in their living area. He typed in Harvey's personal number from memory. The connecting screen flashed. He didn't know which he hoped for more: that she'd answer, or that she wouldn't. There were dig-iprints of her and their daughters on the walls. He didn't look at them but focussed on the screen.

The call went unanswered. He swallowed the rising fear and shut the comm station down. He made himself leave the room, heading to the tech store in his locked office. He began pulling out wristpanels, guns, goggles, gloves, climbing wire and other tech.

Webb appeared in the doorway.

"We'll be lucky to get anywhere near Mars, you know. There's heavy space fighting over Silence City."

"We can slip through in the confusion."

"How?"

"Stop acting like you don't have a plan," Hugo said, moving past Webb into the hall. He went to the bathroom, pulling off his tattered shirt. He ran the water and splashed it on his face, washing away days of grime and Coale's spattered blood. He watched it swirl away down the plughole and felt strength build with every second. The man that looked back at him out of the large mirror over the sink was thin, bent and bruised. But he wasn't beaten.

He stripped off all the bandaging on his hand and leg and cleansed the wounds with the antibac wipes from the cupboard. He redressed them and stepped under the shower, revelling in the feeling of the warm water scrubbing clean his close-shorn hair. He scraped his blunt fingers through it, inhaling deeply the smell of the clean water. When he'd dried and stepped back into the hall he felt more like himself than he could remember feeling in…months.

"Fine, talking straight," Webb said from the office where Hugo could hear him going through the tech. "However this what's-what of mayhem ends, it will be ended by your mom, your brothers, their generals and whoever is idiot enough to take over once she's washed her hands of it. But…"

Hugo stepped into the office doorway. Webb was staring at a grenade, chewing on the inside of his cheek. He waited for the younger man to continue, something between fear and excitement tingling over his skin.

"But you're right," Webb finally said, slowly raising his eyes. "I need to see him. Now my mission's over, I need to figure out…" He faltered, rubbing his forehead. "I need to know if this," he gestured at the nearest display with its images of blast sites, emergency crews and death and injury stats, "is really what he wanted." Webb's pale eyes were bright with need. "I'm not going for the Service. Or for you. It's something coming from here," he bumped a fist against his chest, "that I can't ignore. But I don't believe for a second I'll be able to make him stop. Unless I kill him."

Webb's look darkened, as if realising what he said. For all his talk, Hugo realised that whatever Mac was to Webb, it was more than he'd previously thought.

"Either way, I'm coming."

Webb made an impatient noise. "You should stay here and wait for Harvey to come home."

Hugo turned his back and went to the bedroom.

"Hugo," Webb pestered, following him.

"I can't sit here waiting for Marilyn. If she comes home alone…I couldn't…" he paused, knuckles white as he gripped the wardrobe door. "I could never face her again if I sat by now when I had a chance to do something." He looked Webb in the eye. "You're not the only one whose reality McCullough has turned upside down."

Webb looked at the carpet. "I know that. It's just - "

"Just nothing. Marilyn is either on her way home with our daughters safe or…" He paused for a minute to make sure his voice didn't shake. "Or it's too late anyway. I won't sit here alone, waiting to know. You said you want to look McCullough in the eye and ask him why this is happening. Maybe I do too."

Webb's jaw tightened. There was a long, considered moment when innumerable emotions passed through his expressive eyes. But then he closed them and nodded. "Ok."

Hugo turned back to the wardrobe, pulled on a shirt and steadfastly walled emotion up in his mind. "Help yourself to what you need. There's a medkit in the bathroom. There's no time to waste."

Webb folded his arms and propped himself against the bedroom doorjamb. "I want it noted that I'm only going along with this because I know the only way to stop you coming would be to tie you to the bed and I know to my cost," Webb raised his arm to indicate the bandaging on the wrist, "I'm no match for you."

Hugo winced. "How's the gunshot wound?"

Webb kneaded his shoulder. "It's doing ok. Dana…" Webb took a moment to marshal himself. "Dana saw to it all on Lunar 1. I was feeling pretty shitty, but there was an antibiotic shot in her medkit on the *Thorn* she told me to use. That's helped."

Hugo's face felt hot. "Good," he made himself say and turned his attention back to the wardrobe.

"Either way, Hugo," Webb continued, his forced casual tone betraying how much was going on behind it. "I still think you're optimistic assuming I have a plan." His voice faded as he moved back towards the bathroom. "I'm making this up as I go."

"That's when you do your best planning," Hugo called back, pulling on another pair of boots and one of his old jackets. He was amazed at how the old, familiar clothing felt against his skin. He moved through to the office and strapped on his own weapons belt and shoulder holsters, heart lifting further with every action. He then immersed himself in a full check of all his chosen weapons and tech.

He had a plan. A direction. And he had his mind back. The dark caves and red dust no longer layered his innards with fear, confusion and dread. Mars was just a planet with a rogue colony and a revolutionary leader. With the walls in his mind strong again, he felt a growing certainty that if they could just get to Mac, they would know what to do. They could achieve something, even if it was just slowing the progression of the destruction.

The rest would follow whatever path the Orbit chose for itself. And it should be allowed to choose, he realised suddenly.

"Hey, Hugo," Webb said from the doorway, startling Hugo from his thoughts. "What's up?"

Webb had changed his clothing and found one of Hugo's old baseball caps. It might have even been one the original Webb gave Hugo back on the *Zero*. He had also washed and shaved and his black hair was pushed back under the cap, leaving his blue eyes clear. The cuts and bruises on his face were finally fading and, but for the fresh bandaging on his wrist, he looked almost back to himself. Even the missing teeth in his bottom jaw didn't intrude on the illusion.

For a blissfully painful second it was like last few years had never happened and his friend had just turned up to dinner. He half expected Dana to appear at his shoulder to chide them both for hiding away in Hugo's office with their newest tech when the food was cooling on the table.

Hugo clenched his fists, shaking his head to dispel the image and chased the feelings back behind the protective wall.

"Nothing," he said, keeping his voice level. "Are you ready?"

Webb examined him a moment longer, then shrugged one shoulder. "As I'll ever be."

Δ

"So how are we getting to Mars?" Hugo said as he and Webb stepped into the express lift in Hugo's apartment building. The plexiglass walls gave them a view over Sydney's skyline. The skyways were deserted apart from emergency vehicles and increased security patrols. The sun was higher and had dimmed what remained of the light from fire that was consuming the last of Service HQ. The sky directly above was still black with the smoke.

"*Job*'s berthed in a private dock not far from here."

"She is?"

Webb nodded. He was scanning data on his wristpanel with a slight frown. "I wondered how Osgard caught us up so fast. The *Thorn*'s a good little mover and I've seen her yacht. It's built for stealth but not speed. No doubt she berthed *Job* nearby on purpose, knowing I'd register it on my location scan sooner or later. She'd probably planned to use it as back-up bait if she didn't catch us at HQ."

Hugo blanched. "So the ship's a trap?"

"Only if she survived the explosion," Webb said, looking out to the smoke still rising from the north.

Hugo didn't reply. The lift opened on a suspended walkway between his apartment block and the next high-rise. A few curious civilians stood staring out over the smoky skyline with ashen faces. All public service displays and advertising boards were flashing warnings to stay indoors. It was quiet apart from automated voices over loud speakers and the sound of distant alarms and sirens. As they left the residential area behind the noise rose and there was more sky traffic. Ships were leaving the city, crowding launch lanes from public and private docks, speeding off on space-trajectories or into long-distance airlanes to other parts of Earth, dozens of Service security vessels struggling to keep the launches in check.

"Rats from a sinking ship," Webb murmured, weaving his way through the increasing crowds of nervous people who were pushing their way to the spaceports, flyer pools and interstate shuttle stations with armfuls of belongings.

They reached the flyer pool Webb had been heading for. It was almost empty with a cluster of confused-looking attendants at the entrance bent over a hand-held panel, scrolling through solarnet channels for any form of news. They barely glanced at them before waving them through. Hugo recognised the sleek blue-silver craft in a berth near the wall. The few people around were more concerned with trying to load or launch their own craft to notice them.

Webb circled the ship once warily, scanning what he could from his wristpanel before approaching the boarding ladder. "Seems safe. No life signs registering at any rate."

"What about the contents?" Hugo asked, eyeing the craft. "Does the scan register any usual levels?"

"What, of explosives?" Webb gave a bitter laugh and waved his wristpanel at him. "This thing isn't sophisticated enough for that."

"We'll just have to take the chance."

"Don't we always?" Webb climbed the boarding ladder and tapped a code into the hatch control. Nothing happened and he muttered, tapping another combination in.

"What's wrong?"

"She's changed the codes. Of course. But it won't take me…

there."

The hatch hissed open and Webb climbed in. Hugo followed Webb to the cockpit in something like a dream. He'd been here before, but the memories were blurred, dimmed by the blackness that had been his mind. He sat in the co-pilot seat as Webb ran start-up checks.

"Well, we haven't blown up. I guess that's a good sign."

Hugo searched the unfamiliar panel for the internal scan read-outs. "All looks normal. Cargo hold's empty and we're the only ones here."

"Guess wherever Osgard is she's not in a position to be interfering anymore."

"Good," Hugo said, fists clenching.

"Keep it together," Webb said in a firm voice. A glance at his face told Hugo the younger man was talking to himself as much as Hugo. "We'll have time to fall to pieces after all this is over. We can't let it happen before then."

Webb continued starting up the ship. The dock belatedly started hailing them requesting them check in and wait for a launch space. Webb ignored them and fired the engines. Hugo turned his attention to the comm panel and logged into all the secure information networks he knew. He scanned all the information, statistics, Analyst data, officer statements and ranks of order manifests.

Webb launched the ship and cut through the lines of craft waiting for an open space lane, dodging those that, like him, refused to wait. *Job* was quicker than them all and the flickering hail lights one by one blinked out as they sped out of range. The smoke-stained blue-grey sky darkened to black and pin-pricks of stars winked into view. Webb increased their speed. His face had taken on a determined set.

"So do we know what's going on?"

"The Service and Red Star are at a stand-off," Hugo reported as he came to an end of the data. "Eight buildings have been destroyed. Enough to let everyone know Red Star weren't bluffing."

"How many dead?"

Hugo swallowed. "Unconfirmed."

"Did Coale blow all eight?"

"Negative," Hugo said, skimming more reports. "Sydney HQ, the Service Academy and New Tokyo Commissioning Offices all went at the same time. They may well have all been triggered by him. But the others have all gone up at intervals over the last few hours."

"Bastards," Webb said, thumping his fist into the control panel. "That means Mac's followed through with the maniac's plans."

"Except…"

"Except what?"

"He could have blown them all. He hasn't."

"Small comfort," Webb muttered.

"There have been no more explosions reported for the last hour. The public information is limited but the Analysts' order relay channels imply that the Service is continuing to focus on evacuation and emergency response."

"You're kidding?"

Hugo shook his head. "Their priority is getting people away. They are not negotiating, though Rose has been demanding responses."

"That's your mom that is," Webb said quietly. "Which means…"

Hugo nodded. "Which means, for now, the Service is united under her. Except…"

"Except what?"

Hugo expanded the secret report he'd found copied into a personal comm account. "Expect for Admiral Osgard's fleet."

Webb glanced at his screen. "Great. What exactly are we heading into out there?"

"They're pressing in on the colony, meeting substantial resistance. They sustained heavy losses but are refusing to withdraw."

"What an ass," Webb growled, scrolling the reports, "Doesn't

Osgard realise he's throwing gas on the flames? Wait..." He frowned at the screen. "Kaleb Hugo, have you hacked into your brother's personal message account?"

"It was necessary. Riley has all the highest level reports."

Webb chuckled. "Never thought I'd see the day. I'd believe you were a rebel turncoat before I'd believe you'd spy on your own brother."

"Riley and I have never been...close."

"No, he's never seemed the warm and fuzzy type. The fight for the last piece of pie in your house would have been worth a watch, I bet."

Hugo let the silence stretch on for a moment. "Do you have any memories of your own childhood left?"

"Even if I do," Webb said, not looking at him, "they're not real."

Hugo didn't argue. They'd had this fight before too. Hugo believed he'd won in the past. Now, with all that was his predecessor crumbling from his friend's mind, Hugo wondered whether he'd ever been right.

The thought caused his pulse to quicken. He laid a hand on his chest. His heart was fluttering. He could feel the numbness of the scars under his shirt and for the first time in years the feeling of having an alien presence in his chest took over. Sweat stood out on his skin. His cloned heart sped up, pounding as the emotions behind his mental wall threatened to overspill.

"It's ok, Hugo," Webb's even voice penetrated. "You handled it as best you could."

"Handled what?" Hugo asked, staring out the viewscreen, though he knew very well what the clone was talking about.

"Me," Webb said with a sardonic grin. "What I am. What you have in there," he gestured at his chest, "all that mess. It's not like there's any approved guidance on identity crises in clones. Although, if we get through this in one piece, maybe that's something we could work on."

The man was smiling, but Hugo didn't feel his tension lessen.

His heart skipped and hammered. "Who do you think you are?" Hugo asked softly. "Now?"

Webb blinked. "That's a hell of a question."

"I need to know."

Webb was staring out at the stars. There were bleeps on scopes as they approached inter-Orbit space traffic. Webb adjusted their course to stay out of scan range. "I don't know."

"In the caves you were…different," Hugo heard himself say. "I don't remember very well. I wasn't…myself. But neither were you. You were so certain of yourself. More than you've been in the past. You knew what you believed and you knew what was happening in me before I even understood it. You fought me," Hugo forced the words out though the memories were painful, "and it was nothing to do with my mother's orders or threats. That was all you."

"Hugo, I don't think this is time - "

"No, this is important," Hugo said, leaning forward. He was clenching the front of his shirt over his pounding heart. "What you do when you see Mac will depend on it."

Webb made an impatient noise. "I don't know what you want me to say."

"Tell me who you are."

"I'm me," Webb snapped, cheeks flushing.

Hugo smiled and loosed his grip on his shirt. He flattened his palm against his chest and felt his heart calm. "That's right."

Webb blinked, looking uncertain. He searched Hugo's face, frown gathering on his brow. Hugo turned his attention back to the scopes.

"We're ready to lay in a long-distance course for Mars," he said. "I suggest we take the extra time to circumnavigate the approach lanes to the colony. Osgard's assault offers us a chance to sneak through the edge of the engagement and land on the surface un-detected."

"I feel like something's happened here that you recognise and

I don't," Webb said after a pause. He was still frowning but there was less hardness in his face than there had been.

Hugo clapped Webb on the shoulder, drawing a startled glance from the clone. "And I feel like I've finally met you for the first time, Webb. And that there's no one else I'd rather be facing this with."

"You've gone space-crazy."

Hugo felt a smile of his own spread over his face, but then it faded. "I think you'll agree we've both lost more than is fair in this lifetime. It's time to seize something we can call our own."

"And what's that?"

"Closure," Hugo said, calculating course trajectories and running fuel checks.

Webb shook his head. "Whatever you say, buddy. But if we want to get through this in one piece that isn't one, big flat piece, I suggest we leave the philosophising until we get home."

"Agreed. I've calculated our trajectory."

Webb checked his numbers then programmed the course in, sliding him sidelong glances as he did. "You're a weird guy, you know."

"If you say so," Hugo said, turning his attention back to the screen. "We'll be approaching Mars in approximately fifty-six hours. I'll continue to monitor the Orbit-side situation. I suggest you get some rest."

Webb was silent for a time. When Hugo turned to him he was looking thoughtful. "We've said and done a lot of shitty things to each other in our time, haven't we?"

"We have."

Webb stood. "And yet here we are, still flying together straight towards darkness and danger. What does that say about us?"

"Either that despite everything we're still partners...or we're both a mad as each other."

Webb snorted, but his smile was warm. "I think I'm inclined towards the second one."

"Get some rest," Hugo said. "We don't know when we'll get a chance again."

"Ok, ok, Vice-Admiral," Webb said, waving impatiently at him. "On the condition that in seven hours you wake me and do the same. All mushy stuff aside, we're all we've got for back up."

"Agreed, Captain. I'll wake you in seven hours."

Webb nodded, paused like he was wanting to say something more, but visibly swallowed it and left. Hugo took the quiet moment that followed to examine how he felt and was surprised and bolstered to still discover himself determined.

He only let himself wonder briefly how long that would last before taking the pilot's chair and looking out onto the infinite black they were heading for.

XI

Rest was the furthest thing from Webb's mind when he stepped into *Job's* cabin and sat on the edge of the bunk. Too much had happened and everything yet to come was uncertain. He'd only come here to get some space and, he realised belatedly, to make Hugo happy. The man seemed in control again. Let him enjoy the illusion.

But despite all that, Hugo still had to shake him from dark oblivion the agreed seven hours later. Hugo's face in the harsh light was still too thin and scarred, but there was a strength in it.

Webb left the cabin to allow Hugo to get some sleep of his own and was surprised to find a feeling present in him that was suspiciously close to readiness. Cynical as he had been, he had to admit Hugo was right. He'd needed rest. The last time he'd had the chance was back on Lunar 1 which already felt like a lifetime ago.

Dana had still been alive, then.

He pinched the bridge of his nose with his finger and thumb, taking a moment to breathe through the blackness that welled up in him at that thought. Once he had it under control again, he paced to the cockpit, took the pilot's seat and ran all the checks. The ship was in perfect order. Hugo had monitored their course and readings and kept them within the ideal fuel consumption perimeters and they were making good time. They'd left the Lunar Strip behind already. The view out the screen was vast and dizzyingly empty.

The lightyears and hours stretched on. He attempted to remain in a state of gathered readiness by not thinking too much about what lay ahead or behind. He focussed on the insistent knock in his chest urging him on. Whenever doubt flared, it reminded him how much he needed to look into Mac's face and...understand.

They both took their turns to rest and watch the scopes and dig through what solarnet info they could get as they left the Orbit behind. They consistently found little or nothing on either. Webb wasn't sure if this worried or reassured him.

During one of his rounds of the ship, he found Vergennes's fight stick in the hold. He stopped himself from throwing it in the trash compactor at the last second, turning it over in his hands. The lieutenant's face rose in his mind, all earnest, cobalt eyes and a frank set to the mouth. He remembered the fierce loyalty that hardened that mouth when he'd spoken of McCullough. Mac. His father, but Vergennes's saviour. Webb's hands had started to shake.

How could a man who could so easily convince people to follow him choose, over and over, to lead them to their own destruction? His gut dipped when his thoughts strayed to Hugo and prayed he wasn't making the same mistake.

He set up the fight stick and used it to vent his frustration. It helped.

As the hours started to drag, Webb's impatience increased. It seemed like they'd spent forever in this limbo between two fights, part of neither and running from both. When there was a proximity notification on their sensors and he clinked his feet back onto the deck from where they'd been propped on the control panel to see a bright speck growing in size ahead, glowing red as blood against the black blanket of space, it almost took him by surprise. His pulse quickened.

The hours ticked on and the red dot grew into a russet fingernail and then into a claw then into a curved scimitar that filled the viewscreen. When he was able to make out the flashes of laser cannons and his control panel started flashing warnings, he knew it was too late to turn back.

Hugo had joined him silently, not having to be summoned. His hollow face was set.

"Here we go," Webb said, taking manual control of the ship as they got within scanning range of the Service fleet.

The panel lit up with a dozen warnings, commands and hails.

The glints and bursts of space-combat sprawled across miles of the planet's orbit. They were still too far away to pick much out by eye but the scopes told them that fighters had peeled away from the main engagement and were heading their way.

"The Service fleet have sustained heavy losses," Hugo intoned, studying the readouts, "but still have their most powerful ships left as well as several fighter units. You should probably know, Osgard's troops are considered some of the best in the Space Corps."

"They were never going to go down easy," Webb agreed, scanning all the information the computers were feeding him, "but Silence City won't either. I don't know how there's still anything left of either of them."

"We need to skirt close enough to the engagement to not be noticed from the surface, but not so close that we get caught in it."

"Maybe too late for that," Webb said, the engaging fighters now within visual range. Hugo had noticed them too.

"Service fighters," Hugo muttered. "Osgard's targeting everything that's not his own."

"Target this," Webb said with half a grin. He saw Hugo strap in out of the corner of his eye then let everything else fall away apart from his scopes and the feeling of his hands on the controls.

He veered sharp to starboard. The fighters followed. Webb rolled their craft and accelerated direct through the firing line of Osgard's flagship. The *Perseverance* was firing periodically into the concentrated knots of Red Star forces, pressing toward the colony.

"They've nearly managed to get the *Perseverance* into a position to attack the city," Hugo muttered.

Webb nodded, swinging *Job* around again, registered the medley of craft with red stars painted on their hulls ranged from myriad one-man fighters right up to battle galleons with blinding banks of laser cannons. "Red Star have still got enough here to make that very difficult for them."

"They've been moving towards this for a long time," Hugo

murmured.

Webb concentrated on dodging through the flagship's firing path. Their pursuers followed, finally coming within range to begin shooting. Webb cursed as a laser blast scoured past, his controls reporting that they'd grazed the bow.

"Bear port point 1-5-8," Hugo said, scanning the scopes. Webb obeyed, steering just in time to miss the fire of a Red Star assault frigate that had pushed further into the battle to attempt to engage the flagship. Webb focussed on weaving back to the outskirts of the engagement, dodging fire on both sides.

"More fighters are bearing in on the stern," Hugo said, "Lock lasers."

"No," Webb said, pitching *Job* into a dive.

"What?"

"We're not attacking anyone."

"Why?"

"This isn't our fight," Webb said, pulling out of the dive. He dipped to port then to starboard, shaking off more fighters, then found they were out into empty space. He sent *Job* speeding toward the planet that was bellying huge in the viewscreen, Schiaparelli City a fractured jumble of lights ahead. Both Red Star and Service craft on the outskirts of the battle tried to engage, but *Job* was too fast, Webb was too focussed. No one got close enough to land another hit.

Surface patrols moved to intercept as soon as they breached the invisible atmosphere shield. Webb grinned and pulled the ship round tight enough to jerk them about in the artificial gravity, then shut the engines dead.

"Webb!" Hugo cried, as they plummeted towards the surface. The jagged teeth of scaffolding and holding frames raced up to meet them. The blips that were the surface patrol fell back as their speed increased.

Webb closed his eyes. Hugo growled another warning. Webb counted one more breath then fired the engines. The jerk slammed them against their restraints. He pulled the ship round at a break-neck angle, missed a scaffold by mere feet. The ship ploughed through suspension lines holding access platforms in place and metal and concrete went spiralling into the fog below them. Webb lurched them this way and that as they raced through maze of frames and half-completed buildings. Some smaller craft had caught them up and were attempting to get into position above them, but *Job* was too fast and heading down, deeper into the murk and the denser press of concrete.

"She's too big," Hugo insisted, fielding a thousand beeping scans and proximity warnings on the panel.

"We just need to get to the surface," Webb replied.

"Still intact, preferably." Hugo was sweating, his face tight, eyes darting between the viewscreen and the instruments.

"This is the only way to shake them," Webb replied, spinning them round a cluster of industrial cranes. There was a hideous scraping noise as something clawed against the hull. Webb pressed on.

"Are you planning on slowing down at all for landing?" Hugo gritted.

"Who said anything about landing?"

Webb felt Hugo's look on him and flinched as fire from above caught their hull.

"Webb - "

Hugo was cut off by a screech of tearing metal as a shot knocked *Job* off course into the framework of a suspended walkway. Webb fought for control then his stomach lurched as they plummeted down.

"Hold on," he cried over the blaring alarms and the rattling hull. Hugo gave up trying to wrestle with the console and clutched onto his restraints. Darkness filled the deck as they plunged into the foundation levels. Webb gritted his teeth, fighting with the controls. The engines sputtered and levelled them just enough to get them out of their nose-dive before they were crashing into an unseen obstacle, metal tearing and wires sparking, smoke filling his lungs. The bone-jarring impact threw him against his restraints hard enough to bruise.

"Webb? Webb!"

The voice calling his name penetrated his ringing ears on the second try. A hand was shaking him. He blinked away stars.

"Webb, get up."

Webb shook his head. He was hanging in his straps. The cockpit was tilted at an angle, clustered with shadows and filled with smoke. The viewscreen was cracked and dark. Hugo stood with one foot on the shattered plexiglass and the other propped on the control panel, holding onto the straps of the copilot chair for balance whilst shaking his shoulder.

"Webb, hurry up. We need to get out of here before the patrols find us."

"Yeah, yeah," Webb said, still blinking. He spat blood where his broken teeth had bitten his lip on impact and gingerly undid his straps. "I'm on it."

"Status?"

"Nothing broken," he said, wincing as he climbed out the chair and dropping onto the controls. He flinched and clutched at his ribs. "At least, nothing new."

Hugo began to climb up the tilted deck, grabbing hand holds on anything he could. Webb followed more carefully. They fought the hatch open together and cold air rushed in to meet them.

They scrambled down the side of the ship then Webb's boots were connecting with solid concrete. He craned his neck, staring up into dark, swirling fog obscuring the structures above them. They were so far down the weak sunlight didn't penetrate. It was quiet, the thick air dampening what little sound there was. The bleached patches in the murk from various artificial lights were the only sign that there were anywhere inhabited.

"Where are we?" Webb asked.

Hugo had already started moving down a wide concrete

groundway.

"Somewhere in in the South East quarter of the city," he said. "Relatively central, but away from residential sectors."

Webb cast a glance over his shoulder at *Job* as they moved away. She lay crumpled against the ground, her nose buried in the foundations of something so large and dark it was impossible to tell what it would one day be. Smoke drifted from her engines to mingle with the fog. The remaining lights from her portholes flickered and went out as he watched, then she was enveloped in the mist and vanished. Webb felt a pang, but wasn't given time to think about it as the roar of another engine filled the air and a floodlight stained the mist bright white around the crash site.

"Quick," Hugo hissed and ducked off the groundway to press himself into shadows cast by an exhaust chute. Webb fell in beside him, glancing back in time to see Red Star flyers pull into position over the crashed ship, their floodlights scanning the area.

"This way," Hugo murmured, tugging on his sleeve and leading them further into the darkness.

"Where are we going?"

"The nearest entrance to the caves is this way, not far, but we need to get there before they realise where we've gone."

"How do we know Mac's even in the caves?" Webb asked as he raced to catch up with Hugo.

"We don't. But it's a place to start looking."

"Hugo, stop. We can't just run aimlessly around the city. We'll be recognised."

"How do you suggest we find McCullough without checking his stronghold?" Hugo retorted.

Webb paused, closed his eyes and let out a breath. "I know where he is. And he's not in the caves."

"How do you know?"

Webb opened his eyes. "I don't know how I know. I just know he wouldn't be skulking round underground. He'll be out *here* somewhere, somewhere he can see everything, somewhere he's in touch with it all…"

"Like where?" Hugo asked impatiently.

Webb turned and looked up, up into the foggy darkness that swirled above them. He pulled a mental image of the city into his head, as he'd seen it the first time, all those weeks ago that felt like another lifetime. He saw the groundways, the construction sites, the wide walkways, the wide, airy Appollos Square with its elegant buildings and the rocks red as rust in the Marsquake cliffs rising over the city.

He jolted. "This way," he said, turning back towards the centre, using his wristpanel to check their position and direction.

Δ

"No," Hugo hissed, keeping his voice low. "No way, Webb. Why would he be up there?"

"Because he is," Webb insisted. "I know he is."

"It's a ruin," Hugo argued as his friend crept deeper down a narrow fissure tumbled with red rock. Craning his neck he could only see towering cliff face, stained orange where the sun hit it. He glanced behind them, checking they were out of the light of the nearest walkway. The journey here whilst keeping out of sight hadn't been easy, and his skin still itched being so close to the sections of the city thronging with people. Everyone on the streets had been civilian but they were all ready with weapons and eagerly following instructions from the black-coated red star foot soldiers as they gathered in squares and along roads.

Flyers bustled along the groundways, filled with men and women, constructors and their families, eager to be issued with weapons, goggles and comm devices and to take their place in the standing armies, waiting in the squares and streets and gathering halls for…whatever it was they were waiting for. Every screen and display showed the warm face of Arcadius Rose, telling them that their time was finally here. He assured them that soon the hard part would be over and that it wasn't long before they'd all be celebrating the dawn of a new age.

Hugo knew he didn't have time to feel ill, but he did anyway, drawing close to Webb as he scanned the rock fall for a place to start climbing.

"Webb, stop. This is madness. What makes you think he's up there?"

"I just *know*," Webb insisted again. "And besides, look at him," Webb jabbed his finger up. Hugo followed his gesture to a large display on the wall of the building that overlooked the narrow space. Arcadius Rose was smiling down, telling them the Service fleet over their city would soon be overcome and that then their path would be clear to join their fellows in the Orbit to strength their assult.

"What about him?"

"Look *behind* him, idiot."

Hugo squinted. Behind the governor he could just make out white walls and a high ceiling, moulded columns interspersed with tall windows that looked out onto the sickly yellow sky. "It looks like the New Civic Hall."

Webb shook his head and turned back to the rock. "No, that building's not high enough up to look out on the sky. Rose is up here, away from all the drama but where he can see everything and stay connected. And Mac's with him."

"How do you know?" Hugo asked again.

"You're not telling me those are Rose's words," Webb scoffed as he checked his gloves were fastened on tight and started climbing. "That's Mac speaking. He's with him, feeding him the spiel. Come on, I know they did rock climbing at the Academy. Dana told me, so don't pretend you're scared."

Hugo chewed on his doubt a moment longer before stepping up and clambering onto the bottom of the rock fall beside his friend. Webb climbed fast and sometimes recklessly. Bits of crumbled rock and sand clattered away from his feet and hands.

There was determination in every inch of him and Hugo knew what that meant. It meant he was onto something.

Hugo kicked foot holds into the loose rock, shook the sand away as it fell onto his face and climbed further and further up, trying to keep up with Webb. The months in the caves had taken their toll and he was soon panting for breath and his limbs were aching. The red cliffs rose up above him, turning the colour of freshly refined bloodgrease as the late afternoon sunlight dimmed.

Leaning back as far as he dared, Hugo was able to catch a glimpse of the original Civic Hall perched at the top of the cliff. The untouched white polymer exterior and tall windows flashed in the sun, making it almost blinding compared to the dull, dark surroundings. He could see the ragged edge of the brickwork where half the building was missing, tumbled into an abyss on their right. It looked deserted. But he shook away his doubt and concentrated on keeping pace with Webb.

They both paused when they hauled themselves out of the shadow. Hugo's chest was heaving. His heart was hammering against his sternum. The air was still with no natural breeze to ease his heat in the artificial atmosphere. The city sprawled below, a spread of lights, metal and strangled, muted sound. He knew he'd spent almost a year down there, amongst the metal, the fog, the red dust and the determined people, but from this vantage point it looked entirely alien.

"I think we're ok, no one's seen us," Webb said, voice strained with effort.

Hugo nodded, turned back and continued their climb.

"Remind me again why we didn't use a flyer for this part," Hugo panted.

Webb scrambled up onto a ledge wide enough to crouch on and pulled Hugo up after him. "That would mean stealing one," the younger man said, wincing as he rubbed his bad wrist. "And I don't much like our chances of sneaking one away from this lot," he gestured down to the city, "and getting it up here without anyone noticing. No one will be expecting anyone to climb up."

"I wonder why," Hugo grumbled, massaging his aching arms.

"Come on, Vice-Admiral," Webb said, turning back to the cliff face. "We both know if it's going easy, it's probably going wrong."

Hugo gave no answer other than a glare then recommenced the climb. The rock became steeper and steeper. They both paused and hung, panting, trying to spot a way up. Hugo did not look back or down. His shoulders burned. Sweat dripped into his eyes. His fingers ached even in the grip-gloves as they pinched onto the narrow handhold which were the only thing keeping him in place.

"There," Hugo gasped.

Webb glanced where he was gesturing and nodded. Hugo shimmied to his right, then reached the outcrop that was directly below a thin, vertical fissure in the cliff. Webb followed and got himself onto the outcrop next to Hugo. It was breathtakingly narrow. They turned sideways to allow room for both of them. Hugo glanced down and saw his toes jutting out over nothingness and swallowed.

"Here," Webb said, carefully extricating something from under his jacket and passing it to Hugo. "We're in range. You're in a better position."

Hugo turned the launcher over in his hand and sent a look over his shoulder. "You knew from the beginning we'd be climbing up here, didn't you?"

Webb shrugged one shoulder. "What can I say? I'm a good guesser. At least where that man's concerned. But I'd rather not analyse that too much right now. Hurry up, already."

Hugo shuffled round and raised the launcher, aiming for the dip in the cliff above them and squeezed the trigger. The wire sailed up above their heads, arced over and the dart fell out of sight. The wire stopped feeding and went taught. Hugo tugged on it.

"Secure."

"After you, Admiral," Webb said.

"Vice-Admiral," Hugo corrected, shifting his feet as much as the narrow space would allow whilst he got a grip on the wire.

"Maybe not when this is over," Webb murmured.

Hugo suppressed a snort, tugged the wire one more time then pulled himself up. He got his feet flat against the cliff, took a second to feed the wire through a fastener on his belt, then began climbing, hand over hand, foot after foot. The wire tugged and wobbled in his grip as Webb followed.

Hugo forgot everything except the rock beneath his boots, his breath in his lungs, the thunder of his foreign heart and the burning in his arms. He wasn't sure how long it took them to reach the top, long enough for them to fail any Academy field exam, but they crawled up onto level ground with lungs burning and Hugo saw Webb clutching at his bad shoulder, pain twisting his face. Hugo looked down at his trembling hands, wondering if his old strength would ever return.

He didn't have time to wonder long. Webb was already on his feet and running toward the white walls of the old Civic Hall.

"There are no active scanners in this area," Webb confirmed, consulting his wristpanel as they drew near. "Looks like there's monitoring over the main entrances on the south side, but everything here's higher up."

"Checking for flyers," Hugo said, stepping up beside Webb as they reached one of the windows. The clone peered in, hands shading the glass.

"Clear," he said, stepping back, stooping for a rock.

"Stop," Hugo said, putting a hand on his arm as he pulled it back to throw. "It's shatter-proof," Hugo nodded toward the glass. "This was supposed to be their military HQ as well as a civic hall, before they moved into the caves."

"How do we get in then?" Webb said, desperation edging his voice.

Hugo stepped back, looking the walls up and down. "The main entrance is under surveillance?"

Webb nodded, looking at his wristpanel again. "There's too much active wirework showing around there for anything other than scanners and cameras."

"Then we'll have to do what we always do."

"Oh God, I'm afraid to ask. What's that?"

"Improvise," Hugo said and took off at a trot. They ducked under windows and came to the corner of the building where they stepped into the watery, yellow sunlight. They edged down the remains of the north wall. It ended in ragged stonework and crumbling polymer plaster. Hugo inched up to the edge, toes coming up level with the top of the cliff. The rock sheered down below his boots, smoother than a ship's hull, into the swirling fog of the lower levels of the city. The nearest structures rose up some distance away, the construction taking a wide berth of the nothingness that yawned below them.

"How far does it go down here?" Webb breathed, leaning out, one hand on the broken wall to steady himself.

"Far," Hugo answered, turning his attention to the wall. "Watch out," he said, easing Webb back from the edge and getting his feet firmly planted. He held out his arm to Webb. "Hold on to me."

Webb raised an eyebrow but took a firm a grip of his arm with his good hand. Hugo shifted forward, closed his eyes and breathed, before leaning out and around the broken wall. Nothingness fell away on his right. Webb clung tighter as Hugo leaned further and further until finally he could look round the wall into the exposed interior of the building.

He was looking onto what would have been under other circumstances an extremely lavish ballroom. The floor was tiled in black and white with tiles the size of hull panels made from polished stone. The ceiling arched up to the height of the building, carved columns suspending what was left of the roof at ten-foot intervals. A gallery ran along the inside wall and wide windows offered a view of yellow sky and the city below. A wide staircase at the end of the gallery closest to the north wall was made from slabs of the same black and white stone as the floor.

The thought of the resources it would have taken to get the materials out to Mars made his head spin. The replacement Civic Hall on Appollos Square was lavish enough but nothing compared to this. Had Rose intended to inspire his people through such extravagance but then changed the design under Mac's instruction, or had it been the other way round?

Now this room stood with its western wall and a large part of the floor missing, tumbled away into nothing years ago. Drifts of red sand and dust marred the tiles and some of the windows were missing their glass.

Hugo made himself focus. He was hanging over nothing and Webb was shaking with the effort of holding him. He shifted, reached around for a handhold on the inside but slapped at the smooth plaster vainly.

"Do you have another launcher?" he called back, still reaching.

"No," Webb said through gritted teeth. "What do you see?"

"A way in," Hugo said. "Maybe."

He shifted forward again. Webb uttering a warning, but Hugo reached his foot to connect with the edge of the broken ballroom floor. He straddled the wall, breathing heavily.

"What the hell are you doing?" Webb growled.

"There's a way in. Here. Follow me. Carefully."

Hugo shimmied, getting a better balance on the floor with his right foot, gripping the wall with his left hand. There was a blood-chilling moment where he felt himself hanging over nothing but then bent his knees and flung himself forward. He sprawled onto the ballroom floor, rolled to his feet and pressed against the wall whilst drawing his gun. The room was still silent. The emptiness gaped on his right and his breath echoed in the silence.

"Clear," he whispered. "Hurry, I can head something."

There was the sound of scraping and cursing as Webb straddled then shimmied around to join him. With his longer legs, he had less trouble than Hugo, but he still had to grab him by his sleeve to prevent himself from tumbling off the edge. He regained his feet and stared around the vast room, eyes wide.

"Quiet," Hugo hissed, keeping close to the wall, ears straining to hear the sound again. He heard another mumble, deadened in the thick air but reaching them in the silence like a thunderclap.

"Quick," Webb said, nodding to the staircase. Hugo nodded and they ran, keeping their boots silent on the stone, into the shelter of the curving stairway. Hugo edged around it, peering into the darkened corner of the ballroom under the far end of the gallery. The shadows there were punctured with the light of several computer displays and workstations. The silhouetted shapes of two figures moved between him and the light, one seated, the other stood to attention. Hugo could make out the outline of an automatic rifle in the standing figure's hands. The seated one spoke again to his guard and Hugo froze as he recognised the voice.

He looked at Webb and saw he'd heard it too. He tightened his jaw then gestured with his gun, urging Hugo on.

Hugo took a breath and moved deeper into the shadows, approaching the pair from the left.

"The Northern Caves are well guarded, sir," the guard was saying as they came within earshot. "If you were down there, even if they get any more craft on the ground, we could…"

"No," Mac said, voice firm.

As Hugo came closer he could see the older man's face, bathed in the electric light of the displays. Live combat stats were reeling across the screens, along with troop movements, details of communication lines, order reports and live updates from several solarnet news channels and network sites. His hands moved over the controls of the workstations without looking as he examined and filtered all the data. Hugo couldn't help but feel a grudging admiration at the absolute control he displayed, firing off text commands with one control panel whilst filtering the feedback and sending out blanket orders with another. There was an earpiece in one ear and a wrist panel on both arms, all blinking and flashing as they received communications. "The connections in this building are far more powerful than in those caves. This is where we run everything from, as agreed. This is our moment, soldier. I'm not hiding underground whilst our forces are out here building my future without me."

"But sir - "

A shot rang in the air and the guard dropped to the floor before finishing his objection. Hugo stared at Webb. The younger man's face was unrecognisable as he stepped out of the shadows with his gun raised.

"Should have listened to your men, Mac."

Mac did not turn in his seat. He hadn't even jumped. His only reaction was to still his hands on the console. "Even I didn't expect you to try something as foolhardy as this," he said, voice calm but low.

"Stand up. Get away from those machines."

"Webb," Hugo warned as he stepped up to his friend's side, his own weapon trained on the older man who still hadn't moved. "Be careful."

"Perhaps you should listen to your own men, Ezekiel."

"Get up," Webb ordered.

"No can do, lad."

"Duran McCullough," Hugo intoned, taking another cautious step forward. "You are under arrest for terrorism, revolutionary war crimes, and causing mass destruction and unrest. Order your forces to surrender now and accompany us to Service Command to await trial."

Mac finally turned. His weathered face was cool. He didn't even glance at their raised weapons. His blue eyes were unemotional. "One word from me, Vice-Admiral Hugo, and there is no more

Service Command."

Hugo tensed.

"Don't make it any worse," Webb said, taking another step closer. Hugo thought he was almost pleading. The hard mask of his face had slipped. His eyes looked into his father's earnestly. "Mac, you don't *want* this," he said, nodding to the scrolling combat data and loss stats. "You never wanted this. Tell me you didn't."

Mac stood. He was wearing plain black combat gear and a long black coat. There was an ornate red star patch over his heart. He had a gun clearly visible at his hip but he did not reach for it.

"Kill me now, if you must, boy," Mac said, voice, if anything, slightly weary. "But I warn you, It won't make any difference. *This* is change," he said, gesturing at his displays. "It is bigger than you or me. It's bigger than the Hugos, and their legacy of oppression and control." The pale eyes flicked to Hugo who kept his face blank, then back to his son. "The future is happening. And no amount of frightened children with guns pointed at their elders will stop that."

Webb was shaking. Hugo was struck by how the two men looked like mirror images of each other, but whereas Mac was showing nothing, Webb was wearing everything on his face.

"This is wrong," Webb said, voice breaking. "This is just... wrong. You said to me...you *believed*...that any future that loses you everything before you gain anything wasn't worth it. I know you believed that. You said as much on Haven."

Mac sighed. His face softened. He took a step toward the clone. Hugo examined the console out of the corner of his eye, trying to discern Red Star's position and plans.

"My first revolution failing and the reprisals the Service laid upon the Lunar Strip, yes, that hurt. I'm not a robot, boy. I feel. More than most, probably. And for a long time, I was wounded. I stayed where your mother put me and accepted that I'd failed. Then I found out about you..." Webb stiffened as the older man came so close his chest was almost touching his gun. "I found out about you and what your mother had done," he continued, voice softer than ever, "and it made me look again at what I'd lost. But do you know what you also showed me?"

"What?" Webb said in gritted teeth.

"That there's always a second chance," the old man's smile was warm. "That the things you care about, you don't let go."

"That's a very romantic way of looking at Admiral Pharos killing then cloning her own child in the hope of using him as a political puppet," Hugo said, taking a step toward the console.

"Perhaps you're right," Mac said. "And I was defeated by it. For a long time. I licked my wounds and I buried my head in the sand. But the universe called me back. You think *I* set up Red Star?" He shook his head at Webb, a wry smile on his face. "Lad, Red Star was already here. The seeds were laid generations ago, in the workers that built the colonies, in the families that fled Earth after World War III rendered most of her uninhabitable. Red Star is in the heart of every human being that has suffered because the people at the top can't decide how best to destroy everyone that doesn't agree that they should be in control. And I wouldn't bother with that, Hugo lad," Mac said as Hugo leaned over the workstations. He jumped and refocused himself on the old man, keeping his gun level. "There's no pre-programmed recall command or anything like that. This is where I talk to all my soldiers, where I keep track on what they're doing and guide them on to their next move. Red Star is not commanded by machines or Analyst data. It's lead and guided by the very blood that's in my veins."

"If you sat down there and told them all to withdraw, they would," Webb said.

Mac held his gaze, looking faintly disappointed. "You know that's not going to happen, son."

"Oh yeah?" Webb surged forward and pressed the muzzle of his gun in the centre of Mac's forehead. "Bet your life?"

"Ezekiel…"

"Do it," Webb gritted. "Pull your troops back. Order them the hell away from the rest of the red cement. Surrender now and end this!"

"You know I can't, son."

The gun shook. Webb's face was flushed, his jaw tight.

"The Service has evacuated your target areas," Hugo put in, his voice calm. "They'll regroup and come after you."

"The Service is split. Just look at them," he nodded out into the open space where the furthest wall should be. The yellow sky was darkening to a burnished gold as Martian night approached. In the dimness, the flashes and bursts of the space battle could be seen. Mac took a step back from Webb's gun as the younger man stared up at the silent fire burning above them. "They're tearing themselves apart from the inside, right to their rotten core."

"Not any more. The Special Commander has brought them together. They're readying for retaliation."

Doubt flared in the older man's eyes for the briefest second, but then he shook his head. "It's touching you have faith in your mother," he said. "But she is just one person. She may have successfully nullified the damage from Sydney HQ, but her influence won't last when they lose Command under her watch, evacuated or not." Mac raised his hand and hovered it over his wristpanel.

"You move it you lose it," Webb said, shifting his gun to point at Mac's hand.

"If I don't destroy it, my armies will."

"For the love of God, man, don't you get it?" Webb's voice rose. "*You will not win this.* Whatever you may believe about the power of your cause or other bullshit, this is the *Service* we're talking about. And now they're *united.* And *pissed.*"

"They are rudderless and divided," Mac insisted.

"You need to check your intel," Webb retorted. "I tell you, Admiral Osgard is the only dissenting voice amongst them and you're about to wipe him out," Webb gestured up at the sparking space fight. "You can't win. And if you keep trying, all you're going to do is up the body count."

"If there's one thing I'll be happy to have taught you above everything else, son," Mac said coolly, after a long pause. "It's that some things are worth fighting for. Even dying for."

Hugo swallowed, watching his partner's face intently. A hundred things rose to his lips, but he clenched his jaw shut letting the two men focus only on each other.

"Mac…" Webb sounded different. He lowered his gun. His shoulders slumped. His eyes seemed to have lost what little colour they had. "No more evading. Please tell me that, whatever you hoped for, you didn't want it to go down this way." He gestured at one of Mac's screens that was streaming a news channel with footage from the first wave of explosions. There were shots of rows of stained blankets draped over shapeless bundles, emergency crews battling through panicked people, sweating and straining to reach anyone still alive.

Mac was gazing at the screen, face still calm. When he looked at his son again, a touch of something sad flickered in his eyes. "You need me to tell you this wasn't my plan?"

Webb swallowed. "I do."

"You want me to claim that I wasn't willing to do this? That the only reason it went this way is because of Coale and the mess with your friend here?"

Webb's eyes flicked to Hugo and back to Mac. His hands clenched at his sides, the gun in his right hand quivering. He nodded.

Mac sighed. "I'm not here to make you feel better, lad," the older man said. "As much as I would give anything to be able to."

"Webb," Hugo stepped between them. "This isn't getting us anywhere. The revolution will carry on, if he lives or dies. He's not going to change his mind, and I'm not convinced it would change anything if he did. There's nothing we can do here after all."

Webb didn't seem to have heard him. He was still staring at his father. Tears stood in his eyes. He was stood rigid but somehow looked smaller, defeated.

"I'm sorry, lad," Mac said, softly.

"Are you?"

Mac tilted his head. "I'm sorry that I can't be sorry like you want me to be."

Webb shook his head, dropping his gaze to the floor.

"One day you'll understand."

"McCullough." A loud, clear voice echoed through the room. Webb and Hugo snapped their guns up. Arcadius Rose froze as the door to the ballroom swung shut behind him and he saw Mac wasn't alone. He raised his arms. "What's happening here?"

"Nothing," Mac called, though he didn't move or take his eyes off their weapons. "A small family disagreement, that's all."

Webb snarled. His gun twitched.

"McCullough…" Rose took a few more cautious steps into the room. "This doesn't look like nothing."

"Where are your bodyguard, Rose?"

"I left them at the entrance."

"Call them in, please. We need these men removed."

"Don't move a muscle," Hugo snapped, taking a step toward the governor who stopped where he was, eyes flicking from him to Webb and back again. He nodded amicably. "Very well. I think we can all agree you're calling the shots here, Vice-Admiral," Rose replied. "I'm saddened to see you take a step backward after everything we achieved together. But you've made your choice. I respect that. However, choice or not, under the circumstances you must see your presence here is unlikely to change anything."

"Your revolution might well carry on without you," Hugo snarled, surprised at the emotion now in his voice. "But the world would still be better without you in it."

Rose blinked but otherwise betrayed nothing. Hugo felt fire course under his skin. The governor's mild face was one etched into his mind as one that had overseen his torture at Coale's hands without any visible reaction. He was eyeing him now with the same detached professionalism.

"I can understand how you'd come to think that," the politician said smoothly. "For what it's worth, neither McCullough or I wholly approved of Coale's methods." Hugo tensed. Rose took in the reaction but continued in his level, reasoning tone. "But either way, I did think you above petty revenge. Both of you," he glanced at Webb. "For you must see that this is all this is."

"We've been through all this," Mac said in a slightly bored voice, though the intensity with which he kept his focus on his son, who hadn't moved and was still aiming his gun at him, belied his casual tone. "Our future may take more time, more sacrifice. But it will arrive, with or without me. Or Rose."

"Or Coale," Webb sneered. "He's gooey shrapnel, just so you know."

Mac narrowed his eyes. "We know. He did what was necessary. It's a shame he let his personal desire for glory rule him. I always suspected it would be the end of him. But his work will live on."

Hugo felt his palms sweat in their gloves. He kept his attention riveted on Rose who continued to regard him coolly. His mind spun back and forth, scrabbling after a solution.

"It's all over, son," Mac's voice was soft again. He's taken another step closer to Webb, reaching out a hand as if to touch him. "Please try and see this is the only way."

The shot ringing out had Hugo ducking before he could think. He recovered, blinking around and shouting Webb's name. Mac was down, bleeding onto the tiles next to his prone guard. Webb was staring at him, dumbstruck. His weapon hadn't wavered. Rose hadn't moved but he was stiff as a rod, gaze riveted on the blood. Mac gasped, eyes wide, clutching at his chest.

Hugo swung his gun around as a tall figure stepped out of the shadows under the staircase. His blue eyes blazed. He stopped several paces away, keeping a gun levelled, staring fixedly at Mac with rage hardening his handsome face.

"Vergennes?" Webb said, face slack with surprise. "What the -"

"You were everything to me," the tall young man said, coming forward. His emotion was betrayed by the thickening of a French accent. He wasn't looking at anything but the older man on the floor. His face burned. His muscled frame was rigid. "You were *everything*. But now you're nothing." He raised the gun again but Webb cried out. Hugo shouted a warning, he didn't know who to, and Webb fired.

Vergennes crumpled to the floor, a bullet hole oozing between his fair eyebrows. Webb stood breathing heavily. Hugo rushed forward, but the lieutenant was dead.

Hugo looked up at Webb. His expression was limp with shock. Rose was looking over the scene with a pale face. Hugo considered searching him for any comm devices but it didn't look like it had occurred to him to call for backup.

"He must have followed us," Hugo said, looking back at Vergennes, "escaped from Lunar 1 and tracked us down."

Webb shook his head. "No," he said, voice cracking and unblinking gaze still on the younger man's empty eyes. "He told me he had something he needed to do. I hadn't realised…" His sniffed, wiping his mouth on the back of his glove and shifting from one foot to another, seemingly unable to keep still. "He was like me. He didn't want to believe that Mac would…"

Hugo looked over at the screens. A red light had caught his eye. The warning text flashing next to it sent the blood rushing to his head. He hurried to the workstation, booting up the report details, heart hammering. Rose followed his gaze, registered what was on the screen and went paled further.

Hugo had to say Webb's name twice before the younger man looked up from his dead lieutenant. "What is it?"

"Lunar 1."

"What about it?"

"They've mobilised their own fleets."

"They've…huh?"

Hugo nodded, going back to the report. "Councillor Pope has declared that he is intervening. They're launching as we speak."

Webb's face flickered. "Who has he declared for?"

Hugo took a breath. "The Service."

Webb blinked. "They'll destroy everyone…"

Rose went very still. Hugo glanced at him and saw the man's eyes skimming the report over his shoulder. The face was still a carefully-schooled blank but Hugo could see his mind racing behind the mask.

Hugo glared at him. "Not nice being faced with the reality of your people going down in smoke and blood is it?"

Rose blinked at him. His face suddenly looked pained. "That was never the plan."

"Bullshit," Hugo swore. "You were willing to throw people into the fire of Service cannons when you thought it would help you win."

Rose shook his head. "No, Hugo. You don't understand. You never understood. Sacrifice, yes. I understood the necessity for sacrifice. So did McCullough. But not this…" he nodded at the screen. "Red Star are strong enough for the Service to reckon with, with or without detonating the red cement. And I would never, never had detonated any more."

"Small comfort to families of the smoking corpses they pulled from the Academy," Webb countered.

Rose held out his arms with the palms up. "The Service would have met us to talk. SC Hugo said as much. We were only trying to invoke negotiations. And they would have happened. Eventually. But Lunar 1 have one of the largest independent fleets in the Orbit. With them mounting against us, we're outnumbered but without an order to do so, Red Star will not stop. Not even if it means they're eradicated, down to the last man. But total annihilation of either side was never the plan. How can I build a future if there's no one left to build it for?"

"I don't understand," Webb put in. "Why are Lunar 1 fighting for the Service?"

"Councillor Pope probably considers it'll be easier keeping his power under the Service than a socialist alliance," Hugo gritted, still glaring at Rose. "This is not going to be over quickly. We need to get away while we can," he added, standing.

"No," Webb said slowly, eyes drifting over to the console. "There's still something we can do."

"There isn't," Hugo said. "I've looked. McCullough was telling the truth. There's no pre-programmed retract or surrender command. Even if there were, they wouldn't follow one unless if came from McCullough himself."

"Could you do it?" Webb demanded of Rose.

Rose blinked, looking uncertain for the first time Hugo could remember.

"Do it," Webb hissed, gesturing at the workstation with his gun. "Sit down in that chair and call your armies off. Do it now, before Pope gets his marching orders or one of your people fires off the rest of the red cement."

"I...can't," Rose said, suddenly looking a whole lot less confident. "All Martians know that McCullough and Coale were the military leaders. They would not follow a military order from me...but you..." Rose's eyes widened as he stared at Webb. "You could do it."

"Me?"

Rose nodded earnestly. "Declare yourself heir. Take your inheritance. Say you're taking up your father's role."

"No," Webb said, taking an unsteady step back. "I won't be part of this."

"Webb," Hugo said. "It may be the only way."

"No," Webb said again, pressing his fist to his temple. "No, I won't. This is not how people find out who I am."

"You have to, Zeek," Hugo said standing, feeling his face flush.

"No," Webb said again, glaring at the floor. "This isn't my war."

"Zeek," Hugo put a hand on his shoulder and ducked his head to make the younger man look him in the eye. "This is your chance to prove you could be the man he could never be." He gestured at the still figure of Mac on the floor, face turned to the side and eyes glazed and staring.

Webb glared at his father then at the console. More reports of Lunar 1's fleet numbers were rolling in and urgent requests for orders from Red Star units piled up on the comm unit. Hugo made himself stay silent. He finally stepped aside with relief when Webb slowly lowered himself into the seat, eyes skimming the console and displays. His movements were jerky, stiff, like he was in a dream, but as he typed they became more fluid, like he was growing more certain.

Hugo exhaled a shuddering breath and stepped away, glancing back at the men on the floor and blinked.

"My God, Webb. He's still alive." Hugo rushed to Mac's side. The older man's eyes were flickering. His breathing was barely there and ragged. There was blood soaked into his shirt and coat but when Hugo searched for his pulse it was still strong. Hugo ripped a strip of the man's shirt and pressed it onto the wound, keeping the pressure on. "Webb, hurry, we've got to get him out of here."

"Leave him."

"No," Hugo barked. "He's to face trial. I'm getting him back alive."

Webb glanced over his shoulder. The older man had turned his face to his son. For the first time, Hugo thought he detected weakness in his expression. It may have been the blood loss, but to Hugo it looked like his eyes were pleading.

Webb paused, swallowing, but then turned back to the controls. "Keep him alive. This won't take long."

All the displays went blank. Rose took an uncertain step forward and bent to Webb's ear, saying in a low voice, "Make it convincing, McCullough. Lead them. They will follow."

Webb shot him a poisonous look. Rose nodded firm encouragement, unfazed. Webb took a breath and turned back to the screens. His expression was set. He pressed a few more keys then his own face, pale, drawn, spattered in blood with shadows under his eyes and rock dust smudged across his skin, filled every screen. He pulled off the baseball cap and brushed hair out of his face. He looked startled, scared, but then he visibly gathered himself, his mouth hardening and his look becoming more firm and the resemblance to his father was undeniable.

"My name is Ezekiel Webb," he started. His voice was level, but Hugo could detect the edge in it that betrayed how hard he was fighting to keep it so. "Those of you closest to Duran McCullough will know me as Errol McCullough, his son. My father is dead, killed by a Service double agent that infiltrated the perimeter around Schiaparelli City."

Hugo pressed Mac's hand over his wound, felt the old man gather some strength and apply pressure, then rose to his feet. He paced to one of the tall windows that looked out over the city. Every visible screen, from the large public displays on the megablocks to the smaller screens around the squares and along every groundway, was filled with Webb's face.

"The Service is mobilising. They are uniting for a counter strike. Lunar 1's independent fleet has now added itself to their numbers. They have not responded to your demands because they intend to wipe you out. The threat of red cement has been neutralised as SC Hugo has had all the strike sites evacuated. But there is still hope." He paused. Hugo looked back at him, willed his friend on silently. He saw Webb re-focus and continue. "I believe the Service can still be persuaded to meet with Governor Rose to find a compromise. I believe Special Commander Hugo will take the chance if you…we…give it to her. But Red Star must withdraw. Now. By the power handed down to me by my father, I order you to abandon your posts and hold off from any more violence." He took another shuddering breath, closed his eyes then opened them again. They were clear and his voice was firmer. "You have been heard. Now let the negotiations happen."

The air was thick. Rose was tense, glancing again at Mac who was now trying to get himself up onto his elbows. He was trying to speak. Hugo hurried to him and pushed him back to the ground, gently, but covered his mouth. He looked up at the space battle, but it didn't appear to have diminished in its ferocity.

"Rose," Webb ordered, standing and gesturing at the seat in front of the camera.

Rose blinked and stared at Webb, like he'd just been woken from a nightmare to find a monster from it still in the room.

"This is your chance," Webb said, every word weighted. "This is your only chance to get what you want. Tell them. Make them believe this needs to happen."

Rose took a breath, straightened his tie and sat. He started to talk. He more or less repeated what Webb had said, but he talked well. Calmly. His posture was again assured. Hearing him talk, and what he chose to say at that moment, made the tiniest spark of reassurance ignite in Hugo's chest.

"Red Star, withdraw. Our work is finished. We have provoked a response. This is all we needed. Let me build you a future with no further loss of life. I won't let you down."

The red star pin on his lapel winked in the reflected light of the displays as he stood. He nodded to Webb who came forward and shut down the system. The remaining men still breathing all regarded each other warily. The dead air pressed in on them.

Hugo stood, Mac having given up trying to sit and lay quietly with his eyes shut.

"This is the first step in our negotiation," Rose said in a steady voce. He glanced at Mac. "Take McCullough. Ensure he lives. He and Coale were the ones that designed and executed the violence, not me. He will gladly testify to that, should he survive. I intend this gesture to stand me in good stead and to secure my position as negotiator when the Service agree to meet."

"You're an inciter," Hugo said, stepping forward, drawing his own gun again. "We are taking you in for trial too."

"Then this will all be for nothing," Rose responded smoothly.

"If I am not here to speak for them, Red Star will continue their campaign."

Webb was weighing up the politician with suspicion. "You really think you can still make a change, after all this? And without any more violence?"

Rose put his hands behind his back and tilted his chin up. "I can. Trust me."

"After everything you've been part of," Hugo said, voice low. "After everything that was done to me, to my family, do you honestly expect us to walk away and leave you here?"

"If you want this to be over," Rose returned mildly. "Yes, Vice-Admiral Hugo. I do. And I think you will. All you're doing now is wasting time and lessening the chances of getting Duran McCullough back to your people alive."

Hugo glanced down at the injured man. His eyes were fluttering. Hugo wrestled with himself. He could see a similar struggle going through on in Webb's face. He was not looking at his dying father, or the displays, or at Rose who was standing by calmly, waiting for them to come to the conclusion he knew they had to.

"Webb," Hugo said, and heard his voice was steady. "We need to go." Webb looked at him. He didn't speak. It didn't look like he could. Hugo took a step forward and put a hand on his friend's arm, willing his own growing certainty to seep through from his hand into the other man. "We can still save your father."

Webb's eyes flickered. "Do we want to?"

"Blame is a relative thing, young man," Rose said softly. "The fact that his testimony will be the only thing that can help me salvage this situation is not."

Hugo ignored the politician. "Webb. He's your father," he said, tightening his grip. "Sometimes that's all that matters."

Webb's look slid to the old man on the floor. He swiped his face on his sleeve then nodded. "Let's move."

Webb and Hugo bent down to Mac, moving precisely and efficiently, tearing more strips from their clothing to secure the sodden wad of fabric over his chest wound. Rose was entering commands into some surveillance software at the workstation.

"I'm disabling the cameras around the main entrance, and ordering the guards out there back into the city," he said. "You can take him out that way without being seen. Red Star may or may not have accepted your claim as heir, Webb, but they will certainly think twice about letting you carry McCullough out of here. But this should get you away safely. There will be a ship with all the clearances needed waiting for you at the public dock just south of here. You just need to get past your own blockade."

"We can handle that," said Hugo, bending and pulling one of Mac's arms over his shoulders. "Rose," he said, as the old man gasped as he was pulled to his feet. The politician turned in his chair. "I'm only doing this because I believe this is the only way to end all this. If you mess up, I'll be back for you."

"Along with an entire armoured battle division of the Service Space Corps, I have no doubt. Go."

"Webb. Move," Hugo said.

Webb shook himself, pulled Mac's other arm over his shoulders then looked back at Vergennes. "Goddamn you, Mac. He was a good kid. You crushed him."

Mac whispered something, but it was too quiet to hear. Hugo gave them another nudge and they began shambling to the door. The section of floor that sheered off into nothing yawned on their right and Mac craned his neck to look out over the rocky void to the half-built city.

"Mars is ours," he whispered. "We will survive."

"Save your breath for the Analysts, old man," Webb snapped bitterly.

Hugo didn't speak as they hustled the wounded man out. It was a short distance to the main entrance, the huge doors hanging open at drunken angles where their hinges had buckled with the force of the quake. They found a narrow path down to the city, zig-zagging across the rocky surface of the cliff face. There were footprints in the red dust, but no one was around.

Webb didn't speak as they shambled down the rock path with Mac strung between them. The only noises the old man made were gasps as he was jolted roughly along. Hugo sweated under supporting his weight, which was getting heavier as he grew weaker.

"Don't you dare die, old man," Webb muttered once. "Your work isn't done yet."

The climb down felt like it took hours, but they managed and found their way to the public dock. Good as his word, Rose had cleared all guards and there was a ship berthed apart from all the others, with a dock worker nearby who waved them over. They both kept their faces lowered, but the dock worker gave them nothing more than a cursory glance before opening the ship for them.

"You know, they're treating injuries at the clinic around the corner," the worker muttered. "Don't see why you've been given orders to ship this man out."

Neither of them said anything and the dock worker enquired no further. Hugo kept a close eye on Mac in case he tried to yell for help but the old man was blinking back unconsciousness. The dock worker finished opening the ship then hurried back to the display at the far end of the dock where all the other workers were gathered, listening to Rose's continued broadcast with taut faces. Hugo wondered whether they found the order to withdraw an insult or a relief.

They struggled the unconscious man up the ladder and into the ship. It was an old runner, with no hold and just one tiny cabin. It looked to be built for speed over capacity and Hugo looked at the deathly colour of Mac's face and prayed she lived up to her appearance.

"You look after him," Hugo ordered once they're lowered Mac onto the bottom bunk in the cramped cabin. "I'll get us out of here."

"No way, Hugo," Webb argued. "I'm the faster pilot."

"Someone needs to keep him alive," Hugo returned. "That means not leaving his side and I have to put in half a dozen comm calls to get us back to Command without getting arrested. Besides," he paused at the cabin door. "He's your father."

Webb made a disparaging noise, glaring at the unconscious man.

"Webb, I'm not saying you should forgive him," Hugo said quietly. "But I am saying if you let him die…you'll regret it." Hugo's voice failed him. He left, the sight of Webb looking pained and alone blurring with his vision.

Δ

Webb stared at the hatchway for an immeasurable length of time after Hugo has left. He could barely think above the raging in his head.

Only when the engines roared to life and the deck tilted under his feet did he snap out of his stupor and force himself to turn his attention to Mac. He made himself kneel and take the old man's pulse, feel his temperature and peel back the weak hands from the bloody wound in his chest. His pulse was feeble, the skin of the lined face clammy and grey. The wound, when he pulled the shirt back to examine it, was ugly, but high enough in the chest to have missed his lung.

"Take me back," Mac creaked. "Son, take me back."

"Yeah, *that's* likely."

"I'm still needed."

"Wake up and smell the exit wound, old man," Webb growled. "You're more than done."

"No," Mac said, blinking, but his eyes didn't seem to focus. "Not whilst I'm still breathing."

"Well, that might not be for very long," Webb muttered. "Should have worn a vest, you arrogant old ass."

Mac rolled his head to look at him. "Fighting for what is right is a dangerous game," he rasped. "I guessed anyone getting close enough to get a shot off would go for my head anyway."

"He did," Webb muttered, getting to his feet and opening the cabin lockers. "You were lucky."

"Not lucky," the old man sighed, "I had you."

Webb clenched his jaw. "Don't you dare make this a good thing. He was a good kid," he said, voice shaking a little. The vision of Vergennes's slack face with its neat hole in the forehead wouldn't leave him. "A good man. You destroyed him."

"*I* didn't kill him," Mac's expression was drawn with pain, but Webb thought he detected a shadow of sorrow behind his eyes.

He clenched his teeth and his fists. "You might as well have. You used him. You crushed him."

"He had vision. And loyalty. At least, I thought he had. But you shot him, lad. Not me."

"Because I had to," Webb snapped. There was a bad taste in his mouth. He put his fist to his forehead and closed his eyes, breathing deep and willing the vision to go.

"You saved me," Mac said softly after a pause, meeting Webb's black look with a frank one of his own.

"Lie still and try not to die," Webb said after a heavy silence. "I'm going to see if this crate has a medi-bay."

He had to grab handholds as he staggered down the narrow passageway. The ship juddered and bucked as it broke the atmosphere shield. He fought down the urge to head up to the cockpit to take the controls. He searched all the lockers in the tiny galley until he found a medkit then returned to the cabin.

Mac's eyes were closed again. His breathing was rough. Webb tended to his wound as best he could with hands moving on autopilot. He didn't look at Mac's face as he sliced away his shirt, packed the wound with gauze and bandaged it.

"I should thank you." The old man's voice was so weak Webb barely made out the words.

"I wouldn't bother," Webb said, standing and washing his hands in the sink. "The slug's still in there. And you've lost a lot of blood. Vergennes may still get what he wanted."

"Son - "

"Don't call me that," Webb said. "Enough with the emotional mind-fuckery already."

"I'm not trying - "

"You're alive, old man, only because Rose is right. You're going to tell the Service Analysts that all this red cement shit was your idea. If you have any shred of dignity and mercy for the rest of the miserable people left breathing out there, you'll help convince the Service to meet with Rose for talks. Understood?"

Mac's face was limp, partly in pain but Webb also thought he could see defeat. Webb just recognised the brightening in the old man's eyes to be tears before he closed them, dropped his head back to the bunk and went still. Webb moved to leave but Mac caught his wrist in a weak grip.

"I'm sorry," he murmured, not opening his eyes, "I'm sorry I can't be sorry…"

"Yeah, you said that already," Webb retorted, heat flushing his face, and he left the cabin.

He was nearly jolted off his feet twice before reaching the cockpit and strapping himself into a co-pilot seat that was wedged in alongside the pilot's behind a tiny control panel.

"What the hell is going on, Hugo?"

"What about Mac?" Hugo snapped. His face was shining with sweat and he didn't take his eyes off the panels in front of him that were blinking red and yellow as fighter after fighter dove at them on attack vectors. They flashed past, scattering laser fire as they went.

"He's breathing, which is all we need right now," Webb shouted his reply over the noise of the ship hitching and shuddering. "What's going on here?"

"Trying to get us through Osgard's forces," Hugo bit out, swinging the tiny craft around to starboard as another unit moved to engage them. "We're in a Mars-registered vessel."

"So the fleet hasn't got the memo, huh?"

"Far from it," Hugo said, between manoeuvres. "Your little speech is being beamed out on every channel and connection the Orbit has. What reports I can get show Red Star are responding."

"You're kidding me?" Webb returned, taking control of the few co-pilot controls there were and re-routing power to the engines and weaponry. "It worked?"

"You read it right. Red Star have realised they don't want to sacrifice everything to achieve their goal."

The ship shook as more fire connected with them and the conversation lapsed as they worked together to get the ship away from the blockade. Eventually, they got far enough away from the planet that even the most determined fighters were called back to continue the assault on the Red Star forces still defending the city.

"So what's gonna happen there?" Webb asked as they watched the last of the blips of the battle fade out of scanning distance on their scopes.

"I don't know for sure, but reports suggest there are Service and Lunar 1 units on their way."

"Bad luck, Osgard," Webb said with a rueful grin. "I can't think of anyone more deserving of being on the other end of your mom's wrath."

"Me neither," Hugo said, face hard.

Webb swallowed. His mouth tasted foul. "We did what we could," he said softly, knowing it was all there was to say.

"It's over," Hugo agreed.

Webb stared at the deck. "So how come I feel like shit?"

Hugo turned to him. His face was blank but his eyes were heavy. "Because it's too late for Dana. Too late for my father. And too late for my children."

Webb went still. Hearing Hugo put into words everything he had unconsciously been avoiding thinking about sent what remained of his defences crashing down. He slumped in his chair, feeling each dull throb and pang of every injury in his body, and the built-up strain of having been on the go for weeks…months… years?…without letting himself stop to really think about how he felt. About anything.

"I've been running," he heard himself say, without realising he'd decided to speak. "For years I've been running. And I never knew. You tried to tell me. Dana tried to tell me. And now there's nothing left to run from. Or to."

Hugo didn't give an answer because, Webb knew, there was none to give.

"Did you get through to Command?" he said after a long pause in which they both laid in course corrections without speaking.

"Yes," Hugo replied. "I've informed them we have the rebel leader prisoner and are bringing him in. I've shut off comms now. What happens now is up to them. I'm having nothing more to do with any of it."

"I think that's fair enough."

Hugo didn't respond. When Webb snuck a glance at him, he looked grimmer, thinner and more worn out then when he'd first set eyes on him in the caves.

"We should ask him," Webb put into the silence.

"Ask who what?"

"Mac," Webb clarified, carefully, "where Ayme and Becca are. Or were."

Hugo turned to him slowly. "Coale took them. Not Mac."

"Coale was a wild dog, but Mac was the one that held his leash. Let's ask him."

Hugo stared at him long and hard. He looked to be fighting something inside and in the end he shuddered and looked away. "I can't…" he said, hands tightening on the controls. "If I find out he knew the whole time and I had never made him tell me…I would kill us both."

"Don't be an idiot, Hugo," Webb snapped, standing. "That's the torture talking."

Hugo blinked up at him, eyes red, but didn't respond.

Webb turned on his heel and headed back to the cabin.

Δ

Hugo followed Webb in kind of a dream. It was the kind that felt more like a nightmare that retained a flicker of hope. The worst kind.

Mac was limp and pale on the bed. Blood drenched his clothing, but his breathing was finally steady and his face, though drawn in pain, had regained some colour. Hugo realised the man was going to live and wondered briefly what the revolutionary would think about that once he'd recovered enough to know what that meant.

"Hey, Mac." Webb shook the man by the shoulder. "Wake up. We got something to ask you."

"You mean you haven't already got everything you wanted?" the old man mumbled in a hoarse voice.

Webb's expression tightened. "If you think any of this is what either of us wanted, old man, you're more delusional than I thought."

Mac regarded them both blearily through bloodshot eyes. "If you say so, son."

Webb bristled.

"McCullough," Hugo said, stepping forward. He was surprised to find his voice firm. "Where are my daughters?"

The old man's expression didn't change. He watched Hugo without speaking for a long minute. Hugo held his gaze, not blinking. No one spoke.

"It's over," Webb said eventually. "You know it is. Let the poor guy bury his daughters, for Christ's sake."

Mac's face darkened. There was another painful pause in which Hugo could feel nothing but his pulse thundering in his ears and a black hole of despair open in his gut. He could hear it roaring, ready to suck him in and devour him. It was so loud that when Mac spoke again he almost couldn't hear him.

"Do you honestly think I'd let your god daughters come to any harm, lad?"

Hugo started.

"Is this a game to you?" Webb said, face like thunder. "Cos I don't think Hugo's in the mood for playing."

"No games, boy," Mac said, staring at the bulkhead and not at either of them. "They are safe. Or at least, they were."

The spell broke and Hugo bent over the old man, grabbing his shirt so hard he flinched. "They're alive? Where?"

Mac closed his mouth, eyes belaying a struggle inside him. Hugo squeezed the cloth tighter. "You will tell me."

"Hugo…he's bluffing."

"I'm not bluffing," Mac said, a tired anger creasing his brow. "I'm not a monster, boy. I don't kidnap and kill children. Or allow those I'm working with to do so either."

"You were quick enough to agree to dispatching my father," Hugo growled, leaning closer to the old man. "And what of the countless thousands in the Service strongholds you were ready to destroy? You think there weren't children in the Academy?"

Mac flinched and shuffled away from him but Hugo didn't let go and Webb didn't try to stop him.

"I wanted you to join us of your own free will, Kaleb," he said. "I knew when I met you that you were a man of honour and integrity. But Coale felt you needed persuading. Rightly so, as it turned out." Mac sounded disappointed, and his face was defeated, but whether it was aimed at Hugo or himself he couldn't tell.

"Tell me where my daughters are," Hugo said again.

Mac paused. When he spoke it was slowly, carefully. "I don't know where they are. I did. But they were taken."

"I don't believe you," Hugo growled. "Tell me where they are now or you might not make it back to Command."

"You won't hurt me, Hugo. You need me."

"You can go to hell for all I care," Hugo said, pulling his weapon. "Tell me."

"Hugo," Webb called but Hugo's attention was riveted on the old man.

"You tell me. Tell me now."

"Go ahead. Shoot." Mac said, trying to shift on the bunk and wincing in pain. "It won't make any difference. I don't really want to see what the next stage of history has in store, anyway. And it doesn't make me any more knowledgeable about what happened to them. I'm sorry, I am." Hugo registered, even through his burning anger, that the old man looked sincere. "But I don't know."

"I don't understand," Webb said, laying an arm on Hugo's arm to steady his sudden shaking. "Someone took them from you?"

Mac nodded. "Coale had them on one of the Lunar colonies. I made him swear not to harm them. He was a single-minded soldier, but even he saw they were more valuable alive and, whatever you might think of him, he wasn't going to destroy two children on a whim."

Every inch of Hugo's skin bristled. His palm sweated around the handle of his gun.

"Mac, quit evading," Webb said, voice now firm. "If you do one decent thing in what's rest of your miserable life, tell us what happened."

"Like I said, they were taken." The man's face was sweating with pain now. Hugo didn't care. "A few weeks ago. I had word from their minders that someone had broken in and taken them in the night. There were no demands, nothing left behind. The security cameras caught a shot of her, but no one could identify her and she wore gloves."

"She?" Hugo said, blinking.

"Was it Harvey?" Webb breathed.

Mac shook his head. "Don't you think I would have recognised Hugo's wife? No, it wasn't her."

"What did she look like?" Hugo demanded. "Do you still have the picture?"

Mac groaned and his head fell back on the bunk, face twisted in pain as he tried to grab for his injury.

"Hugo, he's lost too much blood. We need to let him rest up if we want him to make it to Command."

"I don't care if he makes it," Hugo said in a low voice.

"Hugo - "

"I warned you," Hugo said, cutting Webb off. "I warned you that if I found out he knew, I didn't know what I'd do about it."

"Hugo," Webb said again, lifting his hands and taking a step closer. He slid a glance to Mac who'd shut his eyes again. "We know they're alive. We know Red Star didn't hurt them and we know they have a picture of who took them."

"Why are you trying to stop me?" Hugo said, words coming out in a rush.

Webb paused. He swallowed and his face fell. He looked to be searching for words. "I know there are things bigger than us," he said, finally, watching Hugo carefully as he did. "Whatever else he had backwards, my dad was right about that."

Hugo shuddered violently but then his body went still. He couldn't find the strength to reply, hit him or re-focus on Mac, all of which and none of which he wanted to do.

Webb took his elbow and led him towards the hatch, saying soothing words but Hugo didn't hear them.

"Red hair," Mac's croaking voice had them pausing in the doorway.

"What?" Webb said over his shoulder.

"Red hair," Mac repeated, voice a little stronger though he didn't open his eyes. "The woman had red hair. She was tall. Witnesses said she had a Lunar 1 accent."

Hugo and Webb looked at each other then rushed for the cockpit.

"Wait," Webb said as Hugo made for the communications unit.

"You concentrate on getting some more speed out of this crate. I know how to check if this is really what we think."

"It can't be can it?" Hugo said, shaking his head, crushing fear battling with desperate hope in his chest. "Why would she?"

"I don't know," Webb muttered, hands starting to fly over the basic workstation and eyes glued to the screen, "but I can't imagine it was for anything good."

"But...she's locked up, isn't she? Lunar Alpha? She got put away for that bomb attempt. I remember..."

Webb had gone still, staring at the comm unit.

"What is it?"

The younger man looked up, eyes wide. "She got early release. A few weeks ago."

"What? Why?"

"She helped the Service in an investigation and they reviewed her case."

"What investigation?"

"Mine," Webb returned. "For you. I'm sorry, it was the only starting point I had."

"You got Nam Webb released from Lunar Alpha?" Hugo felt his pulse beat in his temples.

Webb blanched. "I didn't know what she'd do. I had no idea - "

"This is not helping," Hugo cut him off, turning his attention to the controls and seeing if there were any more non-essential systems he could divert power from the get more speed from the engines. "Do you think you can find her?"

"Nam may be resourceful," Webb muttered, "but subtle, she ain't. She'll have left a trail. Don't worry, Hugo. I'll find her."

XII

"Hey, Mac. Mac. Wake up."

The man didn't respond. Something Webb didn't want to identify swept up his throat to choke him, but released its hold when the old man took a laboured breath and lifted his head. The strength of the relief he felt was a surprise to him and he wasn't sure it was a welcome one. He bent to help the old man sit up on the bunk.

"What's going on?"

"Here's where you get off."

"What?" Mac blinked, clutching at Webb as he hauled him to his feet. He looked bleary, confused.

"Command, Mac," Webb said, keeping his voice flat. "We're at Service Command. The generals are extremely anxious for a chat with you."

The old man faltered. He clutched at a locker as his knees buckled. Webb held him up but didn't look him in the face.

"You weren't kidding then, huh?"

Webb didn't speak.

"You know, as much as you'll hate to hear this, it appears we're more alike than I thought. You always see done what you think needs to be done too."

"Let's not do this. Move."

Mac let out a gruff sound, pain and resignation equally mixed. Webb walked, helping the old man along who, to Webb's surprise, came peacefully, if not exactly willingly. When they reached the exit hatch, Mac straightened his spine, held his head up. The hatch opened and the cool, processed air of the space station swept in. A swarm of Servicemen climbed the ladder and pushed into the narrow space. They laid eyes on Mac and Webb then fell on the older man in eerie silence, moving like simulants, pulling him from Webb's grip.

"Hey, careful," Webb said. "He's injured."

"Insurgent is now in custody," the captain of the team said into a wrist comm. "Transferring to secure medibay for treatment."

A muffled reply answered him and the man barked an order at his team who hustled Mac to the hatch and down the ladder.

Webb called after them but they ignored him. By the time he was down the ladder, his father had been loaded onto a gurney and was being wheeled across the spacious dock with a group of grey-and-black uniformed guards, weapons drawn, clustered round him. Webb watched him disappear into Service Command with an unwelcome knot forming in his stomach.

"What exactly do they expect him to pull in that state?" he muttered, but no one was listening to him. Hugo was a few paces off, surrounded by Service officers, barraging him with questions about Red Star, his disappearance and how and where they'd apprehended the rebel leader. Hugo was giving them brusque replies whilst trying to detach himself. The blood was rising in his face and Webb recognised him as being on the verge of losing control.

"Hey, Hugo," Webb called. "We leaving, or what?"

Hugo finally raised a hand to dismiss the officers and shouldered his way back toward Webb, face on fire.

"We're wasting time here," he said as he drew level with Webb.

"We did what we had to do," Webb retorted, turning back to their beat-up little ship. "They going to let us go?" he continued, eyeing the Service officers, tech crews and other interested people who were all staring their direction. The rising volume of their chatter along with the changing announcements on all the command displays told Webb word was quickly spreading about who they were and who they'd brought with them.

"They've got no choice," Hugo said, climbing the ladder. "I'm currently the highest ranking officer on board."

"You are?" Webb asked, closing the hatch behind them and hurrying after Hugo toward the cockpit.

"They evacuated most of Command," Hugo explained, taking his seat. "Now they've scanned the whole space station and found no red cement, crews and generals are on their way back, but no one higher than me has landed yet."

"And the fact you've been away on a year-long vacation with the enemy doesn't impact on your influence?" Webb asked doubtfully.

"I've just brought in the enemy's leader. They think I've been on an undercover mission."

There was an uncomfortable silence. At least, it was uncomfortable for Webb. The determined set of Hugo's face told him he wasn't thinking about anything other than the task in hand.

"Hugo, you're gonna have to check in with all this at some point you know."

"What do you mean?"

Webb sighed and took his chair. "I just mean I sense you're pushing stuff down. It'll poison you if you keep on swallowing it."

Hugo paused and gave him a heavy look. "I will do whatever is necessary, once Becca and Ayme are safe. Not before."

Webb nodded heavily. "Yeah, I get that. I just get the feeling you're about ready to fall apart. Maybe I should do this on my own?"

Hugo went still. There was a dangerous look on his face but his hands were shaking slightly, belying the struggle he had holding on to himself. "I'm not spending another second arguing with you, Captain. You said you had a lead. Tell me what it is so we can get going."

Webb nodded, looking away from his friend who he barely recognised, and pulled up a schematic of a Sunside colony on the little display. "Something flagged here. An account code used to rent a suite of boarding pods. I recognised it. Nam's used it in the past, but Hugo…"

"What?" Hugo said, starting the engines.

"It's too obvious. It feels like a trap."

"I don't care. We've waited too long already."

"Well should we at least get a better ship?" Webb grumbled, looking at the sleek fighters and runners in the dock.

"No time," Hugo bit out. "And Nam will be on the lookout for a Service ship. We need to catch her by surprise."

"Fine," Webb said, feeling his own temper rise and getting to his feet. "Then shift your ass, Vice-Admiral. Let me see what this thing is made of."

Hugo eyed him distrustfully for a moment before relinquishing the controls. The hail light had been blinking ever since they'd returned to the ship. Hugo opened the communication channel to harbour control and barked something blunt at the agitated comm officer on the other end and Webb took that as his cue to fire the thrusters.

Curious onlookers scrambled back from the ship. Mac's picture had just started to appear on the displays, along with announcements about his apprehension, as they backed out of the dock's vacuum shield and into open space. With a rush, Webb gunned the engines and blasted them away from the sprawling space station. He ignored the pang of guilt he felt whenever he thought about Mac, pain-withered and looking older than even his years accounted for, being swept away into the depths of Command without even a chance for him to say goodbye.

He caught himself on that thought, silently chastising himself. He didn't want to say goodbye. He hadn't killed the man with his bare hands, which was more than he'd expected of himself. A sideways glance at the haggard and dangerously focussed Hugo at his side, covered in old burn scars and cheeks hollow with the trials of his last year, was almost enough to bolster that thought. Almost.

Δ

Hugo attempted to raise first Giles, then, reluctantly Riley and finally, lastly, desperately, Harvey on the comm as they raced along the inter-Orbit space lane. They were curving around the Earth which looked like a giant swirled marble beneath them, breaking all speed barriers as they careened toward the Sunside Strip. The sparkling glints of the chain of space station colonies grew bigger and brighter out the viewscreen as Webb coaxed more speed than Hugo would have believed was ever possible out of the ragged little ship. He cursed.

"No one's answering," he muttered.

"They'll all have their hands full, man," Webb said. "This is up to us. Don't worry." He threw a tired grin his way. "I think we can handle Nam."

"I just don't understand…why."

Webb shot him another wary glance. Hugo knew he was worried about him, but he also knew he could afford to think about that yet.

"It's obvious, isn't it?" Webb finally said, turning back to the controls.

"Is it?"

"She's still pissed. At us both. For stopping her killing Yoshida and all the Haven Ghosts. This is her way of drawing us out."

"It's been years."

"Years she's spent brooding in Lunar Alpha," Webb pointed out.

"But how did she find my children when no one else could?"

Webb's mouth turned down at the corner. "I don't think Nam takes the bigger picture into account. Harvey will have had to tread carefully when looking for them. But Red Star could have taken your kids to Pluto and Nam would've found a way to get them if she thought she could get to you."

"You seem to understand her very well." Hugo heard himself say.

"She's a classic Lunar 1 screwup," Webb replied after a minute. "I can tell that even without Webb's memories."

Hugo fidgeted. He paced the ship. The clone, thankfully, let him, without passing comment. Finally, they were on the approach to the Sunside Strip and drawing into the traffic heading for Sunside 3. Webb slowed the ship and joined the orderly space lane. At Hugo's protest he pointed out that if they were to surprise Nam, they needed to blend in.

Hugo grumbled, though he knew Webb was right. Webb secured them a dock after a few unpleasant moments wrangling over the ship's Martian registration, then they were landing, though still not quick enough for Hugo. The comm station had periodically bleeped with various calls coming through as one then another Service general, high-ranking Analyst or family member had heard about what had happened at Command, identified the ship and attempted to contact him. It was bleeping again as they landed, and this time he could tell from the code signature that it was direct from his mother.

"Surprised she's got time for a call," Webb mumbled, as he carefully berthed the ship in the busy public dock. "You not gonna answer her?"

"No one but Marilyn has got answers we need right now," Hugo said, standing from his seat and heading for the exit.

Webb replied something that Hugo didn't hear. He was already climbing out the exit hatch and joining the throngs of people disembarking their ships and heading for the colony gates.

"We don't exactly blend in here," Webb commented as a well-dressed couple stepped hurriedly out of their way when they rushed out onto a moodily-lit plaza that passed for an entry lounge. "Especially at the beginning of the night-cycle."

Hugo didn't reply. He checked their location on his wristpanel and turned them down a dark walkway. As they hurried along, Hugo saw the surroundings were familiar. Webb's face had taken on a grim, set expression. He was about to ask what he wasn't being told when they halted outside the large, ornate entrance to an exclusive-looking club. There were a number of sporty one-man flyers and two-wheelers pulled up in the parking pool and everyone coming and going was finely dressed in evening wear. Some sent them questioning looks, though most were more engaged with each other than them. Except for the overly-large private enforcers at the entrance who were looking over their way with unfriendly expressions on their faces.

"This is where Nam is?" Hugo asked in a small voice.

"This is where she used her account to rent a boarding suite," Webb said, voice expressionless. "I told you, she's done it on purpose."

Hugo hadn't been to the *Lagrange Lounge* in years. It shouldn't have struck him the way it did. But as they drew closer and he could see the oriental interior and smelt the mix of spirits and the expensive colognes of the clientele, he was catapulted back in time.

"She's…in there?"

Webb shrugged one shoulder. "She's rented one of the suites, at least. And she did it in such a way she knew someone would spot it if they knew what they were looking for."

"She's chosen this place to hurt."

"But, how would she know?" Webb said. His voice was catching. "About Dana?"

"She's always kept a very close watch on all of us," he said with gritted teeth, before taking a step toward the doors.

Webb put a hand on his elbow. "We won't get in that way," he said, eyeing the Enforcers who were eyeing them. "Come on."

Hugo followed Webb away from the front door and toward a supply entrance between the club and the 4D theatre next door.

"Dana used to complain that you knew a back way into her club," Hugo said as Webb punched keys on the secure keypad next to the door.

"What did she expect me to do when she kept barring me?" Webb smile was sad. "I was courteous last time and went in the front door. I'm not feeling the need to be polite this time…"

The door hissed open and Webb hurried down the service passage beyond. There were cameras in the walls and ceiling, but Webb moved them along at a fast pace and they came to some stairs before anyone came looking. There was an express lift but Webb chose the stairs. Hugo didn't question. His heart pounded in his chest. Webb checked the floor numbers at each turn of the stairs before finally taking them through a door on the sixth floor that opened out onto carpeted corridors, mutely painted walls and a series of numbered doors.

"Which suite is it?" Hugo murmured.

"Moonlight Suite," Webb said as they turned a corner and stopped outside double doors with the suite's name engraved in the metal. Hugo had started to shake. The door had a key-card lock. Webb pulled his sleeve back and started tapping commands into his wrist panel.

"Let's see if the applications on this high-grade tech of yours really work," Webb mumbled as he shuffled closer to the lock, tapping more commands.

"If it doesn't, we break the door down."

"Just hold your horses, Vice-Admiral," Webb admonished. "We don't want to be arrested before we've got the girls, ok?"

Hugo shifted from one foot to another as Webb continued to work, but then the doors opened of their own accord. They were faced with the tall figure of Nam, wearing all black and holding a semi-automatic rifle. Her black eyes burned coldly, though the rest of her face was set and expressionless.

"I was beginning to think you weren't coming," she said into the stony silence.

Hugo's chest heaved. His mind whirled. He wanted to fling himself on her, shoulder into the room, cry out his daughters' names. But he couldn't do any of it. He was paralysed by the look on her face that told him he was too late.

"We know you've got them, Nam," Webb said.

"I would hope so," she said, voice toneless. "I left an obvious enough trail."

"Let me see them." Hugo's voice was hoarse.

Nam regarded him for an interminable minute, eyes blacker than space and just as empty, then took a step back and twitched her gun to gesture them inside.

Hugo barrelled in. He registered the plush sitting room was empty apart from themselves. He hurried across it and rattled the door handle on the locked bedroom door, calling out.

"Step back," Nam ordered. She had kept up position by the door, keeping her weapon trained on both of them.

"Let me see them," Hugo said, voice loaded. "Let me see them now, or God help you, you will be sorry."

Nam tilted her chin. "Not as sorry as you will be if you don't do as I say."

"What do you want?" Webb demanded. "I thought you were all set you run off and get your sister cloned?"

A dangerous stillness stole through Nam's face. "Maybe I've had time to think," she said evenly. "Maybe I decided tying up loose ends is more important than unraveling more."

Webb glared. "If you just wanted to kill us you could have gunned us down already."

"Death was for the perpetrators," Nam said, voice still devoid of expression. "You're just the obstructers of my revenge. Death is not for you. *Pain* is for you."

"You will tell me where they are," Hugo said, taking three steps forward despite the trained gun.

"I plan on telling you. What would be the point otherwise?"

"You - "

She raised the gun, halting Hugo as he started toward her. "Would be a huge shame for their mom and dad to have come this far only to die within hearing range, don't you think?"

Hugo started, looked around again at the closed doors around the suite. "Marilyn?"

The woman didn't smile. Hugo wasn't sure she ever smiled. But a light came into her eyes. It sent a shudder through him.

"Take a seat, Vice-Admiral Hugo. Captain Webb."

The two men looked at each other. Webb gave an infinitesimal nod. Hugo was too angry to think, but followed his friend's example as he sat stiffly on the edge of one of the armchairs. Hugo sat on the sofa, soft with rich, black fabric. Blue-painted walls and the fine digiprints hung on them swam in and out of focus as he watched Nam seat herself in a chair opposite, laying the rifle across her lap. She leant forward with her elbows on her knees and stared right at him, almost into him.

"I can tell you're planning to jump me," she said in a low voice. "Or hope you can shoot me quicker than I can shoot you. I wouldn't recommend it." She pulled up her sleeve. There was a blinking control on a strap around her wrist. "This is linked to a gas grenade. I'll let you guess where it is. If I don't tap my own series of changing codes into it at regular intervals it will go off and suffocate anyone in the room within minutes."

Hugo's fingernail beds dug into his palms.

"Go on then," Webb snapped. "What do you want? This game is getting real old real quick."

She slid her unblinking gaze to Webb and then back to Hugo. "I wonder how much of what I've heard is true," she said softly.

"About what?" Hugo demanded. His palms were itching, his feet twitching on the plush carpet. He was trying to scan the room for the grenade. He strained his hearing for any other noises from the rest of the suite but it was eerily quiet.

"About you," she murmured. "It's amazing what you can find on you two if you know who to ask."

"Nam, you're mad as a barrel of angry ants," Webb said, "but we all know you're not stupid. If you want to deliver some kind of dramatic judgment you better get the fuck on with it, because it's only a matter of time before SC Hugo sends someone after us."

Hugo watched Nam carefully for a reaction but she showed none.

"You've been tortured," she said, ignoring Webb entirely, her black eyes lingering on Hugo's face.

"Yes."

"By Red Star?"

He nodded again.

"And you, well," she gave Webb an up-and-down look. "Looks like you've had a rough time of it since I saw you."

"Again," Webb said, "your point?"

"I told you," she said coolly, "death is not for you. Pain is for you." Her eyes took on a dangerous glint. "You used me, derailed my plans and lied to me. For that, for your arrogance, for your condescending attitudes that imply nothing else matters but your own little ego-boosting suicide missions, it was necessary you learn just how insignificant and unimportant you really are."

She reached out a hand and both Webb and Hugo started, but she was just reaching for the entertainment display control on the arm of her chair. She turned on the huge screen that hung over a mock fireplace on their right. The channel was pre-tuned to one of the news networks. A woman in smart suit was issuing a statement about Red Star continuing to withdraw from Service space and the scheduling of initial negotiations to be opened with Arcadius Rose about Red Star's demilitarisation. In a banner along the bottom of the screen were text updates on the places already destroyed, the losses of Service and civilian crews, updates on Lunar 1's mercenary fleet continuing to patrol the Lunar Strip for any Red Star craft attempting to sneak into or out of the Orbit. It also mentioned Duran McCullough being in Service custody and Special Commander Hugo's continued role in organising the Service's movements, despite her own personal losses.

"And what exactly is the point here?" Webb said, though his voice had lost some of its swagger.

"If you don't know what the point is, then you really haven't learned anything," Nam said.

"I understand," Hugo heard himself say softly. They both

looked at him. He felt his eyes start to sting. "We believed it was our lot to fight the universe, or hide from it," he said, with a look at Webb who blanched. "I've lost my father, both my sisters and now possibly my wife and daughters because I thought that was what happened when you fought for something. I almost lost my mind, too…"

Everyone was quiet. Nam had muted the display. Webb was watching him with something like fear on his face. The air felt almost as thick as that in Schiaparelli City.

"Webb's life has been manipulated by power and politics ever since he was born. His answer was to hide from it. That brought its own problems. We were both arrogant enough to assume we had the right to do what we wanted to protect our chosen lives, whoever else it impacted on." Colour rose in Webb's face. Hugo made himself go on. "We're both at fault. And we both failed you when all you had done was ask us to stay out of your way."

Nam's eyes glinted. She sat very still. Her wrist control started blinking and Hugo's heart jumped. She looked at him a moment longer before slowly turning her attention to the control, hitting a few commands and it stopped blinking. Then she looked at Webb.

"As that came from Hugo and not from you, who I imagine to be a more skilled liar, I'm happy to believe he understands. What about you?"

Webb scowled. "I think you're as arrogant as you think we are to judge us like this."

Hugo started, but all Nam did was to tilt her head to the side.

"I suppose there was always little or no hope for you," she said.

"You don't even know us," Webb stood up, glaring.

"Webb," Hugo said, almost pleading, but the younger man ignored him.

Nam looked as close as he had ever seen her to smiling. "I've had a long time to learn all about you, Ezekiel Webb," she murmured. "Or should I say Errol McCullough? Lunar Alpha may have been secure, but solarnet access was allowed for good behaviour. And I can behave very, very well when I need to. So, believe me, I know a lot more about you than you do about me."

Webb bristled.

"I sense this reaction is coming from a raw nerve," she said as she got to her feet. "Perhaps you should think on that after this."

She strolled across the room. Hugo stood, unsure what was going on. She pulled a card from her pocket, swiped it on the control of one of the doors. She pulled it open.

"Come on then," he heard her say in a voice that sounded so different to the one she'd used on them it didn't even sound like the same woman. "Your dad came for you. I told you he would."

Time slowed down. Hugo's knees went weak. He heard voices. High, happy voices. Two young girls with curly, dark hair appeared in the doorway, scanning the room until their excited eyes landed on him.

"Papa!" the younger one cried and moved to run to him.

"Ayme," the older one chided, grabbing her sister's elbow and shaking her head. The younger one bit her lip, nodded then they both strode forward and saluted, backs straight and shoulders square, but both sets of eyes shining with restrained excitement.

Hugo choked. He dropped to his knees, gathered them to him and clung on, breathing in the smell of their hair and feeling his eyes prickle.

"Papa," Becca said, patting at him nervously. "It's ok, Papa."

He couldn't breathe. He clung tighter.

Ayme giggled. "Papa, you're crushing us."

He kept saying their names over and over until they finally pulled back far enough to look into his face. All the joy fled their faces.

"Why are you crying?" Ayme asked, looking scared.

"What happened, Papa?" Becca said, reaching fingers toward the scars on his face then letting her hand drop as if afraid to touch him.

"Nothing you need worry about," Hugo said, fighting to keep

his voice under control. "All you need to know is you're safe. I'm taking you home."

They nodded, still looking a little nervous.

"Are you both ok? Have you been hurt?"

They exchanged glances and Hugo's heart kicked at his ribs.

"Not hurt," Becca spoke up for them both. She'd gone a little stiff. "Ayme was scared, for a while."

"You were scared too," Ayme hissed.

Becca shushed her sister. "It was a bit scary. No one spoke to us, but no one hurt us, but we had to do as we were told and stay quiet. But I told Ayme it was a field exercise and we were to just stay calm and do as we were told and wait to see what happened. We didn't understand why it went on for so long…but we were good, we did as we were told. It was practice, right Papa? The men were helping us practice what we learned in survival class?"

Their glance slid nervously to Nam who was stood watching in silence then back to Hugo. He took a deep breath, his throat tight. He swallowed again to try and loosen it. "Yes," he said. "It was an exercise. A very long exercise. And you both did very well."

The girls flushed and smiled, Becca straightening her back with pride. Ayme grinned, then glanced at her sister then copied her straight back and proud smile.

"We passed, Papa?"

"Yes, Ayme," he said. "You both passed."

Hugo stood, took his girls firmly by the hand and only then noticed that Harvey was stood in the bedroom doorway. She was looking at him with a smile on her face, her eyes tired and ringed in dark shadows but shining as she looked at him.

Hugo blinked the blurriness from his eyes, staring between her and Nam. The red-haired woman stood off to one side, a dispassionate expression on her face. She had propped the rifle out of sight behind the chair.

"Marilyn?" he breathed. His wife came forward, wrapped him in here arms and kissed him. Hugo wanted to clutch her to him but couldn't bring himself to let go of his daughters' hands. When she pulled back he finally was able to choke out, "I don't understand."

"Don't ever, ever think about running out on me ever again, Kaleb Hugo," Harvey said in a thick voice, her own eyes brimming. "If you even think about it - "

"I…"

"What the hell is going on here?" Webb suddenly thundered. His voice held the anger that comes from not daring to hope.

"Leave," Nam said, going to the suite door and opening it. "Now."

"What, just like that?"

Nam gave Webb a level look. "I said you were owed pain. I didn't say I had to be the one that delivered it. The Orbit has punished you both far more effectively than I could have done. Now go. I just pray you've learned from it. Leave."

"Come on," Harvey said, reaching down and gathering Ayme up into her arms and grabbing Becca's other hand. "It's time to go home."

Hugo stared at Nam who was gazing at him with eyes that could be threatening murder as easily as they could be just wishing him out of her sight, but didn't stop to think. He grabbed the indignant Webb by the elbow and pulled him along. Nam slammed the door behind them.

"What the hell, Harvey?" Webb sputtered as they hurried along the corridor. "You were in league with that bag of bat-shit mental the whole time?"

"Language, Webb," Harvey hissed over her shoulder as Ayme covered a grin with her hand. "I'll explain later, ok? For now, let's just get the girls home."

"There was no gas grenade?" Webb said.

"Oh no, there was a grenade," Harvey said, voice hard. "Nam likes to keep up appearances. But she wouldn't have hurt us."

"Jesus, Mary and Joseph," Webb said, clutching his head. "This is so messed up."

"I told you'd I'd explain," she said as they all bundled into an express lift. "Just not yet," she added, with a significant glance at the two girls. Webb held his tongue though he wasn't able to keep his dissatisfaction from his face.

"Are you ok, Zeekal?" Ayme's face crumpled with concern.

"Ayme," Becca chided. "It's Captain Webb."

Webb blinked at the girls but couldn't seem to find words to answer them.

"Captain Webb's tired, girls," Harvey said softly, sending a grateful smile his way. "He's been working very hard. Let him alone"

Hugo didn't listen to any of this. He didn't think. At last, he didn't need to. He just held on to Becca's other hand, watching his wife as she led them out the lift and across the *Lagrange Lounge*'s main bar. Many of the patron's faces turned their way but Hugo felt nothing apart from the sensation of pain slowly numbing. Even the reminders of Dana all around only served to remind him, for once, of what he still had rather than what he'd lost.

Harvey hailed them a taxi flyer outside the club. The girls were yawning as they bundled them in the back. Harvey climbed in next to them, saying they'd be home soon and to just be patient a little longer. Webb sat in the chair facing them, staring at the girls like he couldn't quite believe they were real. Even when they tried to draw him into a game of finger-snap, he was distant and un-responsive. They soon gave up and played with each other. Harvey sat with one hand on Hugo's knee the whole flyer ride to the docks. He covered his wife's hand with his own and let himself be comforted.

Harvey refused to talk to either of them until the girls were set-tled top-to-toe in the tiny cabin of their ship, asleep before they'd even left the cabin and Webb was piloting them out into space and laying in a course for Sydney.

"Ok, ok," she said, lowering herself into the co-pilot's chair like she'd lost all her strength. Hugo was stood at her side, holding the back of her chair. She smiled up at him and took his hand, then faced Webb's accusing look. "And you can drop the attitude, Ezekiel. Especially when you only know half the story."

"So tell us," he said, voice harsh. "Your husband's been driven half mad with worry. If we'd known you were with them..."

"I *haven't* been with them, alright?" Harvey said, raising her voice a little. "Not the whole time."

"Marilyn," Hugo said softly, gently squeezing her hand. "It's ok. I don't care what happened, just that we're going home."

"Well *I* care," Webb said. "I care big time. And I think after having Nut-job Nam wave a rifle at us whilst you're sat in the next room, we're owed an explanation."

Harvey narrowed her green eyes. Webb's set expression didn't soften. Harvey sighed and rested the back of her head against the chair like she couldn't summon the energy to stay angry.

"I went looking for them right after you left to find Kaleb," she began softly, eyes far away. "It had to be an absolute secret. I'm not an idiot," she said, emotion bleeding into her voice. "Kaleb and the girls were at Red Star's mercy, I guessed that much. No one could know. Even when I found where they were held and that someone else had taken them from there, no one could know. Not even your mother," Harvey said, craning her head to look up at Hugo. "She and Anita Rami were the only ones I trusted with what I was doing. But when I got close, no way could I risk sending communications. I had to act alone."

"You found out Nam had taken them?"

A corner of a tired smile twitched Harvey's mouth. "Kaleb, she didn't take them. She rescued them."

"Come again?" Webb said, frowning.

Harvey nodded, face warming. "You should engage your brain with your mouth. She's not what you think she is."

"Harvey, she's exactly what I think she is."

"And what's that?"

"A shipment short of a cargo," Webb muttered, checking their course as they pulled into a spacelane.

Harvey shrugged one shoulder. She rubbed the back of Hugo's hand where it rested on her chair back absently. "She has a... unique way at looking at things."

"She tried to kill us," Webb protested. "Several times."

"That was a long time ago. And she was different then. Hurting."

Webb gave her a disbelieving glance.

"It's true," she insisted. "You of all people should understand what dumb shit you can do when you feel betrayed."

That shut Webb up. He glared out the viewscreen with a tight jaw. Hugo knelt next to Harvey, took her hands in his, not able to take his eyes of her face.

"She wanted to confront me. Us," he said, with a glance at Webb

Harvey nodded. "She wanted to get you to come to her, but she never wanted to hurt the girls. She believes in justice. And she was majorly hung up on you two after Haven." Her green eyes flickered. "She wouldn't let me take them until she'd seen you. She needed to know that you'd learned something."

"And if we hadn't?" Webb muttered. "She'd have killed us?"

Harvey's face went dark for a second. "Maybe. I can't tell. But I was right in the next room. I wouldn't have let her hurt you."

Webb shook his head. "Messed up."

"Yes, it is," Harvey replied. "But I think in all of this, she was the one who saw things the most clearly. She knows all that matters is those who are important to you. She wanted you to realise that too."

Harvey's words hung in the quiet air. No one said anything for a long time, until she turned to Hugo and seemed like she looked at him properly for the first time. "Kaleb," she choked. "You look like death. We're hours away from Sydney. Go and rest."

He clung to her hands. "I'm sorry."

Her eyes swam. "I know."

He squeezed her hands, feeling rushing under his skin like hot water. Realising she knew everything he was sorry for without having to say it out loud reminded him again of why he married her.

"Go on," she said again, giving him a small push. "Get yourself to bed."

He glanced back toward the cabin. "Were they hurt?" he dared to ask. "Becca says they weren't. Was that true?"

Harvey shook her head. "Don't ask me why, but whoever took them didn't threaten or frighten them. It sounds like they were sedated. Becca's convinced it was year-long boarding trip or training exercise. They never understood what had really happened."

"And they never will," Hugo said firmly. He looked again back toward the cabin. "It must have been Mac," he said softly. "He made sure they weren't hurt, just like he said he did."

"Mac?" Harvey frowned. "Who?"

"Far too long a story," Webb said bitterly.

Harvey frowned but took in the look on Webb's face and didn't venture any questions. "Kaleb," she said instead. "I won't tell you again."

Hugo leant down and kissed her. The smell of her skin was so familiar it made him ache. He detached himself, took a moment to drink in the smile on her face, then left the cockpit to sneak into the darkened cabin, lay down on the deck and let himself be lulled to sleep by the sound of his daughters' breathing.

XIII

Almost the minute they landed, Hugo was swept out of Harvey's grasp to be subjected to hours of questioning by Service Analysts about his actions, his knowledge of Red Star, Duran Mc-Cullough, Arcadius Rose and Christof Coale. Only when he was nearly passing out from exhaustion and his mother intervened was he released from questioning to be admitted to a medicentre for surgery to try and mend all the ageing injuries he'd sustained since being taken away by Red Star.

Webb was admitted at the same time. The fact that the younger man acquiesced to the hospital stay without such as a murmur of protest told Hugo just how badly he really had been hurt and how long he'd been hiding it for. Knowing that a lot of that had been caused by him hurt more than recovering from surgery.

As soon as he was physically capable, the Analysts' agents started arriving at his hospital room with more questions. He answered everything honestly, not denying any of his own involvement and willingly giving up all he knew. Even as he heard his own voice admitting to the things he'd thought, done and said at the behest of Coale, saying the words out loud felt like the lancing of some black and ugly wound. He offered everything happily, not caring what it meant for his future and just glad to be rid of it all from his still-riotous mind.

At some point, Giles had turned up and forced the Analysts to leave.

"You'll have to answer for this all someday soon, little brother," he said with a hand on his shoulder. "But not just yet."

The days all blurred into one grey haze of painkillers and drug-induced sleep, punctuated by the bright spots of visits from Harvey and his daughters. They came every day. Every time he saw their faces appear in the door, every single ache and stab of pain, the physical ones and the darker, deeper, more sinister ones that lingered in the back of his mind when he was completely alone, were easy to forget.

Eventually he was allowed back to their apartment for further recuperation, though the Service guard on his door twenty-four-seven didn't let him forget that he wasn't out of the woods as far as the Service generals were concerned. He didn't care. He carried on touching the familiar shapes and textures of his furniture, apartment walls and old clothes, as if to constantly remind himself it was over. At least, on the outside.

"Hey, Hugo."

Hugo blinked himself awake. He'd been dozing in his armchair on the balcony as he'd taken to doing in the afternoon when Harvey was out. He looked up and saw the tall figure of Webb in the doorway, leaning on a cane but with a half-smile on his face and a brightness in his eyes that Hugo hadn't seen for months. All the bruises and cuts that had been a constant reminder to Hugo for weeks of what he'd been capable of under Coale's thrall had finally faded. The young man more looked like himself again, though perhaps with sharper cheekbones and a more crooked smile. Somehow, it suited him. He'd tided up his hair too, wearing is in a small tail at the back of his neck. Hugo couldn't recall him ever wearing it so tidy in the past. But again…it worked.

"Webb," he said, sitting up in his chair. "They let you in?"

Webb shrugged, came forward and lowered himself into the other armchair. "You're the one under house arrest, not me. At least, not anymore."

Hugo nodded, scrubbing a hand over his face. "How are you feeling?"

"Better," Webb said with another smile, leaning the stick against his legs. "This is just until my ribs heal properly."

Hugo winced, looked out over the Sydney skyline without answering.

"Hey, Hugo, relax. I'm not here to make you feel guilty. So how are you holding up?"

"I'm fine."

Webb snorted, leaning further back into his seat and following Hugo's gaze out of the skyline of megablocks and skyways. The gap where HQ used to stand looked like a missing tooth in a familiar mouth.

"Sounds like they're going to elect an Orbit Alliance after all," Webb ventured into the silence.

"I heard."

"Rose is overseeing it all. You know, as much as I might not agree with the means to the end, I think he might end up making a difference after all."

Hugo still didn't answer. He rubbed his palms down the armchair's arms, sinking himself into the feeling of that which he knew, closing his eyes against the spiralling darkness which threatened every time he thought about any of those men.

Hugo didn't hear Webb saying his name, but he did feel the firm hand he placed on his forearm. He blinked his eyes open and looked over.

"It's ok, Hugo," Webb said softly. "It is over, you know."

"It's never over though, is it?" Hugo said, putting words to the fear. "If any of this has taught us anything, it's that the war is only over for you when you're dead."

Webb's face darkened for a second. "It's over for us," he said, firmly. "I've resigned my commission."

Hugo blinked at him. "You have?"

His face twisted a moment. "Well, even if I hadn't wanted to… which I did, in the end anyway…I kinda had to. I'm not sure how you cope."

"With what?"

"With everyone knowing your face. For all the wrong reasons."

Hugo looked at the floor. "Yeah. That's fun."

Webb shook his head. "Seems anyone who doesn't want me executed as a revolutionary is screaming for me to join the Orbit Alliance."

Hugo couldn't suppress a small smile. "Maybe you should."

Webb snorted. "Jesus wept. I'm only just starting to figure out taking responsibility for myself. How the hell am I supposed to do it for an entire solar system?"

"I don't know. I'd say you've got some good experience in that area."

Webb gave him an assessing look. "Speak for yourself."

Hugo met his look with an open one of his own. "So you're leaving?" he said, pleased he kept his voice level.

"Yeah. It's time."

Hugo nodded, staring hard at the wall.

"I…" Webb started, rubbed his mouth and sighed. "I'm not good at this."

"At what?"

Webb grimaced. "Saying goodbye."

A lump formed in Hugo's throat. "Then don't."

Webb looked like he was fighting something. "Ok, Hugo. Not goodbye. How about…see you round?"

"When do you go?"

"Tomorrow. If I don't go then…I know I won't go at all. And I need to. Really."

"Are you sure?"

"I am. No more running for me. No more letting other people make decisions for me. I might have pretended for a long time that that was the easier road. And maybe it was." He turned and looked back over the skyline. "But easy don't mean right."

Hugo nodded to himself. "And how about…I mean how is…?"

"My head?" Webb's grin was wry. "It's ok. You can ask. You've had a ringside seat for the whole roller-coaster. I think you've a right to know."

"Ok. How's your head?"

Webb shrugged on shoulder, looking wary. "I've had no more blackouts. No more headaches. A few weeks now."

"That's…good?"

Webb chewed on the inside of his cheek for a moment. "I think so. Yes. I know so. It means it's gone, all of it. *He's* gone. But that's the way it should be."

"I think the man you are now," Hugo said slowly. "Is down to the choices you have made and not the ones you used to remember. And I am proud to know that man." He raised his eyes. "You should be proud too."

Webb glanced away, like he was unable to hold his look. "Jeez, rack out the feels why don't you."

"It's true."

"Well," Webb said, shifting in his seat. "Thank you. That…well. Yes, that means something."

"I'm glad."

"You know I…we…you know," Webb tried, face screwing up.

"Know what?" Hugo said, letting a small smile turn up the corner of his mouth.

"Oh man, you're going to make me say it?"

Hugo smiled, wider.

Webb made an impatient noise. "For the love of Jesus, ok, yes I'm proud to know you too. More than proud. I…" Webb finally met his eyes. "I might not be dead without you. But I wouldn't be alive. Not in the way I am. You saved me. Several times, if I remember rightly," he added, rubbing the back of his neck. "And. Well. I'm looking forward to leaving it all behind, if I'm honest. But I'm not looking forward to seeing how I manage without you to kick my ass when it needs it. And I've learned it does need it from time to time."

Hugo looked back over the balcony, waiting for his voice to return. "So what will you do?"

"There's a little cottage I know, out in the middle of nowhere. Away from everything. Everyone. It's been empty for a while, but I reckon I could make a home of it."

"And what will you do there?"

Webb shrugged again. "Fish. Read. Breathe. Rest." He turned a suddenly warm smile on Hugo. "Live. And try and forget."

Hugo nodded. "Sounds good."

"What about you?"

Hugo stiffened. "I haven't let myself think about that. I don't know what's going to happen yet."

"They're not going to throw you in the brig. Your mom won't allow it."

"Mother's not the SC anymore," Hugo said. "She has no influence over what the court-martial decides."

"I'll be a ship's skivvy before I believe that your mom can't make anything she wants happen."

Hugo closed his eyes. He didn't want to think about it. He didn't want to think about anything.

"Kaleb, you gotta let it go."

"Let what go?" Hugo's voice was hoarse.

"Everything. You're hanging on to it all. I can see it."

"I don't know what you're talking about," Hugo said, once again resolutely turning away from the black pit lurking just behind his mind.

"The *guilt*, man," Webb said, sitting forward in his chair and forcing Hugo to look at him.

"You don't understand."

"You're talking to a man who would have crashed a flagship into Tranquility if it hadn't been for you," Webb said softly. "I understand what it is to do shit you wouldn't if your head were on straight. Everyone's forgiven you. You should forgive yourself."

"You're wrong. Everyone blames me. And they're right."

"If you're talking about the conspiracy theory nuts and the Osgard sympathisers, they wouldn't' have been happy with anything but a more puritanical Service. They ain't gonna get it. Your mom and Rose have seen to that. Things are changing, but not the way they wanted. They're bitter."

Hugo looked away.

"Hey, it's true," Webb insisted. "Everyone that matters doesn't care anymore. They know it wasn't your fault."

"Is this why you came by?" Hugo said after a pause. "To tell me this before you left?"

"Your wife gets you," Webb said after a moment. "She understands exactly what's going on in that self-flagellant head of yours. But whereas she thinks she needs to give you time to pull yourself out of the mire, I think you need a good hard smack round the head. *That's* why I'm here."

Hugo looked at him, saw the smile take the sting out the words and smiled himself. But then his smile dropped. "So much has happened," he said. "I don't remember all of it. What I do remember makes me want to scream every time I think about it. I don't even know where to begin understanding what I've done."

Webb's face softened. "Then don't try," he said with a shrug. "We're not meant to understand everything, Hugo. It happened, but it's over now. Let it go."

"Have you managed to let it go?" Hugo said softly.

"I'm beginning to," Webb said after a pause long enough that Hugo knew he'd had to think about it.

He met Webb's pale eyes and saw the sincerity in them. Despite everything, he felt a lift in his chest. Something must have showed on his face because Webb patted his shoulder and rose stiffly.

"You know I'm right. I'm always right."

Hugo got to his feet too. "I don't know if that's entirely accurate."

Webb's crooked smile widened. "Even when you managed to forget everything else, remember this." He put a hand on his shoulder and his smile changed, opening up and lightened his face. "Living well is the best revenge. We've had our share of shit. Time to show this damn world it's not beaten us, yeah?"

"I will if you will."

Webb smiled again, held out his hand. "Deal."

Hugo shook his hand. It was a long time before either of them let go. When they finally let their hands drop, Hugo hesitated then pulled the other man into a hug. Webb went rigid before returning it, briefly but tightly, then pulled away. Hugo let him.

"Visit sometime," Webb said as he moved to the door. His voice had changed. "I think you know where to find me."

"Yeah, I think I do," Hugo said. "It'll be a lot quieter round there now they've moved the Academy to Johannesburg."

"It'll just be me and the wind," Webb said, pausing at the door. "It's the way I've always wanted it."

"It's about time you realised that," Hugo said. "Dana would be pleased."

Webb's face tightened. "Yeah, I know she would."

"Live well, Webb," Hugo reminded him and the younger man nodded, a little too forcefully, and looked away to hide his face.

"It's time I did," he said. "Time we both did."

"You're right," Hugo said, finding he believed it.

"What did I say? I'm always right." Webb said with one last lop-sided smile.

Hugo would remember that smile for years. He couldn't know it then, but the memory of it would be the thing that kept him going in the times to come.

There were to be many more trials, accusations and tensions to ride out. He knew that, even then. What he didn't know was the strain it would put on his marriage, his relationship with his children, or the rest of his family. Neither did he know that it would be another in a long line of strains that they would weather together and that would one day make them stronger.

There was no way he could know that the troubles in turn would lead him and Harvey to take their girls out of the New Academy and move their family into the mountains of Old Europe to find their own life, far away from still-delicate and often fractious struggle for power between the newly elected Orbit Alliance and the Service, which was now under their direct command. Hugo predicted it would be a few generations before the Service would get used to answering to a civilian body. But then he'd put the thought away as none of his concern.

He also couldn't know that his mother would keep her word and leave the Orbit to sort itself out, or that she would visit them at their new home and somehow regain some of the years she had lost, seeming younger than he'd ever known her. He couldn't know that she was a completely different woman out of uniform, or that she would take his daughters hiking in the mountains and encourage them to follow their own paths and put their own freedom and dreams first in all matters.

He also couldn't know that one day she would bring them news that Webb had finally visited his father in prison, now that the old man's health was failing. She wouldn't be able to tell Hugo much, her connections would no longer be what they were, but she would say that the younger man had arranged to have his father transferred somewhere less secure and more homely for his last days. This would make Hugo believe that forgiveness of some kind had been built between the two McCullough men and the realisation would ease a tension he hadn't realised had been carrying in him for years.

That still-lingering memory of Webb's smile led, many years later, to Hugo buying a shuttle ticket to the Former United Kingdom. From there, he would take a ground-flyer as far as it would go into the Highlands before he had to disembark, pay the driver and continue on foot until he found the closed-up remains of the old Service Academy. Then it was a case of striking out into the woods towards a loch on the shores of which he hoped to find a small cottage, smoke from a real wood fire drifting from the chimney and warm glow in the windows.

There would be a boat tied up at the small jetty, fishing nets laid out to dry on the stony beach. The towering, abandoned turbines that had once powered the Academy and its medical research centre would be standing eerily still against the burnished sunset. Hugo would take a moment to imagine what it must have been like for Webb's clone, before he realised what had happened or what he was, when he staggered though these woods to this very same cottage, perhaps seeing a very similar glow in its windows, to happen upon a man who was more significant to him than he could possibly understand at the time.

Hugo would wonder at the fact that that brief time with that man would sow the seeds for Webb to one day finally understand what he needed to make himself happy, but that it would take a cycle of pain, hatred and betrayal for the same man to make him realise it.

Then he would let the thought go and tread carefully over the loose stones, being sure to make plenty of noise to announce himself as he approached the door.

It would be the first time he would truly understand that everything that had happened had been worth it. It would be the first time he would understand he was finally free.

But it was still some time off.

THE END

NOTE FROM THE AUTHOR

I find it really hard to describe what it feels like to finish my first ever series of novels. The only thing that I know for certain is that's it's been one hell of a ride.

I am definitely sad to be saying goodbye to these characters. I've loved working with them and discovering their stories. We've come a long way together and they've helped me figure out how to write books. But I also know in my heart their tales are done.

I am, also, overwhelmingly grateful to all readers that have journeyed this far. I hope you've enjoyed the ride as much as me.

ABOUT THE AUTHOR

J S Collyer is a Science Fiction writer from Lancaster, England. She lives there with her partner and two cats and enjoys reading, writing and walking.

The Orbit Series is her first novel series and has been received well by fans of Science and General Fiction alike. The first novel, Zero, was listed in Northern Soul Magazine's 'Best Reads of 2014'.

She has plans to release a new series in the near future.

Find out more at:

http://jcollyer.wordpress.com
http://www.facebook.com/jscollyer
http://www.twitter.com/jexshinigami

ACKNOWLEDGEMENTS

Writing the Orbit Series has been the most wonderful journey of discovery for me and the people along the way who have supported and encouraged me are too numerous to list but are, to a one, living legends. I always knew I wanted to write books. These people made me realise I could.
However, there are a few that have to be mentioned for being so instrumental to me reaching this point.

Ray Robinson, George Green and Jo Baker, my creative writing tutors, because without them I would never have learned to learn.

My parents Ann and Phil cannot escape being mentioned for the constant encouragement they've given me since school as well as the moral and financial support to pursue my dream, not to mention driving copies of my books to conventions for me in the wee hours of the morning.

My mother's parents also, Derek and Sheila, who both sadly passed within seven weeks of each other earlier this year, I have to thank as they, also, helped me pay for university and never faltered, right to the end, in making sure I knew that making yourself happy is the most important thing there is.

I'd also like to thank my brother Chris and my Uncle Adam and Aunt Cheryl for being among my best readers and most supportive fans. Thanks to Chris also for lending me his name, though not his character (I wouldn't want anyone to think that anyone I liked had anything in common with the man), for Christof Coale.

My partner Andy needs a thank you for putting up with me shutting myself away in rooms for hours on end with my manuscript, only surfacing to cry out for tea, as well as my best friend Anna for always being there with joyful expectancy of my stories.

Becky and Amy not only gave me their names for Silence but also gave me their time and support by reading the series and being so wonderfully positive about it as well as flashing the books round plane cabins whilst making appreciative noises and encouraging colleagues, friends and family to read them as well.

I also need to thank Victoria Osgood for not only being an encouraging reader but for lending me her name and passionate character for that of Vee Osgard in Silence.

I also have to thank Reg Davey of Dagda publishing for all his hard work formatting, uploading and publishing my books. Without him, literally none of it would be possible.

I'd also like to thank Hugo and Webb because, though fictional, they have been very real to me over the last two years. They constantly surprised me, grew and developed and drove me to want to explore more of their stories. They have done well by me and, I hope, I have done well by then.
It is said to say goodbye to them, so I will just say 'Good luck, guys!'

Because never say never.